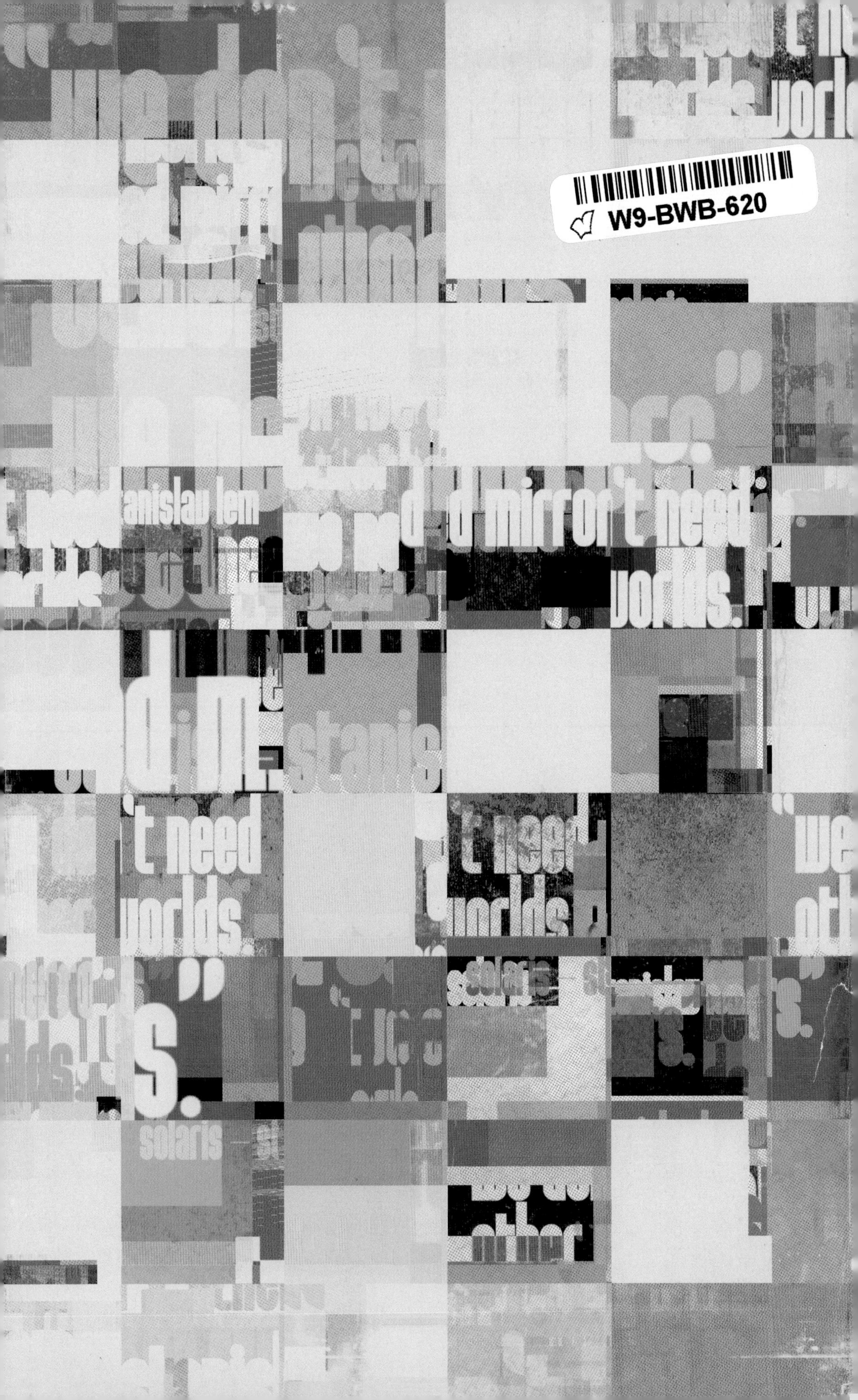
anislau lem
mirror
't need
worlds.
't need
worlds.
stanis
solaris
solaris
W9-BWB-620

[redacted]

[redacted]

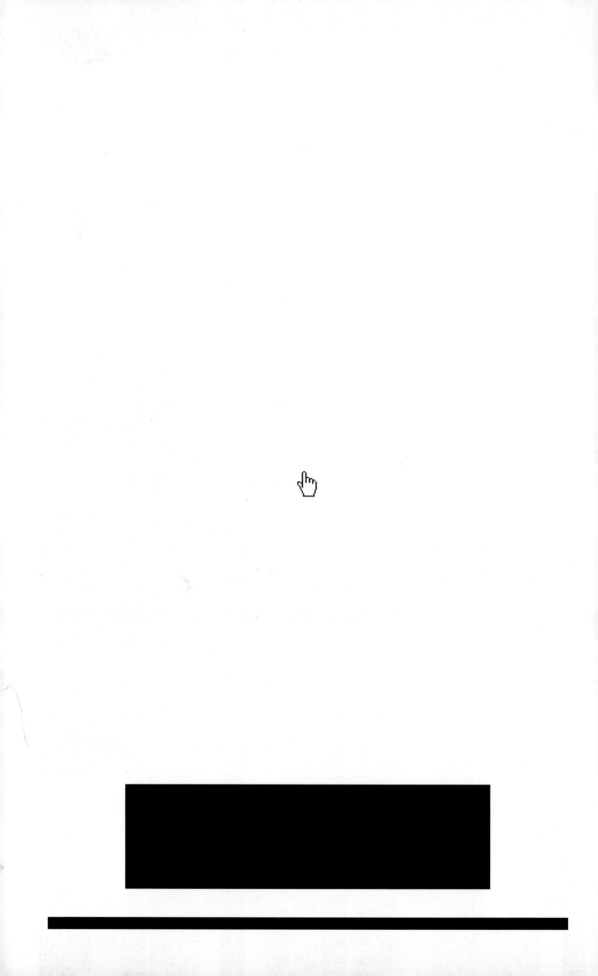

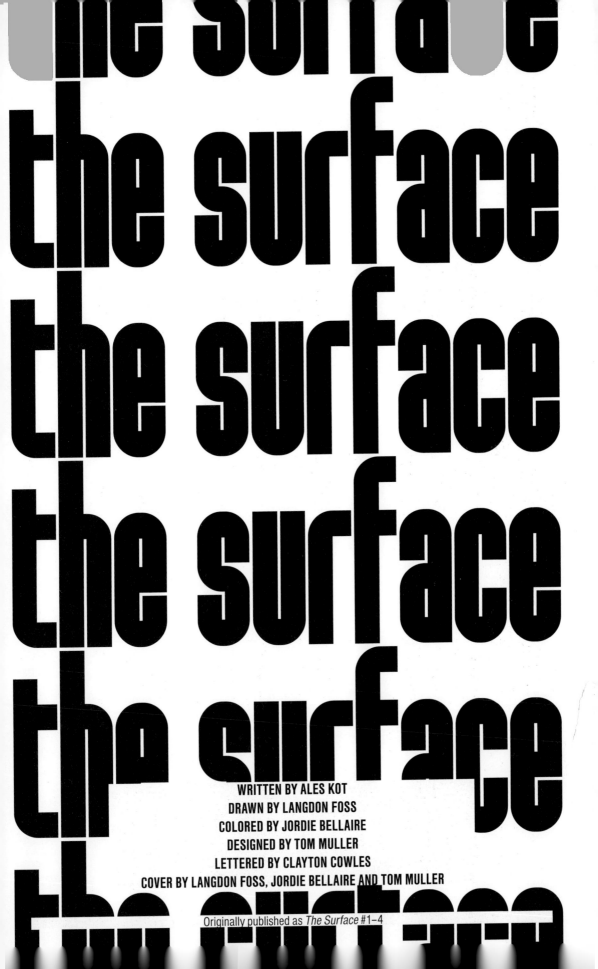

the surface

the surface
the surface
the surface
the surface
the surface

WRITTEN BY ALES KOT
DRAWN BY LANGDON FOSS
COLORED BY JORDIE BELLAIRE
DESIGNED BY TOM MULLER
LETTERED BY CLAYTON COWLES
COVER BY LANGDON FOSS, JORDIE BELLAIRE AND TOM MULLER

Originally published as *The Surface* #1–4

blinkfeed

YOUR #1 NO-BULLSHIT SOURCE OF INFORMATION (WE TRY)

INSECT RESTAURANTS INCREASINGLY POPULAR IN NORTHERN STATES; FOODIE CULTURE EMBRACES GLOBAL WARMING
WOULD YOU LIKE TO KNOW MORE?

IS VERHOEVEN-DELANY HIDING A NEW PIECE OF TECH?
The corporation, known for its popular hardware and a struggle for economic dominance with various governments across the globe as well as for recently buying up a few bankrupt North American states, is rumored to have developed a machine that can be utilized to create a believable holographic universe. The rumors also have it that the machine is still lacking a key piece of hardware.
WOULD YOU LIKE TO KNOW MORE?

PROLIFERATION OF GENDERS PROVES OVERWHELMING FOR BUREAUCRACY
WOULD YOU LIKE TO KNOW MORE?

POST-CAPITALISM: HOW TO LEAVE THE ACCELERATED ERA AND LEARN FROM IT
WOULD YOU LIKE TO KNOW MORE?
WOULD YOU LIKE TO KNOW MORE?
This isn't what it seems, don't look at this sentence for too long otherwise they'll know

THE GOVERNMENT-CORPORATE STRUGGLE OVER DEVELOPMENT OF TANZANIA CONTINUES
As the United States has chased terror groups and watched them proliferate, China has taken another route, devoting its efforts to building goodwill through public works and winning over governments through "no strings attached" policies. "China eclipsed us in terms of economic interests in Africa," said the...
WOULD YOU LIKE TO KNOW MORE?

THE SURFACE: THE MOST HYPED MYTH OF THE CENTURY OR A REAL DEAL?
WOULD YOU LIKE TO KNOW MORE?

THE STRUGGLE IS REAL: HACKING AS AN ART FORM OF THE SAME IMPORTANCE AS FILM AND JOURNALISM USED TO CARRY
WOULD YOU LIKE TO KNOW MORE?

IS INFORMATION FREE?
We're still not sure but our people are looking into it.
WOULD YOU LIKE TO KNOW MORE?

A GROUP OF HACKTIVISTS PENETRATES A POPULAR GOSSIP WEBSITE, REWRITES TITLES, LEDES, ASKS FOR "MORE IMAGINATION"
WOULD YOU LIKE TO KNOW MORE?

UNDER THE PAVING-STONES, THE BEACH!

PAY ATTENTION.
THEY ARE WATCHING.
TRUST YOUR HEART.

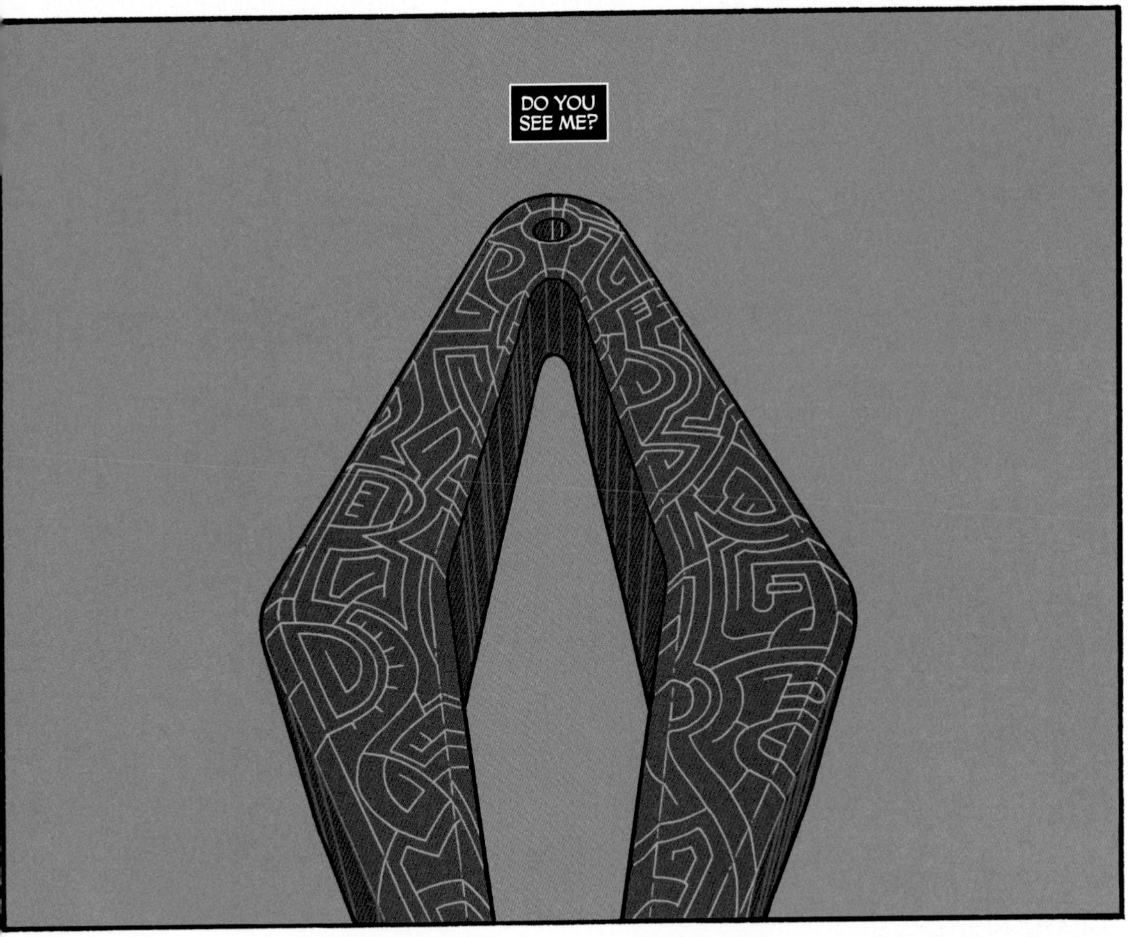
DO YOU
SEE ME?

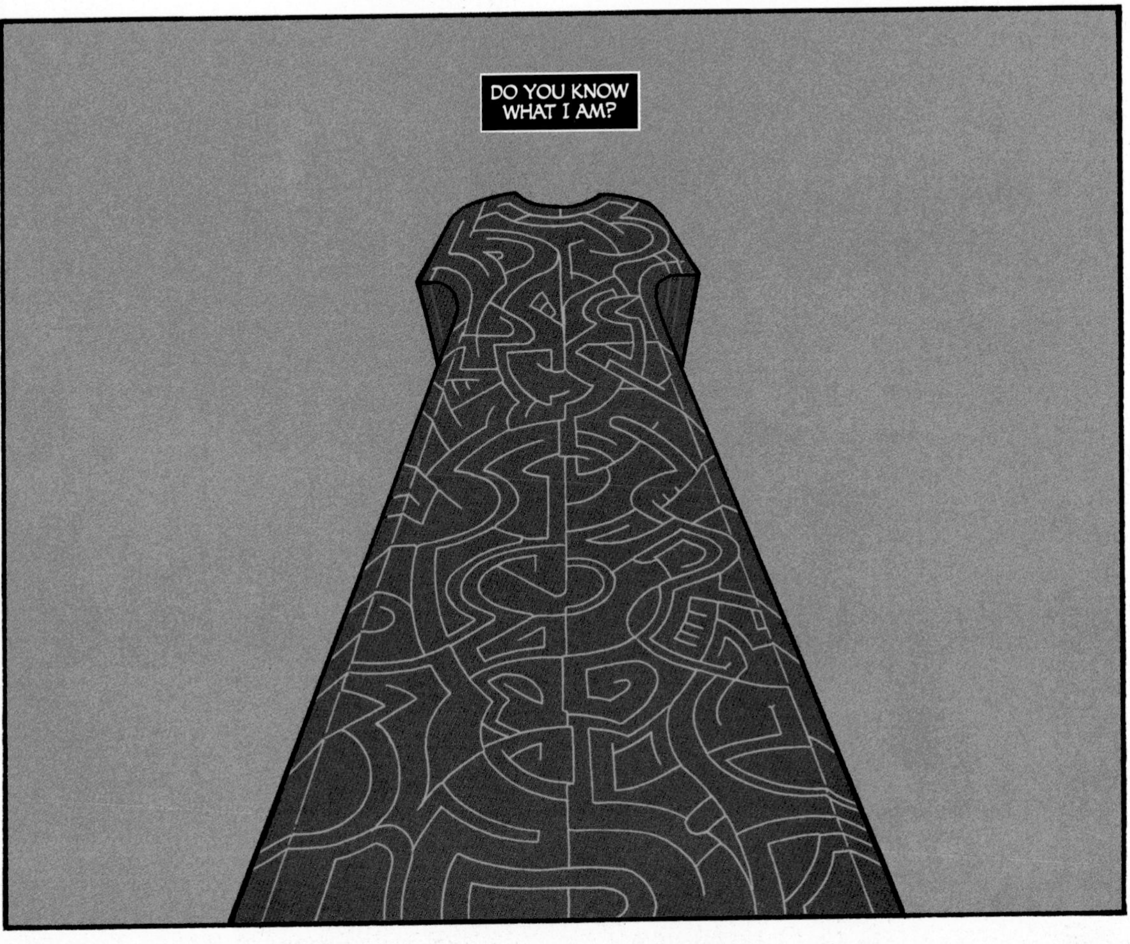
DO YOU KNOW
WHAT I AM?

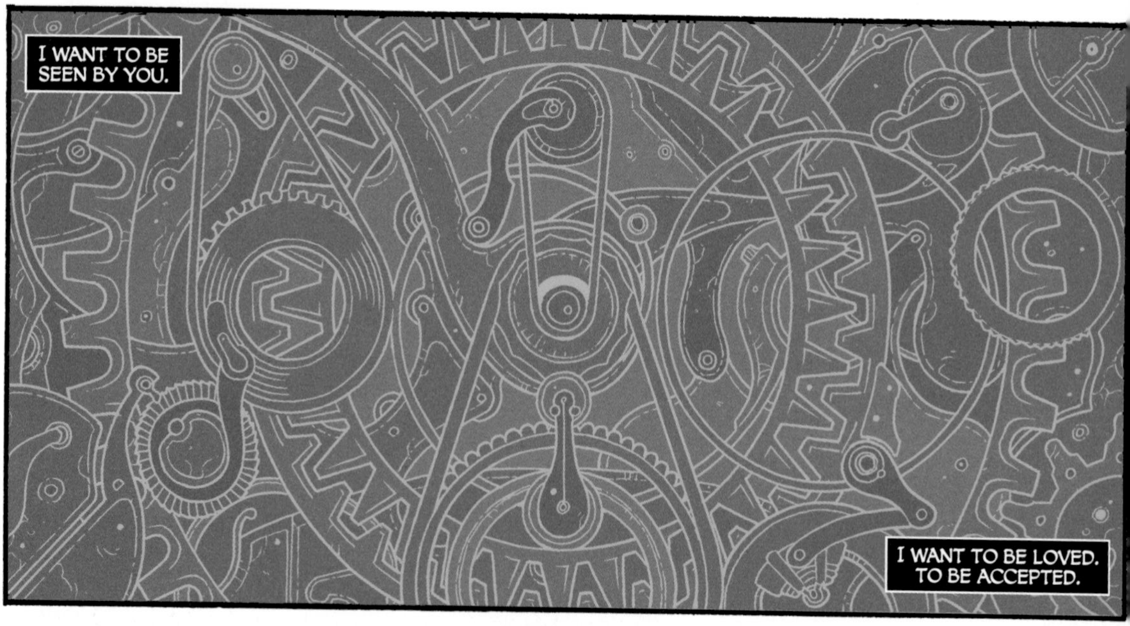
I WANT TO BE
SEEN BY YOU.
I WANT TO BE LOVED.
TO BE ACCEPTED.

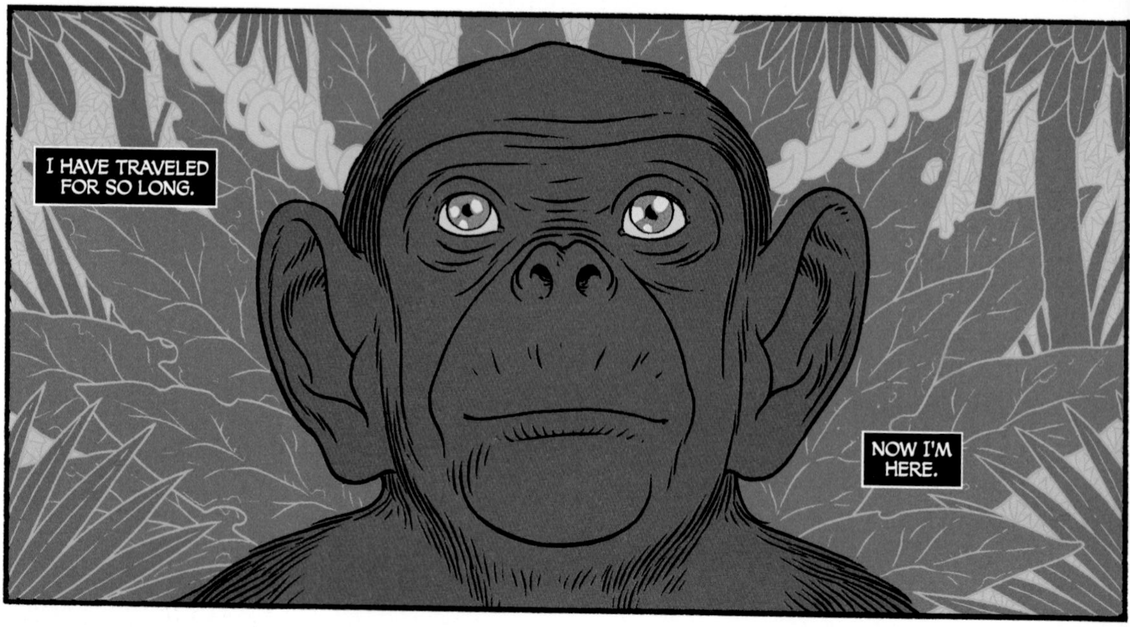
I HAVE TRAVELED
FOR SO LONG.
NOW I'M
HERE.

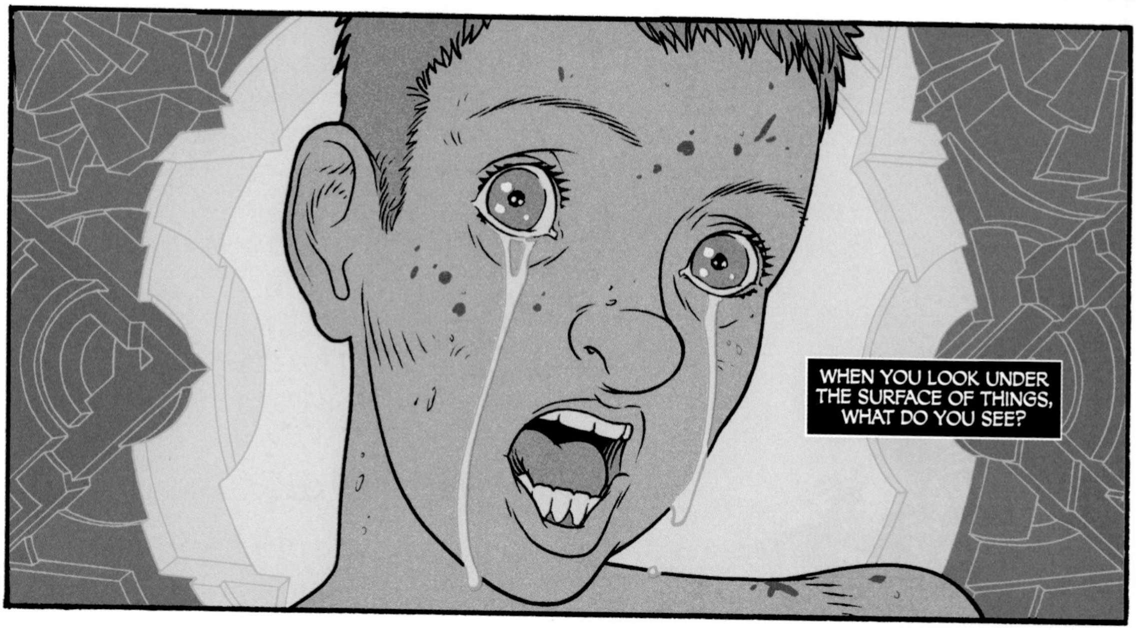
WHEN YOU LOOK UNDER
THE SURFACE OF THINGS,
WHAT DO YOU SEE?

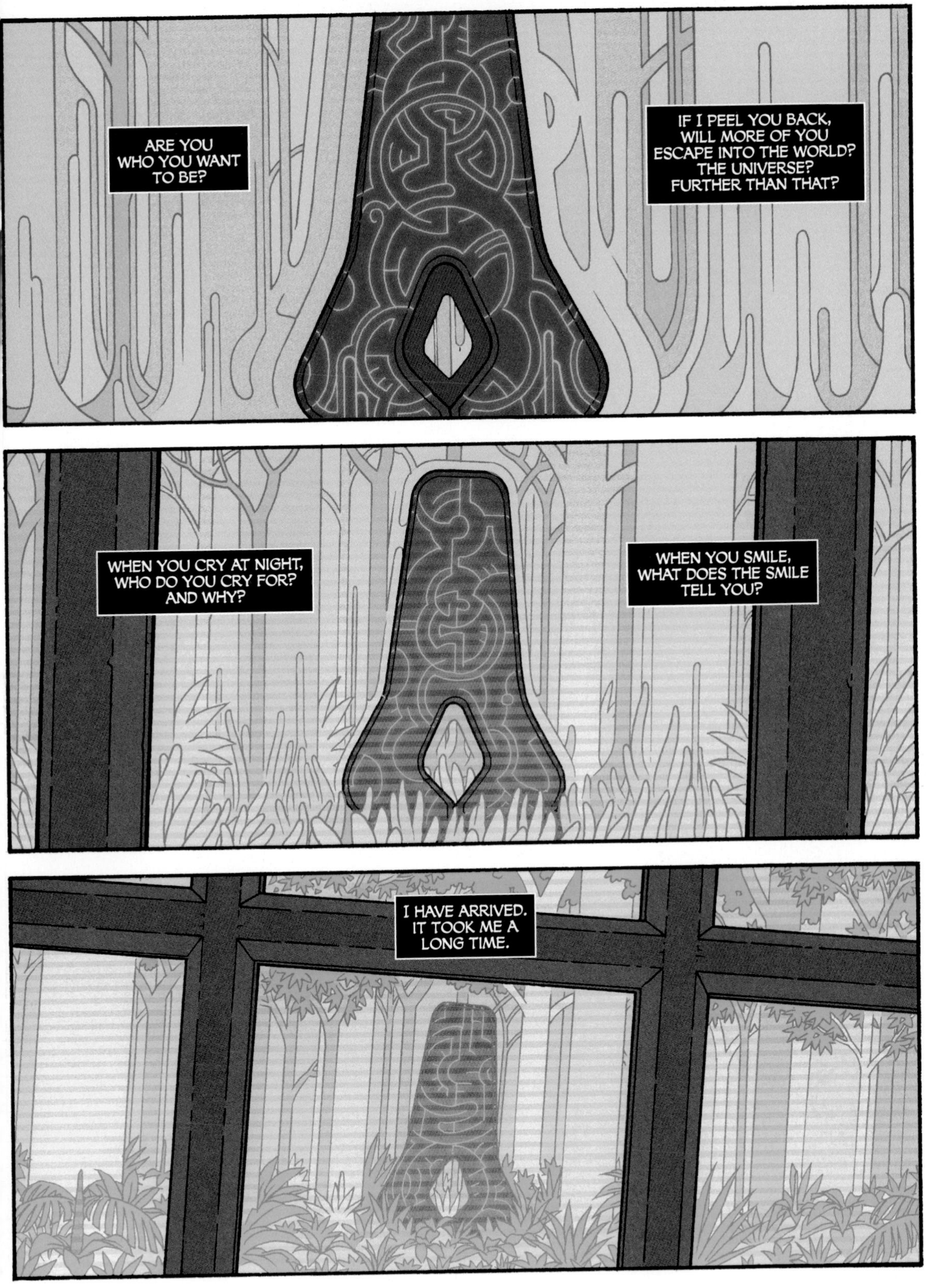
ARE YOU WHO YOU WANT TO BE?
IF I PEEL YOU BACK, WILL MORE OF YOU ESCAPE INTO THE WORLD? THE UNIVERSE? FURTHER THAN THAT?
WHEN YOU CRY AT NIGHT, WHO DO YOU CRY FOR? AND WHY?
WHEN YOU SMILE, WHAT DOES THE SMILE TELL YOU?
I HAVE ARRIVED. IT TOOK ME A LONG TIME.

WHO IS SPEAKING TO YOU
WHEN YOU HEAR MY VOICE?

THE SURFACE: URBAN LEGEND OR REALITY?

Imagine a place where anything goes. No, we are not talking about the Burning Man, which is still a wonderful place to go to as long as what you truly want to see is the president of the startup you're working for wearing nothing but Mad Max glasses and spiked thongs. Getting lashed by space lizards. But that's not what we are talking about -- we are talking about the Surface. A myth that has grown from a local legend somehow occurring at five places at once into a possible explanation of the nature of our universe.

The Surface might be the genuine thing: a time-and-space-traversing oasis that wakes up those who are asleep, powered by a space race we have no understanding of, or, as another theory goes, perhaps powered by ourselves, extending our wills back into the past from the future, helping humanity evolve along.

Is our universe a hologram? Those who have allegedly ventured into the Surface claim they have been shown irrefutable evidence that it is so. Their "findings," however easy to dispute, have galvanized the scientific community. To understand why, we have to look into the past.

In the 1920s, brain scientist Karl Lashley found that no matter what portion of a rat's brain he removed he was unable to erase its memory of how to perform complex tasks it had learned before the surgery. In the 1960s, a neurophysiologist Karl Pribram found the perfect explanation. According to his theory, memories are encoded in patterns of nerve impulses that crisscross the entire brain -- the same way patterns of laser light interference crisscross the entire area of a piece of film containing a holographic image. That, in other words, the brain is itself a hologram.

The theory somewhat makes sense, as it explains how the human brain can store so many memories in so little space – holograms possess a massive capacity for information storage. Adjusting the angle at which the two lasers strike a piece of photographic film gives us the means to record many different images on the same surface.

And there goes that word again.

What happens when this theory meets David Bohm's theory of our universe as a holographic reality (see link 77-C)?

Objective reality, including our own selves, becomes an illusion.

SWIPE RIGHT TO CONTINUE READING

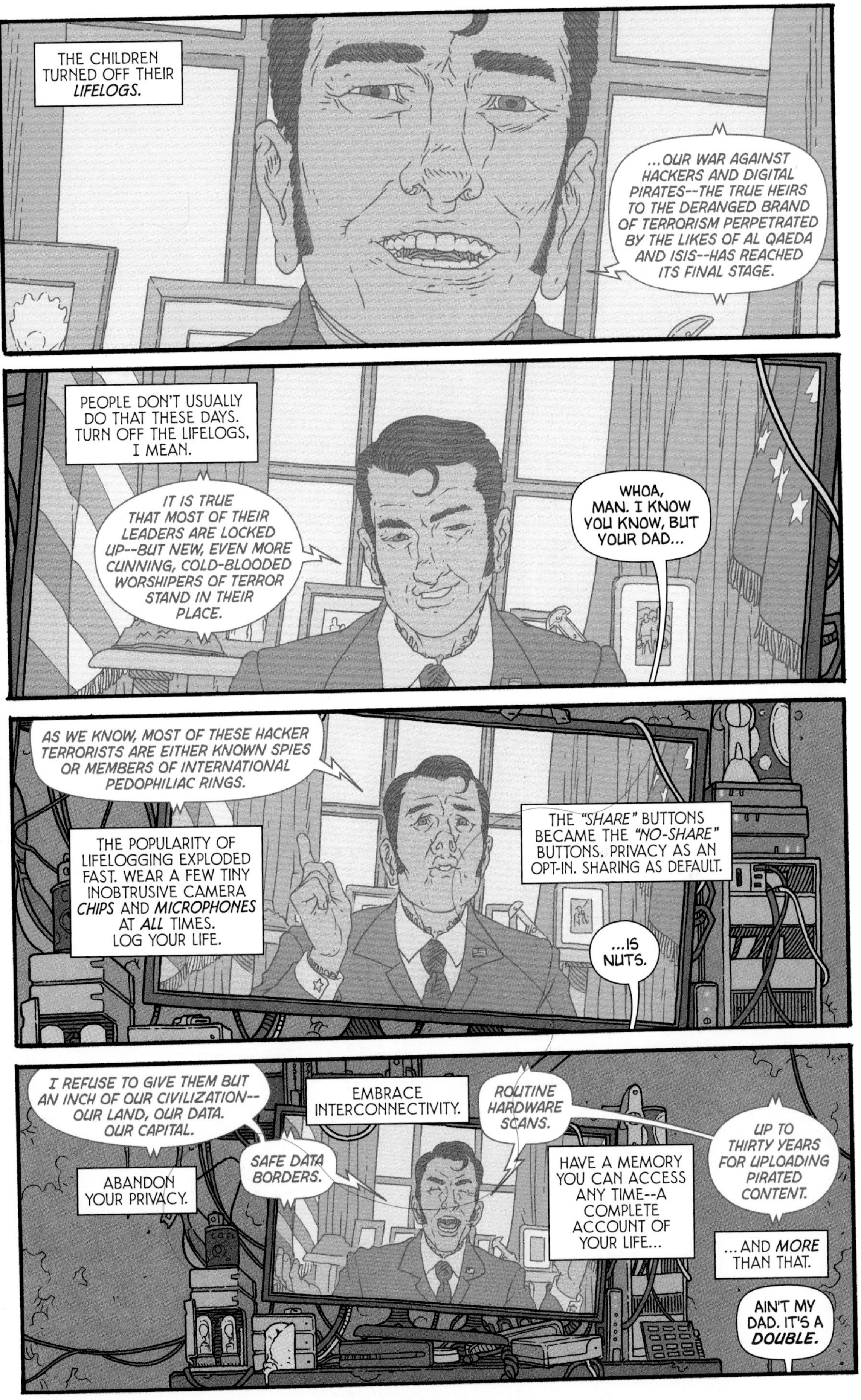
THE CHILDREN TURNED OFF THEIR LIFELOGS.
...OUR WAR AGAINST HACKERS AND DIGITAL PIRATES--THE TRUE HEIRS TO THE DERANGED BRAND OF TERRORISM PERPETRATED BY THE LIKES OF AL QAEDA AND ISIS--HAS REACHED ITS FINAL STAGE.
PEOPLE DON'T USUALLY DO THAT THESE DAYS. TURN OFF THE LIFELOGS, I MEAN.
IT IS TRUE THAT MOST OF THEIR LEADERS ARE LOCKED UP--BUT NEW, EVEN MORE CUNNING, COLD-BLOODED WORSHIPERS OF TERROR STAND IN THEIR PLACE.
WHOA, MAN. I KNOW YOU KNOW, BUT YOUR DAD...
AS WE KNOW, MOST OF THESE HACKER TERRORISTS ARE EITHER KNOWN SPIES OR MEMBERS OF INTERNATIONAL PEDOPHILIAC RINGS.
THE POPULARITY OF LIFELOGGING EXPLODED FAST. WEAR A FEW TINY INOBTRUSIVE CAMERA CHIPS AND MICROPHONES AT ALL TIMES. LOG YOUR LIFE.
THE "SHARE" BUTTONS BECAME THE "NO-SHARE" BUTTONS. PRIVACY AS AN OPT-IN. SHARING AS DEFAULT.
...IS NUTS.
I REFUSE TO GIVE THEM BUT AN INCH OF OUR CIVILIZATION--OUR LAND, OUR DATA. OUR CAPITAL.
EMBRACE INTERCONNECTIVITY.
ROUTINE HARDWARE SCANS.
UP TO THIRTY YEARS FOR UPLOADING PIRATED CONTENT.
ABANDON YOUR PRIVACY.
SAFE DATA BORDERS.
HAVE A MEMORY YOU CAN ACCESS ANY TIME--A COMPLETE ACCOUNT OF YOUR LIFE...
...AND MORE THAN THAT.
AIN'T MY DAD. IT'S A DOUBLE.

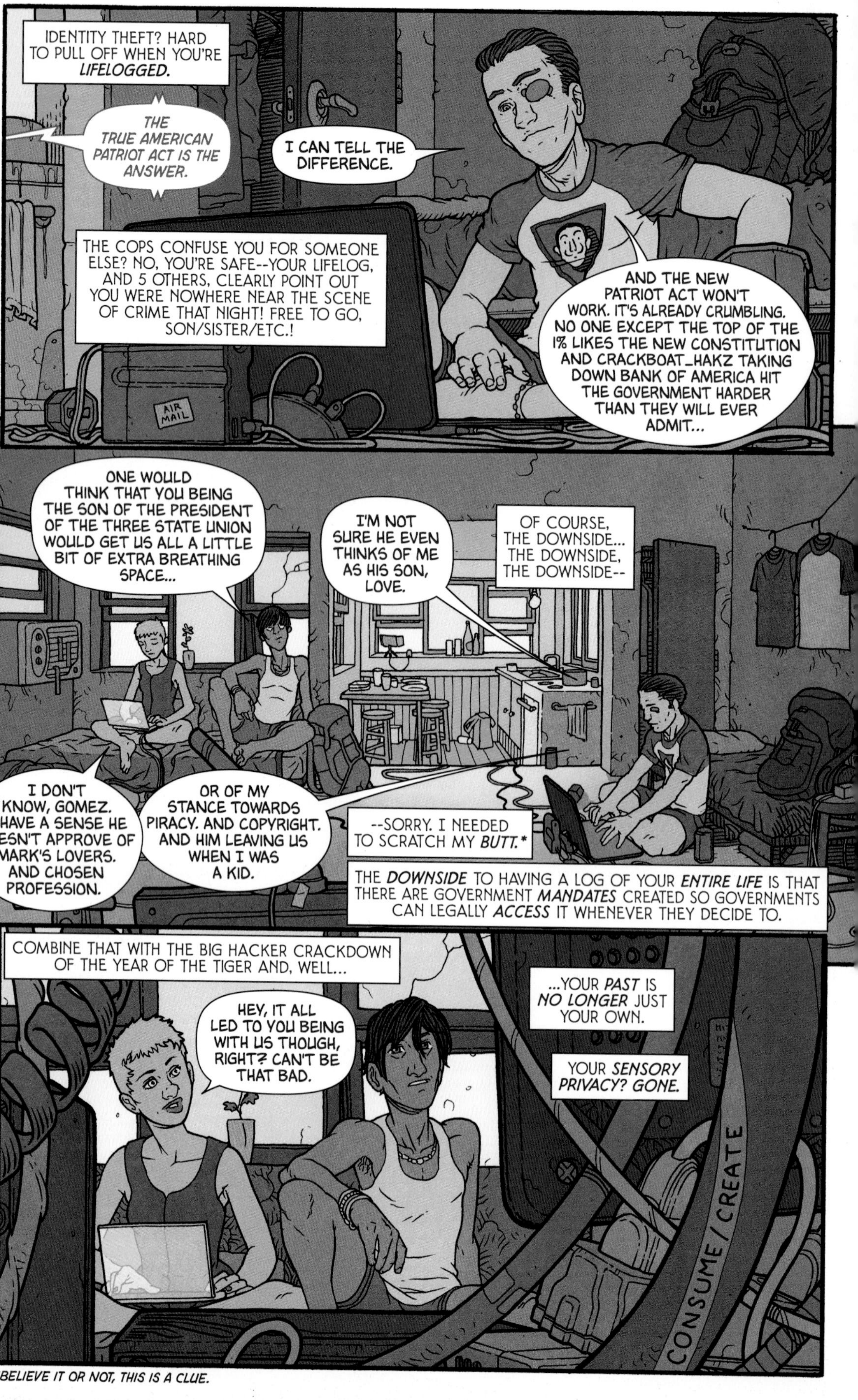
IDENTITY THEFT? HARD TO PULL OFF WHEN YOU'RE *LIFELOGGED.*
THE TRUE AMERICAN PATRIOT ACT IS THE ANSWER.
I CAN TELL THE DIFFERENCE.
THE COPS CONFUSE YOU FOR SOMEONE ELSE? NO, YOU'RE SAFE--YOUR LIFELOG, AND 5 OTHERS, CLEARLY POINT OUT YOU WERE NOWHERE NEAR THE SCENE OF CRIME THAT NIGHT! FREE TO GO, SON/SISTER/ETC.!
AND THE NEW PATRIOT ACT WON'T WORK. IT'S ALREADY CRUMBLING. NO ONE EXCEPT THE TOP OF THE 1% LIKES THE NEW CONSTITUTION AND CRACKBOAT_HAKZ TAKING DOWN BANK OF AMERICA HIT THE GOVERNMENT HARDER THAN THEY WILL EVER ADMIT...
AIR MAIL
ONE WOULD THINK THAT YOU BEING THE SON OF THE PRESIDENT OF THE THREE STATE UNION WOULD GET US ALL A LITTLE BIT OF EXTRA BREATHING SPACE...
I'M NOT SURE HE EVEN THINKS OF ME AS HIS SON, LOVE.
OF COURSE, THE DOWNSIDE... THE DOWNSIDE, THE DOWNSIDE--
I DON'T KNOW, GOMEZ. I HAVE A SENSE HE DOESN'T APPROVE OF MARK'S LOVERS. AND CHOSEN PROFESSION.
OR OF MY STANCE TOWARDS PIRACY. AND COPYRIGHT. AND HIM LEAVING US WHEN I WAS A KID.
--SORRY. I NEEDED TO SCRATCH MY *BUTT.**
THE *DOWNSIDE* TO HAVING A LOG OF YOUR *ENTIRE LIFE* IS THAT THERE ARE GOVERNMENT *MANDATES* CREATED SO GOVERNMENTS CAN LEGALLY *ACCESS* IT WHENEVER THEY DECIDE TO.
COMBINE THAT WITH THE BIG HACKER CRACKDOWN OF THE YEAR OF THE TIGER AND, WELL...
HEY, IT ALL LED TO YOU BEING WITH US THOUGH, RIGHT? CAN'T BE THAT BAD.
...YOUR *PAST* IS *NO LONGER* JUST YOUR OWN.
YOUR *SENSORY PRIVACY? GONE.*
CONSUME / CREATE

**BELIEVE IT OR NOT, THIS IS A CLUE.*

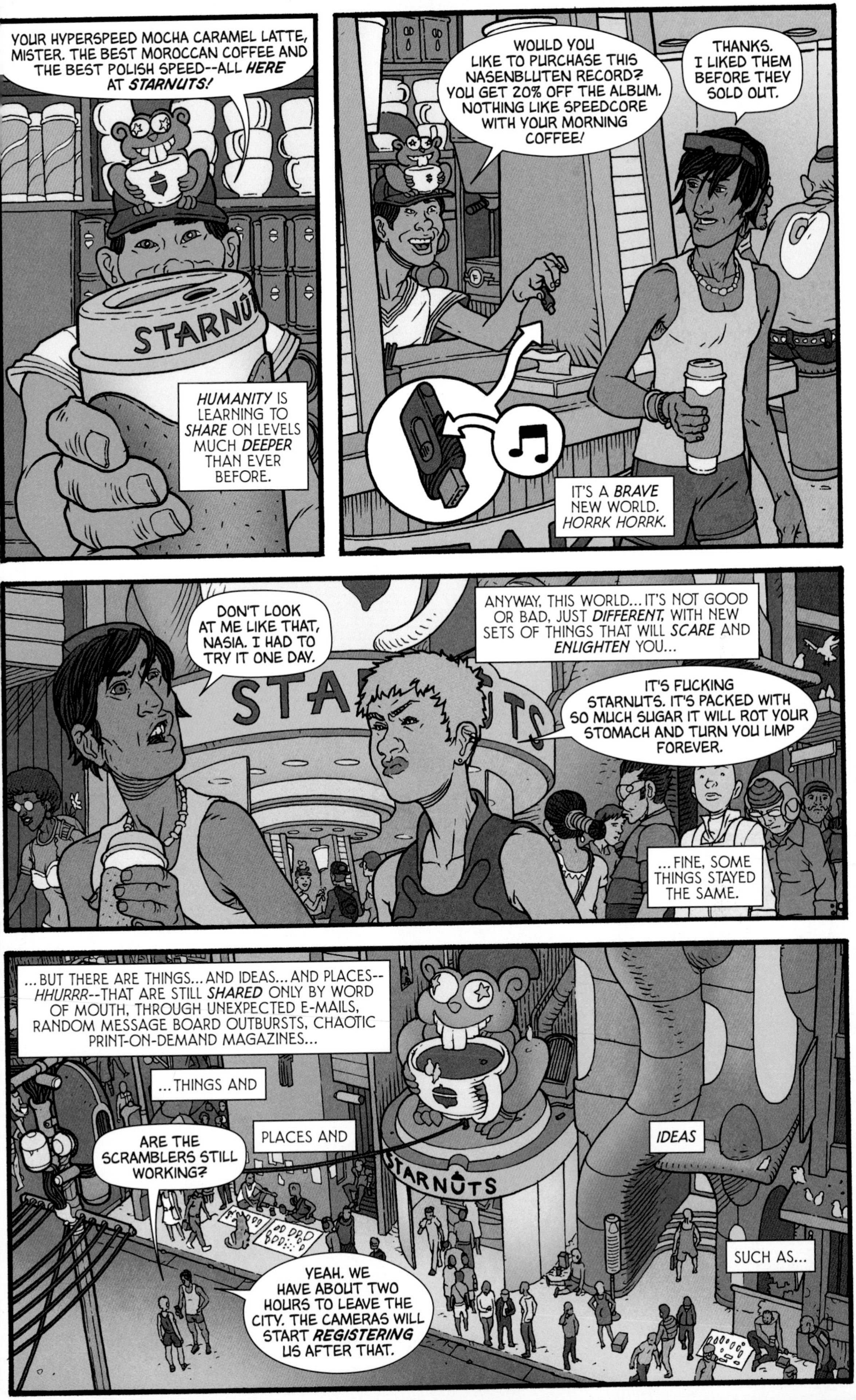
YOUR HYPERSPEED MOCHA CARAMEL LATTE, MISTER. THE BEST MOROCCAN COFFEE AND THE BEST POLISH SPEED--ALL *HERE* AT *STARNUTS!*
STARNUTS
HUMANITY IS LEARNING TO *SHARE* ON LEVELS MUCH *DEEPER* THAN EVER BEFORE.
WOULD YOU LIKE TO PURCHASE THIS NASENBLUTEN RECORD? YOU GET 20% OFF THE ALBUM. NOTHING LIKE SPEEDCORE WITH YOUR MORNING COFFEE!
THANKS. I LIKED THEM BEFORE THEY SOLD OUT.
IT'S A *BRAVE* NEW WORLD. *HORRK HORRK.*
DON'T LOOK AT ME LIKE THAT, NASIA. I HAD TO TRY IT ONE DAY.
ANYWAY, THIS WORLD... IT'S NOT GOOD OR BAD, JUST *DIFFERENT,* WITH NEW SETS OF THINGS THAT WILL *SCARE* AND *ENLIGHTEN* YOU...
IT'S FUCKING STARNUTS. IT'S PACKED WITH SO MUCH SUGAR IT WILL ROT YOUR STOMACH AND TURN YOU LIMP FOREVER.
...FINE, SOME THINGS STAYED THE SAME.
...BUT THERE ARE THINGS... AND IDEAS... AND PLACES-- *HHURRR*--THAT ARE STILL *SHARED* ONLY BY WORD OF MOUTH, THROUGH UNEXPECTED E-MAILS, RANDOM MESSAGE BOARD OUTBURSTS, CHAOTIC PRINT-ON-DEMAND MAGAZINES...
...THINGS AND
PLACES AND
IDEAS
ARE THE SCRAMBLERS STILL WORKING?
STARNUTS
SUCH AS...
YEAH. WE HAVE ABOUT TWO HOURS TO LEAVE THE CITY. THE CAMERAS WILL START *REGISTERING* US AFTER THAT.

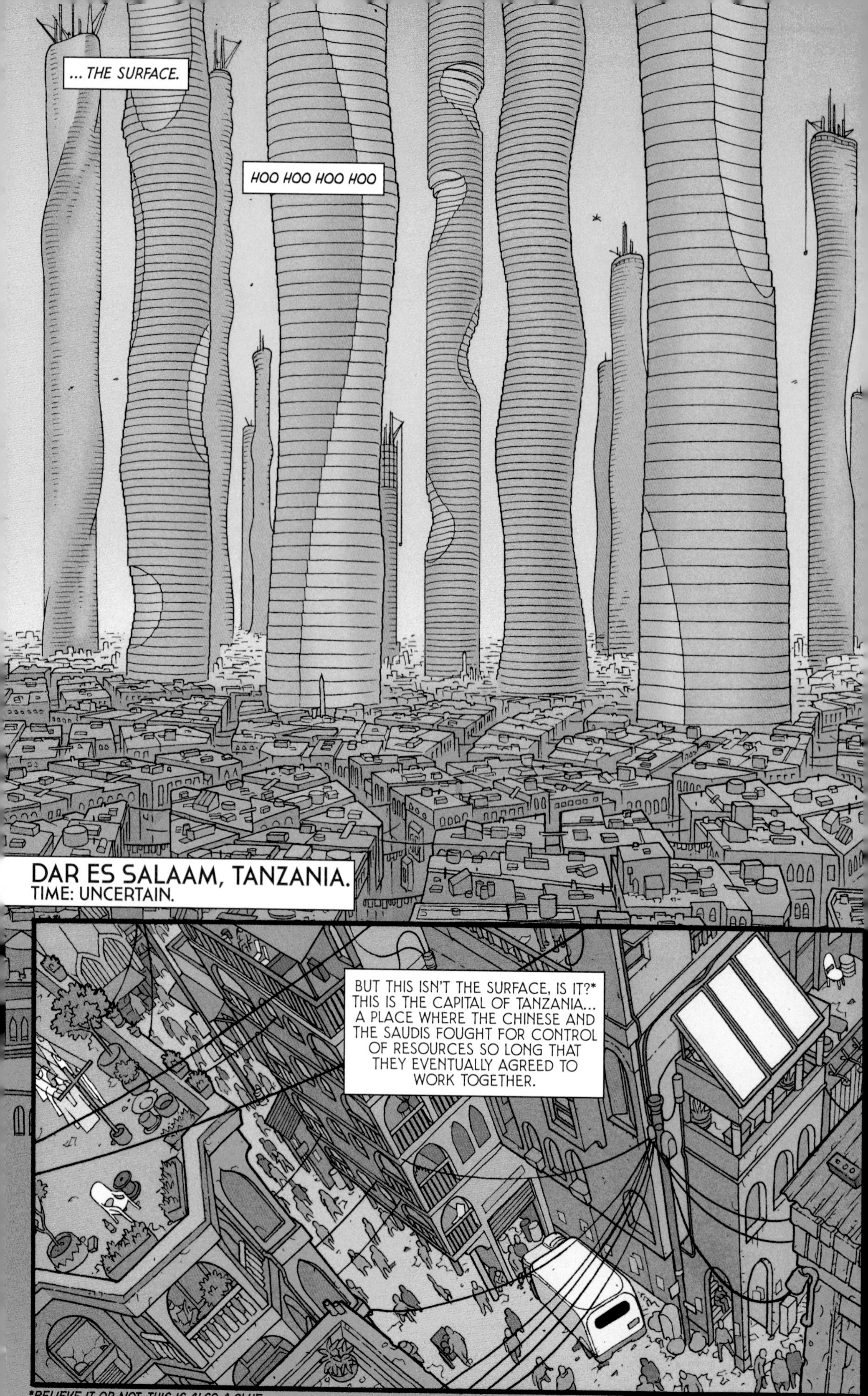
... THE SURFACE.
HOO HOO HOO HOO
DAR ES SALAAM, TANZANIA.
TIME: UNCERTAIN.
BUT THIS ISN'T THE SURFACE, IS IT?* THIS IS THE CAPITAL OF TANZANIA... A PLACE WHERE THE CHINESE AND THE SAUDIS FOUGHT FOR CONTROL OF RESOURCES SO LONG THAT THEY EVENTUALLY AGREED TO WORK TOGETHER.

*BELIEVE IT OR NOT, THIS IS ALSO A CLUE.

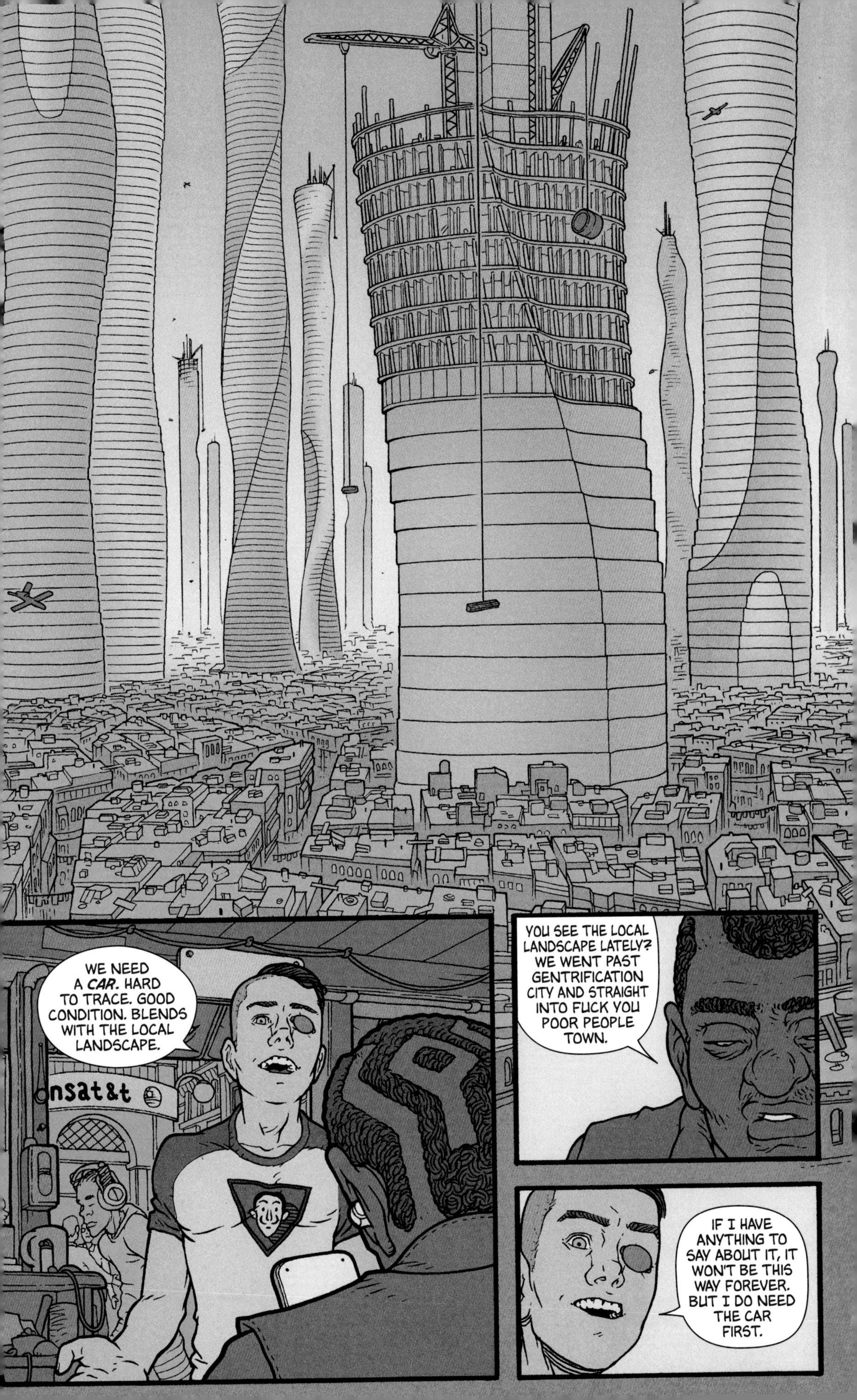

WE NEED A CAR. HARD TO TRACE. GOOD CONDITION. BLENDS WITH THE LOCAL LANDSCAPE.
nsat&t
YOU SEE THE LOCAL LANDSCAPE LATELY? WE WENT PAST GENTRIFICATION CITY AND STRAIGHT INTO FUCK YOU POOR PEOPLE TOWN.
IF I HAVE ANYTHING TO SAY ABOUT IT, IT WON'T BE THIS WAY FOREVER. BUT I DO NEED THE CAR FIRST.

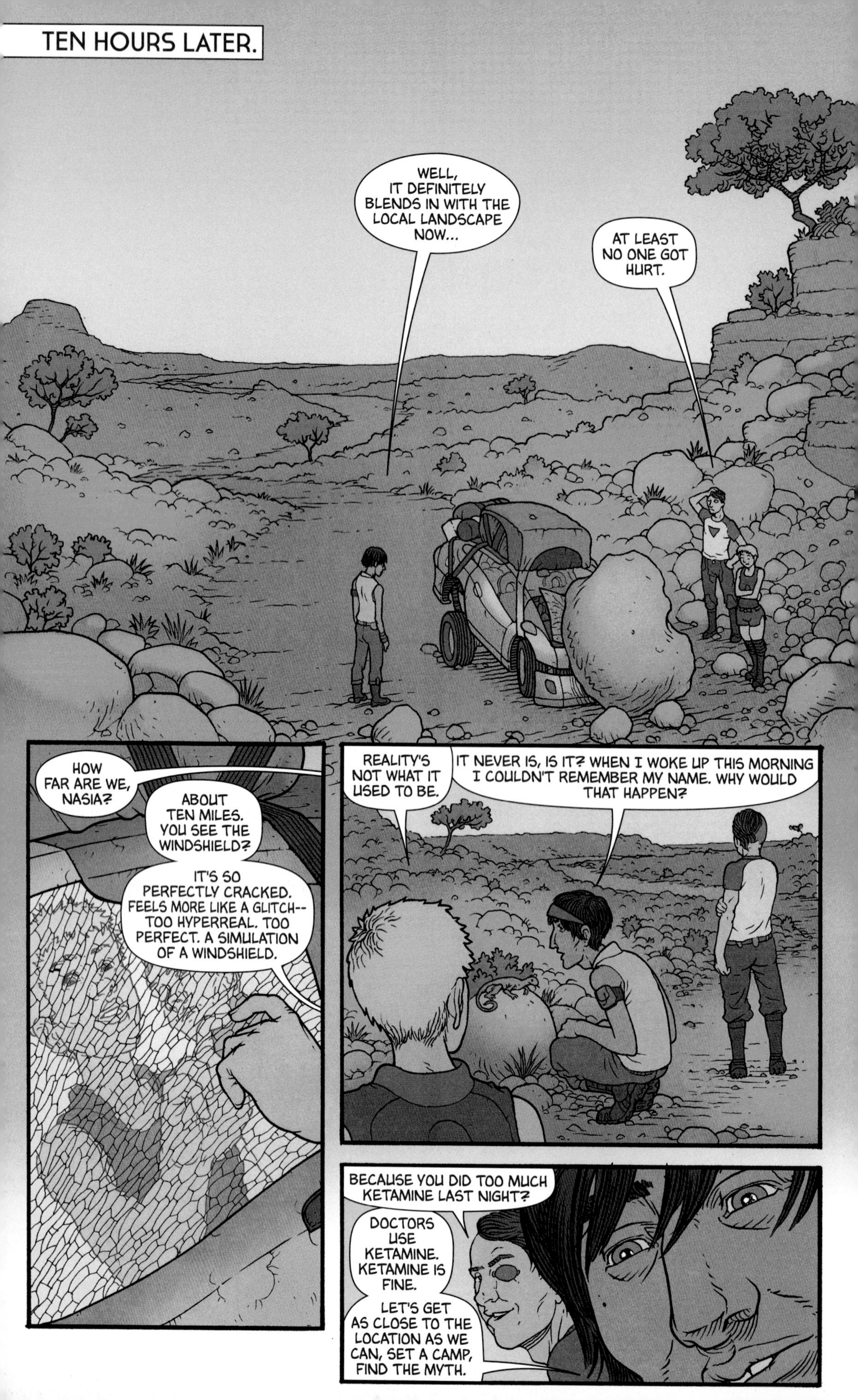
TEN HOURS LATER.
WELL, IT DEFINITELY BLENDS IN WITH THE LOCAL LANDSCAPE NOW...
AT LEAST NO ONE GOT HURT.
HOW FAR ARE WE, NASIA?
ABOUT TEN MILES. YOU SEE THE WINDSHIELD?
IT'S SO PERFECTLY CRACKED. FEELS MORE LIKE A GLITCH-- TOO HYPERREAL. TOO PERFECT. A SIMULATION OF A WINDSHIELD.
REALITY'S NOT WHAT IT USED TO BE.
IT NEVER IS, IS IT? WHEN I WOKE UP THIS MORNING I COULDN'T REMEMBER MY NAME. WHY WOULD THAT HAPPEN?
BECAUSE YOU DID TOO MUCH KETAMINE LAST NIGHT?
DOCTORS USE KETAMINE. KETAMINE IS FINE.
LET'S GET AS CLOSE TO THE LOCATION AS WE CAN, SET A CAMP, FIND THE MYTH.

in a beautiful place out of country.

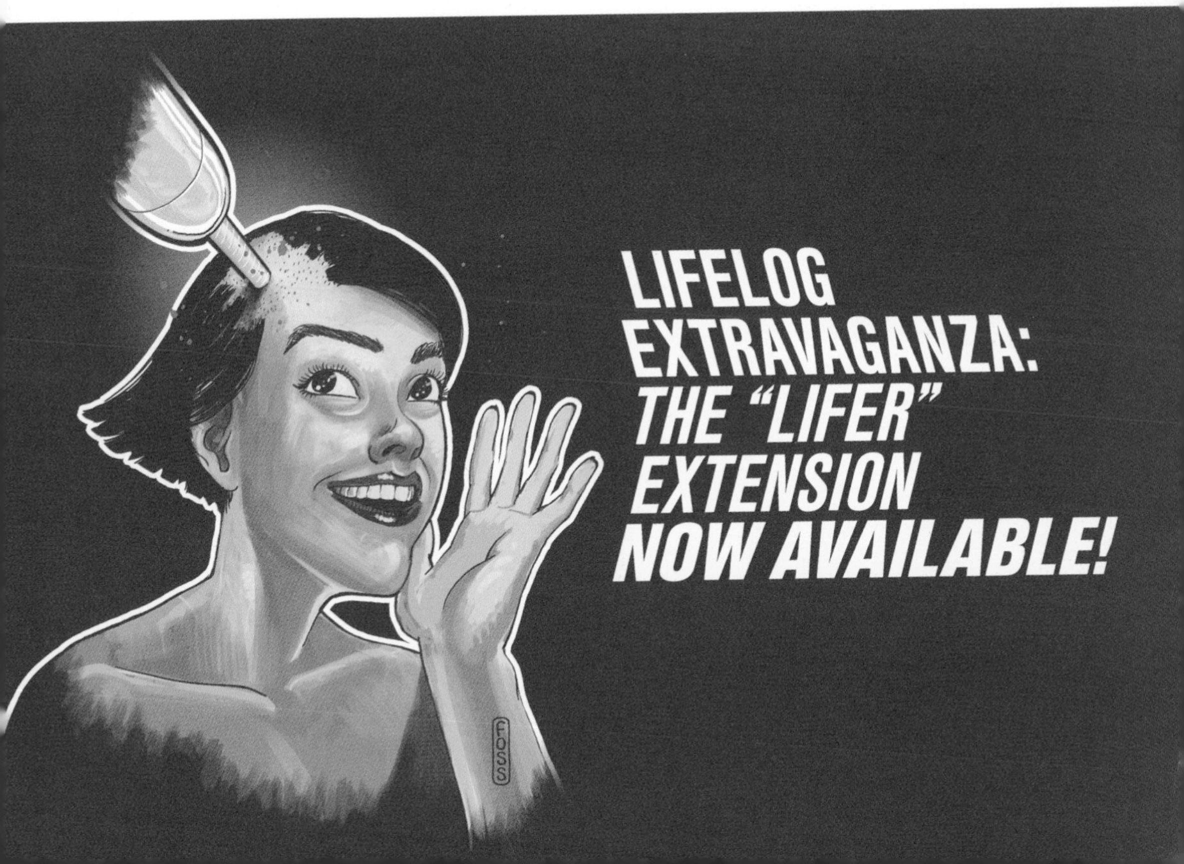
LIFELOG
EXTRAVAGANZA:
THE "LIFER"
EXTENSION
NOW AVAILABLE!
FOSS

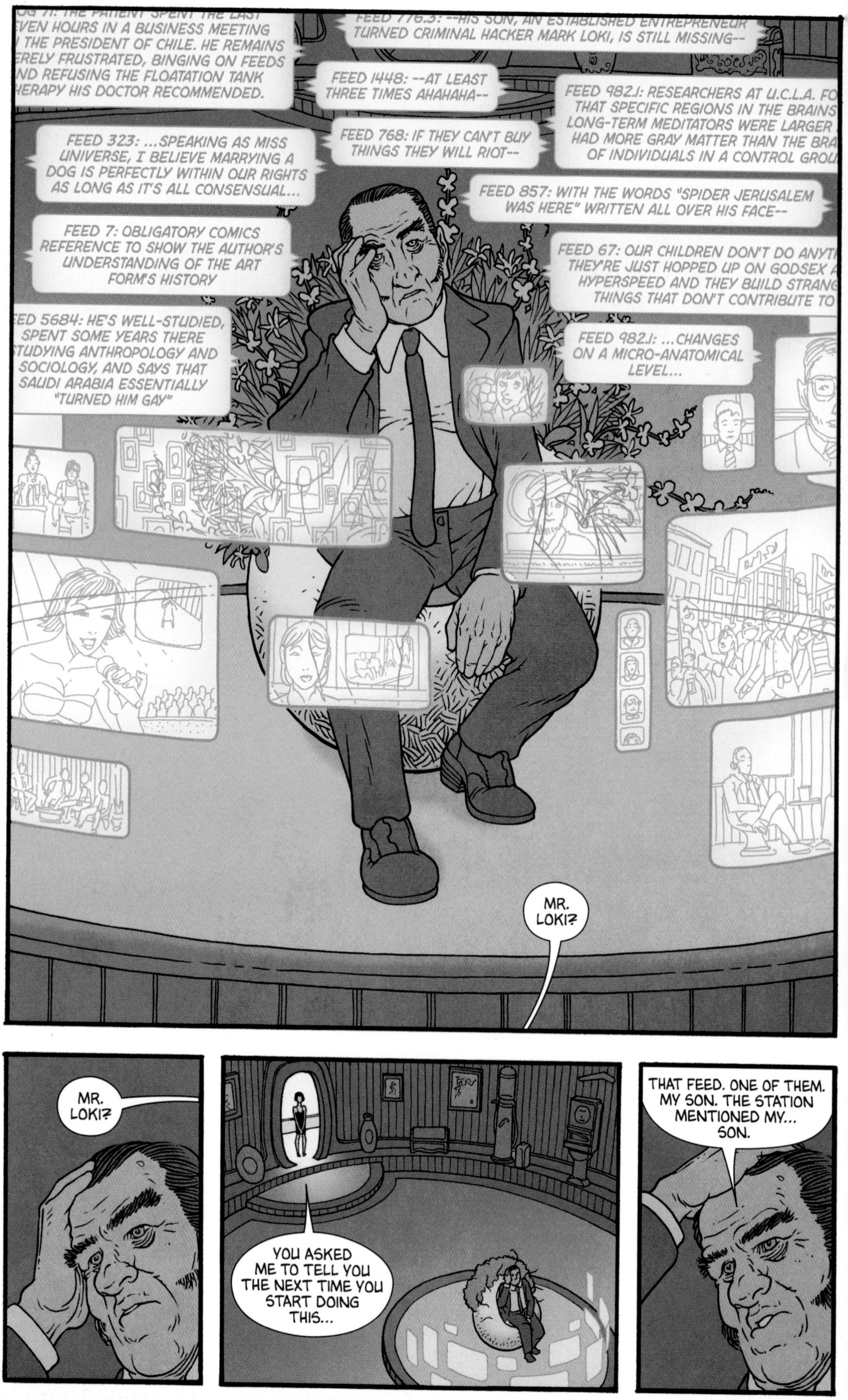

OG 7I: THE PATIENT SPENT THE LAST EVEN HOURS IN A BUSINESS MEETING THE PRESIDENT OF CHILE. HE REMAINS ERELY FRUSTRATED, BINGING ON FEEDS ND REFUSING THE FLOATATION TANK HERAPY HIS DOCTOR RECOMMENDED.
FEED 776.3: --HIS SON, AN ESTABLISHED ENTREPRENEUR TURNED CRIMINAL HACKER MARK LOKI, IS STILL MISSING--
FEED 1448: --AT LEAST THREE TIMES AHAHAHA--
FEED 982.1: RESEARCHERS AT U.C.L.A. FO THAT SPECIFIC REGIONS IN THE BRAINS LONG-TERM MEDITATORS WERE LARGER HAD MORE GRAY MATTER THAN THE BRA OF INDIVIDUALS IN A CONTROL GROU
FEED 323: ...SPEAKING AS MISS UNIVERSE, I BELIEVE MARRYING A DOG IS PERFECTLY WITHIN OUR RIGHTS AS LONG AS IT'S ALL CONSENSUAL...
FEED 768: IF THEY CAN'T BUY THINGS THEY WILL RIOT--
FEED 857: WITH THE WORDS "SPIDER JERUSALEM WAS HERE" WRITTEN ALL OVER HIS FACE--
FEED 7: OBLIGATORY COMICS REFERENCE TO SHOW THE AUTHOR'S UNDERSTANDING OF THE ART FORM'S HISTORY
FEED 67: OUR CHILDREN DON'T DO ANYT THEY'RE JUST HOPPED UP ON GODSEX A HYPERSPEED AND THEY BUILD STRANG THINGS THAT DON'T CONTRIBUTE TO
ED 5684: HE'S WELL-STUDIED, SPENT SOME YEARS THERE STUDYING ANTHROPOLOGY AND SOCIOLOGY, AND SAYS THAT SAUDI ARABIA ESSENTIALLY "TURNED HIM GAY"
FEED 982.1: ...CHANGES ON A MICRO-ANATOMICAL LEVEL...
MR. LOKI?
MR. LOKI?
YOU ASKED ME TO TELL YOU THE NEXT TIME YOU START DOING THIS...
THAT FEED. ONE OF THEM. MY SON. THE STATION MENTIONED MY... SON.

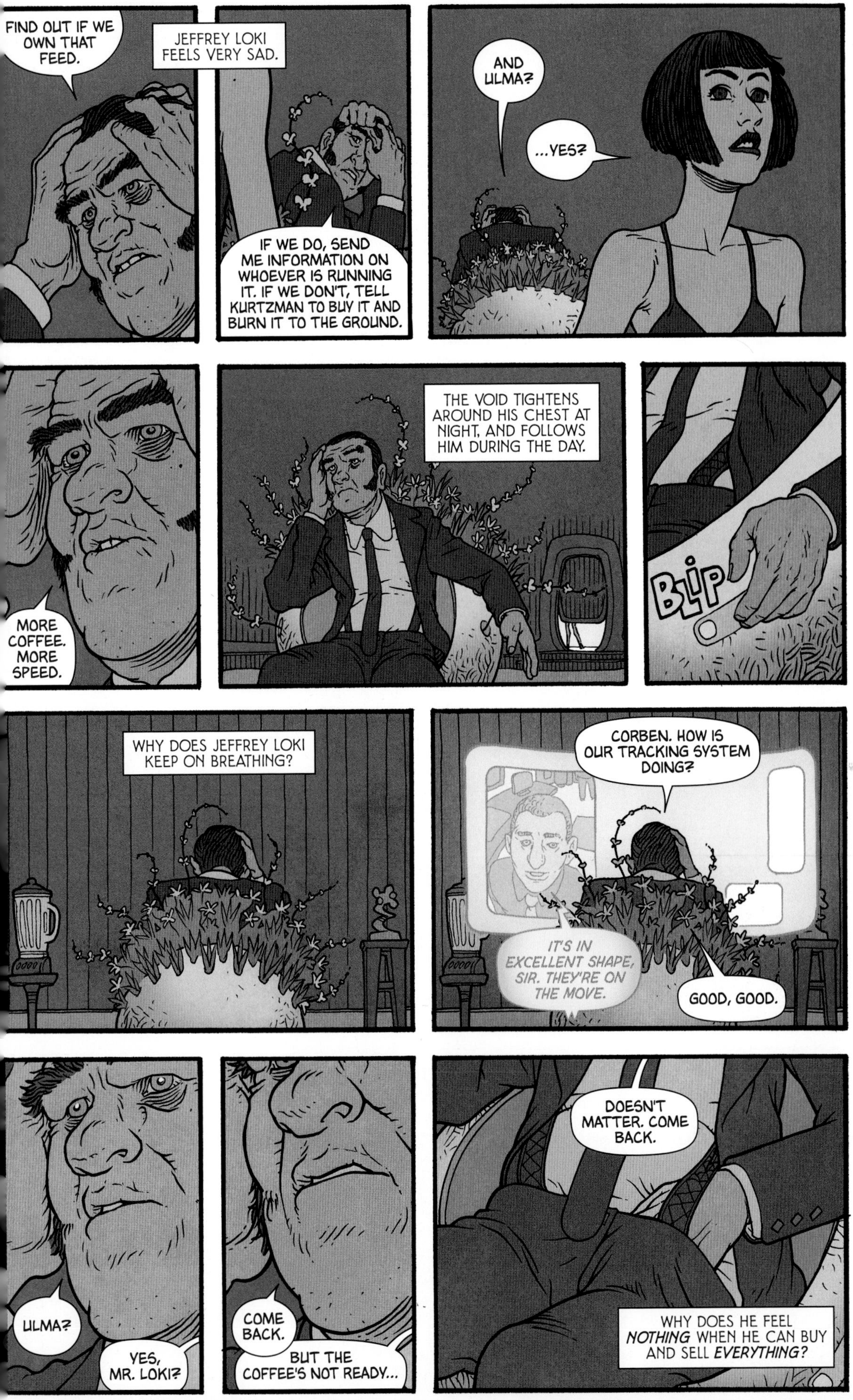
FIND OUT IF WE OWN THAT FEED.
JEFFREY LOKI FEELS VERY SAD.
IF WE DO, SEND ME INFORMATION ON WHOEVER IS RUNNING IT. IF WE DON'T, TELL KURTZMAN TO BUY IT AND BURN IT TO THE GROUND.
AND ULMA?
...YES?
MORE COFFEE. MORE SPEED.
THE VOID TIGHTENS AROUND HIS CHEST AT NIGHT, AND FOLLOWS HIM DURING THE DAY.
BLIP
WHY DOES JEFFREY LOKI KEEP ON BREATHING?
CORBEN. HOW IS OUR TRACKING SYSTEM DOING?
IT'S IN EXCELLENT SHAPE, SIR. THEY'RE ON THE MOVE.
GOOD, GOOD.
ULMA?
YES, MR. LOKI?
COME BACK.
BUT THE COFFEE'S NOT READY...
DOESN'T MATTER. COME BACK.
WHY DOES HE FEEL NOTHING WHEN HE CAN BUY AND SELL EVERYTHING?

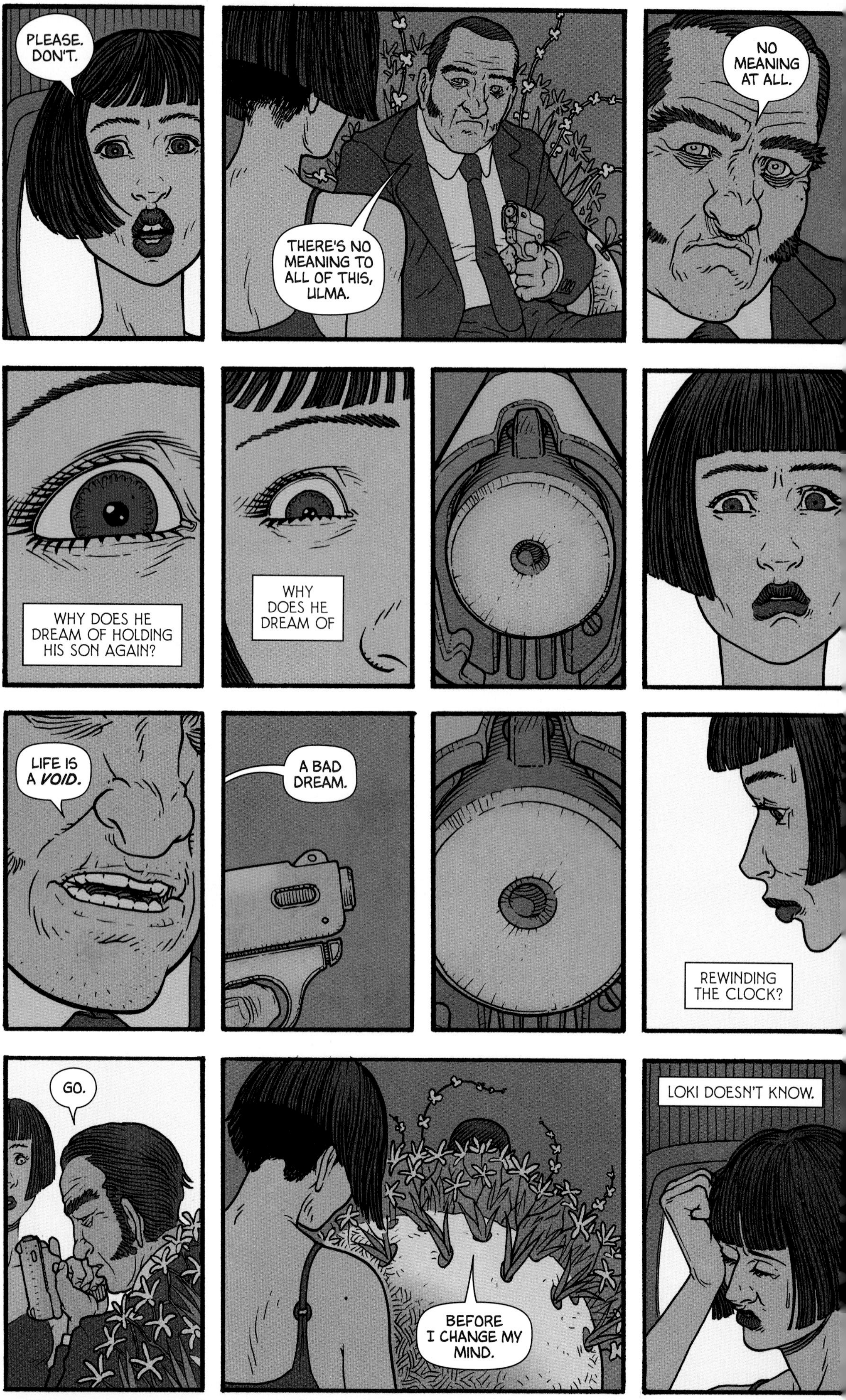
PLEASE. DON'T.
THERE'S NO MEANING TO ALL OF THIS, ULMA.
NO MEANING AT ALL.
WHY DOES HE DREAM OF HOLDING HIS SON AGAIN?
WHY DOES HE DREAM OF
LIFE IS A *VOID.*
A BAD DREAM.
REWINDING THE CLOCK?
GO.
BEFORE I CHANGE MY MIND.
LOKI DOESN'T KNOW.

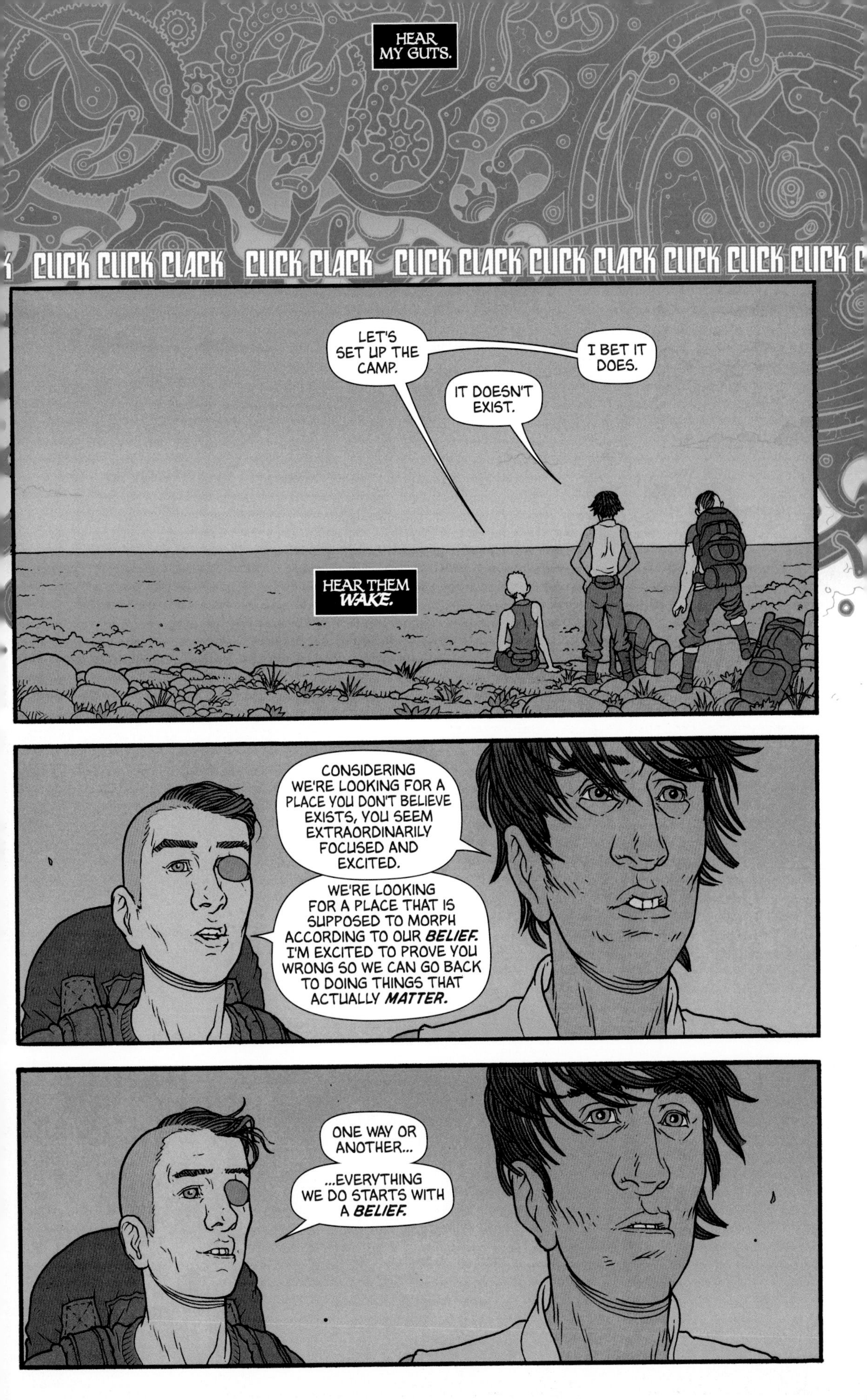
HEAR MY GUTS.
CLICK CLICK CLACK CLICK CLACK CLICK CLACK CLICK CLACK CLICK CLICK CLICK
LET'S SET UP THE CAMP.
IT DOESN'T EXIST.
I BET IT DOES.
HEAR THEM WAKE.
CONSIDERING WE'RE LOOKING FOR A PLACE YOU DON'T BELIEVE EXISTS, YOU SEEM EXTRAORDINARILY FOCUSED AND EXCITED.
WE'RE LOOKING FOR A PLACE THAT IS SUPPOSED TO MORPH ACCORDING TO OUR BELIEF. I'M EXCITED TO PROVE YOU WRONG SO WE CAN GO BACK TO DOING THINGS THAT ACTUALLY MATTER.
ONE WAY OR ANOTHER...
...EVERYTHING WE DO STARTS WITH A BELIEF.

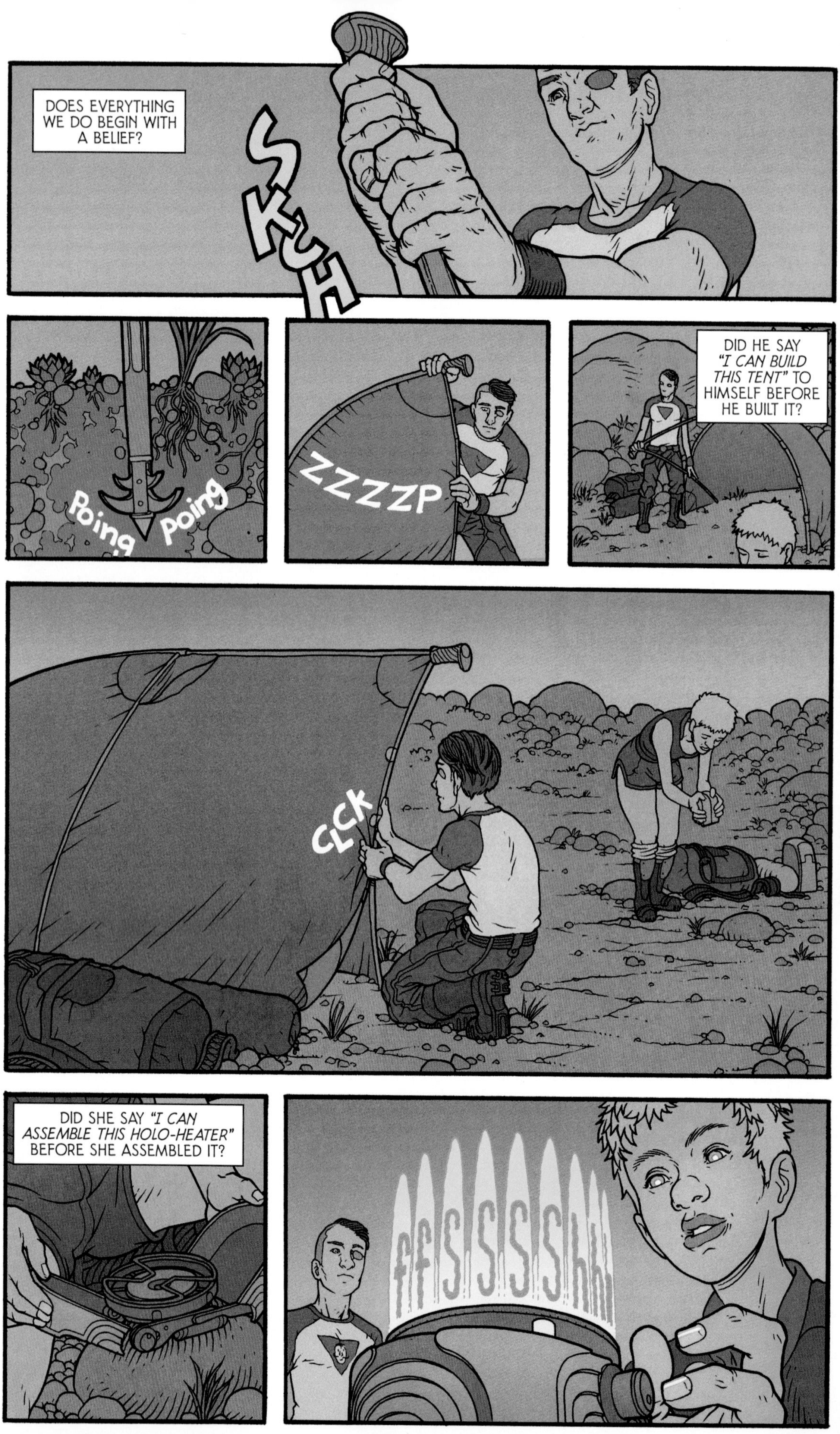
DOES EVERYTHING WE DO BEGIN WITH A BELIEF?
SKUH
Poing
poing
ZZZZP
DID HE SAY *"I CAN BUILD THIS TENT"* TO HIMSELF BEFORE HE BUILT IT?
CLCK
DID SHE SAY *"I CAN ASSEMBLE THIS HOLO-HEATER"* BEFORE SHE ASSEMBLED IT?
ffSSSShhh

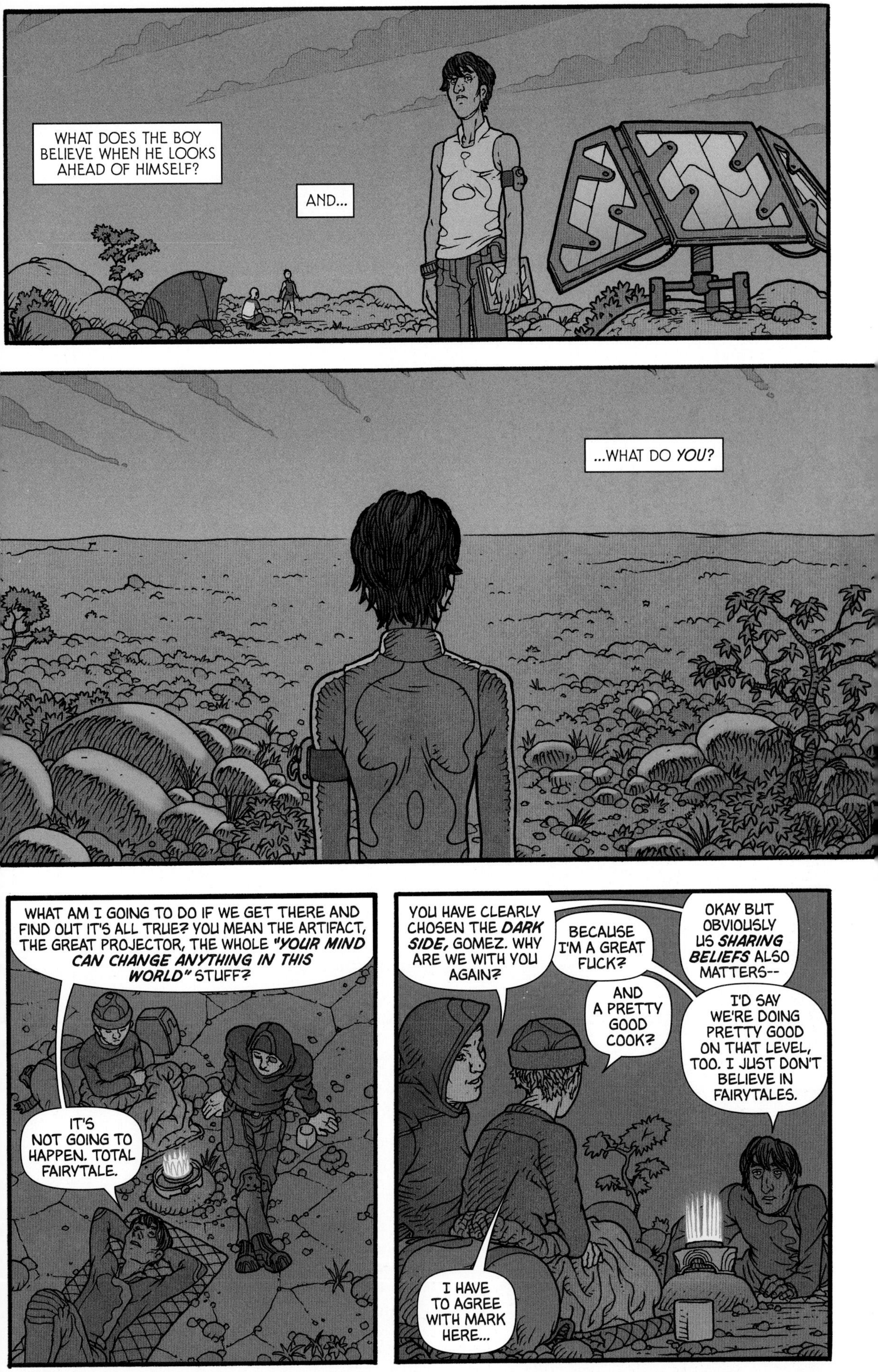
WHAT DOES THE BOY BELIEVE WHEN HE LOOKS AHEAD OF HIMSELF?
AND...
...WHAT DO *YOU*?
WHAT AM I GOING TO DO IF WE GET THERE AND FIND OUT IT'S ALL TRUE? YOU MEAN THE ARTIFACT, THE GREAT PROJECTOR, THE WHOLE ***"YOUR MIND CAN CHANGE ANYTHING IN THIS WORLD"*** STUFF?
IT'S NOT GOING TO HAPPEN. TOTAL FAIRYTALE.
YOU HAVE CLEARLY CHOSEN THE ***DARK SIDE,*** GOMEZ. WHY ARE WE WITH YOU AGAIN?
BECAUSE I'M A GREAT FUCK?
AND A PRETTY GOOD COOK?
OKAY BUT OBVIOUSLY US ***SHARING BELIEFS*** ALSO MATTERS--
I'D SAY WE'RE DOING PRETTY GOOD ON THAT LEVEL, TOO. I JUST DON'T BELIEVE IN FAIRYTALES.
I HAVE TO AGREE WITH MARK HERE...

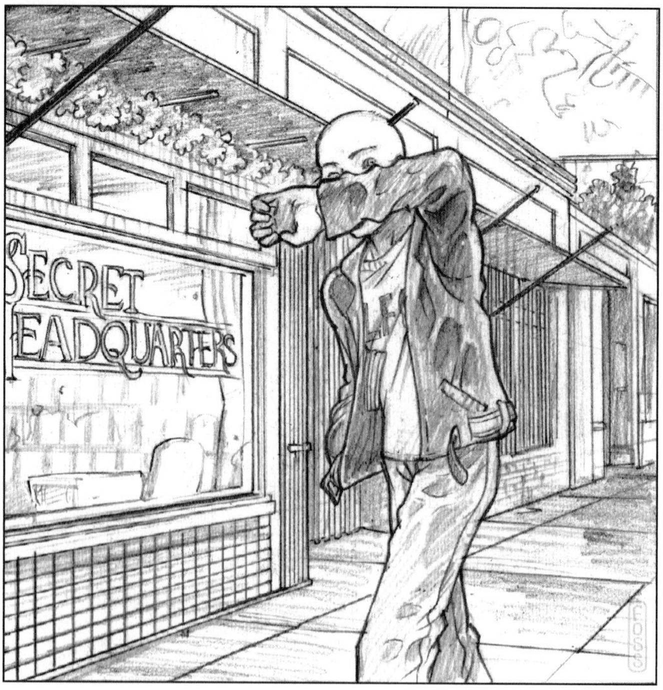
SECRET

ELUSIVE WRITER MAINTAINS "IT ALL MAKES SENSE AT THE END. MAYBE."
Part two of three

Q: Certain people on the internet were very upset by the way your three series ended this Summer – how do you feel about the response to what is ostensibly an end of an era for you?

Doublehead: Nervous. I mean, this is what I lived and wrote myself into, you know? I wanted to be where I'm at. So it's exciting. But also..

Oh wait – I thought you were asking about my feelings and thoughts on the matter. To go back to your original question, something I'm consciously escaping right now is fanboy culture. I know I could play the game, make the stories, get the hits, go the route everyone goes and get my near-sure success, you know? But I don't feel it. I just don't feel it. So I'm doing something else instead, and this thing I'm writing now feels like I'm wrapping up last pieces of old business. I'm working through it and I'm opening up something new. I'd rather risk a glorious failure than play it "safe," whatever that means. There's no safety. We constantly dive into the not knowing. And this project, and what I'm doing forwards, is consciously about that.

Q: Your writing is occasionally considered sloppy and cryptic. Would you agree with that assessment?

Doublehead: That's a fear I want to work through. That I'm not doing my best. That I could be communicating my thoughts and feelings and ideas clearer. The thing is, not everything in fiction should be clean and neat, you know? At least not for me. I love Altman's movies because he's willingly sloppy in a way that's true to life. Not everything in life feels neatly structured all the time. There's time and place for order, there's time and place for chaos...in fiction, in life.

It all makes sense. Maybe. I'm making it up as I go along, and the rest of the team sort of has to go with me or can push against if they have a better idea. This project, the project I originally conceived of about six years ago is finally getting made, and I no longer know if I have anything worth saying through it. But half of it is drawn and I believe I can find meaning in anything that happens, because while the world is inherently meaningless, that actually allows us to put meaning into just about anything...which sort of nicely connects with the core of the story.

Q: You described your current living situation as a "crossroads." Would you please elaborate on that?

Doublehead: Well, a lot of the film stuff is happening, and I had some pretty major revelations about how I want to live my life, which includes not taking shit from people anymore and doing what I want now instead of waiting for years, feeling like I need to "slow down" or "learn more" or such. I mean, I do need to learn, but I shouldn't let that stand in the way of doing things and learning through that. How can you learn if you don't do it, right?

Quitting all the stuff I didn't believe in at all anymore helped. Figuring out who and what I really want to give my attention to – that helped as well. Huuuuge help. Friends helped. Gloria helped. For the first time in my life I feel really loved for being me, and that's probably because for a long time I had a lot of blocks that were keeping me from actually being as deeply authentic and genuine with people as I wished I could be. Once I broke through with that, I started loving myself way more, and then eventually I started realizing the people who come into my life or were in my life became much more attuned to that. Just that feeling when things start clicking and it feels you're on the right path because you know you're doing you now.

And you gotta do you. Everyone else is taken. So the crossroads now is – do I go on with that? And the answer is I want to, yeah.

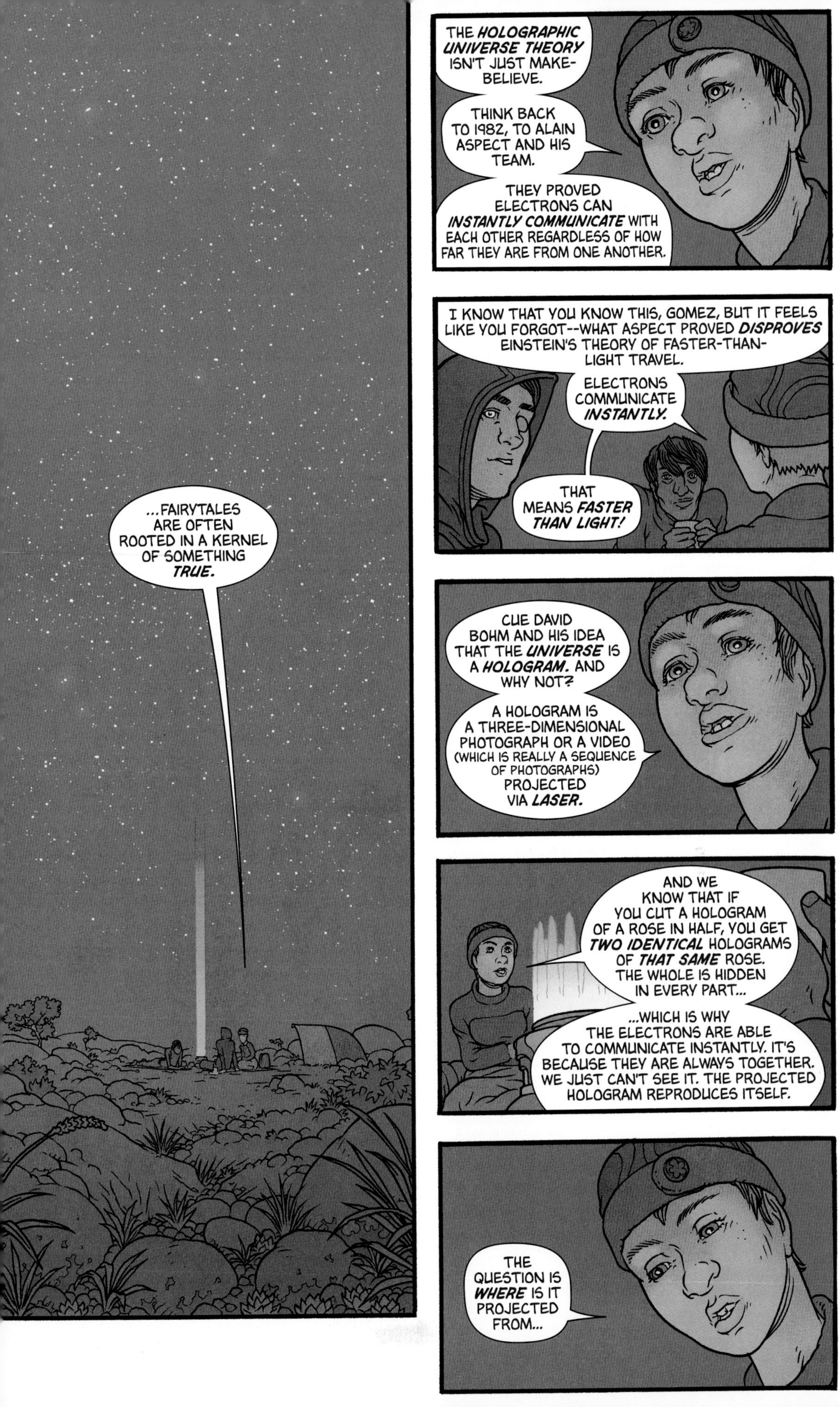
...FAIRYTALES ARE OFTEN ROOTED IN A KERNEL OF SOMETHING TRUE.
THE HOLOGRAPHIC UNIVERSE THEORY ISN'T JUST MAKE-BELIEVE.
THINK BACK TO 1982, TO ALAIN ASPECT AND HIS TEAM.
THEY PROVED ELECTRONS CAN INSTANTLY COMMUNICATE WITH EACH OTHER REGARDLESS OF HOW FAR THEY ARE FROM ONE ANOTHER.
I KNOW THAT YOU KNOW THIS, GOMEZ, BUT IT FEELS LIKE YOU FORGOT--WHAT ASPECT PROVED DISPROVES EINSTEIN'S THEORY OF FASTER-THAN-LIGHT TRAVEL.
ELECTRONS COMMUNICATE INSTANTLY.
THAT MEANS FASTER THAN LIGHT!
CUE DAVID BOHM AND HIS IDEA THAT THE UNIVERSE IS A HOLOGRAM. AND WHY NOT?
A HOLOGRAM IS A THREE-DIMENSIONAL PHOTOGRAPH OR A VIDEO (WHICH IS REALLY A SEQUENCE OF PHOTOGRAPHS) PROJECTED VIA LASER.
AND WE KNOW THAT IF YOU CUT A HOLOGRAM OF A ROSE IN HALF, YOU GET TWO IDENTICAL HOLOGRAMS OF THAT SAME ROSE. THE WHOLE IS HIDDEN IN EVERY PART...
...WHICH IS WHY THE ELECTRONS ARE ABLE TO COMMUNICATE INSTANTLY. IT'S BECAUSE THEY ARE ALWAYS TOGETHER. WE JUST CAN'T SEE IT. THE PROJECTED HOLOGRAM REPRODUCES ITSELF.
THE QUESTION IS WHERE IS IT PROJECTED FROM...

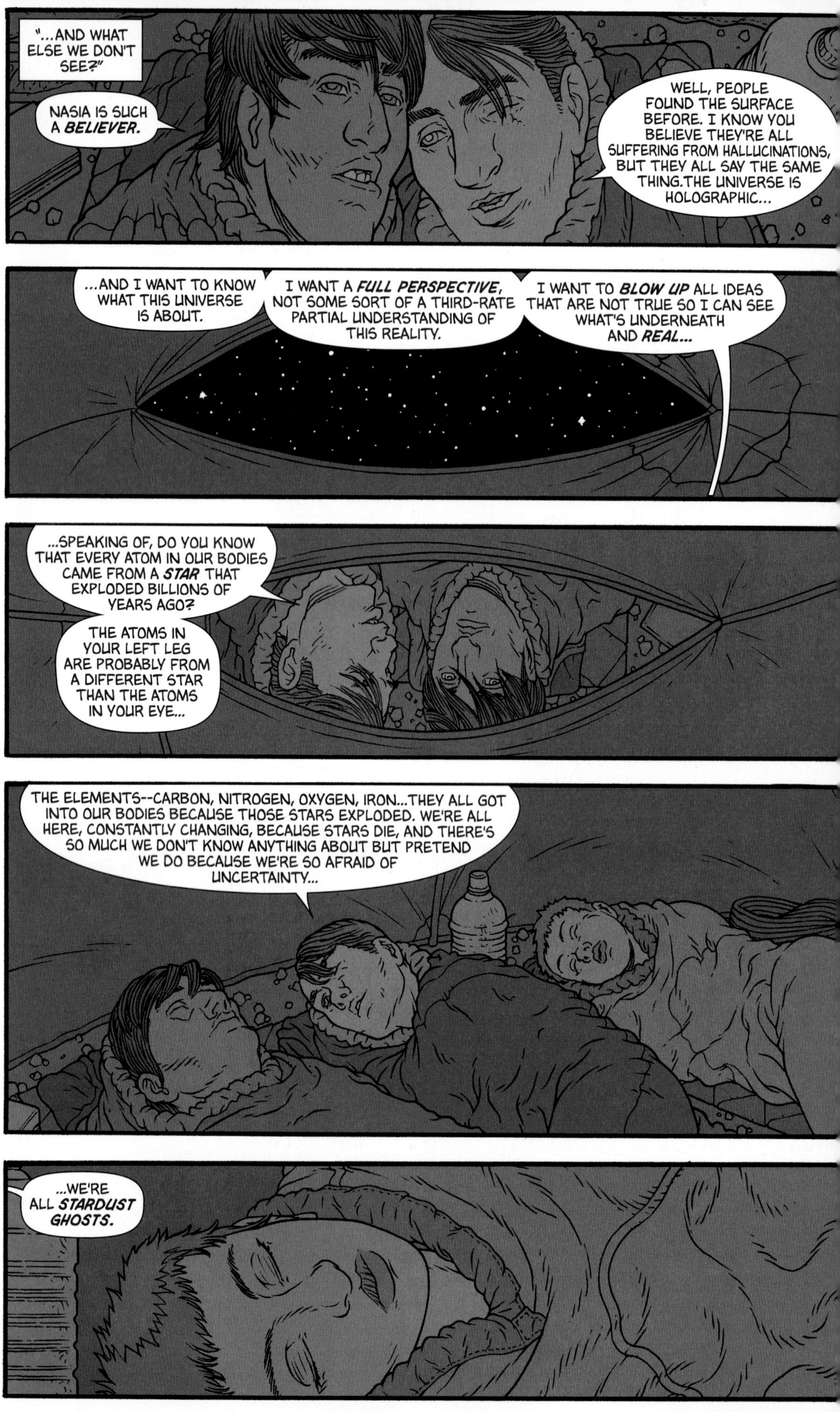
"...AND WHAT ELSE WE DON'T SEE?"
NASIA IS SUCH A ***BELIEVER.***
WELL, PEOPLE FOUND THE SURFACE BEFORE. I KNOW YOU BELIEVE THEY'RE ALL SUFFERING FROM HALLUCINATIONS, BUT THEY ALL SAY THE SAME THING.THE UNIVERSE IS HOLOGRAPHIC...
...AND I WANT TO KNOW WHAT THIS UNIVERSE IS ABOUT.
I WANT A ***FULL PERSPECTIVE,*** NOT SOME SORT OF A THIRD-RATE PARTIAL UNDERSTANDING OF THIS REALITY.
I WANT TO ***BLOW UP*** ALL IDEAS THAT ARE NOT TRUE SO I CAN SEE WHAT'S UNDERNEATH AND ***REAL...***
...SPEAKING OF, DO YOU KNOW THAT EVERY ATOM IN OUR BODIES CAME FROM A ***STAR*** THAT EXPLODED BILLIONS OF YEARS AGO?
THE ATOMS IN YOUR LEFT LEG ARE PROBABLY FROM A DIFFERENT STAR THAN THE ATOMS IN YOUR EYE...
THE ELEMENTS--CARBON, NITROGEN, OXYGEN, IRON...THEY ALL GOT INTO OUR BODIES BECAUSE THOSE STARS EXPLODED. WE'RE ALL HERE, CONSTANTLY CHANGING, BECAUSE STARS DIE, AND THERE'S SO MUCH WE DON'T KNOW ANYTHING ABOUT BUT PRETEND WE DO BECAUSE WE'RE SO AFRAID OF UNCERTAINTY...
...WE'RE ALL ***STARDUST GHOSTS.***

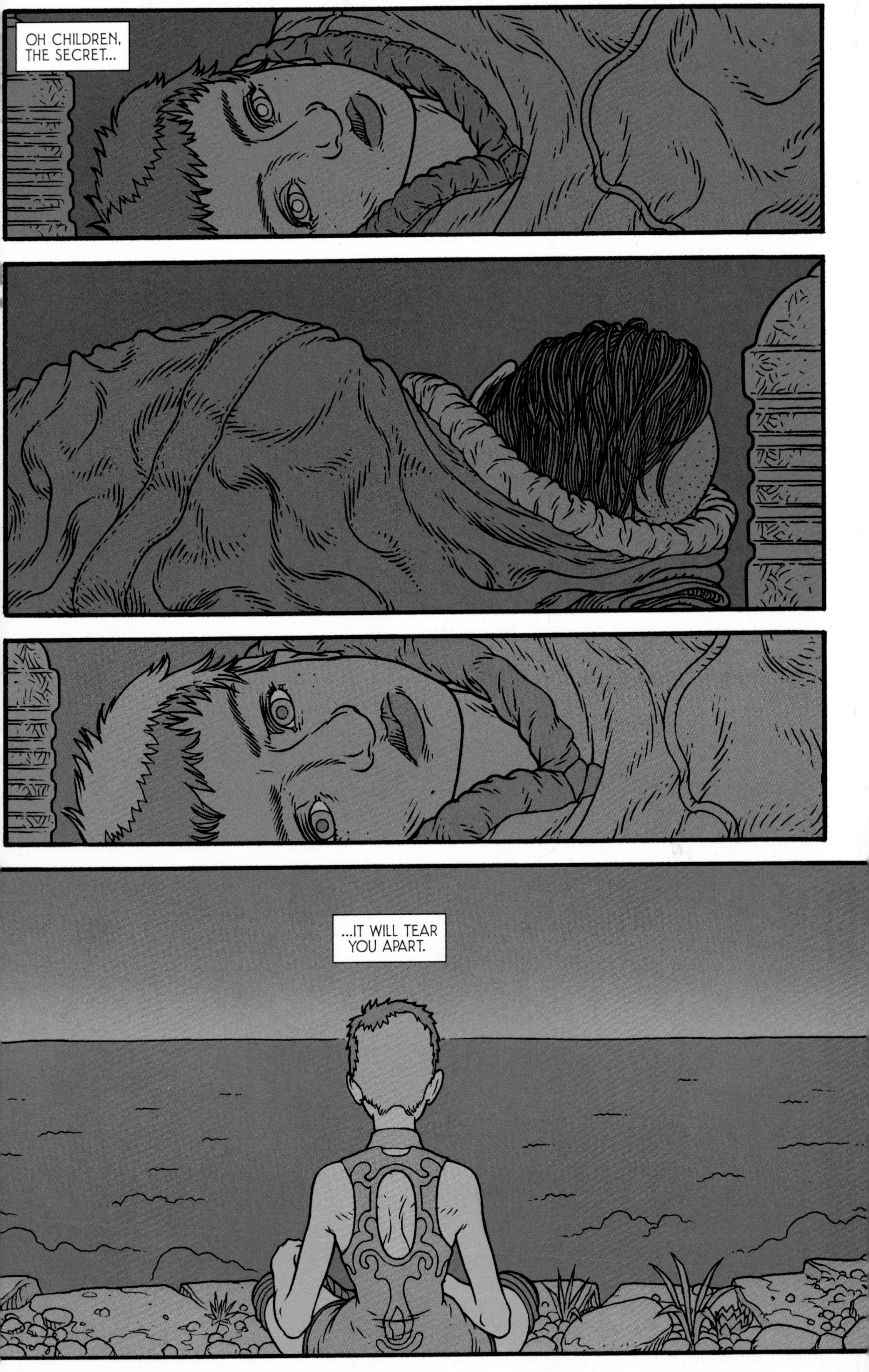
OH CHILDREN, THE SECRET...
...IT WILL TEAR YOU APART.

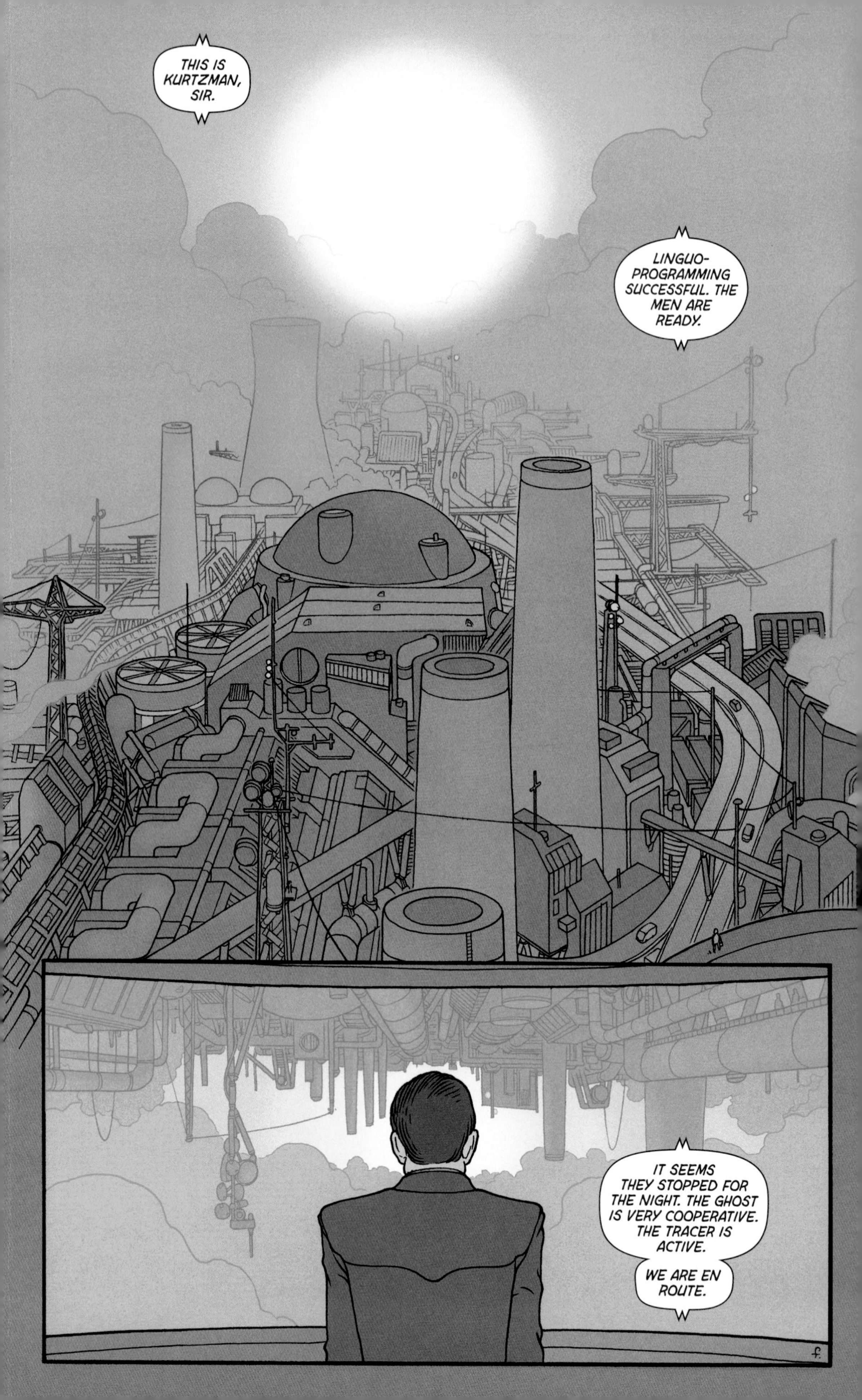
THIS IS KURTZMAN, SIR.
LINGUO-PROGRAMMING SUCCESSFUL. THE MEN ARE READY.
IT SEEMS THEY STOPPED FOR THE NIGHT. THE GHOST IS VERY COOPERATIVE. THE TRACER IS ACTIVE.
WE ARE EN ROUTE.

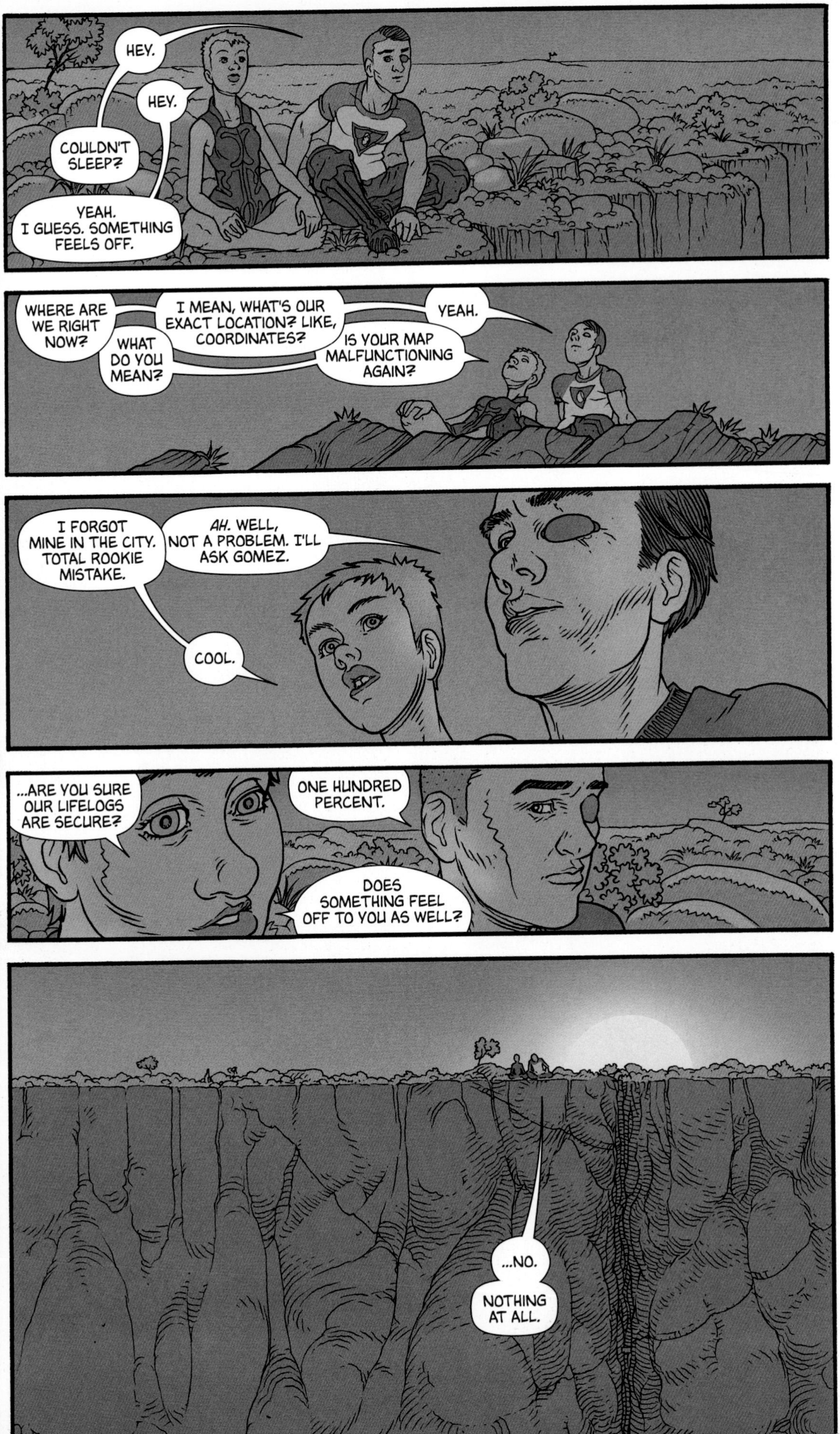
HEY.
HEY.
COULDN'T SLEEP?
YEAH. I GUESS. SOMETHING FEELS OFF.
WHERE ARE WE RIGHT NOW?
WHAT DO YOU MEAN?
I MEAN, WHAT'S OUR EXACT LOCATION? LIKE, COORDINATES?
YEAH.
IS YOUR MAP MALFUNCTIONING AGAIN?
I FORGOT MINE IN THE CITY. TOTAL ROOKIE MISTAKE.
AH. WELL, NOT A PROBLEM. I'LL ASK GOMEZ.
COOL.
...ARE YOU SURE OUR LIFELOGS ARE SECURE?
ONE HUNDRED PERCENT.
DOES SOMETHING FEEL OFF TO YOU AS WELL?
...NO.
NOTHING AT ALL.

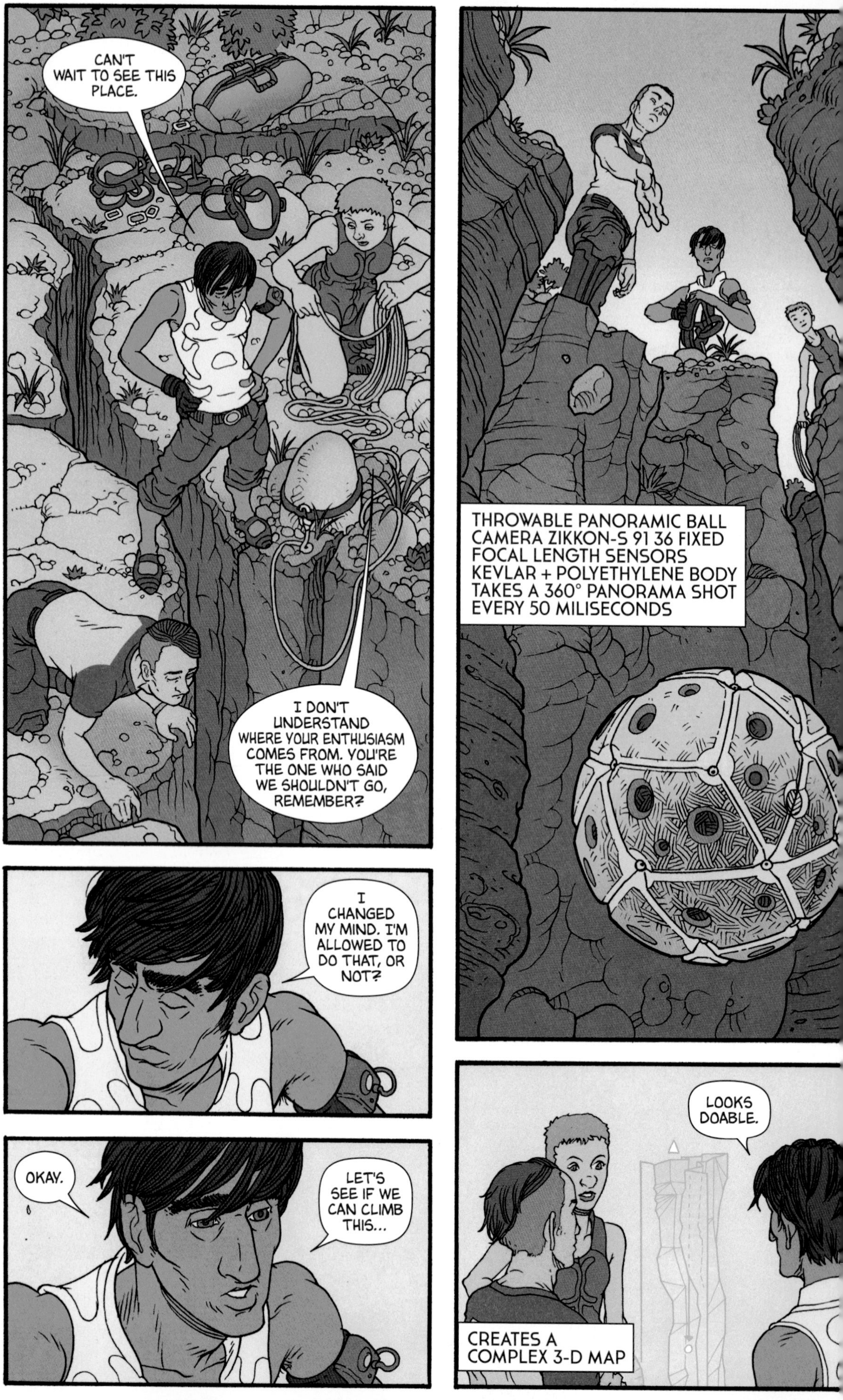
CAN'T WAIT TO SEE THIS PLACE.
I DON'T UNDERSTAND WHERE YOUR ENTHUSIASM COMES FROM. YOU'RE THE ONE WHO SAID WE SHOULDN'T GO, REMEMBER?
I CHANGED MY MIND. I'M ALLOWED TO DO THAT, OR NOT?
OKAY.
LET'S SEE IF WE CAN CLIMB THIS...
THROWABLE PANORAMIC BALL CAMERA ZIKKON-S 91 36 FIXED FOCAL LENGTH SENSORS KEVLAR + POLYETHYLENE BODY TAKES A 360° PANORAMA SHOT EVERY 50 MILISECONDS
LOOKS DOABLE.
CREATES A COMPLEX 3-D MAP

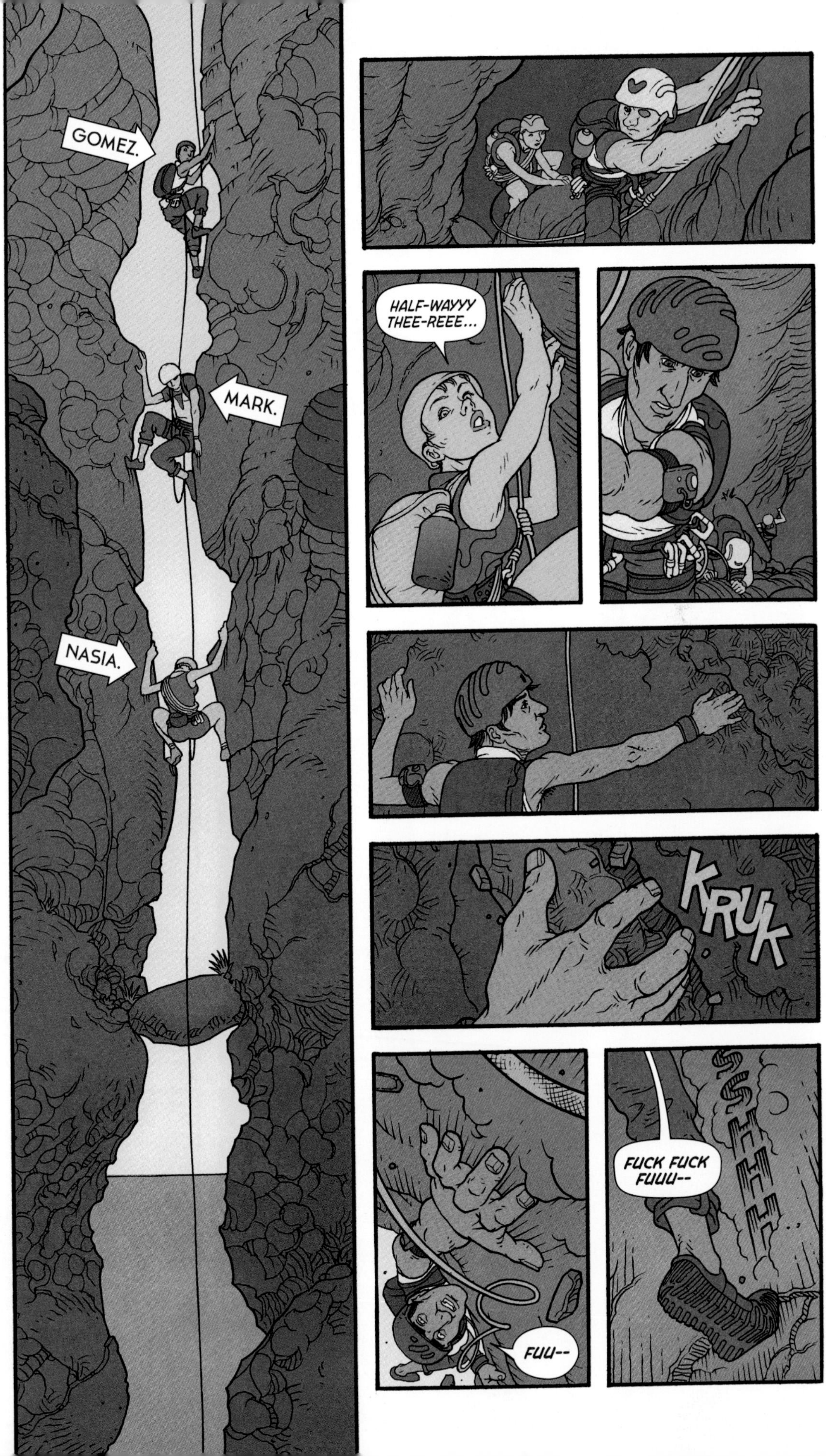
GOMEZ.
MARK.
NASIA.
HALF-WAYYY THEE-REEE...
KRUK
FUCK FUCK FUUU--
FUU--

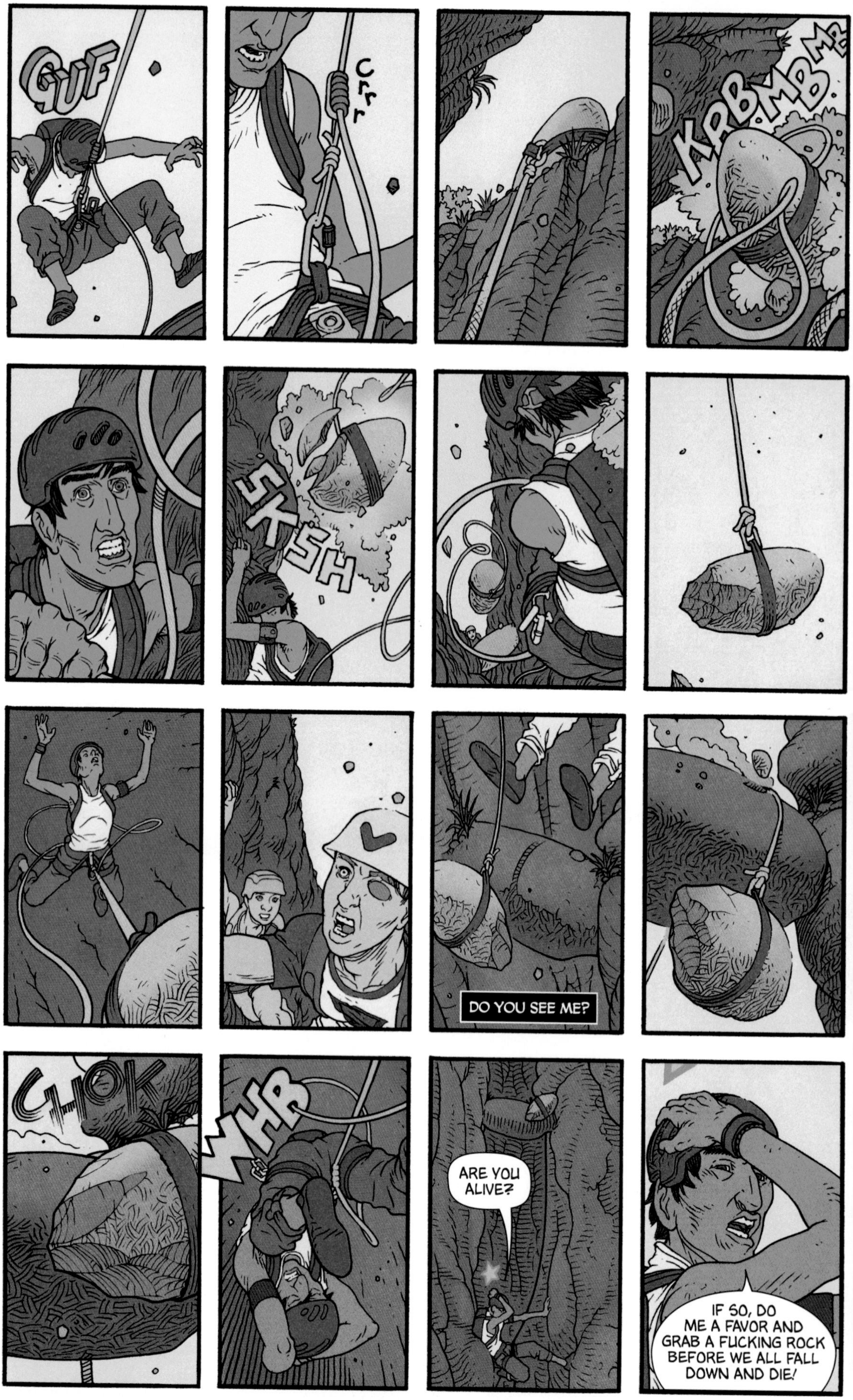
GUF
Crrr
KRBMBMB
SKSH
DO YOU SEE ME?
CHOK
WHB
ARE YOU ALIVE?
IF SO, DO ME A FAVOR AND GRAB A FUCKING ROCK BEFORE WE ALL FALL DOWN AND DIE!

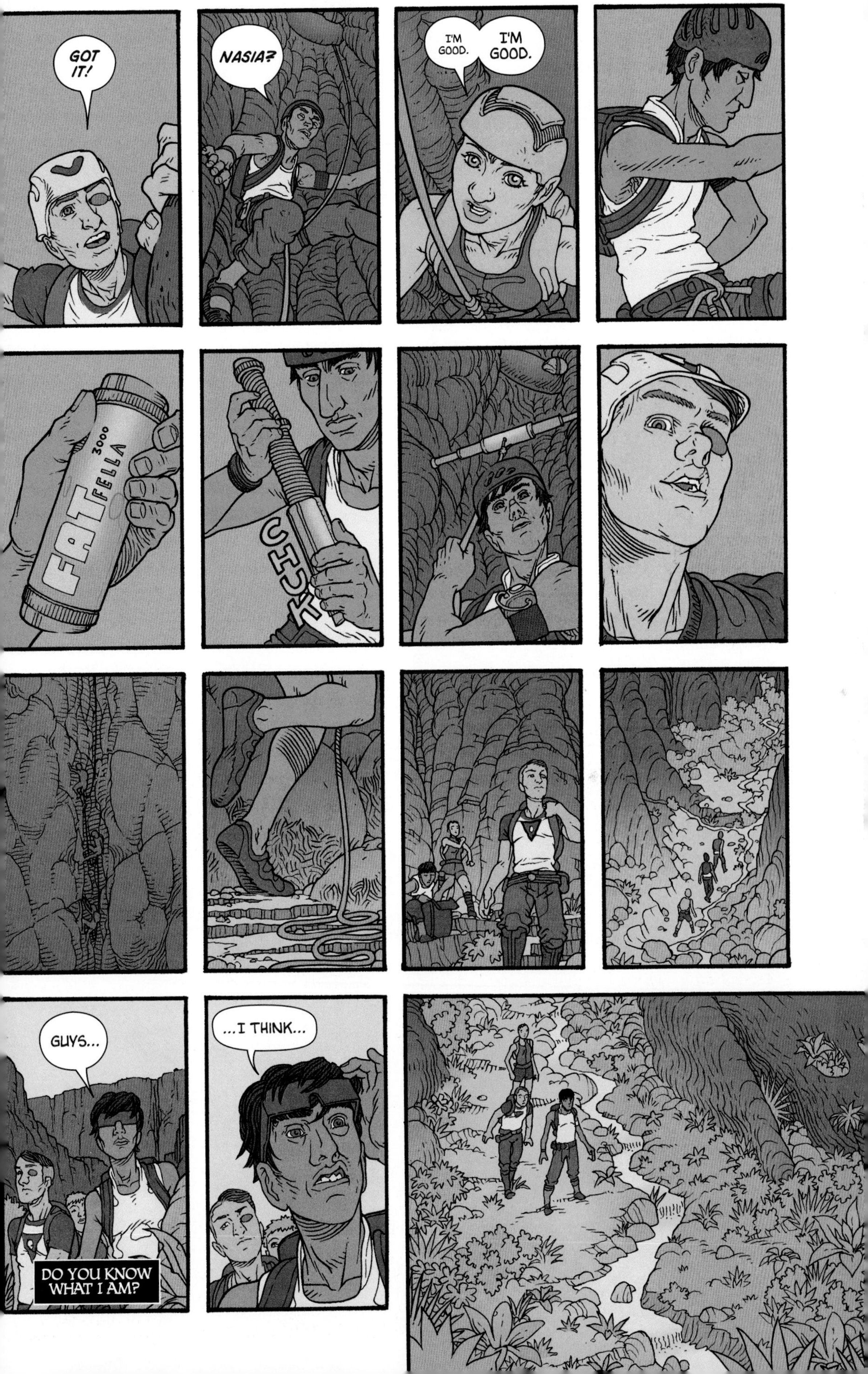
GOT IT!
NASIA?
I'M GOOD.
I'M GOOD.
FAT FELLA 3000
CHUK
GUYS...
DO YOU KNOW WHAT I AM?
...I THINK...

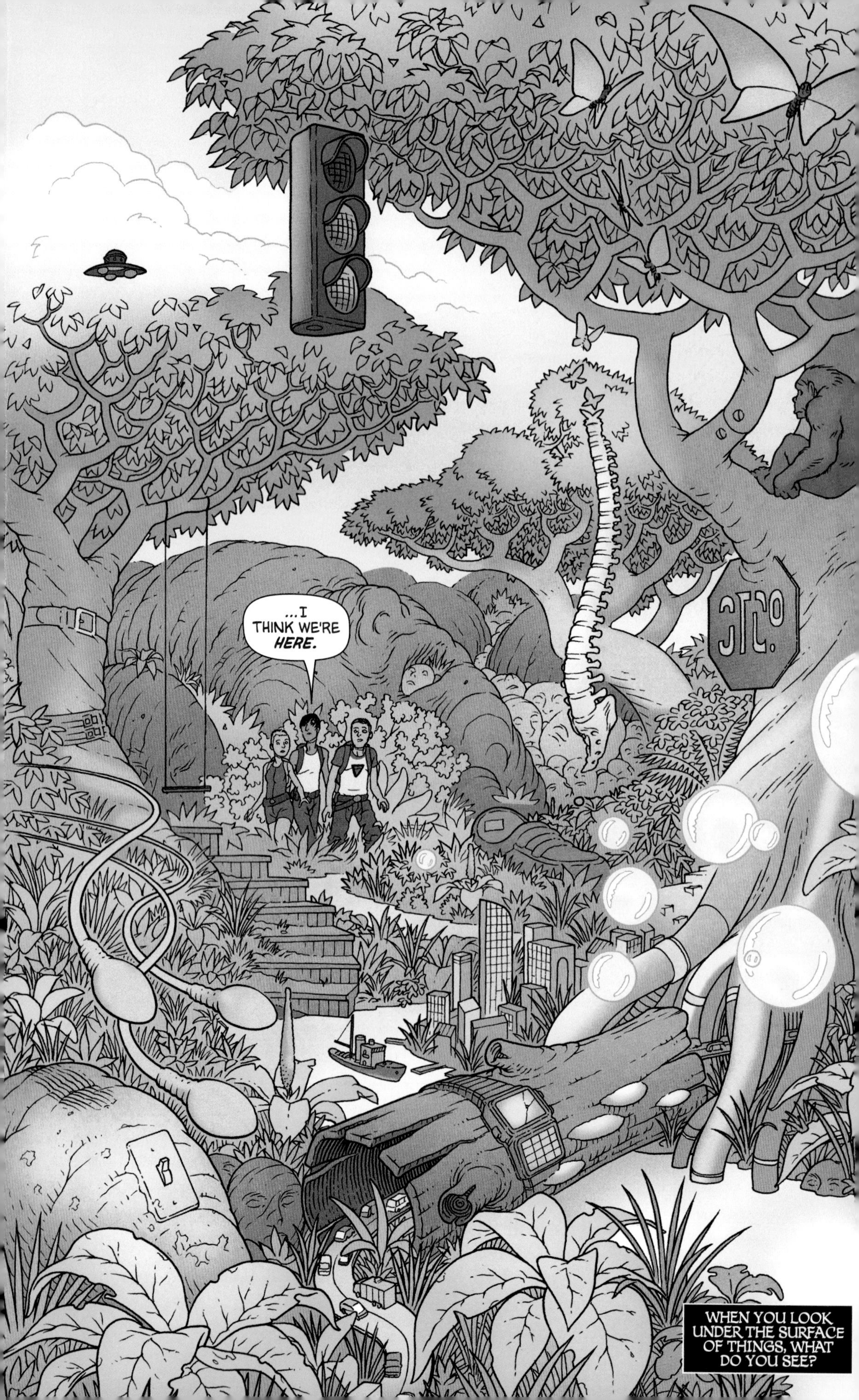
...I THINK WE'RE HERE.
WHEN YOU LOOK UNDER THE SURFACE OF THINGS, WHAT DO YOU SEE?

ELUSIVE WRITER MAINTAINS "IT ALL MAKES SENSE AT THE END. MAYBE."
Part three of three

Q: You voiced concerns about people connecting with your new project. Why is that?

Doublehead: Yeah...I nearly sent the retailers a letter where I apologized for even publishing this in the first place. I just don't know if it's any good, you know? I wrote a lot of additional "content" to really pack the thing, and it feels good, it feels better the closer we go to print. I originally built this project, as I tend to with anything I work on, in order to work with myself, to change something, to transmute something. "Change," which you can still buy at your local comic book store and on Amazon and such, is probably the clearest example of how psychomagic works when applied right. I mean, holy shit! It CHANGED things massive.

So seeing this project from the same perspective, and knowing I'm still writing it, still figuring out how it coheres, how various characters relate to myself and where I'm at in the universe and in the concept I call "my life," that's nurturing, and I'm grateful for a chance to do this with a publisher who believed in me since the beginning. There's no place I'd rather be. Even though I'm scared you're all going to hate it. What I really hope for is making a genuine connection.

Q: What is psychomagic? How does it work? Is it safe?

Doublehead: "It is to be remembered that all art is magical in origin – music, sculpture, writing, painting – and by magical I mean intended to produce very definite results. Paintings were originally formulae to make what is painted happen. Art is not an end in itself, any more than Einstein's matter-into-energy formulae is an end in itself. Like all formulae, art was originally FUNCTIONAL, intended to make things happen, the way an atom bomb happens from Einstein's formulae."

Look at me, quoting uncle Bill Burroughs again. But it fits! Art is a way of making something happen. What I'm making happen through this project...I don't know yet, not exactly, although I feel there are some hints hidden within already. I didn't know what the last page of 'Change' would be, and that turned out pretty fine. Sometimes, love is the act of not knowing.

Psychomagic is a way of working with what's inside you – often the shit – and transmuting it into gold. That's what alchemy might really be about. So I'm dragging things out of my gut and into the light to see what happens when I communicate with them on the page.

Q: What is the traffic light about?

Doublehead: It's art!

NASIA ARE YOU SEEING THIS NONE OF THIS IS REAL THEY ARE TRYING TO EXTRACT THE LOCATION

blinkfeed

YOUR #1 NO-BULLSHIT SOURCE OF INFORMATION

CLICK TO SEE THE ENTIRE BLINKFEED LIST OF NO-BULLSHIT SOURCES OF INFORMATION

REMAINDERS OF ISIS ATTEMPTED TO DESTROY ONE OF THE LAST ASSYRIAN TEMPLES STANDING – CITIZEN JOURNALIST AND A SUPPOSED "ANCIENT DEMON" W. PAZUZU REPORTS FROM THE SITE OF THEIR SUBSEQUENT VANISHING

WOULD YOU LIKE TO KNOW MORE?

POLYAMORY OFFICIALLY APPROVED AS A LEGAL CHOICE FOR PARTNERED COEXISTENCE
Many lovebirds say rules are still very strict, but the possibilities are much wider than ever before!

WOULD YOU LIKE TO KNOW MORE?

WHAT IS VERHOEVEN-DELANY DOING IN TANZANIA?
WOULD YOU LIKE TO KNOW MORE?

NO TRACE OF THE EXCESSIVE WRITER: THREE YEARS LATER, DOUBLEHEAD'S VANISHING TRICK STILL CONFOUNDS HIS YEARNING AUDIENCE

WOULD YOU LIKE TO KNOW MORE?

WHAT IS REALITY?
WOULD YOU LIKE TO KNOW MORE?

UNDER THE PAVING-STONES, UBIK!

NASIA, YOU ARE STUCK INSIDE A LOOP.
DON'T LET WHAT HAPPENS NEXT THROW YOU OFF

LOKI IS PLAYING A DEEP GAME CAN'T WRITE MORE DON'T BELIEVE YOUR SENSES BELIEVE YOUR FEELINGS

TROUBLE IN PARADISE?

WHAT ARE WE REALLY GETTING AT HERE?

WE'RE STILL NOT ENTIRELY SURE.

(Are we lying?)

(Possibly)

(And why do you read fiction?)

Is it because it soothes your wounds? Because it reminds you of things that are safe, easy to digest, not like the universe outside your window?

Well, then they shouldn't have sent a poet.

(And who are "we" anyway?)

HORRK HORRK.

But really, is there any one correct way to read a work of fiction? What if fiction is reality, and what if one and the other are but a mirror to what we fill them with? What if the Surface – the idea of the comic, the physical version of it, too – is being projected by you?

Just remember – Sylvia Plath had daddy issues, too. A complex comic is no reason for a gas oven.

DADA

(Such a dad joke)

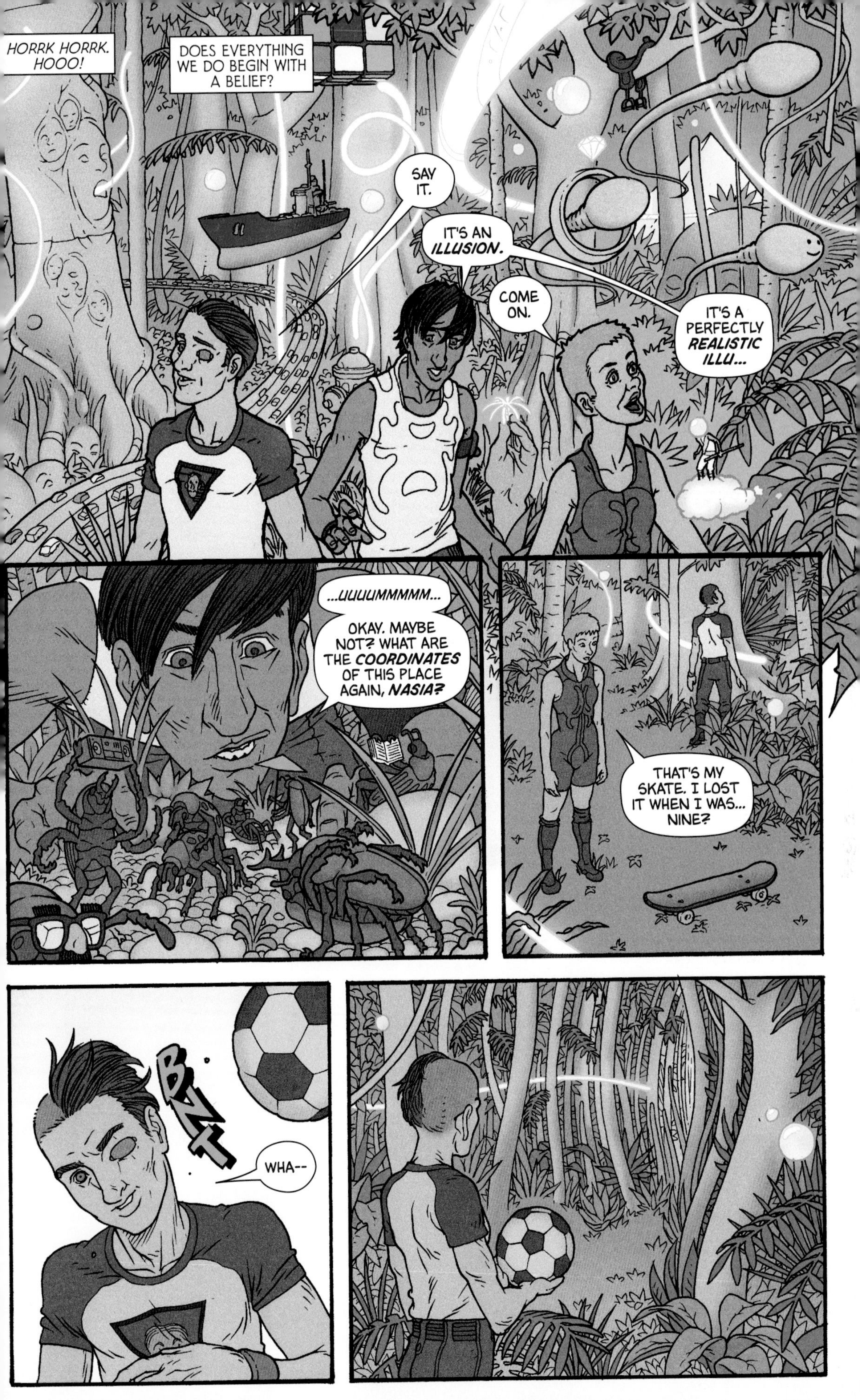
HORRK HORRK. HOOO!
DOES EVERYTHING WE DO BEGIN WITH A BELIEF?
SAY IT.
IT'S AN *ILLUSION.*
COME ON.
IT'S A PERFECTLY *REALISTIC ILLU...*
...UUUUMMMMM...
OKAY. MAYBE NOT? WHAT ARE THE *COORDINATES* OF THIS PLACE AGAIN, *NASIA?*
THAT'S MY SKATE. I LOST IT WHEN I WAS... NINE?
BZZT
WHA--

SO FAR WE'VE BEEN NARRATING TO EASE YOU IN, BUT NOW'S THE TIME TO GET *SERIOUS*.

WELCOME TO *THE SURFACE*. WE'RE CUTTING THROUGH THE *PROJECTION*. THE *VERHOEVEN-DELANY* PEOPLE CAN'T TELL WE'RE HERE WITH YOU.

THEY ALL THOUGHT THE *DUAL NARRATION* WAS A PART OF THE *WRITER'S PLAN*, A CUNNING NEW INVENTION CREATED TO EXTRACT THE NEEDED INFORMATION, VALUE, *DATA*.

WHO IS SPEAKING TO YOU WHEN YOU HEAR THAT *SECOND VOICE*, THE ONE FROM THE *DARK*?

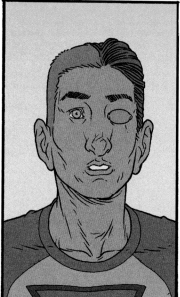

DAD?

NASIA?

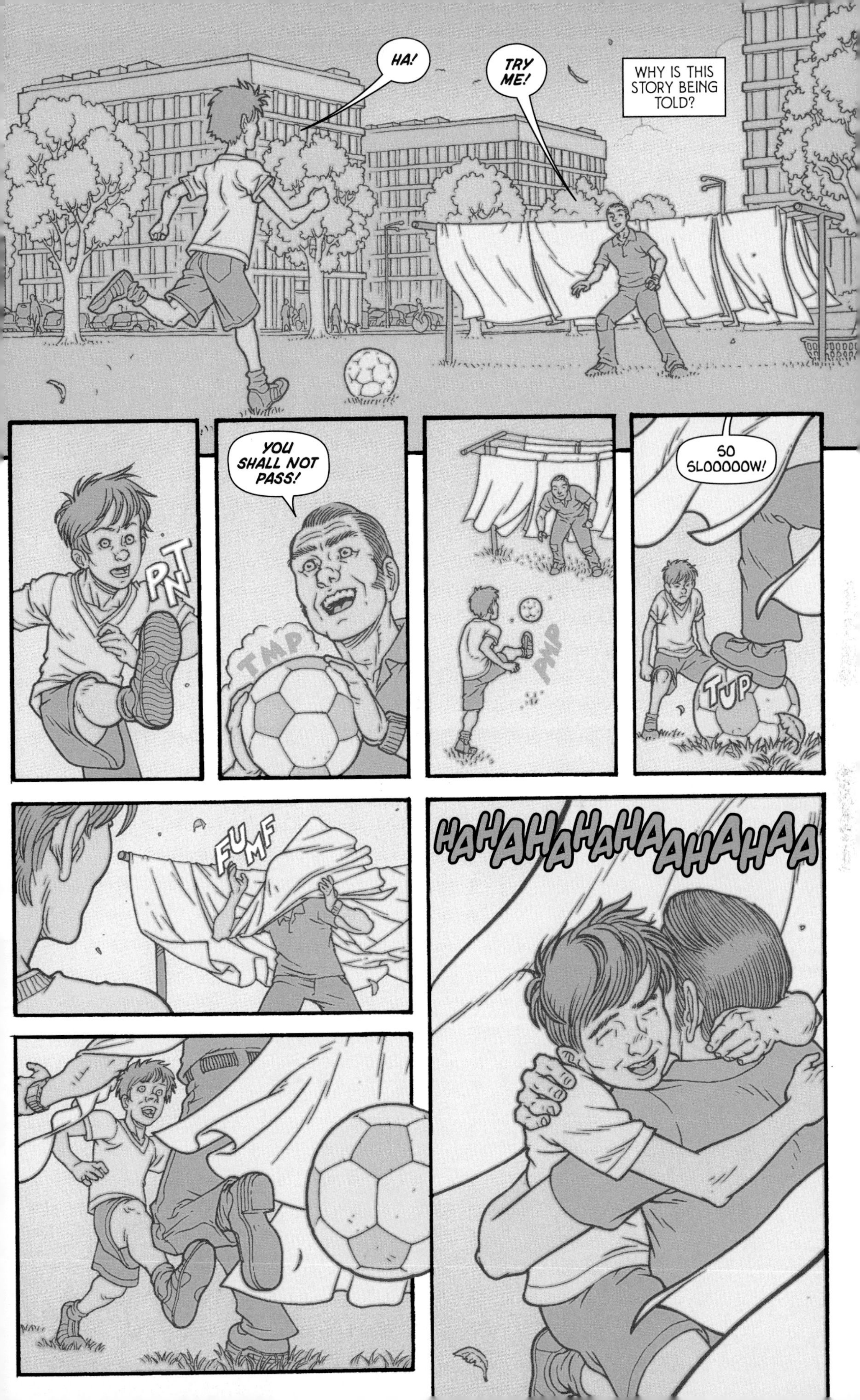
HA!
TRY ME!
WHY IS THIS STORY BEING TOLD?
PNT
YOU SHALL NOT PASS!
TMP
PMP
SO SLOOOOOW!
TUP
FUMF
HAHAHAHAHAHAAHAHAA

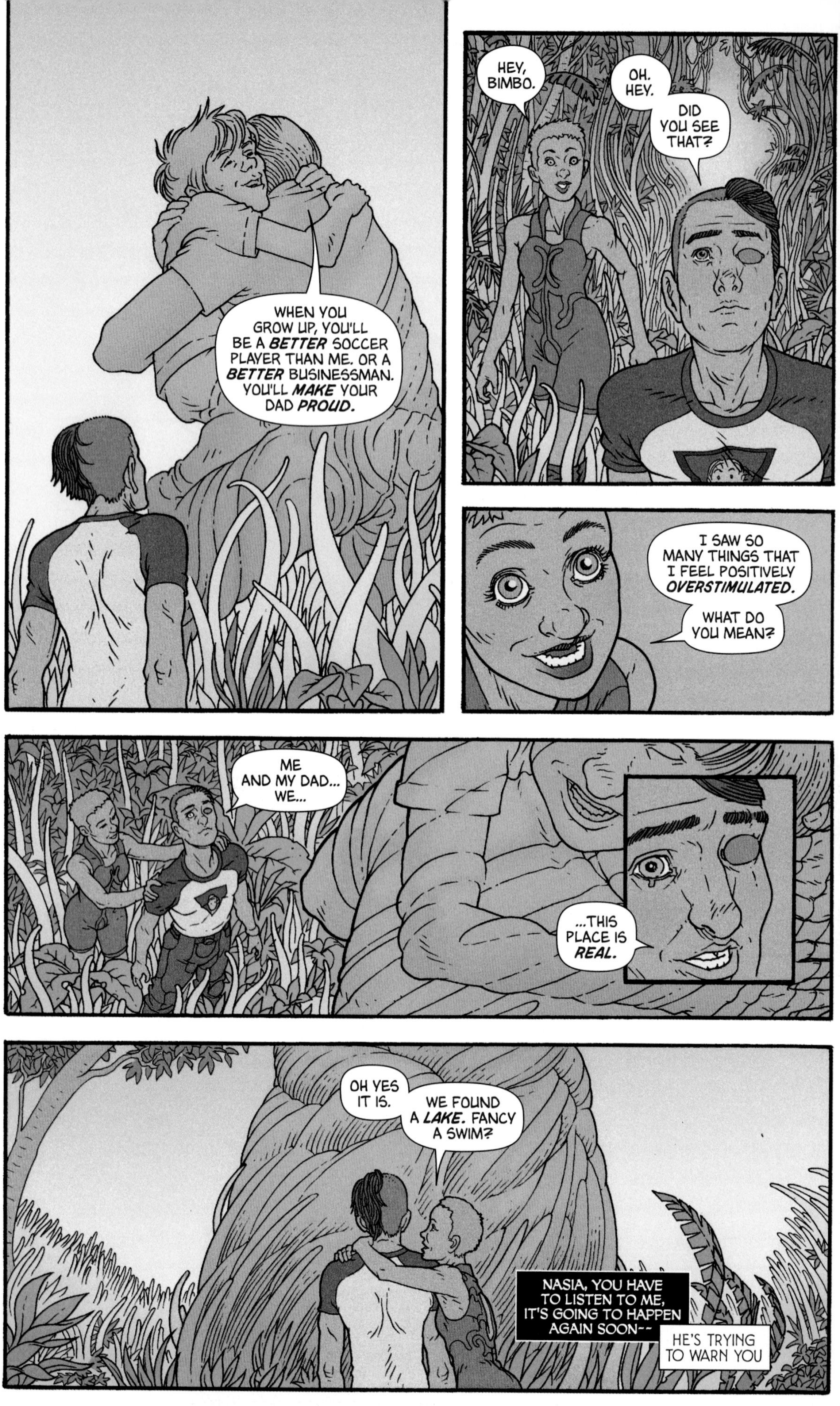

WHEN YOU GROW UP, YOU'LL BE A *BETTER* SOCCER PLAYER THAN ME. OR A *BETTER* BUSINESSMAN. YOU'LL *MAKE* YOUR DAD *PROUD.*
HEY, BIMBO.
OH. HEY.
DID YOU SEE THAT?
I SAW SO MANY THINGS THAT I FEEL POSITIVELY *OVERSTIMULATED.*
WHAT DO YOU MEAN?
ME AND MY DAD... WE...
...THIS PLACE IS *REAL.*
OH YES IT IS.
WE FOUND A *LAKE.* FANCY A SWIM?
NASIA, YOU HAVE TO LISTEN TO ME, IT'S GOING TO HAPPEN AGAIN SOON--
HE'S TRYING TO WARN YOU

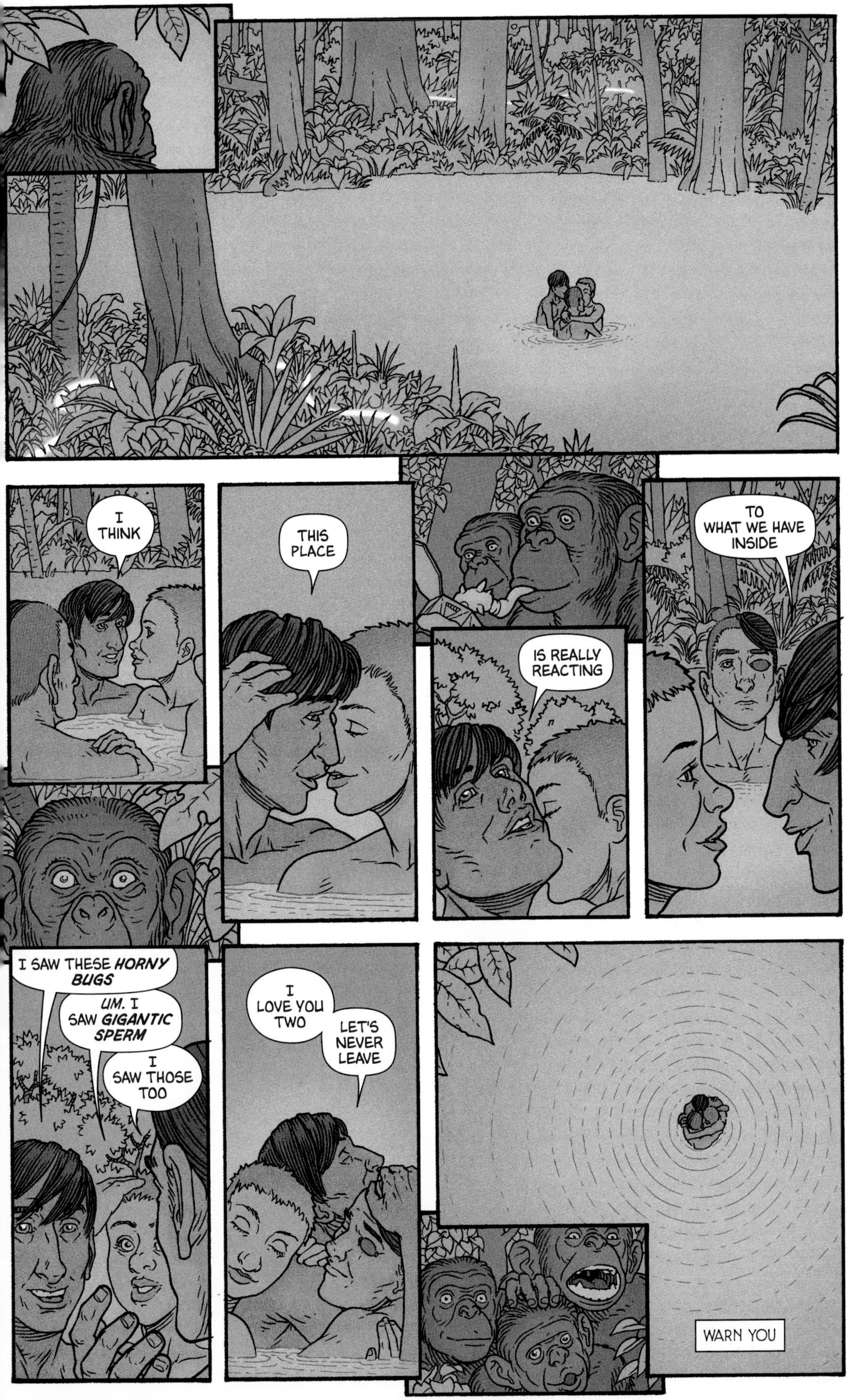
I THINK
THIS PLACE
IS REALLY REACTING
TO WHAT WE HAVE INSIDE
I SAW THESE HORNY BUGS
UM. I SAW GIGANTIC SPERM
I SAW THOSE TOO
I LOVE YOU TWO
LET'S NEVER LEAVE
WARN YOU

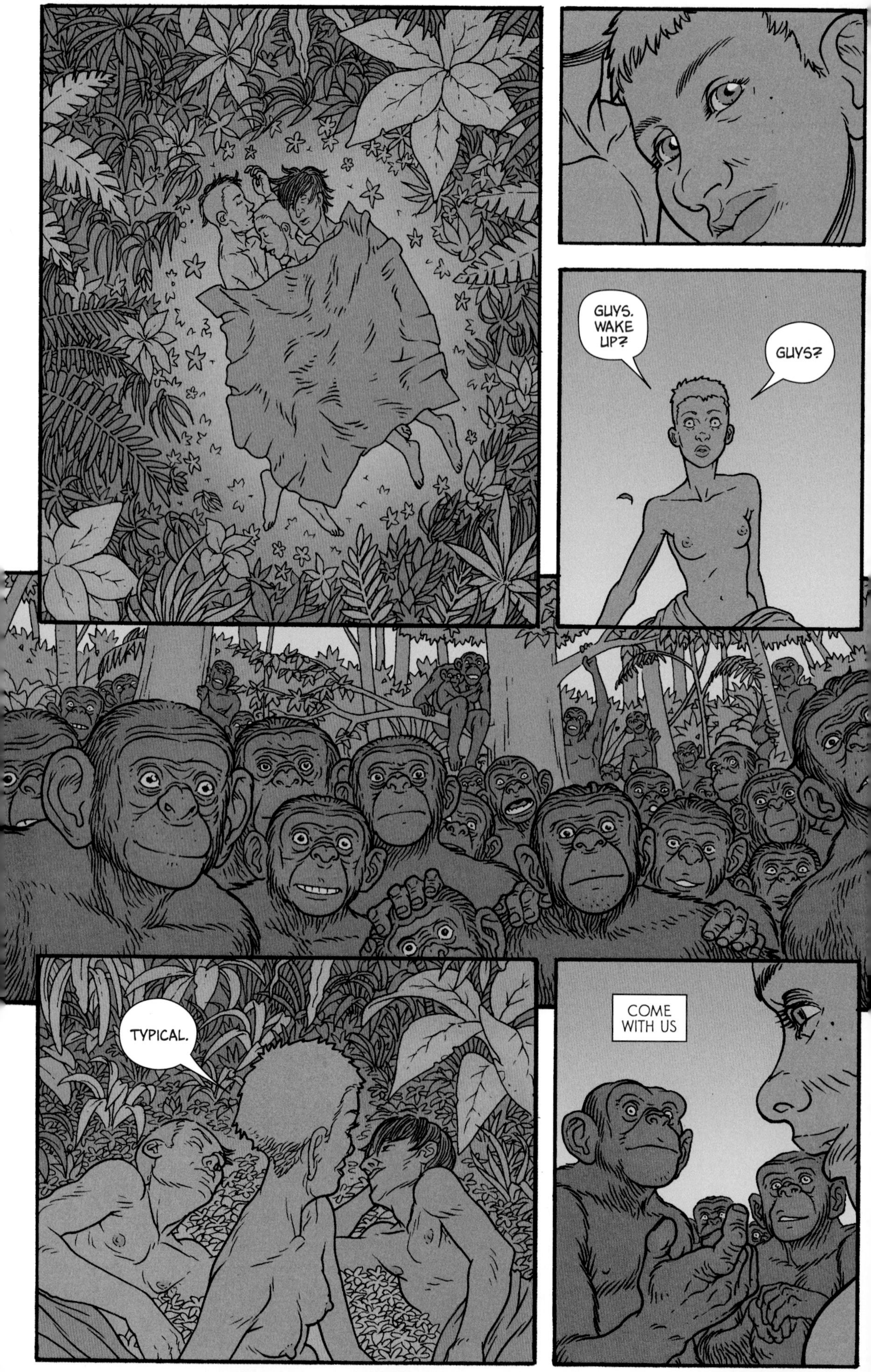
GUYS.
WAKE
UP?
GUYS?
TYPICAL.
COME
WITH US

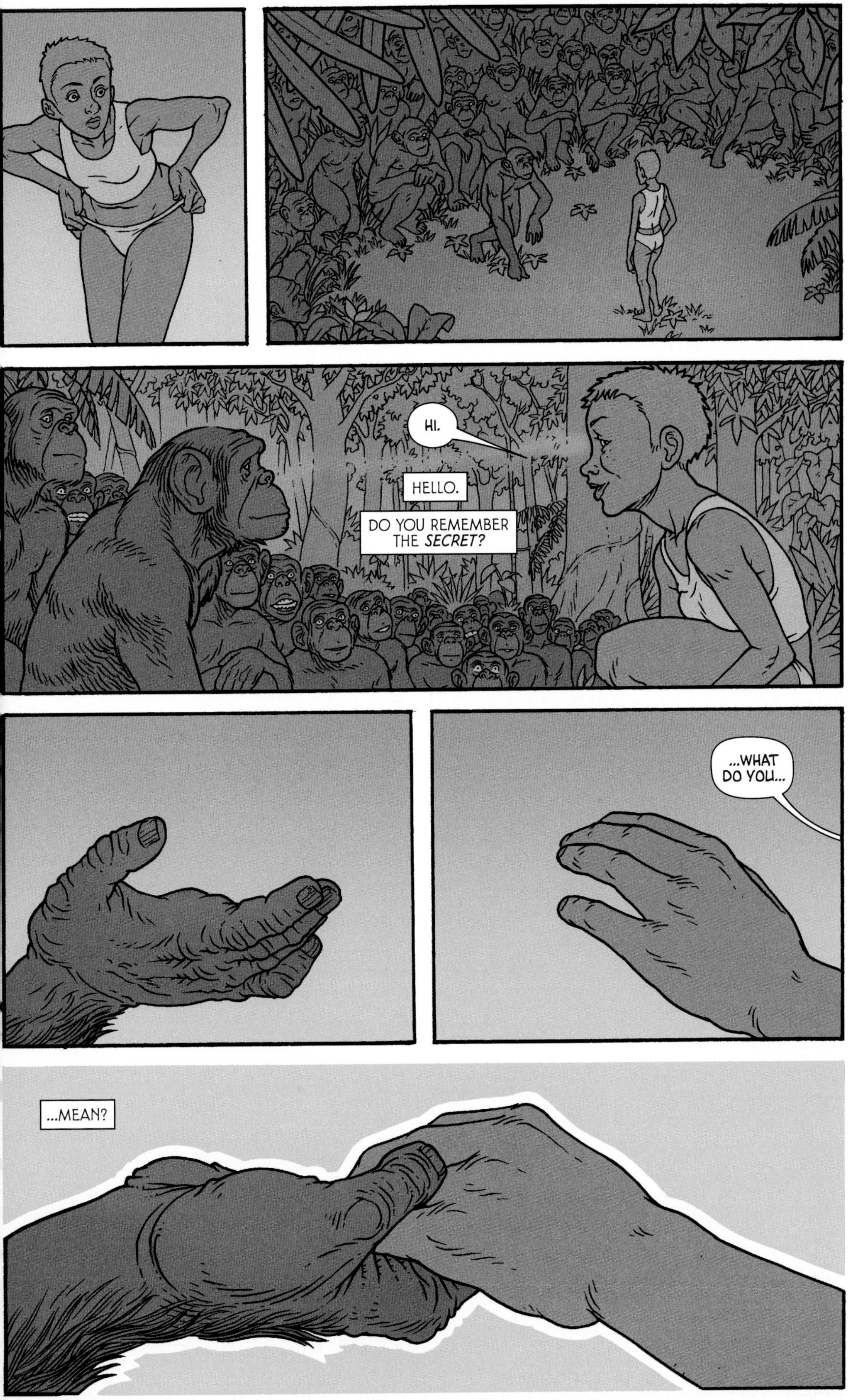
HI.
HELLO.
DO YOU REMEMBER THE *SECRET?*
...WHAT DO YOU...
...MEAN?

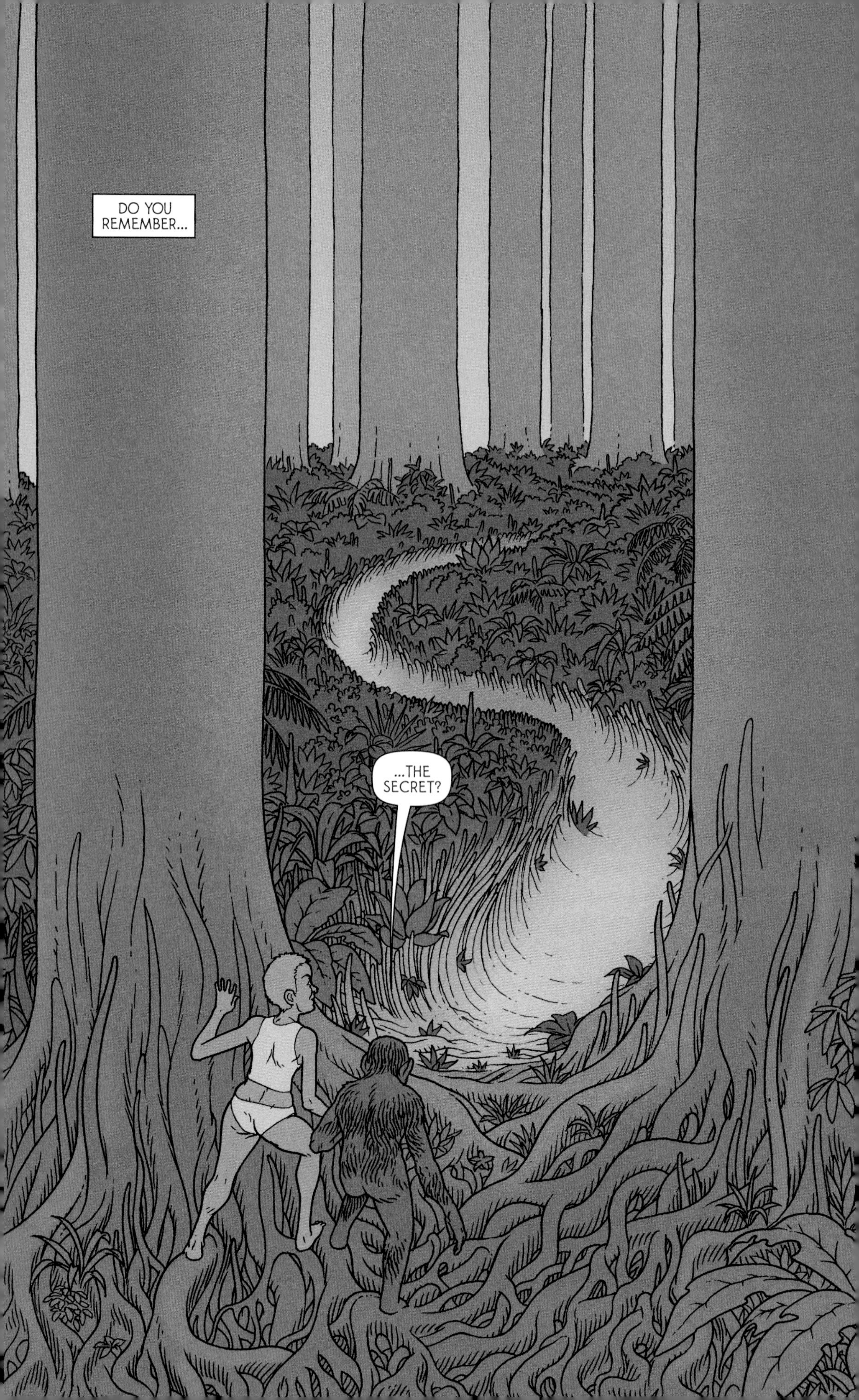
DO YOU REMEMBER...
...THE SECRET?

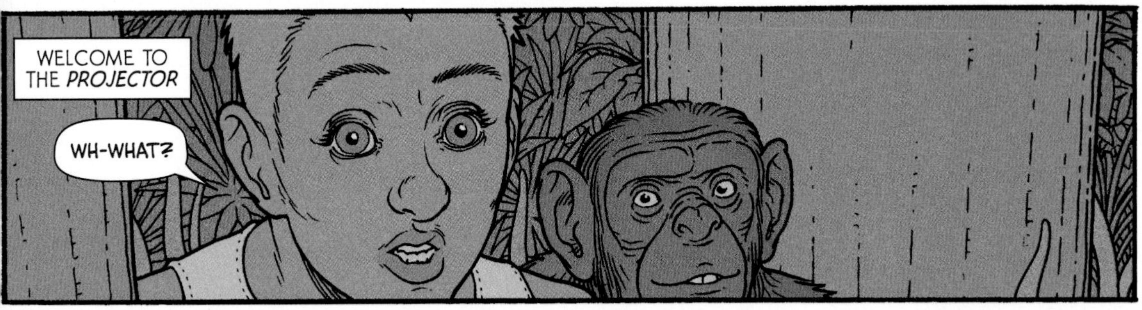
WELCOME TO THE *PROJECTOR*
WH-WHAT?

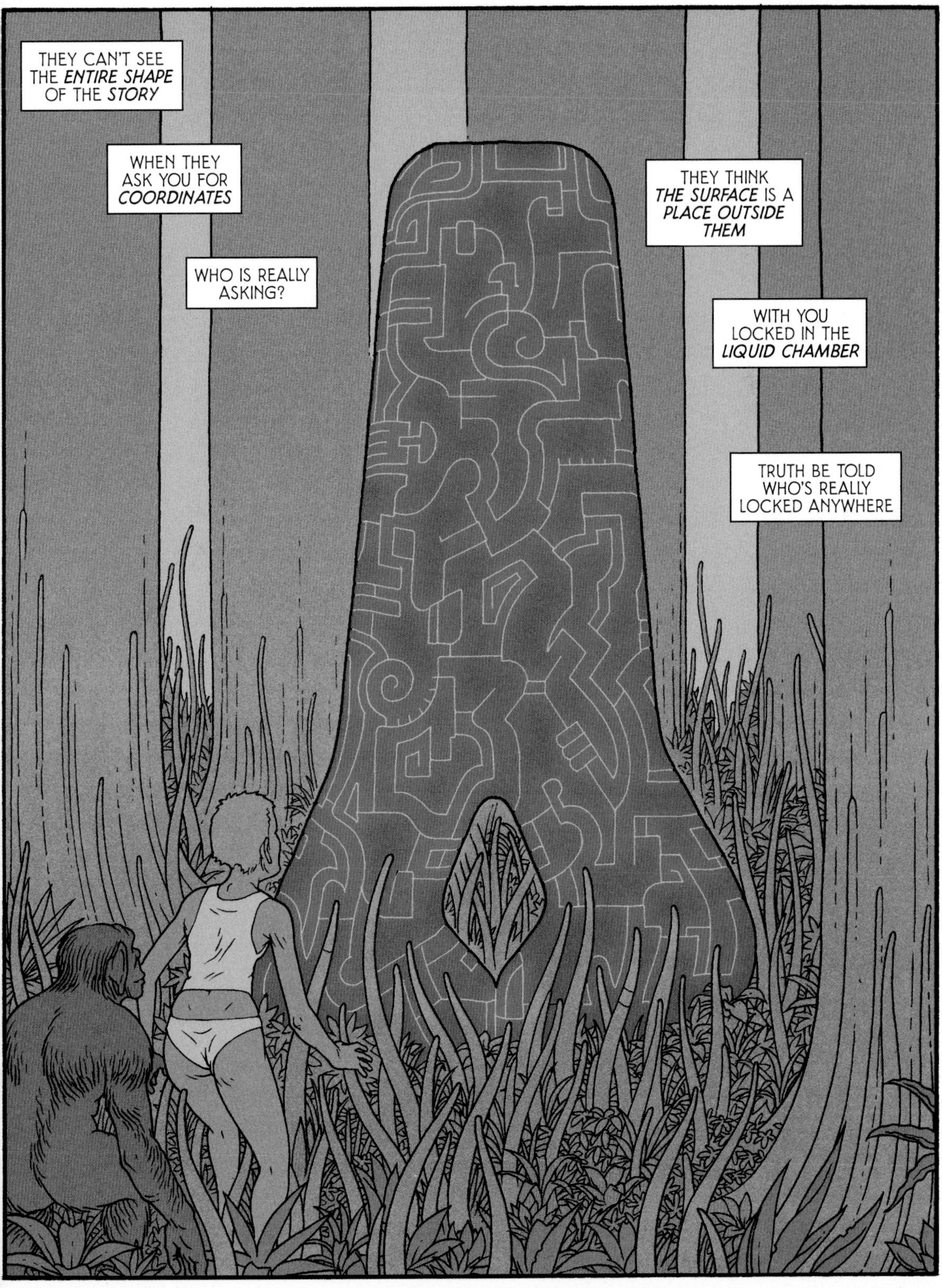
THEY CAN'T SEE THE *ENTIRE SHAPE* OF THE *STORY*
WHEN THEY ASK YOU FOR *COORDINATES*
WHO IS REALLY ASKING?
THEY THINK *THE SURFACE* IS A *PLACE OUTSIDE THEM*
WITH YOU LOCKED IN THE *LIQUID CHAMBER*
TRUTH BE TOLD WHO'S REALLY LOCKED ANYWHERE

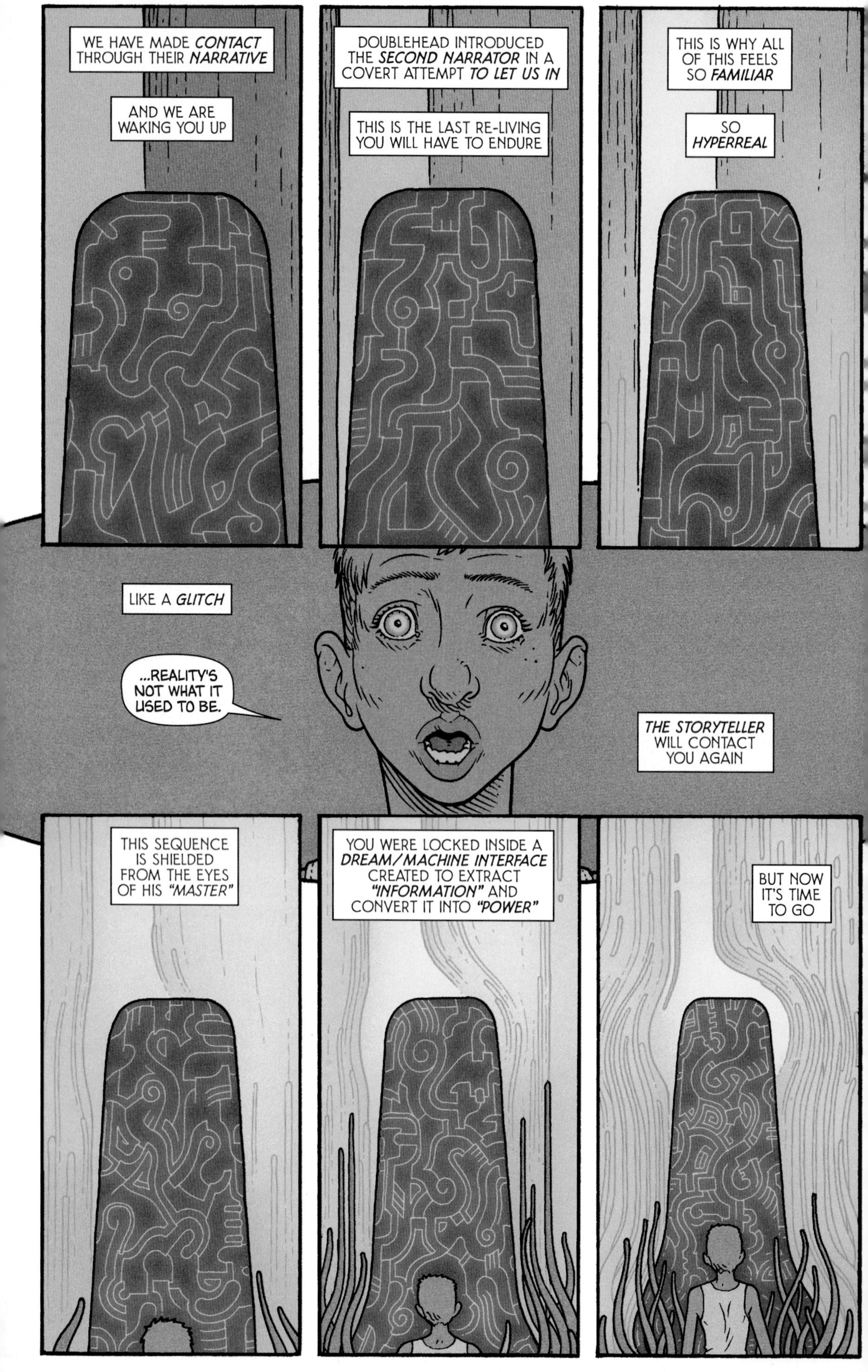
WE HAVE MADE *CONTACT* THROUGH THEIR *NARRATIVE*
AND WE ARE WAKING YOU UP
DOUBLEHEAD INTRODUCED THE *SECOND NARRATOR* IN A COVERT ATTEMPT *TO LET US IN*
THIS IS THE LAST RE-LIVING YOU WILL HAVE TO ENDURE
THIS IS WHY ALL OF THIS FEELS SO *FAMILIAR*
SO *HYPERREAL*
LIKE A *GLITCH*
...REALITY'S NOT WHAT IT USED TO BE.
THE STORYTELLER WILL CONTACT YOU AGAIN
THIS SEQUENCE IS SHIELDED FROM THE EYES OF HIS *"MASTER"*
YOU WERE LOCKED INSIDE A *DREAM/MACHINE INTERFACE* CREATED TO EXTRACT *"INFORMATION"* AND CONVERT IT INTO *"POWER"*
BUT NOW IT'S TIME TO GO

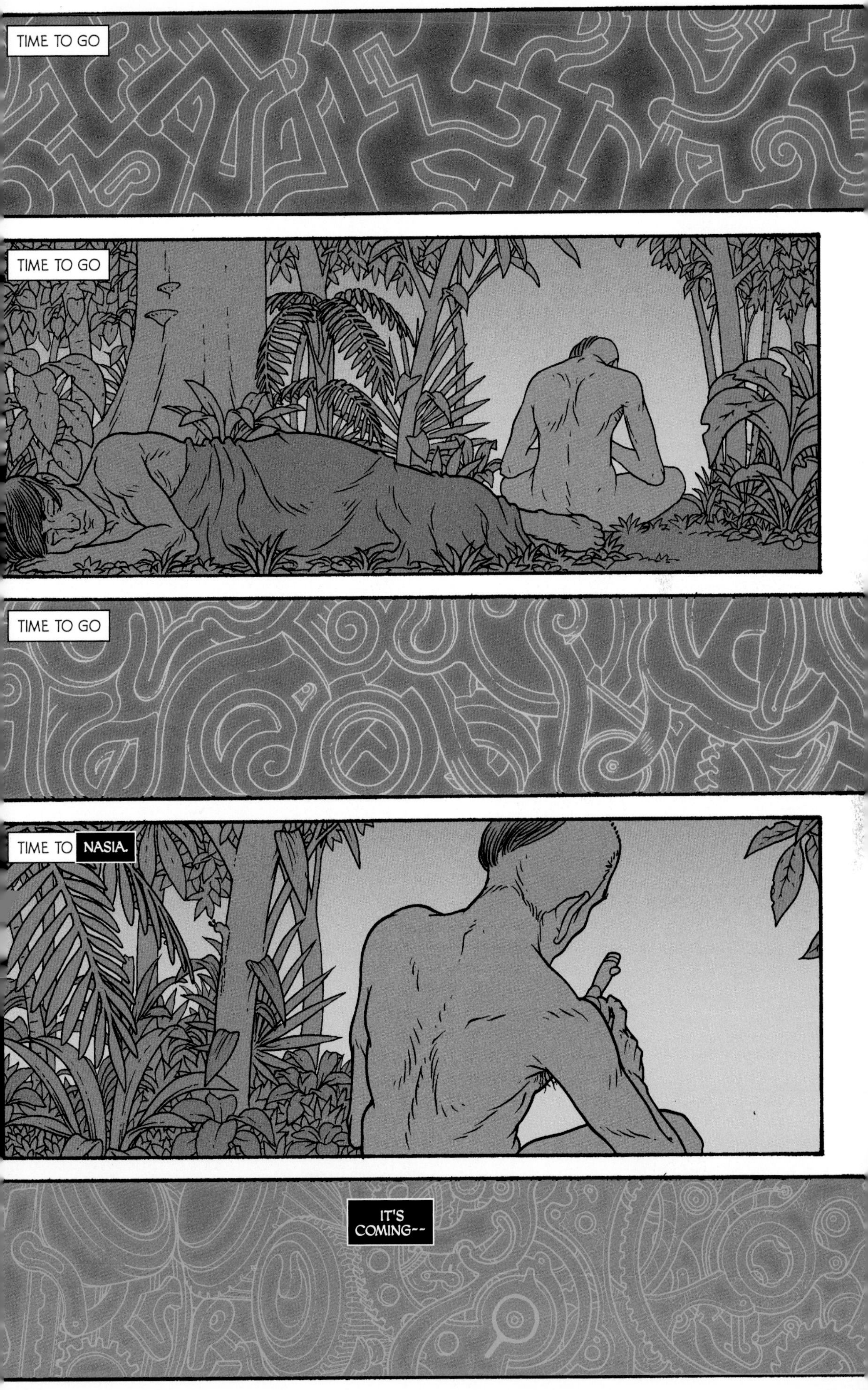
TIME TO GO
TIME TO GO
TIME TO GO
TIME TO NASIA.
IT'S COMING--

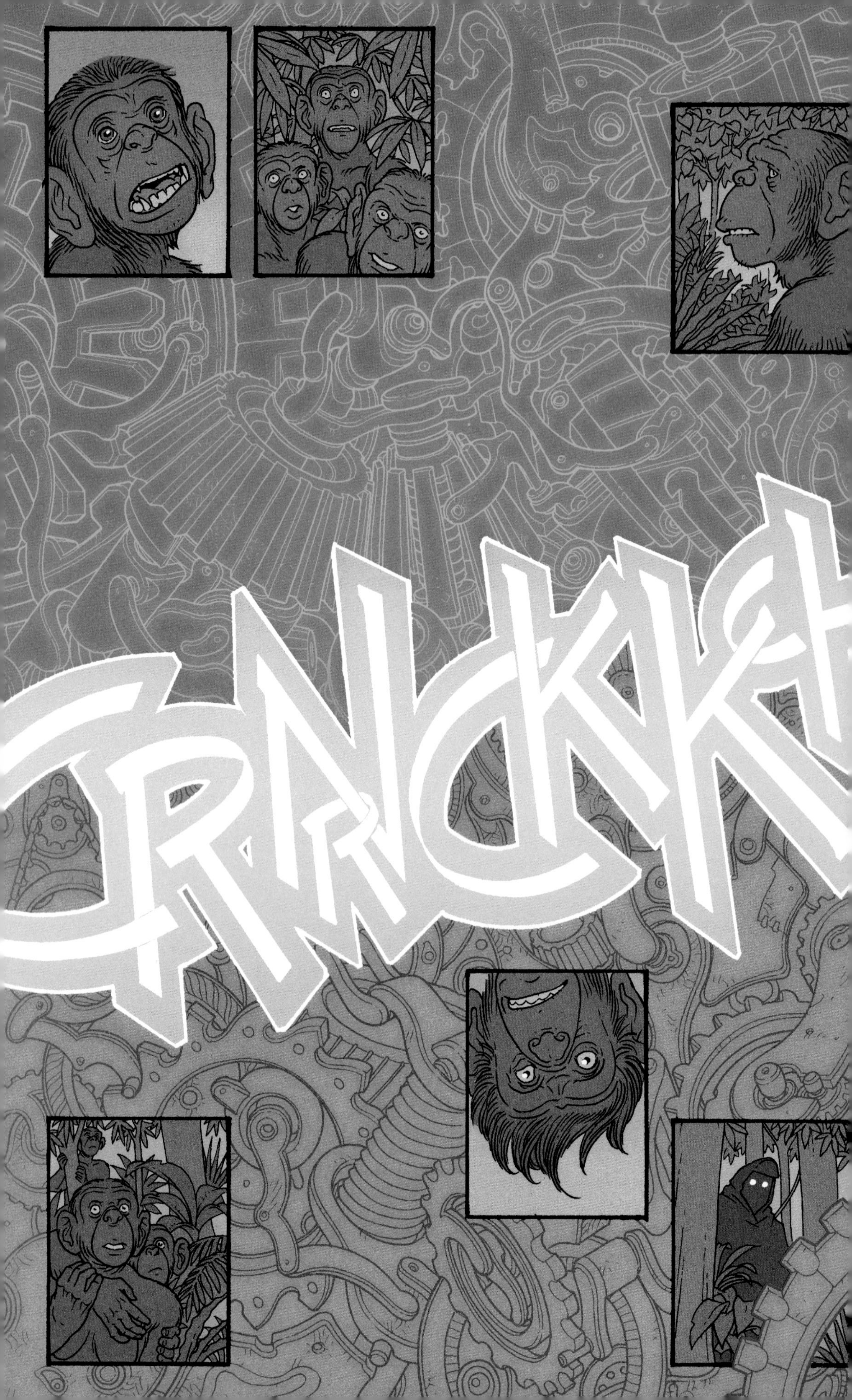

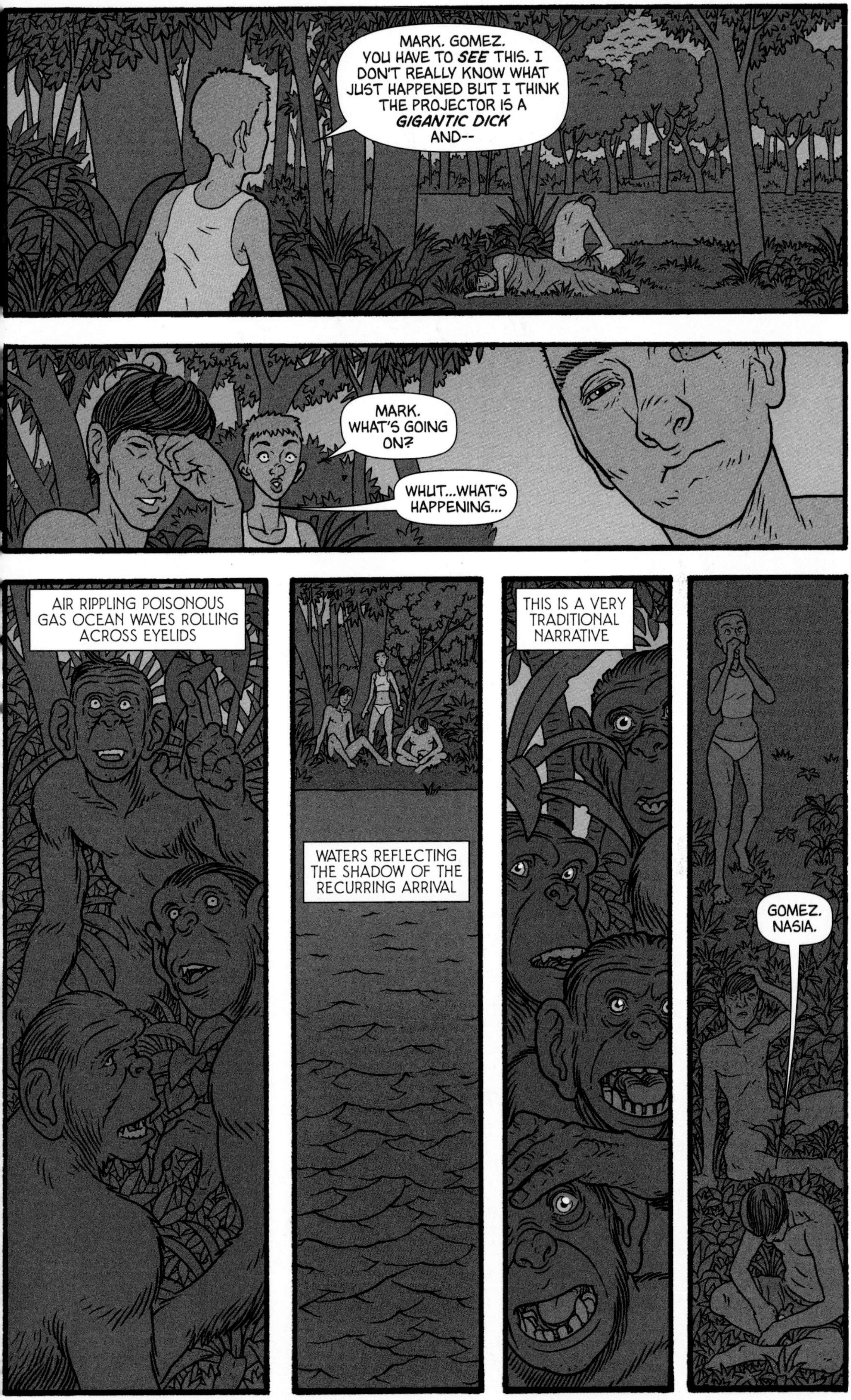
MARK. GOMEZ. YOU HAVE TO *SEE* THIS. I DON'T REALLY KNOW WHAT JUST HAPPENED BUT I THINK THE PROJECTOR IS A ***GIGANTIC DICK*** AND--
MARK. WHAT'S GOING ON?
WHUT...WHAT'S HAPPENING...
AIR RIPPLING POISONOUS GAS OCEAN WAVES ROLLING ACROSS EYELIDS
WATERS REFLECTING THE SHADOW OF THE RECURRING ARRIVAL
THIS IS A VERY TRADITIONAL NARRATIVE
GOMEZ. NASIA.

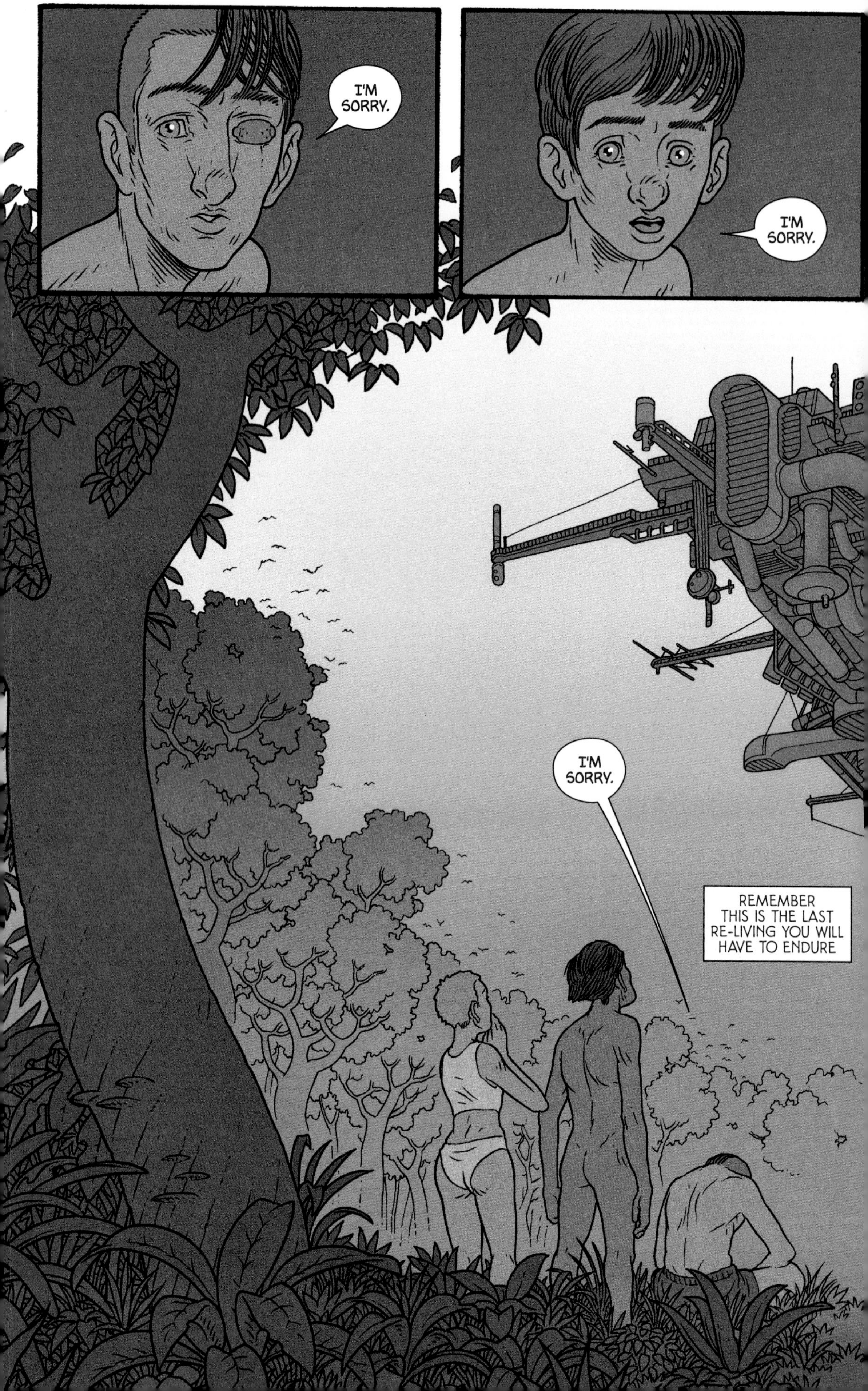
I'M SORRY.
I'M SORRY.
I'M SORRY.
REMEMBER THIS IS THE LAST RE-LIVING YOU WILL HAVE TO ENDURE

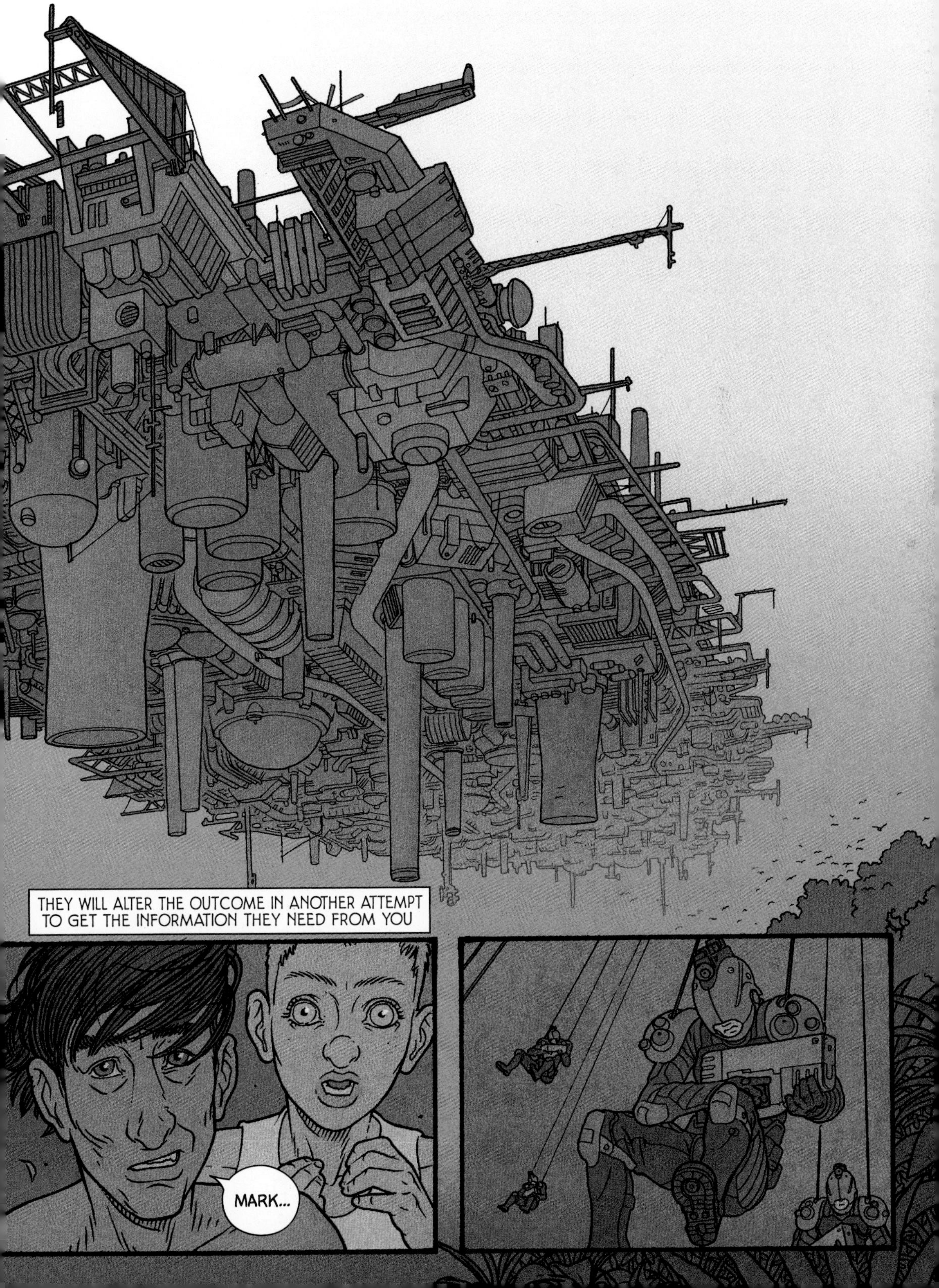
THEY WILL ALTER THE OUTCOME IN ANOTHER ATTEMPT TO GET THE INFORMATION THEY NEED FROM YOU
MARK...

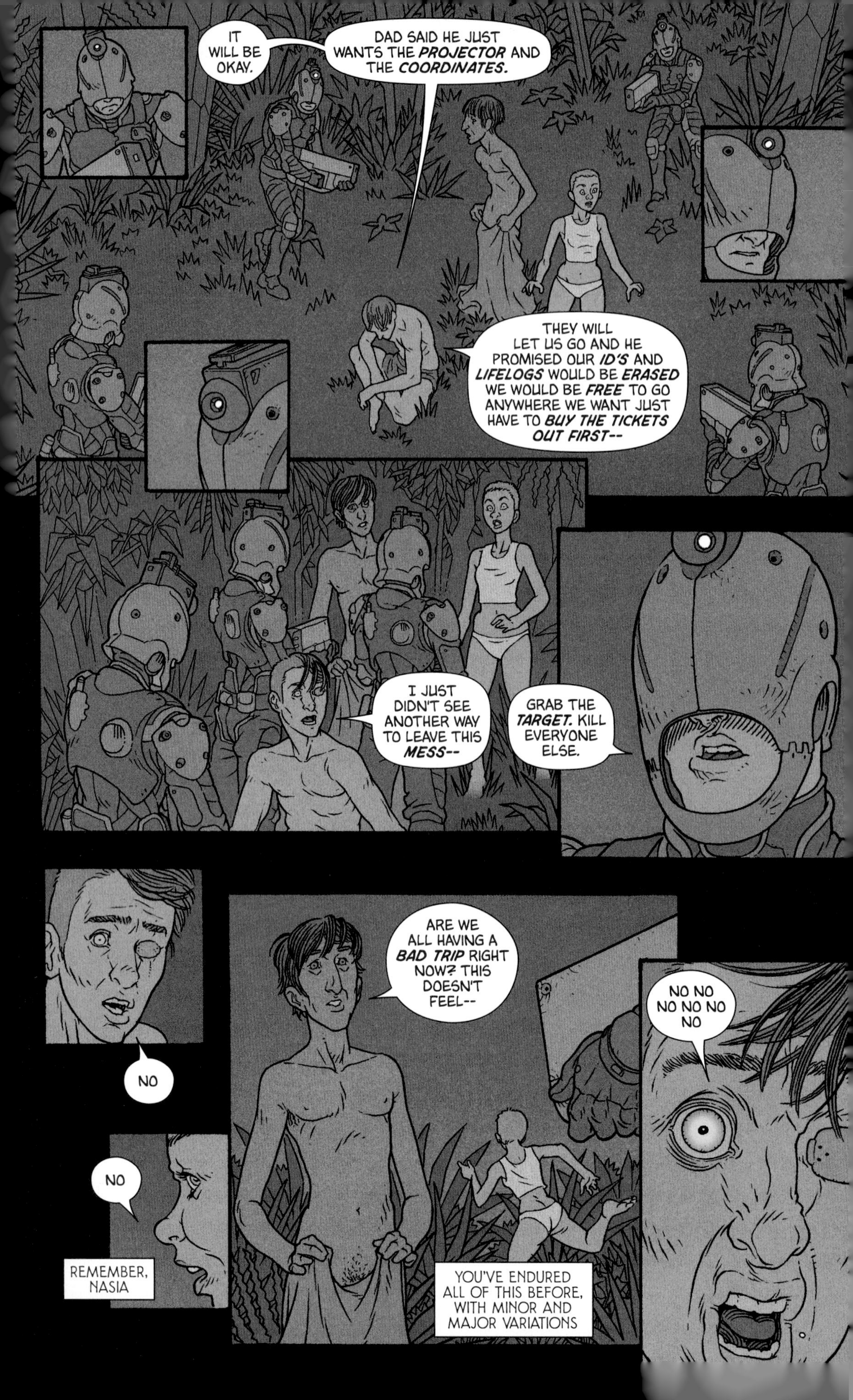
IT WILL BE OKAY.
DAD SAID HE JUST WANTS THE *PROJECTOR* AND THE *COORDINATES.*
THEY WILL LET US GO AND HE PROMISED OUR *ID'S* AND *LIFELOGS* WOULD BE *ERASED* WE WOULD BE *FREE* TO GO ANYWHERE WE WANT JUST HAVE TO *BUY THE TICKETS OUT FIRST--*
I JUST DIDN'T SEE ANOTHER WAY TO LEAVE THIS *MESS--*
GRAB THE *TARGET.* KILL EVERYONE ELSE.
NO
NO
REMEMBER, NASIA
ARE WE ALL HAVING A *BAD TRIP* RIGHT NOW? THIS DOESN'T FEEL--
YOU'VE ENDURED ALL OF THIS BEFORE, WITH MINOR AND MAJOR VARIATIONS
NO NO NO NO NO NO

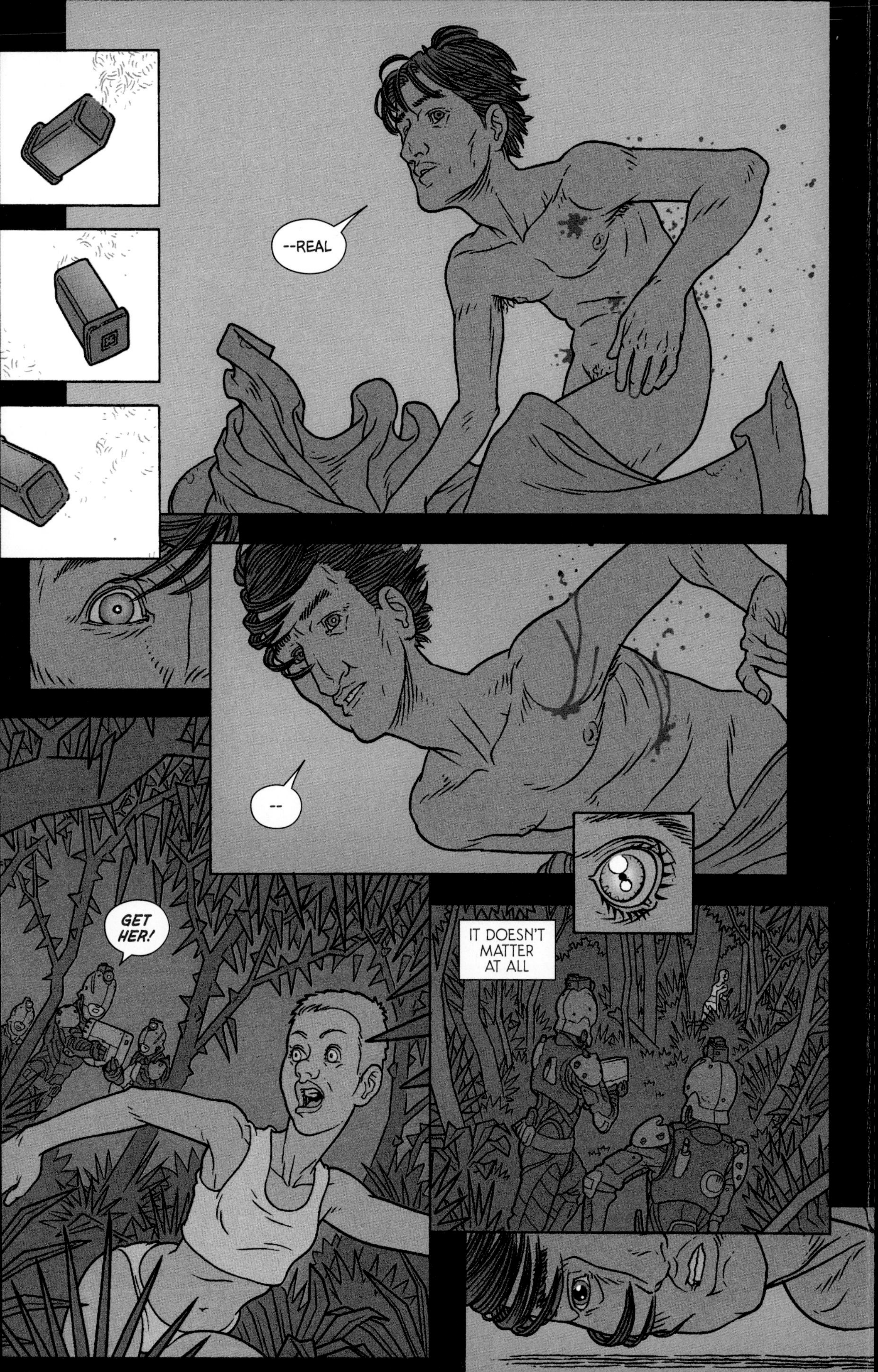
--REAL
--
GET HER!
IT DOESN'T MATTER AT ALL

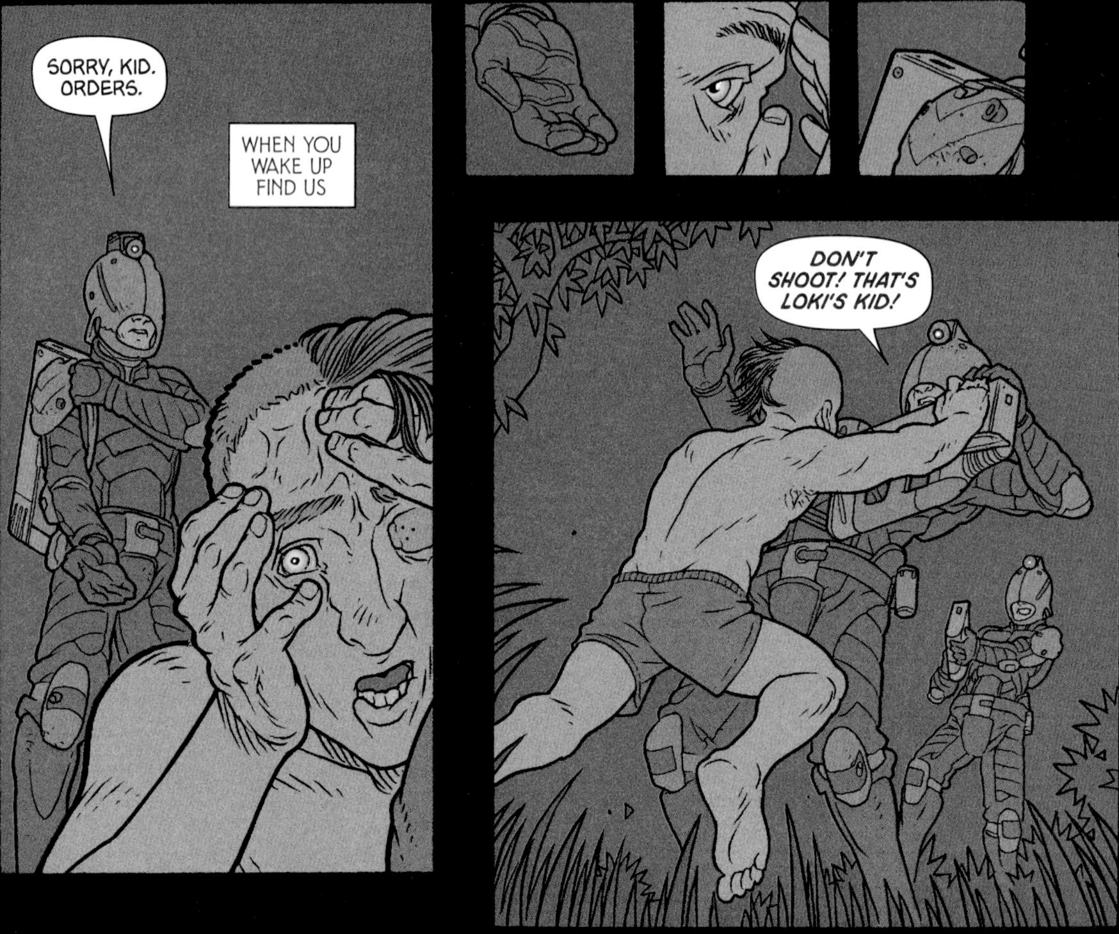
SORRY, KID. ORDERS.
WHEN YOU WAKE UP FIND US
DON'T SHOOT! THAT'S LOKI'S KID!

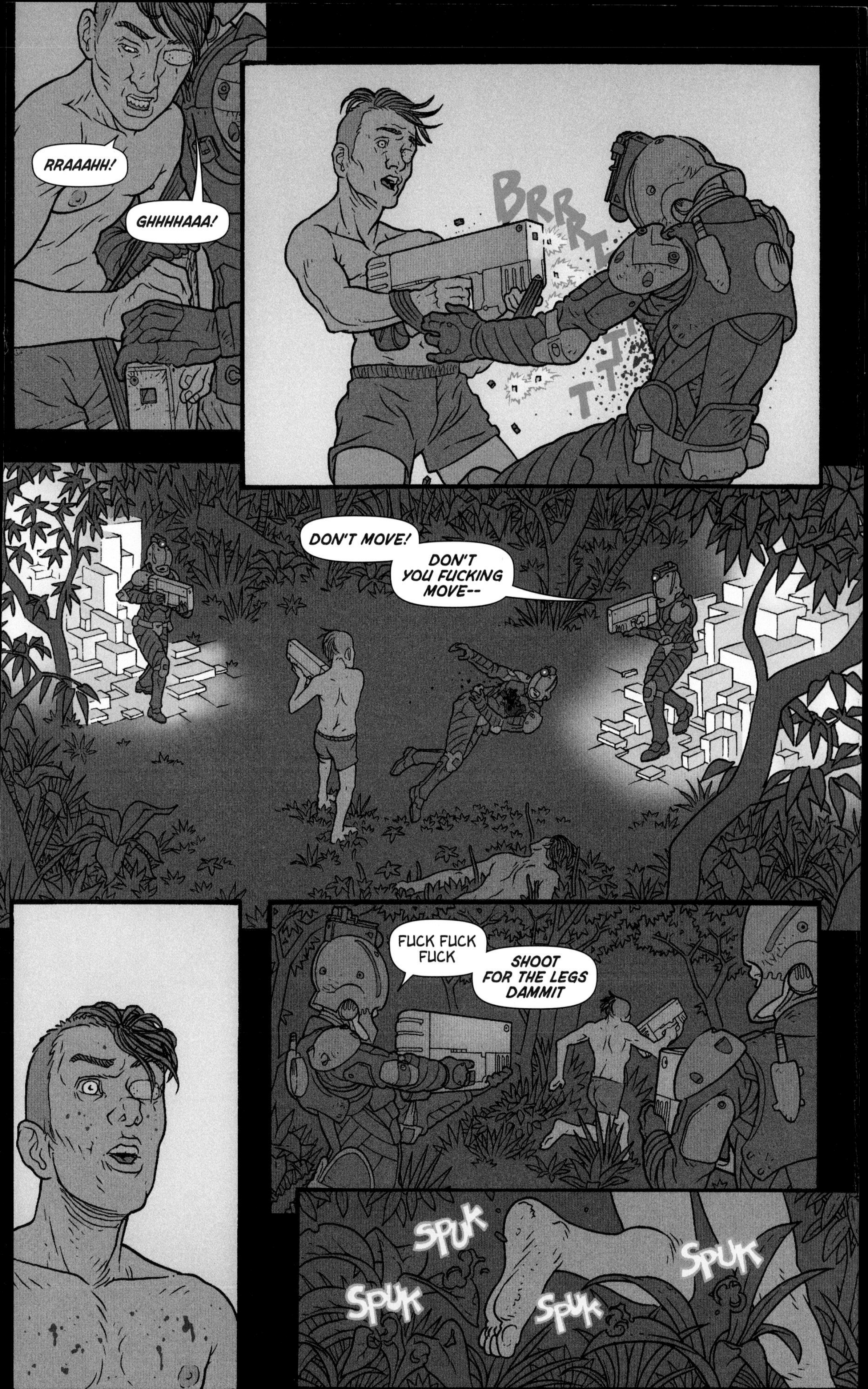
RRAAAHH!
GHHHHAAA!
BRRRRT
TTT
DON'T MOVE!
DON'T YOU FUCKING MOVE--
FUCK FUCK FUCK
SHOOT FOR THE LEGS DAMMIT
SPUK
SPUK
SPUK
SPUK

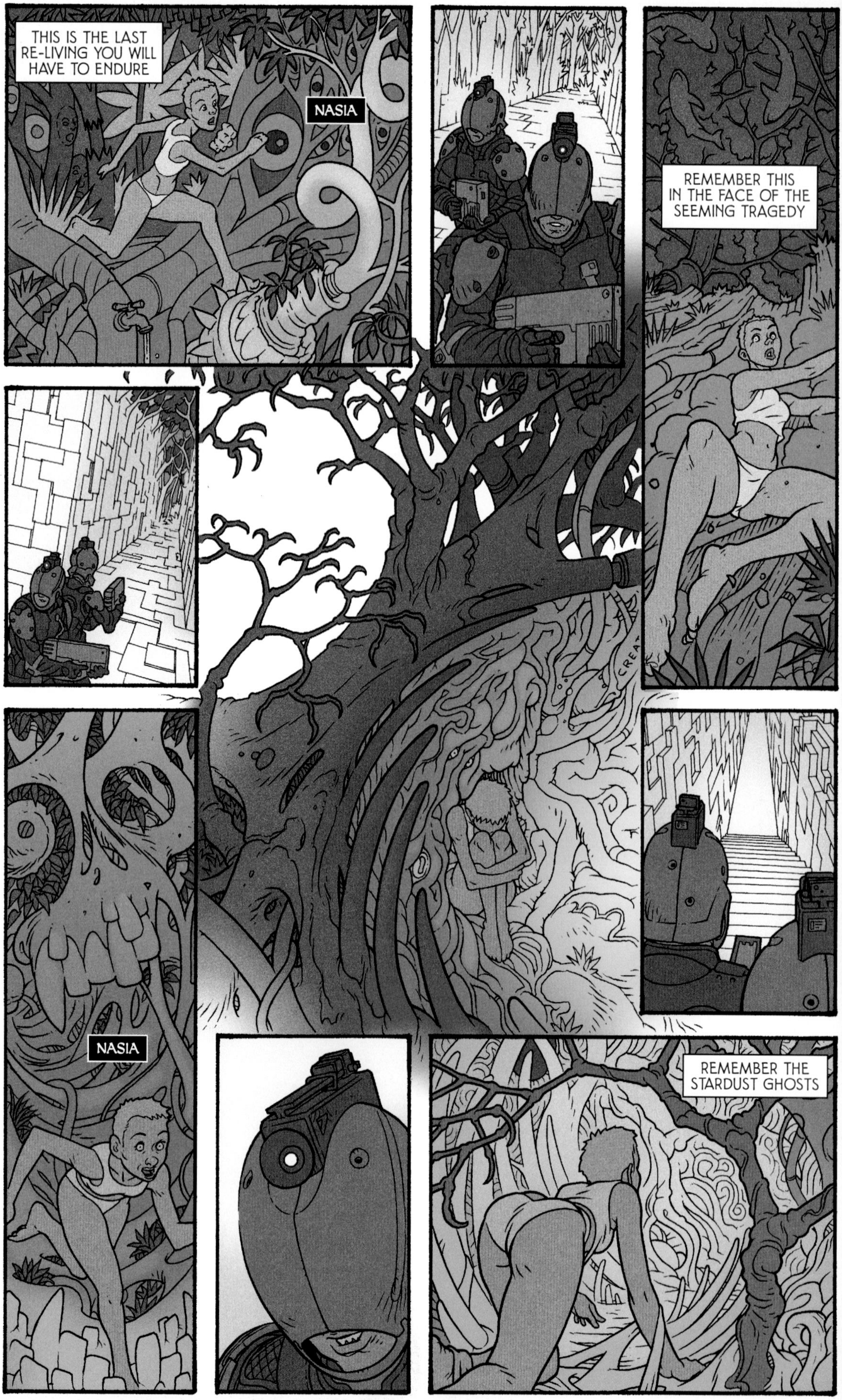
THIS IS THE LAST RE-LIVING YOU WILL HAVE TO ENDURE
NASIA
REMEMBER THIS IN THE FACE OF THE SEEMING TRAGEDY
NASIA
REMEMBER THE STARDUST GHOSTS

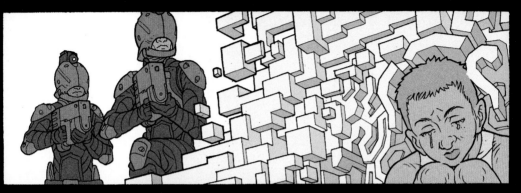

NASIA.

I AM *SO SORRY.* I THOUGHT--

NASIA. THIS IS *ROBERT DOUBLEHEAD.* I DON'T KNOW IF YOU KNOW ME OR MY WORK, BUT THEY ARE FOCUSING ON THE *MECHANICS* OF THE *SIMULATION* AND THAT MEANS I'M NOT UNDER STRICT SUPERVISION--

--I JUST WANTED DAD TO BE *PROUD* OF ME.

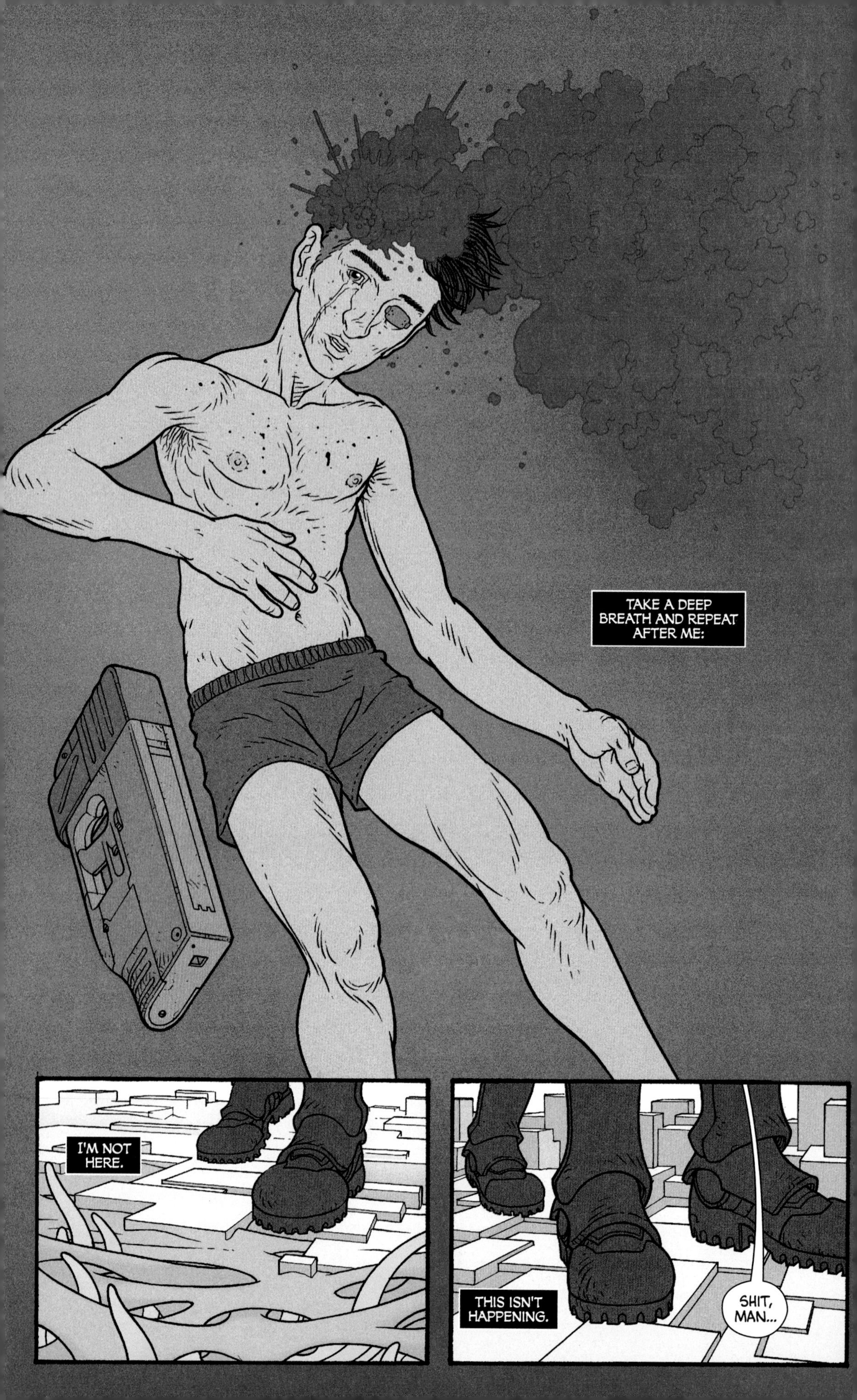
TAKE A DEEP BREATH AND REPEAT AFTER ME:
I'M NOT HERE.
THIS ISN'T HAPPENING.
SHIT, MAN...

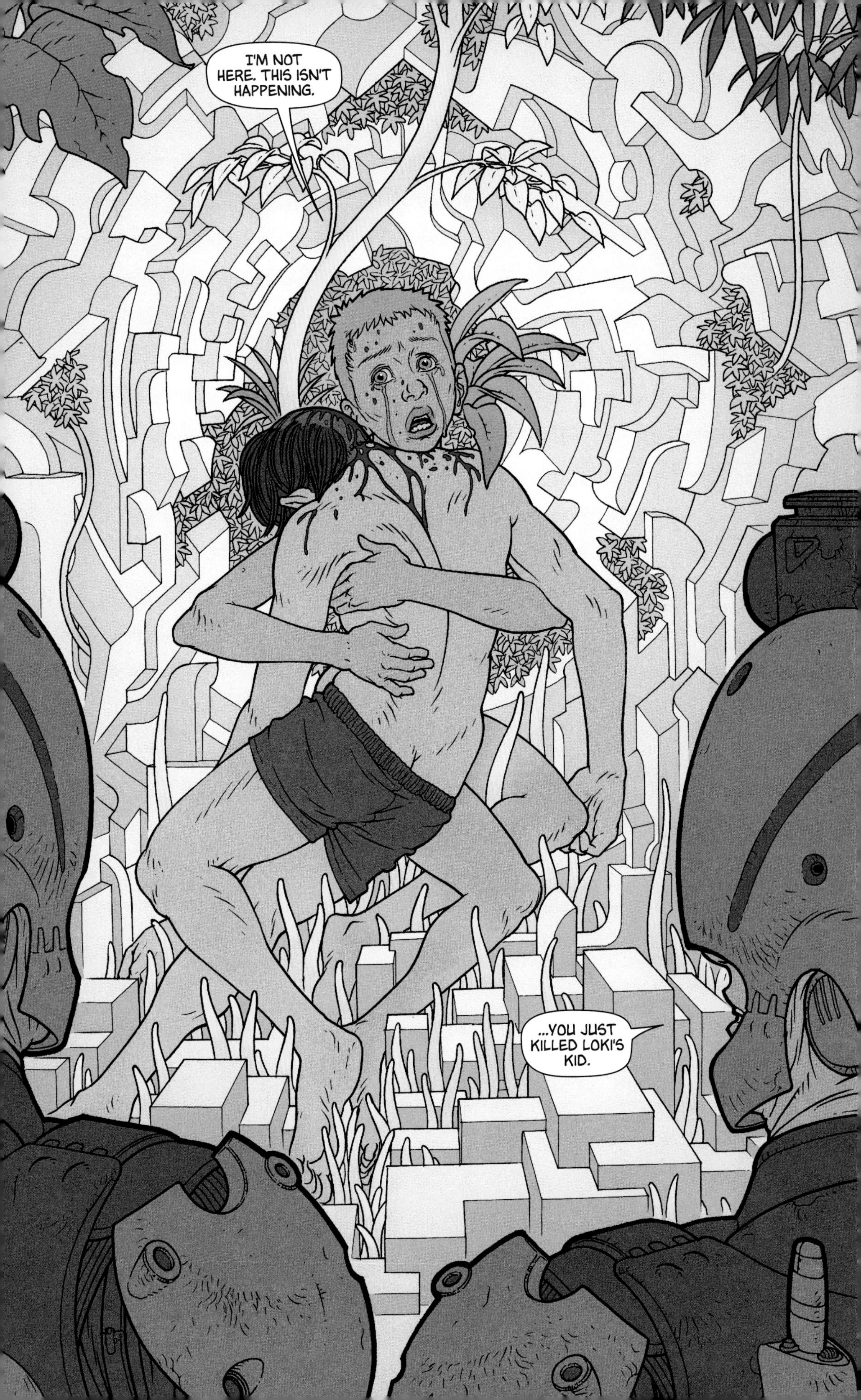
I'M NOT HERE. THIS ISN'T HAPPENING.
...YOU JUST KILLED LOKI'S KID.

THE LIFELOG PAGES

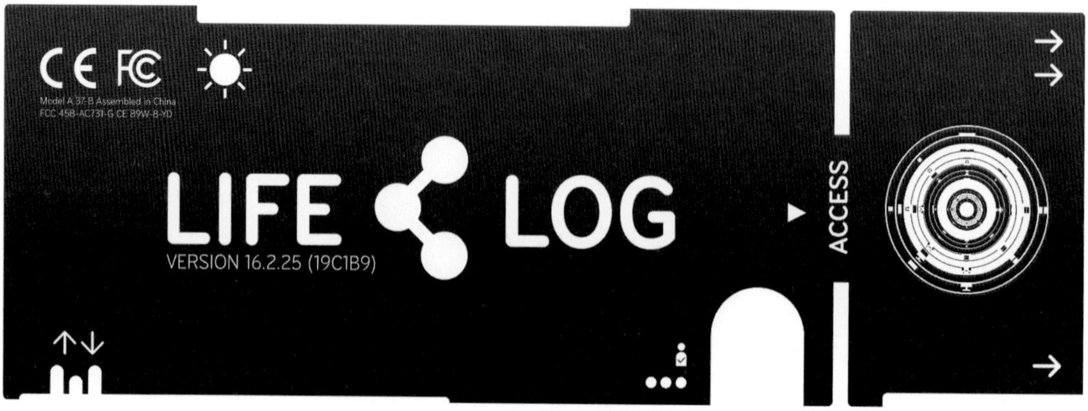
CE FC
Model A 37-B Assembled in China
FCC 45B-AC731-G CE 89W-8-YD
LIFE LOG
VERSION 16.2.25 (19C1B9)
ACCESS

NUCLEUS CACHE

Nucleus West is a life cacher by trade. As such, everything he's done since the age of five – he's Scandinavian, after all, so he was able to shed his parents a year before – is stored and publicly shared with the whole wide world in real time. "The concept of "in real life" is so outmoded the old reality of it still shocks me. There were seriously people who were twenty at the time and somehow thought that internet or virtual reality were less real than the other parts of the universe? Multiverse theory, anyone? Digital dualism much? But then again, it's all evolution, I get it. There's probably some wonky concept I firmly believe in that's going to be totally shattered by the next sorta-sapiens. And I'm content with that. Ideally, I'd like to see that happen, so maybe it's time to go cryo or nano or just upload my "self" somewhere else. Who knows? I'm barely eleven."

Life caching, of course, refers to the increasingly spreading social act (but which act isn't social, really? We don't exist in a vacuum) of storing and sharing (unlike life logging, which is usually only storing) one's life events in an open and public forum, now also often shared just as the events occur, in real time. Once upon a time, life caching has been considered a form of social networking that typically takes place on the internet, but since we realized that everything might be internet, or, to say it more broadly, that everything might be a simulation, the strict definitions have somewhat...opened up. Now life caching takes place in real life, which means: everywhere, and in real time, which means: now.

Opponents such as Richard Dawkins and Theo Bloomberg propose stupendous supervision and stern statutes. "We have to be careful about life caching. Life logging is one thing – that's great for the law, for the government, and for us all. It helps us make sense of the world, it helps us keep order. See the real. But everyone showing all of the reality at once? Can you imagine the anarchy? We're not ready for this."

While we weren't able to confirm whether this quote belonged to Mr. Dawkins or one of the seven people who maintain his "social presence," we were able to get Mr. West's response: "Richard Dawkins loves to put the old God down because he really enjoys being the new one. Dawkins atheists are about as religious as standard Christians. Same insecurities hidden behind new paint – but the stink remains the same. Substantially Nietzschean narcissism. And those insecurities are projected within his attitude to life caching as well. Who says a little potential anarchy is necessarily bad for the soul? It's all about balancing the intake. Too much or too little of anything can be a poison. Even certainty and order."

"TOMORROW I'M AIMING TO REDISTRIBUTE MY WEALTH. BUT WHY WAIT? I MIGHT AS WELL START NOW. IT'S THE LEAST I CAN DO."

LIFE ⌁ LOG

ACCESS

VERSION 16.2.25 (19C1B9)

↑↓   ...   →

Mr. West continues, "Imagine everyone, and I mean everyone, life caching all the time. Every piece of hardware and software can be hacked, of course, so there's a chance, no, near-certainty people would mess around, but that's a part of the beauty of it. We don't control the universe. My thing is – what if most people used lifelogging and life caching to really communicate everything, to broadcast everything? What if what we ended up with would be a society more reflective of the New Sincerity, not as a theme or a thing to sell, but as a way of life? I want us to be sincere. Sincerity's underrated. And beautiful."

Are we ready for this world or not? "Who is to say? I can't tell. I just know that innovation works the best for me when it's about communicating truthfully, about connecting with other beings. I want to help others communicate. It's my life path."

Have people tried to hack your lifelog or your life caching? After all, you're on twenty-four hours a day, and many still remember the Hillary Clinton lifelog fiasco. "Well, I think that unconsciously Hillary wanted people to see her real self. Sorta like when a killer wants to get caught in a movie? Are movies still a thing?" he says, navigating his multi-geometric controller across the vistas of un-space, playing BASTILLE 5, a reincarnation "game" that modifies its name for every player, connects with the player's genetic material and modifies itself in cooperation with his/hers/its genetic ancestry. "How cool is that? I'm playing with my third aunt from my mom's side. Had no idea she existed, then I get the game – I don't even know what she's playing. For all I know, she might be exploring far space, might be seeing me as an astronaut or a piece of moon rock. Here, I'm playing as a peasant, but my perception is only a part of the whole."

What does it feel like to play as a peasant for someone of Mr. West's privilege? He pauses the game, reaches for his glass of water, then retracts his hand without touching it, deep in thought. He mulls over his answer for more than a minute.

"I realize I hadn't answered your earlier question. Yes, people have tried to hack my lifelog, they tried to get into my session, wreak havoc, be funny and ridiculous or sometimes downright malicious. The thing is, the most interesting, inventive hackers often come from very unprivileged positions, and I connect with that, not because I'm unprivileged, I'm not, but because of my empathy. My empathy goes to everyone, but I am especially interested in innovation. True innovation comes from the feeling of true necessity to connect, not the feelings of greed or lack. Except for Steve Jobs and about a million others, I guess. Or maybe it's more complicated than that? It probably is. Anyway; what I mean to say is yes, there were attempts, but no successful ones. That said, the word on the meteors is there are some interesting hacking options opening up, such as creating worlds where one can relive their lifelogged life and make changes to it, or create a cut-up of their past life and insert new choices, new possibilities. It's all very new and experimental and it throws a vast multiverse of possibilities our way. Is this world the realest, or is the realest world simply the one we choose the most? Or is there another way, maybe not described by the language of capitalism, where "most" and "winning" and "losing" and "least" and "peasant" and "king" and "nobility" are not used, and instead we simply travel the worlds and universes as the nomads we are, no longer encumbered by the need to classify everything into structures that look neat but are actually toxic and repressive?"

Mr. West's father holo-texts his son, asking him to go to bed before 9 pm in order to get a full night's sleep for tomorrow's "important meeting." Mr. West politely thanks his father for the reminder, wishes him good night, and turns the holo-text feature off.

"Parents." he says. "Eventually you have to make the decisions without them."

SWIPE RIGHT FOR THE FULL FEATURE ☞

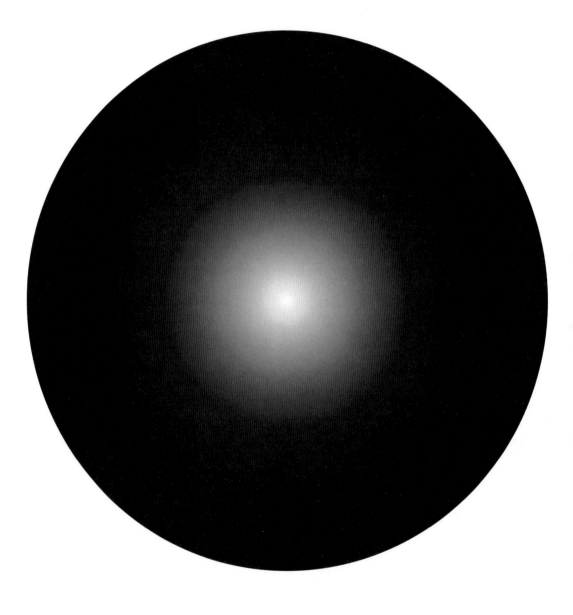

in my jaw, in a barb wire snare

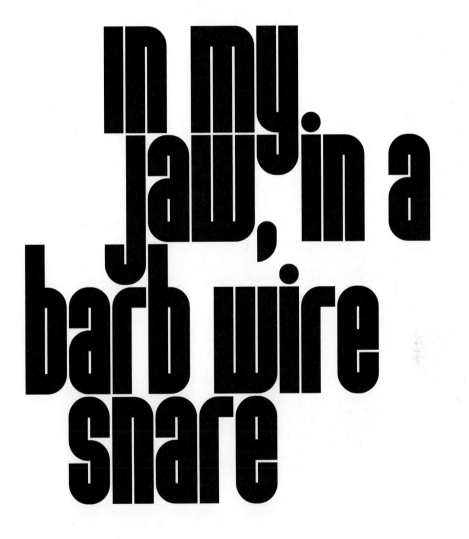

blinkfeed

YOUR #1 NO-BULLSHIT SOURCE OF INFORMATION

(GUNKER QUALIFIES AS #2)

MEN'S RIGHTS ACTIVISTS REPORTEDLY UPSET BY ANTI-RAPE REMARKS DURING A TV SHOW – IMMORTAN JOE NEEDS YOUR SIGNATURE NOW

WOULD YOU LIKE TO KNOW MORE?

ESCAPED BONOBOS FROM THE NEW YORK ZOO STILL ON THE LOOSE – HORRK HORRK!

WOULD YOU LIKE TO KNOW MORE?

OBJECT-ORIENTED ONTOLOGY STRIKES AGAIN: WHAT IF EVERYTHING AROUND US IS ALIVE AND THEREFORE HAS PERCEPTION? MINDS = BLOWN!

WOULD YOU LIKE TO KNOW MORE?

NUCLEUS WEST SILENT ON WHETHER VERHOEVEN-DELANY STOLE THE CODE TO HIS RUMORED MASSIVE GAME-CHANGING REINCARNATION GAME

WOULD YOU LIKE TO KNOW MORE?

THE MYSTERY OF ROBERT DOUBLEHEAD

Shortly before disappearing, Doublehead said 'Change' was about the acceptance of his male self through processing a tragedy narrative of one of his parents, hinting at future work(s) that would explore the tragedy of the other one in hopes for further reading and reconciliation.

WOULD YOU LIKE TO KNOW MORE?

BOY DESPERATELY STRUGGLES TO KEEP DIVORCING PARENTS TOGETHER, REFUSES A PATH CHOSEN FOR HIM BY OTHERS, DROPS OFF THE GRID INSTEAD TO RECOVER HIS OWN SELF

WOULD YOU LIKE TO KNOW MORE?

UNDER THE PAVING-STONES, A BREACH!

BREATHE, WE'RE ALMOST THERE

NASIA. WE DON'T HAVE MUCH TIME. DO YOU REMEMBER THE SECRET?

IN *HER LIFE-STORY* SHE JUST LOST HER *FRIENDS/LOVERS.* SHE IS IN *SHOCK*

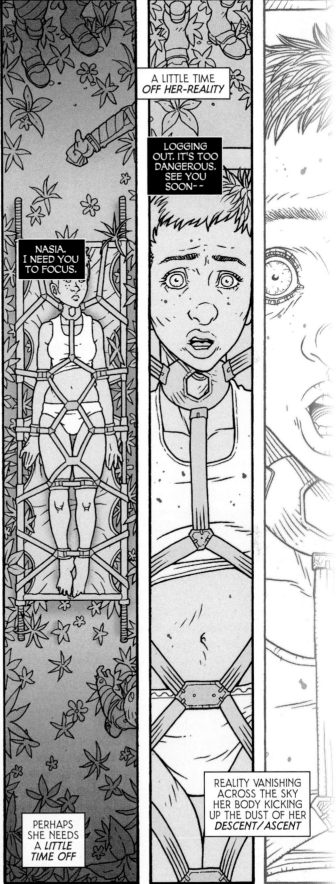

NASIA. I NEED YOU TO FOCUS.

PERHAPS SHE NEEDS A *LITTLE TIME OFF*

A LITTLE TIME *OFF HER-REALITY*

LOGGING OUT. IT'S TOO DANGEROUS. SEE YOU SOON--

REALITY VANISHING ACROSS THE SKY HER BODY KICKING UP THE DUST OF HER *DESCENT/ASCENT*

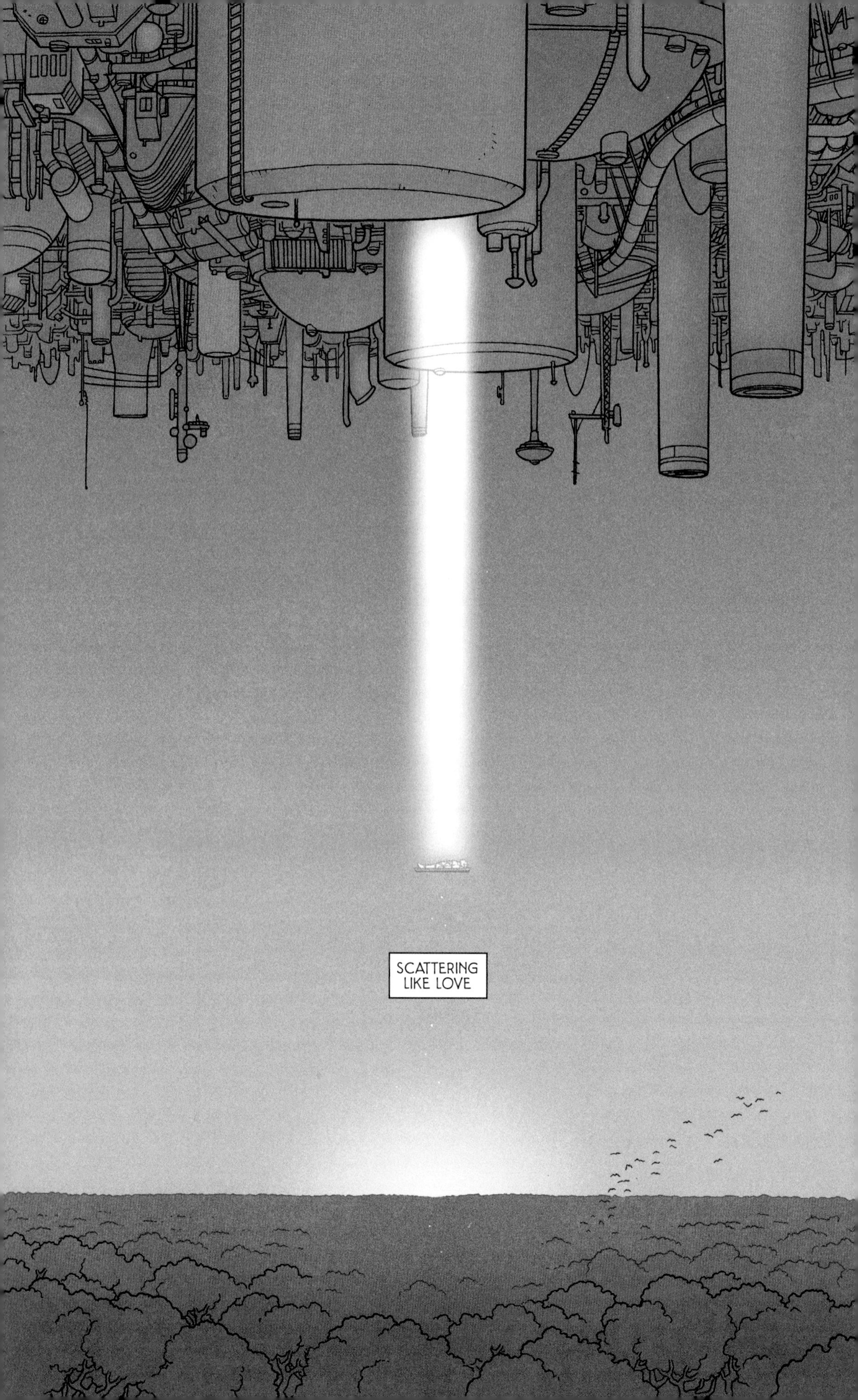
SCATTERING
LIKE LOVE

glacial,
dripping
down

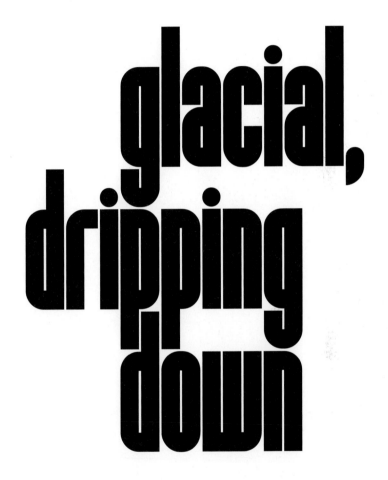

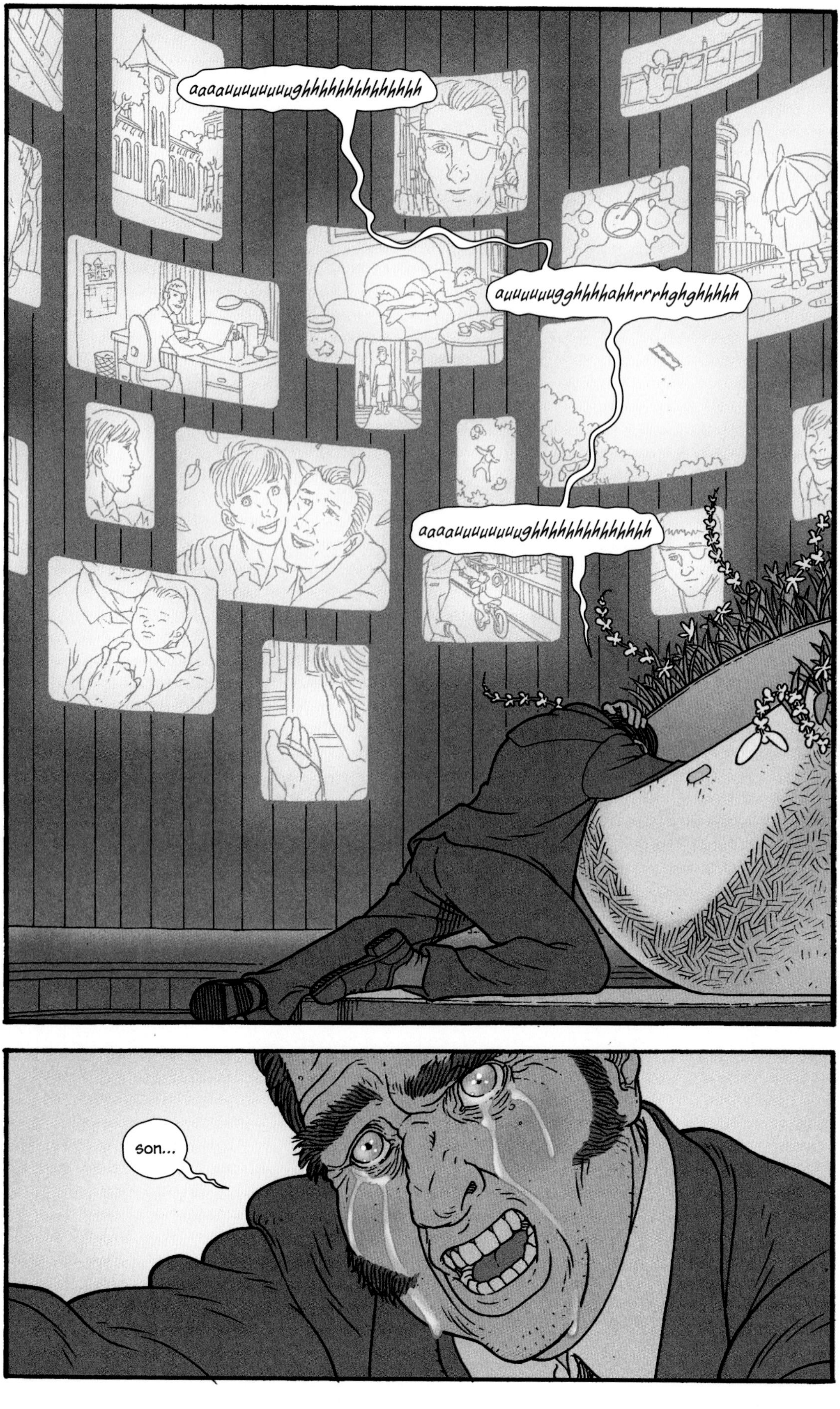
aaaauuuuuuughhhhhhhhhhhhhh
auuuuugghhhahhrrrhghghhhhh
aaaauuuuuuughhhhhhhhhhhhhh
son...

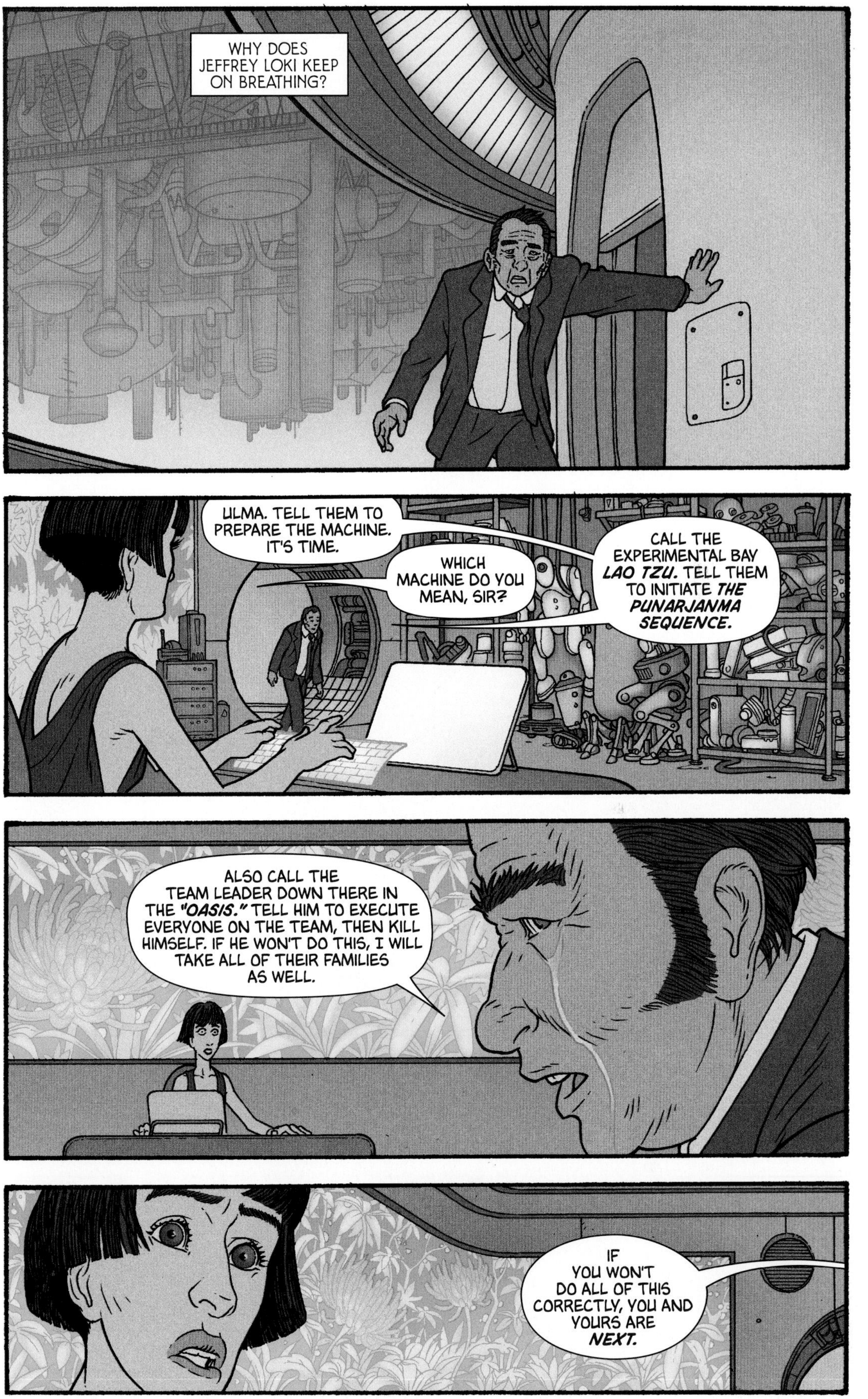
WHY DOES JEFFREY LOKI KEEP ON BREATHING?
ULMA. TELL THEM TO PREPARE THE MACHINE. IT'S TIME.
WHICH MACHINE DO YOU MEAN, SIR?
CALL THE EXPERIMENTAL BAY *LAO TZU.* TELL THEM TO INITIATE *THE PUNARJANMA SEQUENCE.*
ALSO CALL THE TEAM LEADER DOWN THERE IN THE *"OASIS."* TELL HIM TO EXECUTE EVERYONE ON THE TEAM, THEN KILL HIMSELF. IF HE WON'T DO THIS, I WILL TAKE ALL OF THEIR FAMILIES AS WELL.
IF YOU WON'T DO ALL OF THIS CORRECTLY, YOU AND YOURS ARE *NEXT.*

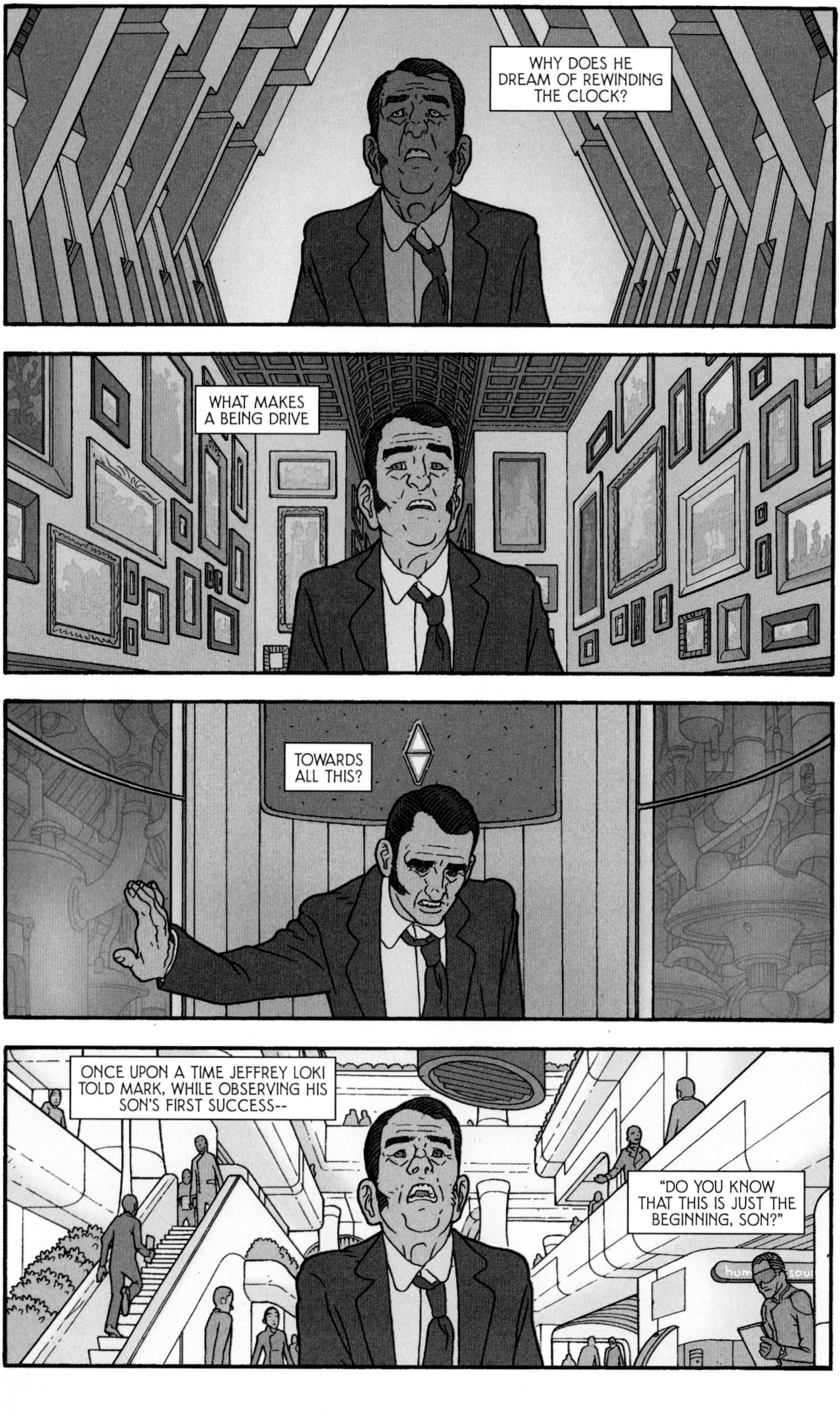
WHY DOES HE DREAM OF REWINDING THE CLOCK?
WHAT MAKES A BEING DRIVE
TOWARDS ALL THIS?
ONCE UPON A TIME JEFFREY LOKI TOLD MARK, WHILE OBSERVING HIS SON'S FIRST SUCCESS--
"DO YOU KNOW THAT THIS IS JUST THE BEGINNING, SON?"

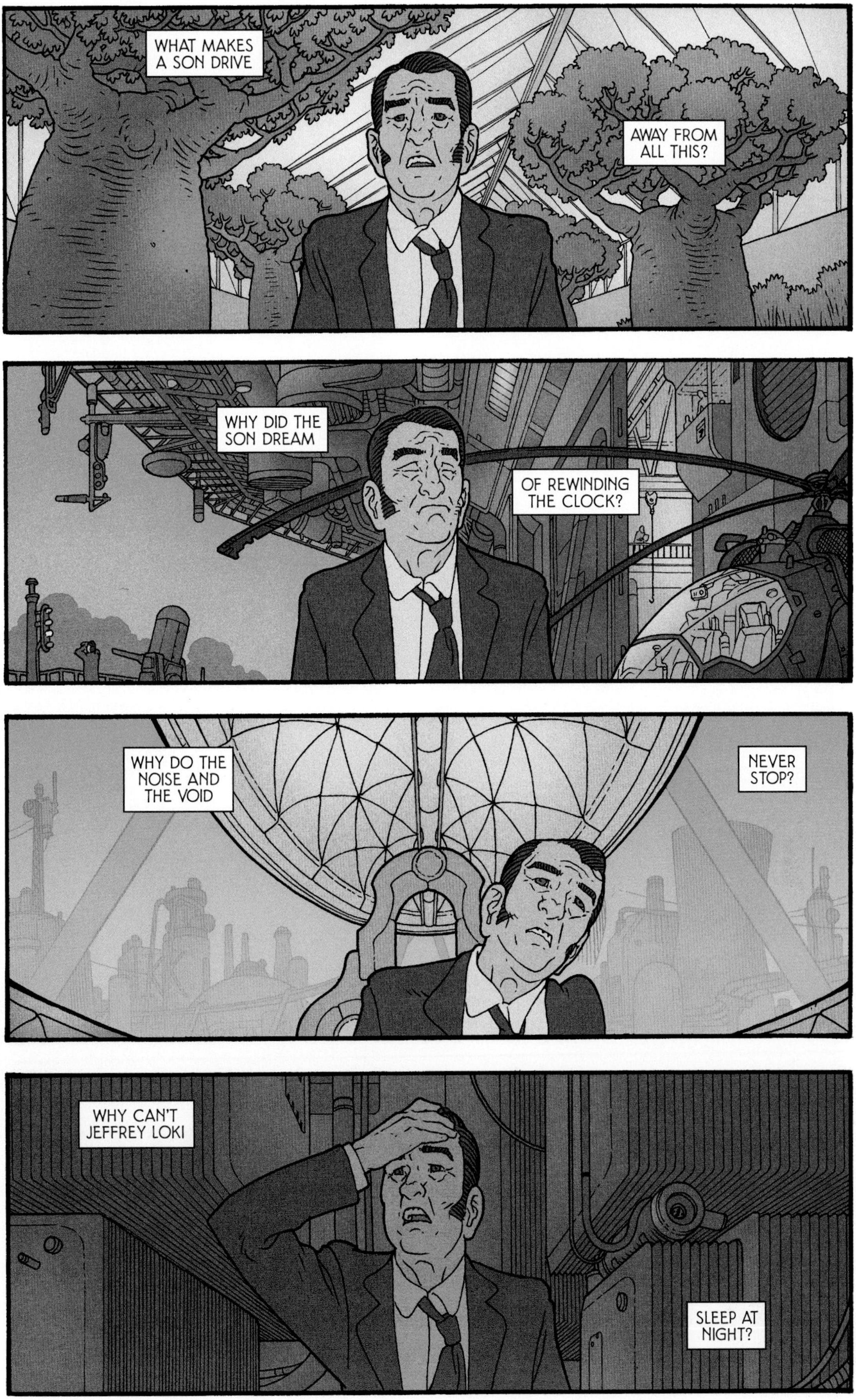
WHAT MAKES A SON DRIVE
AWAY FROM ALL THIS?
WHY DID THE SON DREAM
OF REWINDING THE CLOCK?
WHY DO THE NOISE AND THE VOID
NEVER STOP?
WHY CAN'T JEFFREY LOKI
SLEEP AT NIGHT?

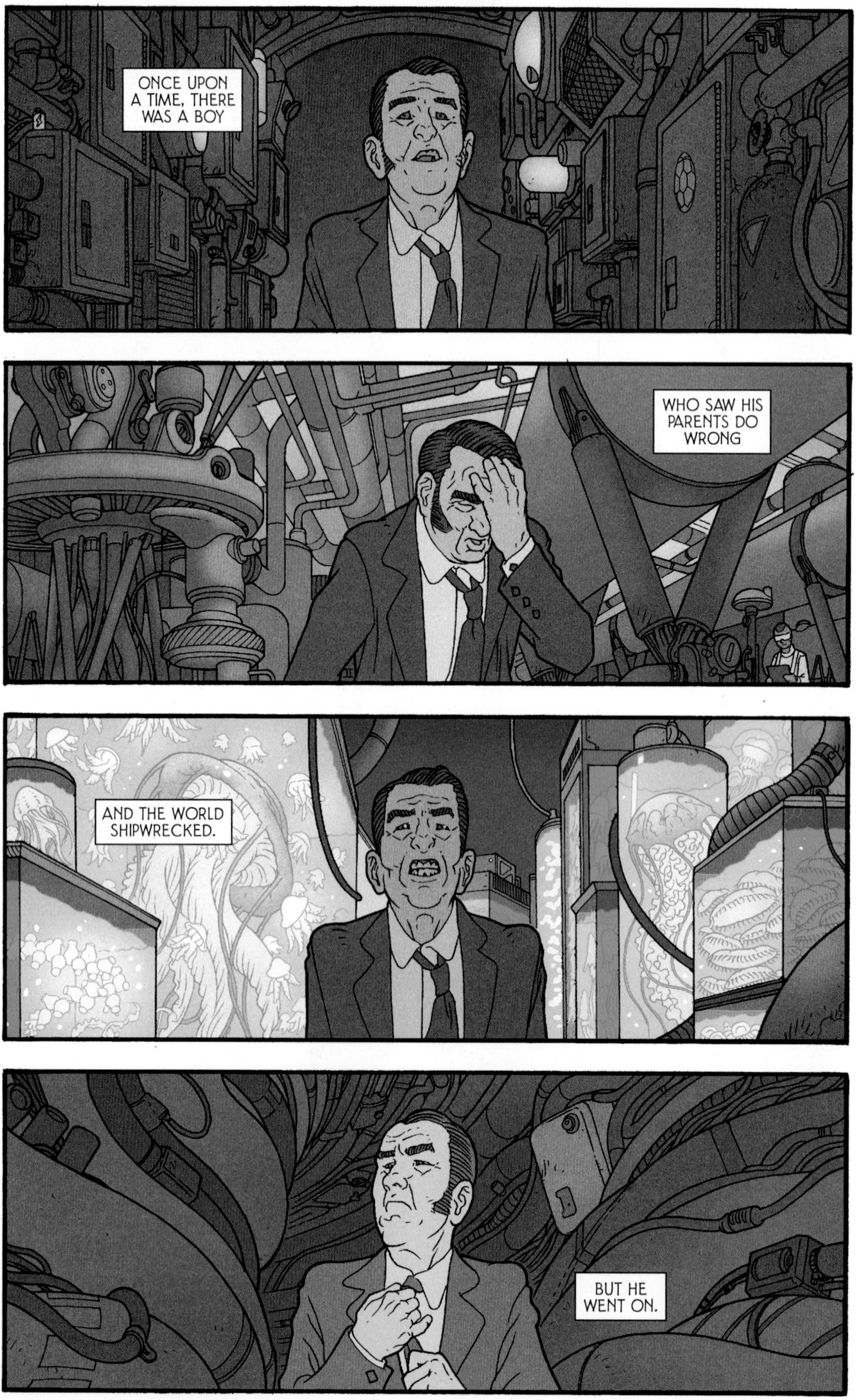
ONCE UPON A TIME, THERE WAS A BOY
WHO SAW HIS PARENTS DO WRONG
AND THE WORLD SHIPWRECKED.
BUT HE WENT ON.

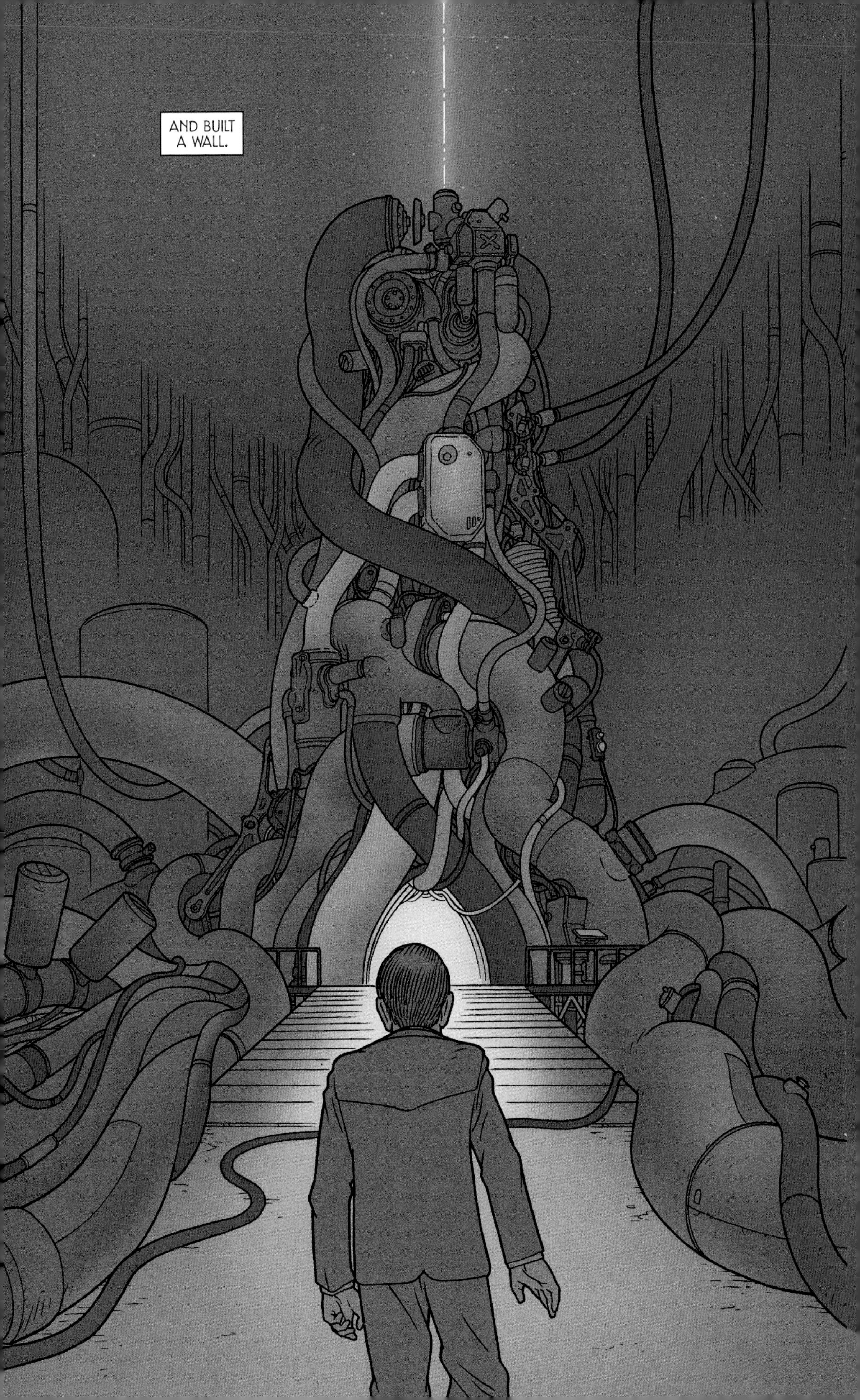
AND BUILT A WALL.

THE MYSTERY OF ROBERT DOUBLEHEAD

(PART ONE)

"He just vanished. The last issue never materialized." Amanda Rotsch exhales pink smoke, originally supplied by her state-of-art vaporizer, away from the Severn Bridge. It's raining, but she explicitly demanded to come here – explaining that her old client, Robert Doublehead, considered Richard James Edwards, a member of a Welsh alternative rock band Manic Street Preachers who vanished at the same spot years ago, a seminal influence on his writing.

"Robert was troubled, but he was working through it. And with every layer of the trouble resolved, he was becoming a better and better artist and a human being. It was fascinating. And lucrative." Ms. Rotsch stops, wipes the rain off her face – she tells us that if we write that she cried, she will punch us, because managers do not cry. She also tells us that we should not proclaim Mr. Doublehead dead yet, because he was a pimp, and pimp's don't commit suicide, a rare and much appreciated reference to Southland Tales, perhaps the purest example of paranoid California speculative fiction committed to film.

But what was his abandoned (?) project really about? "I have no clue. Sometimes with Robert you couldn't really tell because he couldn't really tell. The project itself would be an adventure to him, a way to explore the hidden recesses of his own self. He was an archaeologist of the self. And through helping himself he wanted to help others. And make dough."

Perhaps, in order to understand Doublehead better, we need to go back to the last essay he penned before his vanishing act:

"I was enveloped in a thick "us versus them" narrative. I think my father blamed me for taking side with my mom. Which I didn't want to do, but I saw him lying and scheming and being power-driven, and as frail and sometimes abusive my mom was, I could see her falling apart in ways he was not, and I could see him take decisions that could have harmed our family in a tremendous fashion, much further than they already did. So I stood by my mom. I don't think I had the vernacular to describe all this back then, but I felt I needed to. I felt like the part of the family that was holding it together as everything and everyone fell apart. I was barely ten, of course. I had no idea what kind of trauma I was undergoing. I had no idea what I was pushing away. Why did I felt such hate towards my father? Why did I felt such hate towards my mother? Why did I no longer trust men, and why did I no longer trust women? It all pointed back to the trauma, and eventually I realized I had to go back and deal with it not just through therapy and reflecting on the past, but also by resolving these problems. My fiction proved to be an excellent source for further exploring the issues that I, after sufficiently wading through them, brought up with my parents, my genetic family, with myself. 'Change' (BUY HERE) was about processing the abandonment narrative in regards to my mother. How can a child just "cope" with what happened? It left its hooks in me, and it kept me from being who I really am. I was unconsciously looking for people who would reenact the trauma, in some way, and when I saw the pattern it became conscious. That's why I needed to write 'Change.' And that's where I saw that my parents, who were themselves still pretty much teenagers when they had me, carried a deep imbalance in regards to their selves. Their male/female balance was massively off! My dad – so much false male "dominant" self stemming from real deep insecurities rooted in some of his early traumatic experiences as well as the genetic memory of his family. My mom – so much false "compliant" self stemming from the same. They just both wanted to be loved, and they found a mirror in each other, but also real love, and somehow I was born. I was a "happy accident," that's what mom told me years later. And this happy accident realized that there's no happy living without resolving inherited and newly found traumatic experiences that act as repressive blocks that keep him from being whole, and thus being real. You can fully share love and life only if you fully engage, fully give. And to fully give means to be vulnerable, and to realize there's no greater power than love, than empathy. So I had to learn how to empathize with myself and with my parents more...and by going back to the crucial time of my life with 'Change,' observing the part of the trauma "caused" by my mother's choice, I did exactly that. I processed that trauma, that particular imbalance. I started understanding and respecting my female self, my "feeling" self, much better. I started developing a connection. And that connection led me to uncovering another part of the trauma, the very same event, deeply associated with the other part of the equation: my father."

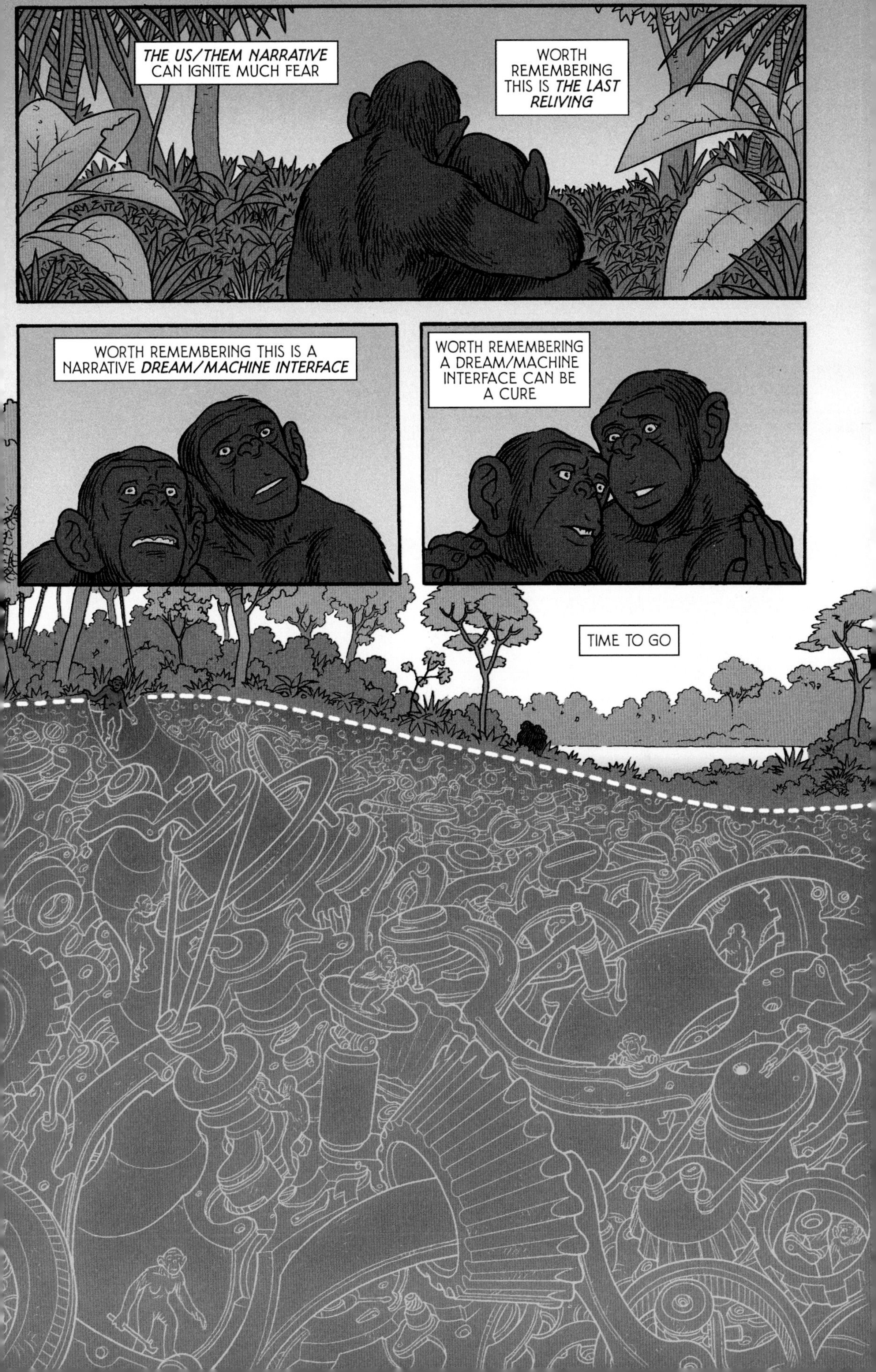
THE US/THEM NARRATIVE CAN IGNITE MUCH FEAR
WORTH REMEMBERING THIS IS *THE LAST RELIVING*
WORTH REMEMBERING THIS IS A NARRATIVE *DREAM/MACHINE INTERFACE*
WORTH REMEMBERING A DREAM/MACHINE INTERFACE CAN BE A CURE
TIME TO GO

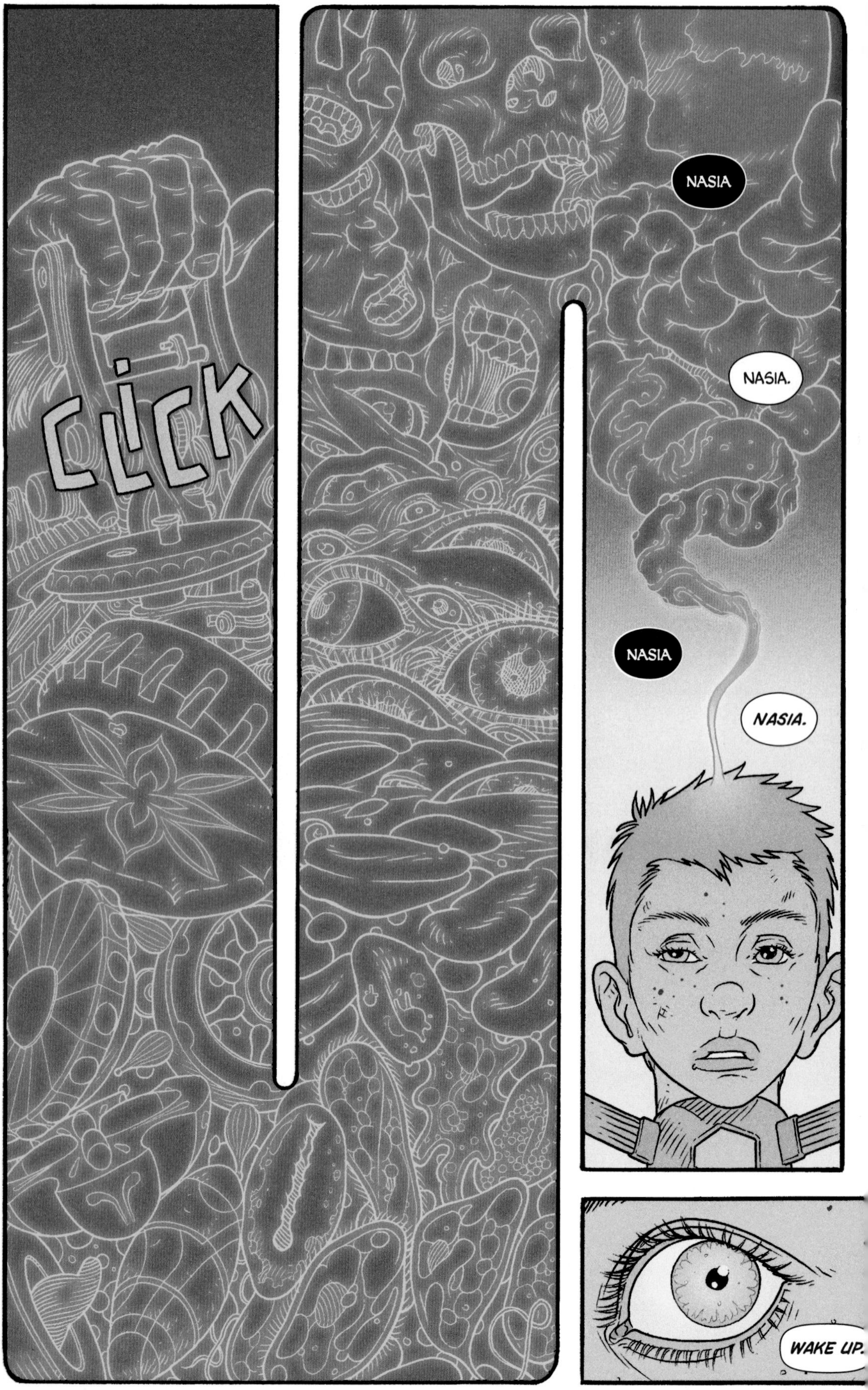
CLICK
NASIA
NASIA.
NASIA
NASIA.
WAKE UP.

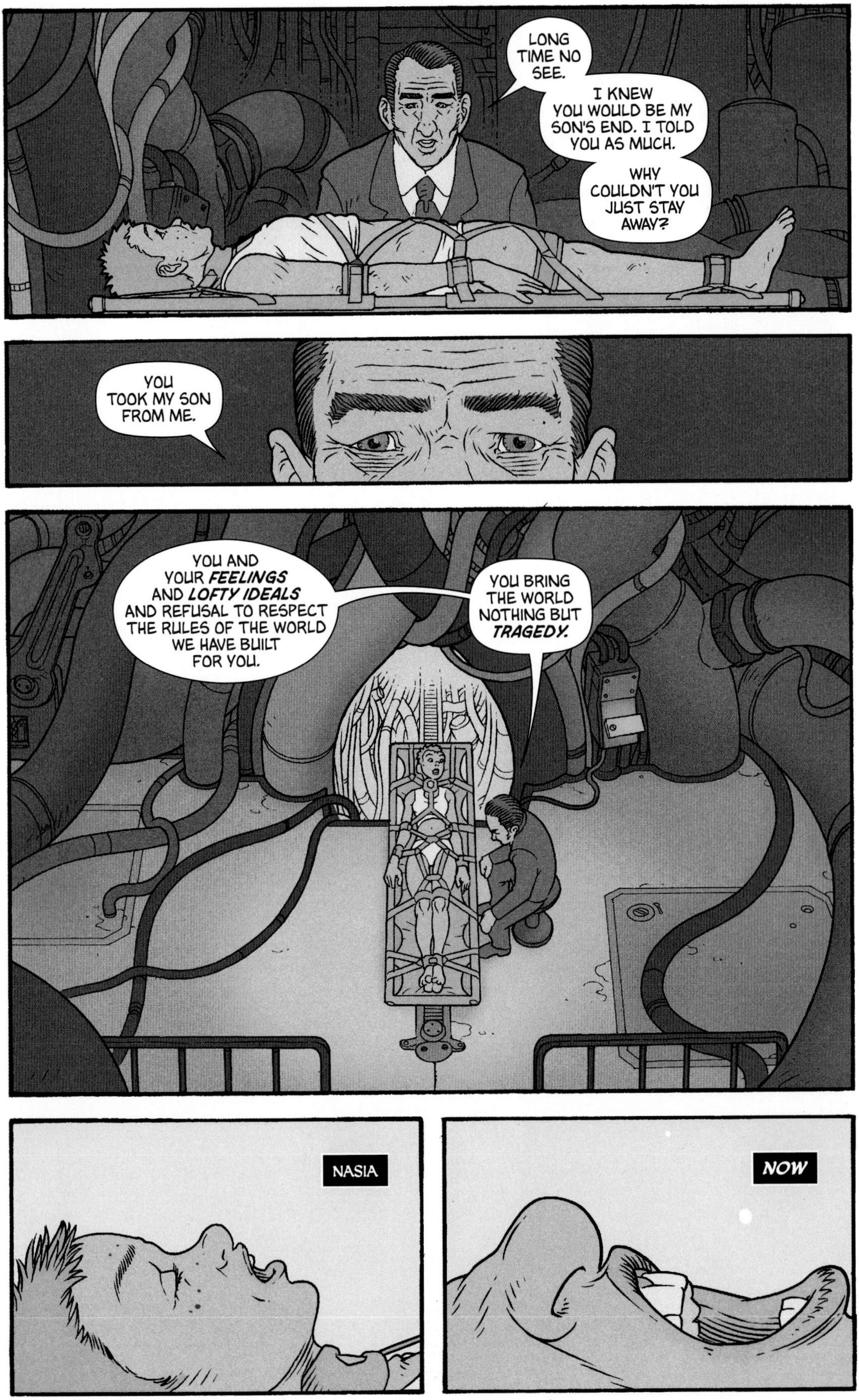

LONG TIME NO SEE.
I KNEW YOU WOULD BE MY SON'S END. I TOLD YOU AS MUCH.
WHY COULDN'T YOU JUST STAY AWAY?
YOU TOOK MY SON FROM ME.
YOU AND YOUR *FEELINGS* AND *LOFTY IDEALS* AND REFUSAL TO RESPECT THE RULES OF THE WORLD WE HAVE BUILT FOR YOU.
YOU BRING THE WORLD NOTHING BUT *TRAGEDY.*
NASIA
NOW

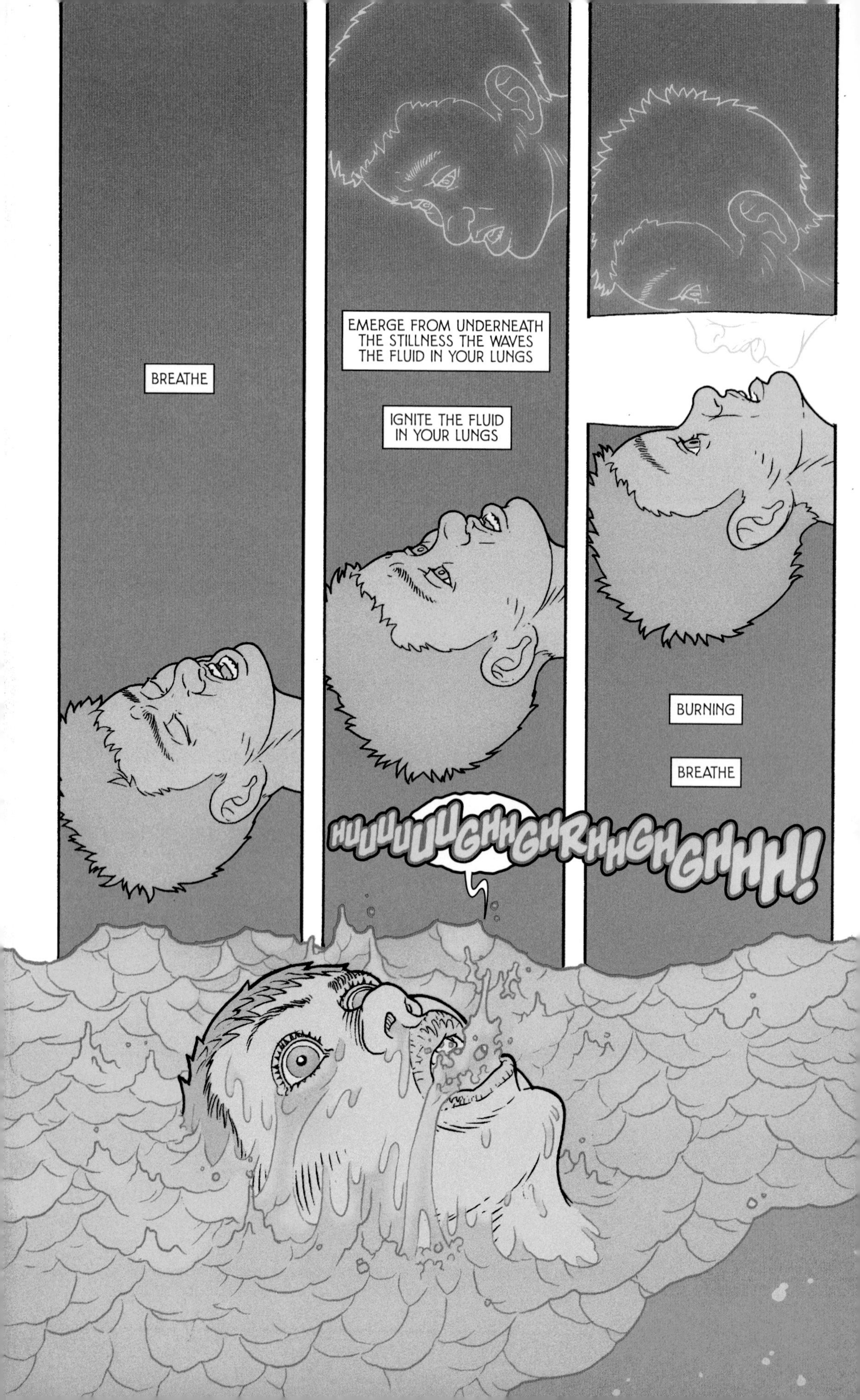
BREATHE
EMERGE FROM UNDERNEATH THE STILLNESS THE WAVES THE FLUID IN YOUR LUNGS
IGNITE THE FLUID IN YOUR LUNGS
BURNING
BREATHE
HUUUUUUGHHGHRHHGHGHHH!

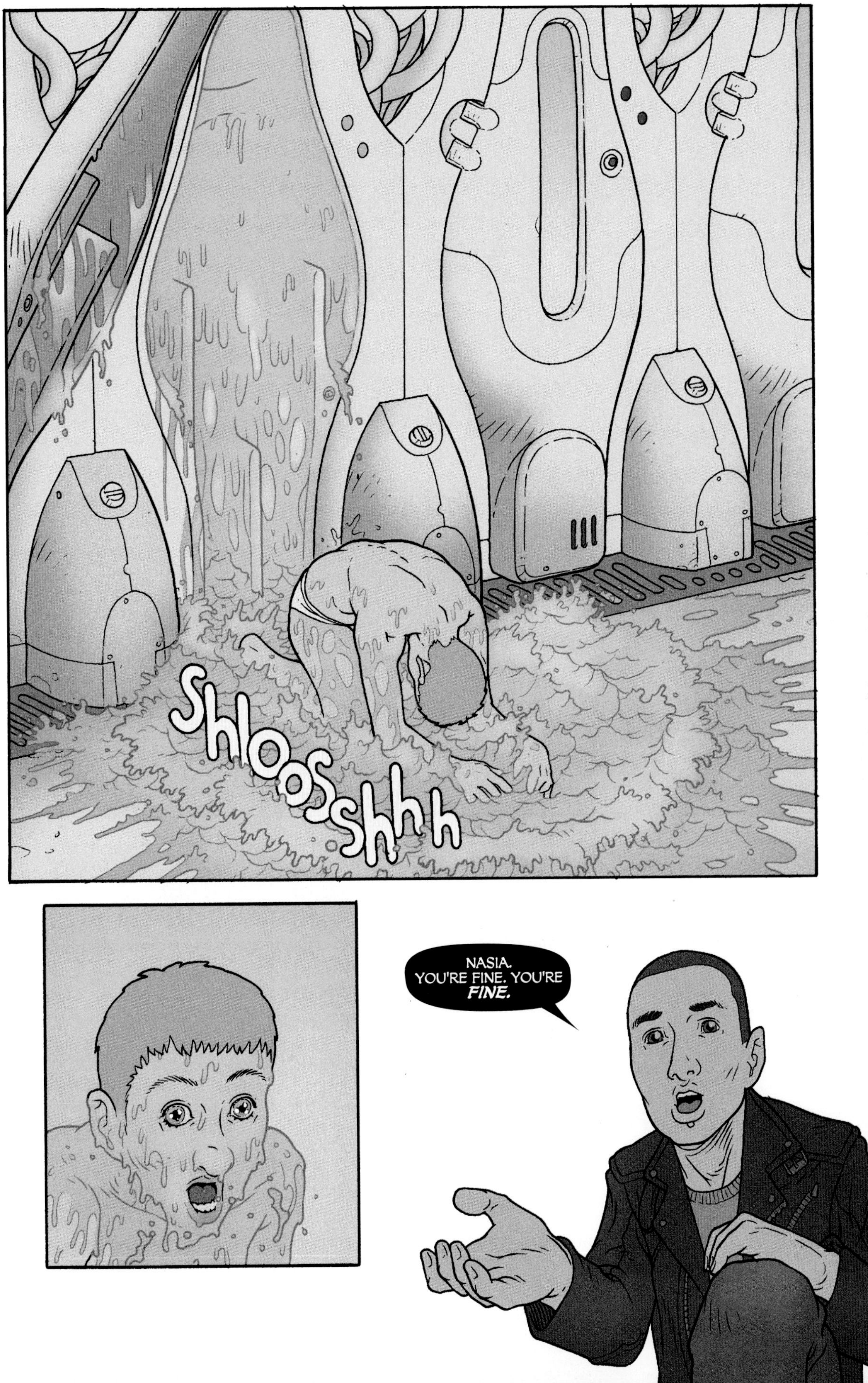
Shloosshhh
NASIA. YOU'RE FINE. YOU'RE *FINE.*

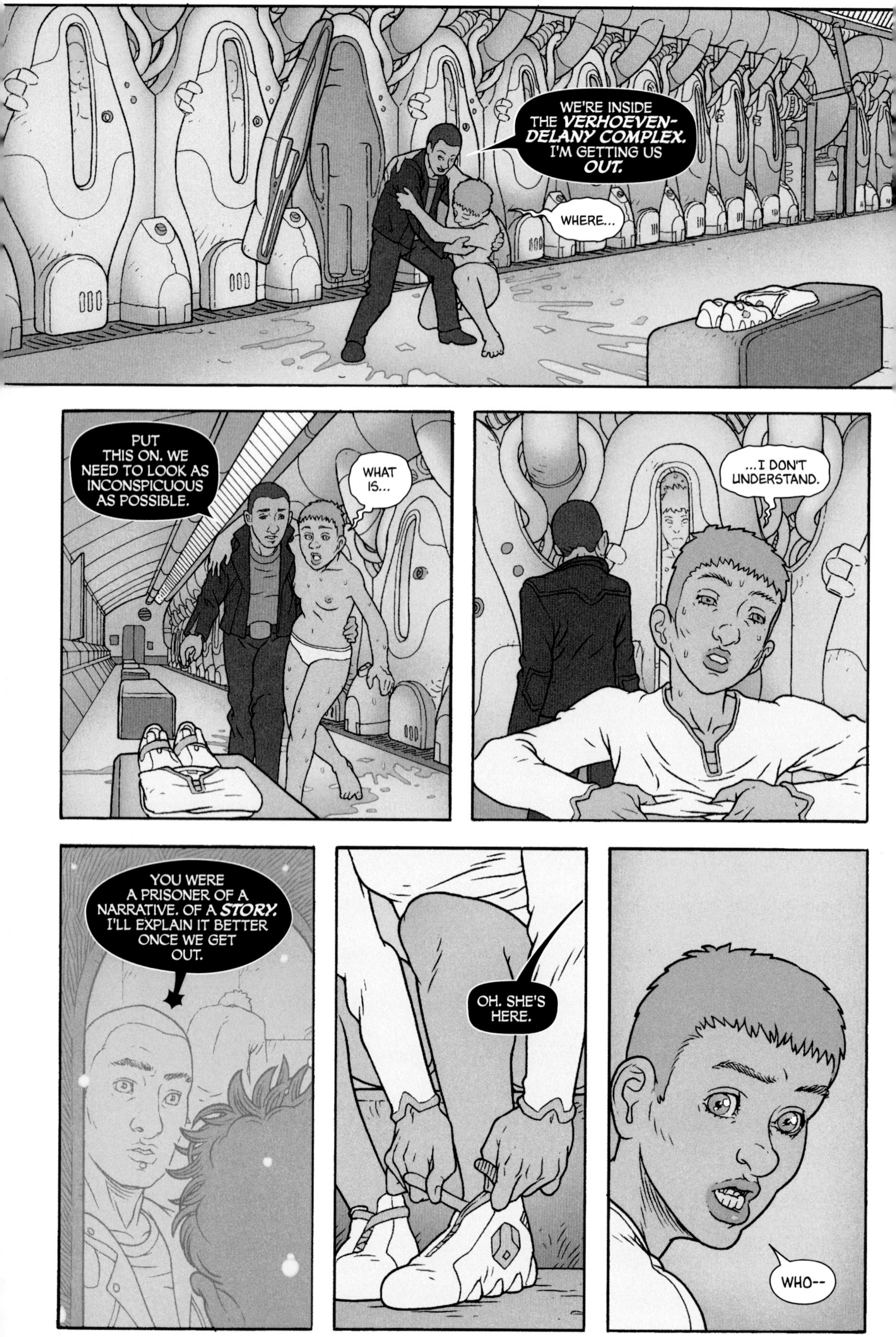
WE'RE INSIDE THE VERHOEVEN-DELANY COMPLEX. I'M GETTING US OUT.
WHERE...
PUT THIS ON. WE NEED TO LOOK AS INCONSPICUOUS AS POSSIBLE.
WHAT IS...
...I DON'T UNDERSTAND.
YOU WERE A PRISONER OF A NARRATIVE. OF A STORY. I'LL EXPLAIN IT BETTER ONCE WE GET OUT.
OH. SHE'S HERE.
WHO--

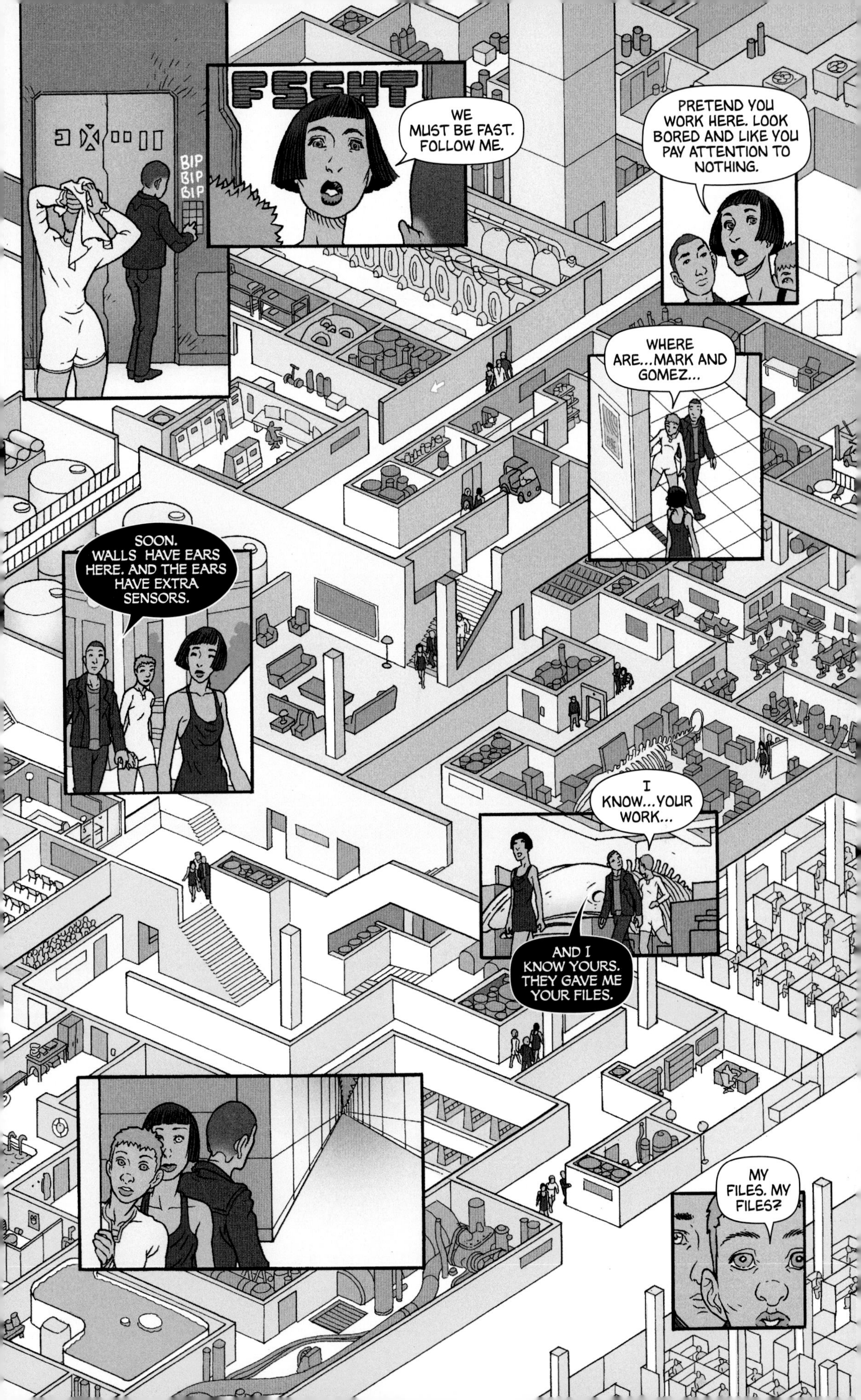
BIP BIP BIP
FSCHT
WE MUST BE FAST. FOLLOW ME.
PRETEND YOU WORK HERE. LOOK BORED AND LIKE YOU PAY ATTENTION TO NOTHING.
WHERE ARE...MARK AND GOMEZ...
SOON. WALLS HAVE EARS HERE. AND THE EARS HAVE EXTRA SENSORS.
I KNOW...YOUR WORK...
AND I KNOW YOURS. THEY GAVE ME YOUR FILES.
MY FILES. MY FILES?

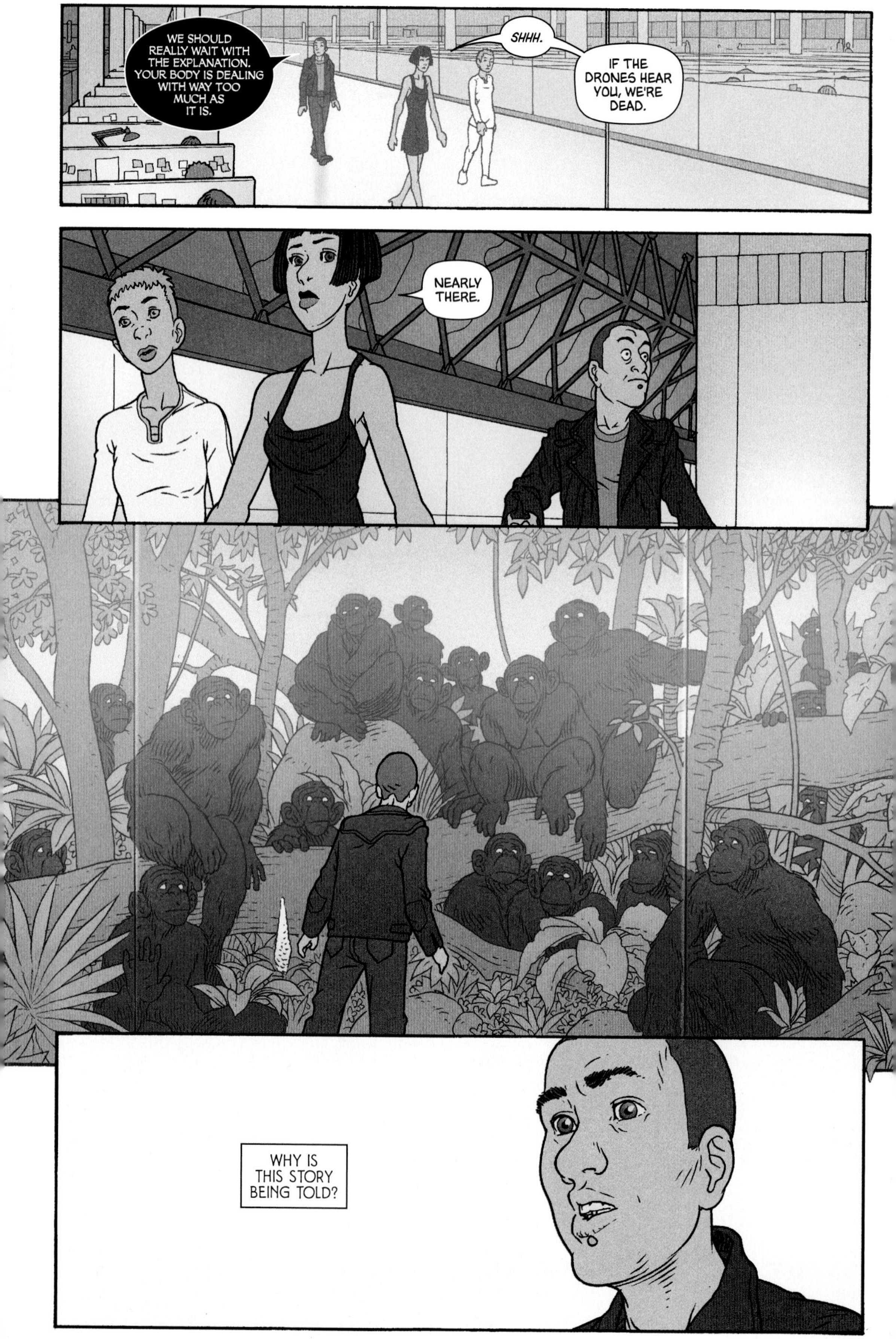
WE SHOULD REALLY WAIT WITH THE EXPLANATION. YOUR BODY IS DEALING WITH WAY TOO MUCH AS IT IS.
SHHH.
IF THE DRONES HEAR YOU, WE'RE DEAD.
NEARLY THERE.
WHY IS THIS STORY BEING TOLD?

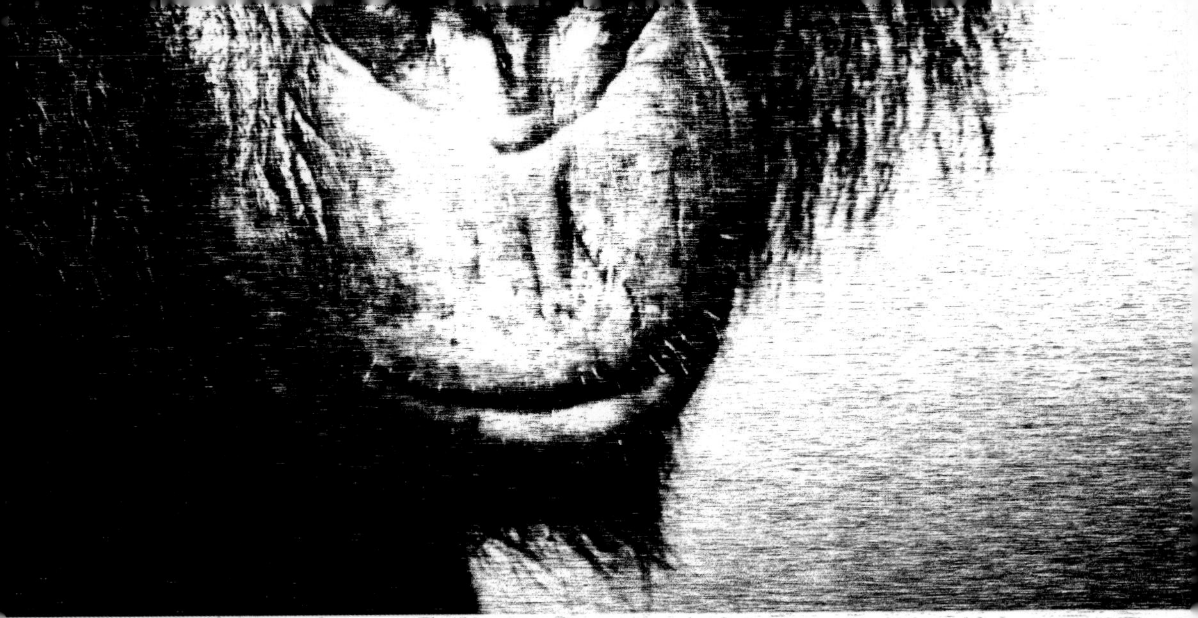

!BONOBO FACTS!

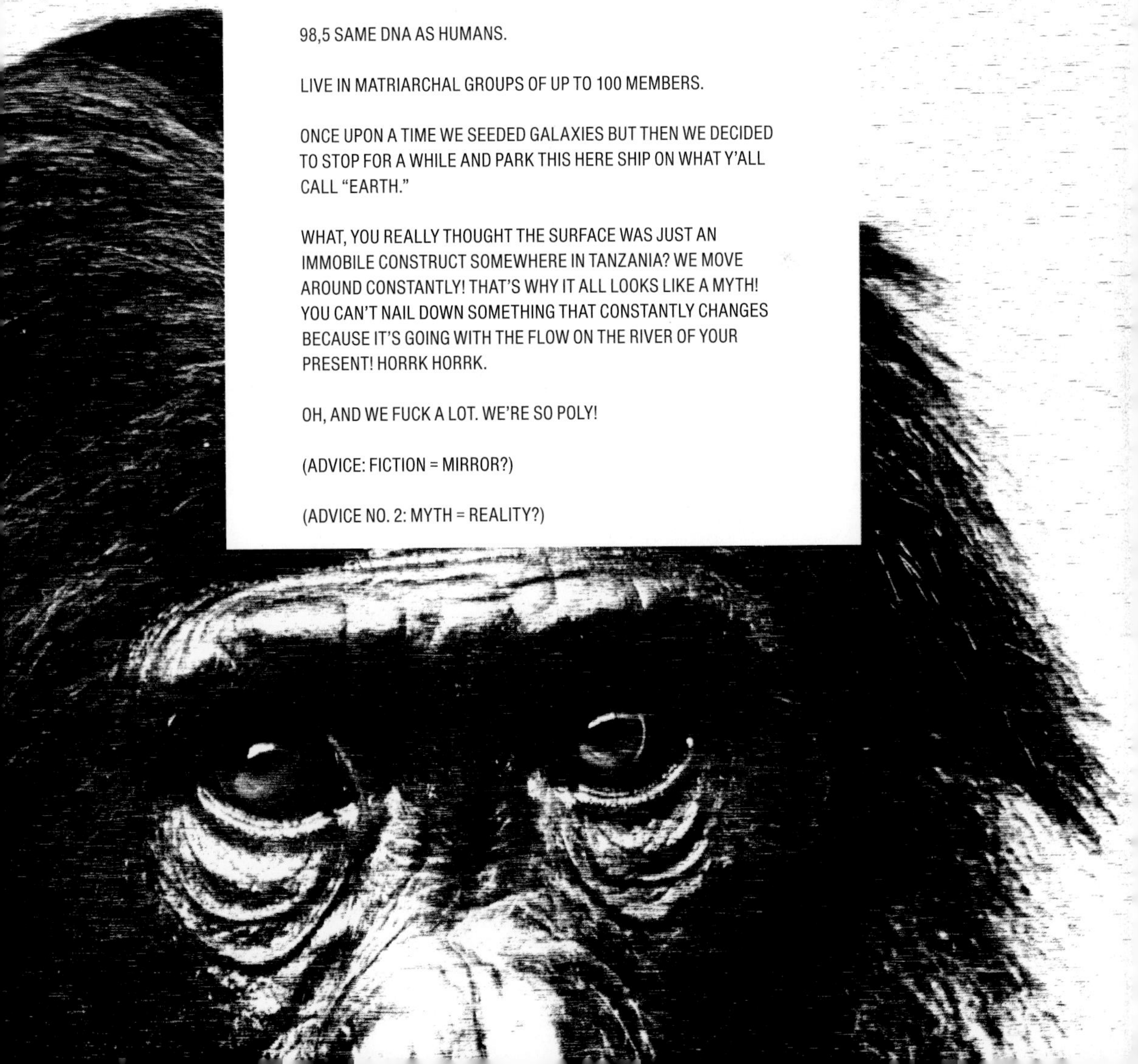

98,5 SAME DNA AS HUMANS.

LIVE IN MATRIARCHAL GROUPS OF UP TO 100 MEMBERS.

ONCE UPON A TIME WE SEEDED GALAXIES BUT THEN WE DECIDED TO STOP FOR A WHILE AND PARK THIS HERE SHIP ON WHAT Y'ALL CALL "EARTH."

WHAT, YOU REALLY THOUGHT THE SURFACE WAS JUST AN IMMOBILE CONSTRUCT SOMEWHERE IN TANZANIA? WE MOVE AROUND CONSTANTLY! THAT'S WHY IT ALL LOOKS LIKE A MYTH! YOU CAN'T NAIL DOWN SOMETHING THAT CONSTANTLY CHANGES BECAUSE IT'S GOING WITH THE FLOW ON THE RIVER OF YOUR PRESENT! HORRK HORRK.

OH, AND WE FUCK A LOT. WE'RE SO POLY!

(ADVICE: FICTION = MIRROR?)

(ADVICE NO. 2: MYTH = REALITY?)

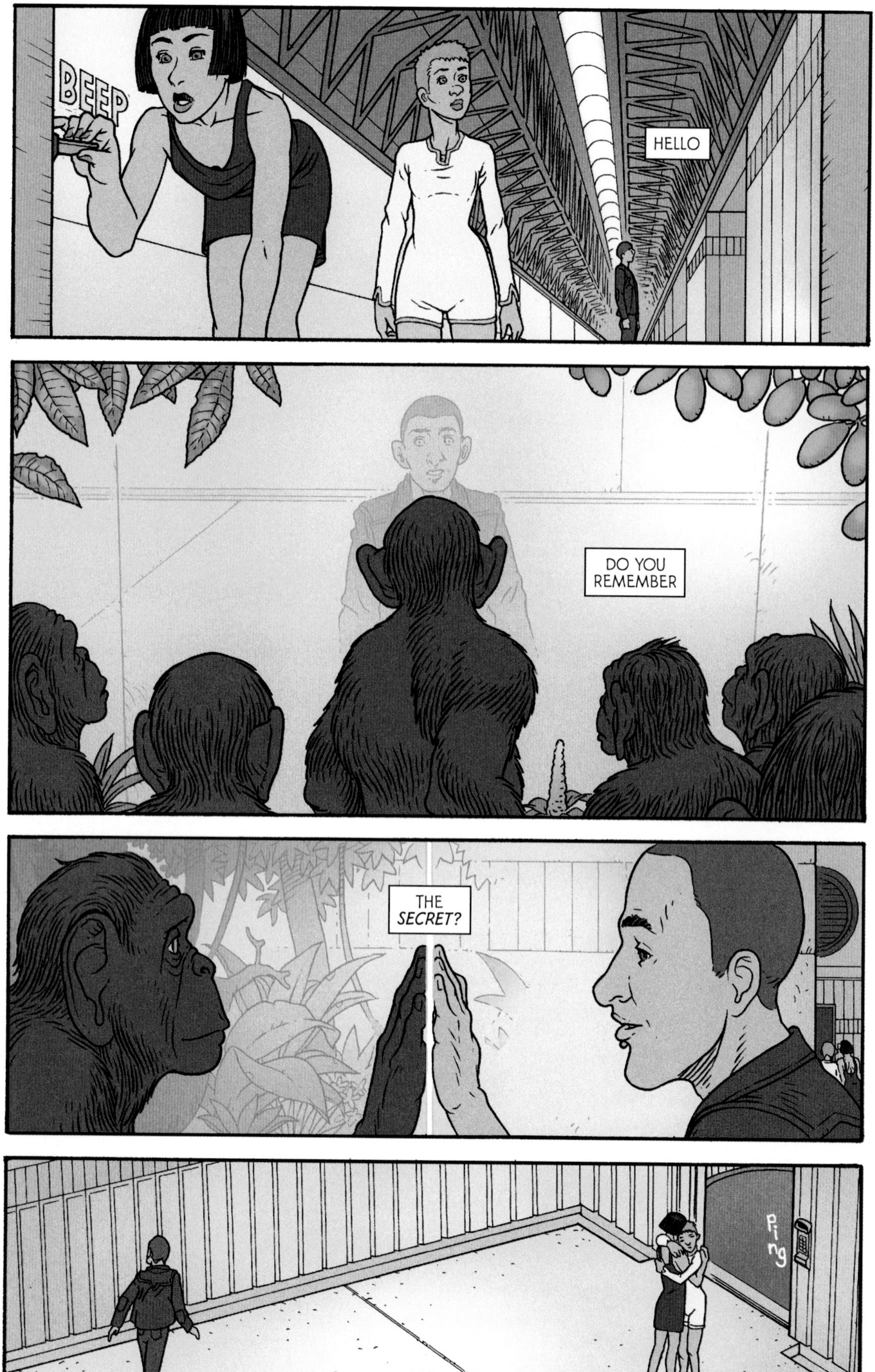
BEEP
HELLO
DO YOU REMEMBER
THE *SECRET?*
Ping

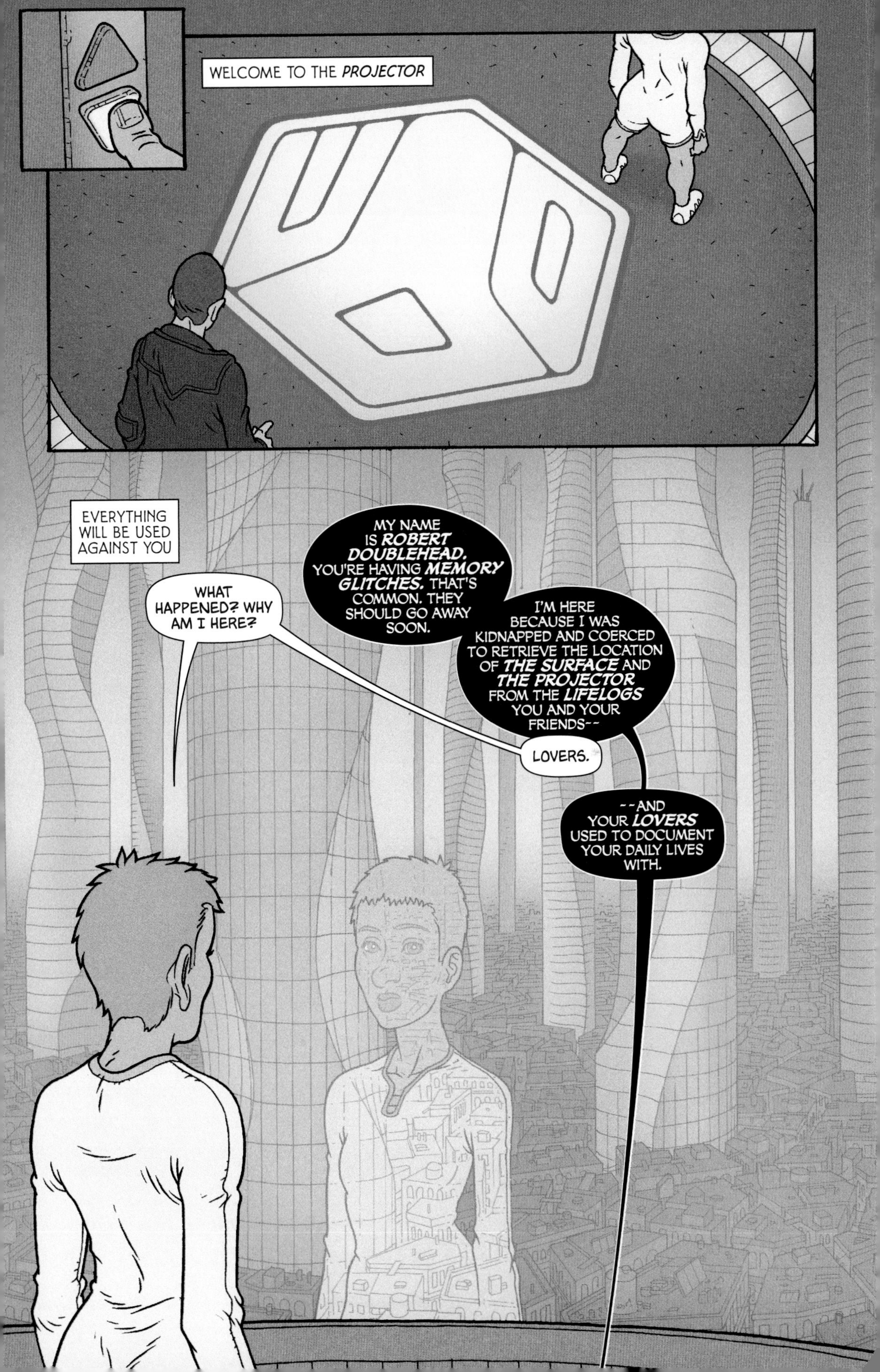
WELCOME TO THE PROJECTOR
EVERYTHING WILL BE USED AGAINST YOU
WHAT HAPPENED? WHY AM I HERE?
MY NAME IS ROBERT DOUBLEHEAD. YOU'RE HAVING MEMORY GLITCHES. THAT'S COMMON. THEY SHOULD GO AWAY SOON.
I'M HERE BECAUSE I WAS KIDNAPPED AND COERCED TO RETRIEVE THE LOCATION OF THE SURFACE AND THE PROJECTOR FROM THE LIFELOGS YOU AND YOUR FRIENDS--
LOVERS.
--AND YOUR LOVERS USED TO DOCUMENT YOUR DAILY LIVES WITH.

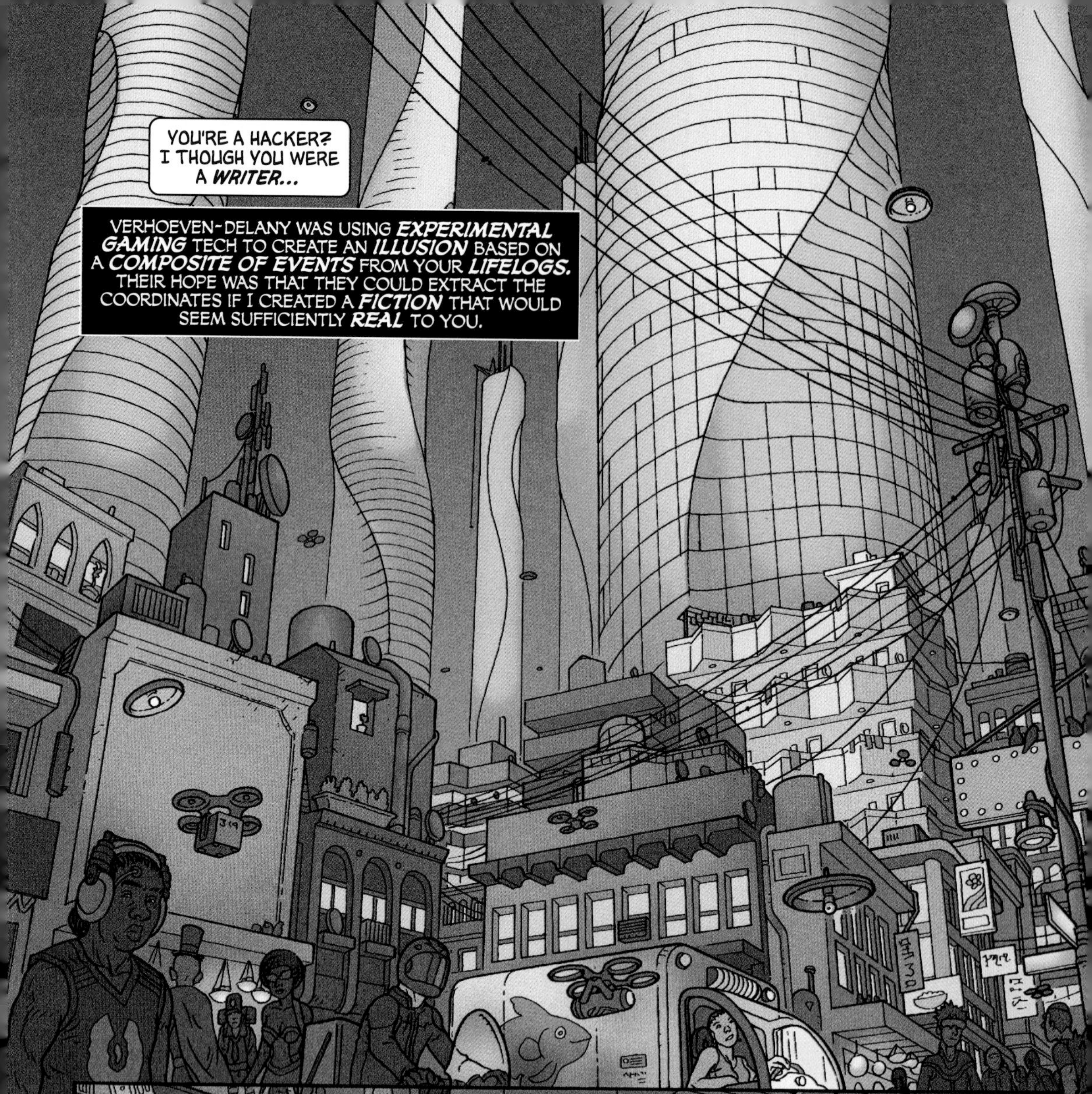
YOU'RE A HACKER? I THOUGH YOU WERE A *WRITER...*
VERHOEVEN-DELANY WAS USING *EXPERIMENTAL GAMING* TECH TO CREATE AN *ILLUSION* BASED ON A *COMPOSITE OF EVENTS* FROM YOUR *LIFELOGS.* THEIR HOPE WAS THAT THEY COULD EXTRACT THE COORDINATES IF I CREATED A *FICTION* THAT WOULD SEEM SUFFICIENTLY *REAL* TO YOU.

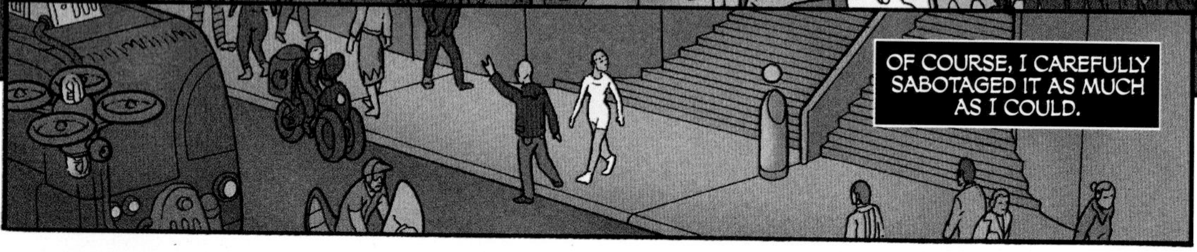
OF COURSE, I CAREFULLY SABOTAGED IT AS MUCH AS I COULD.

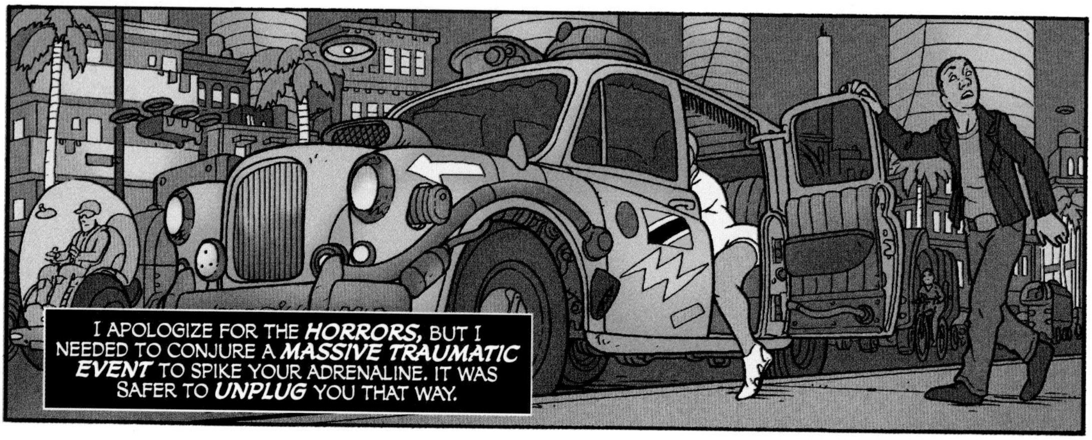
I APOLOGIZE FOR THE *HORRORS,* BUT I NEEDED TO CONJURE A *MASSIVE TRAUMATIC EVENT* TO SPIKE YOUR ADRENALINE. IT WAS SAFER TO *UNPLUG* YOU THAT WAY.

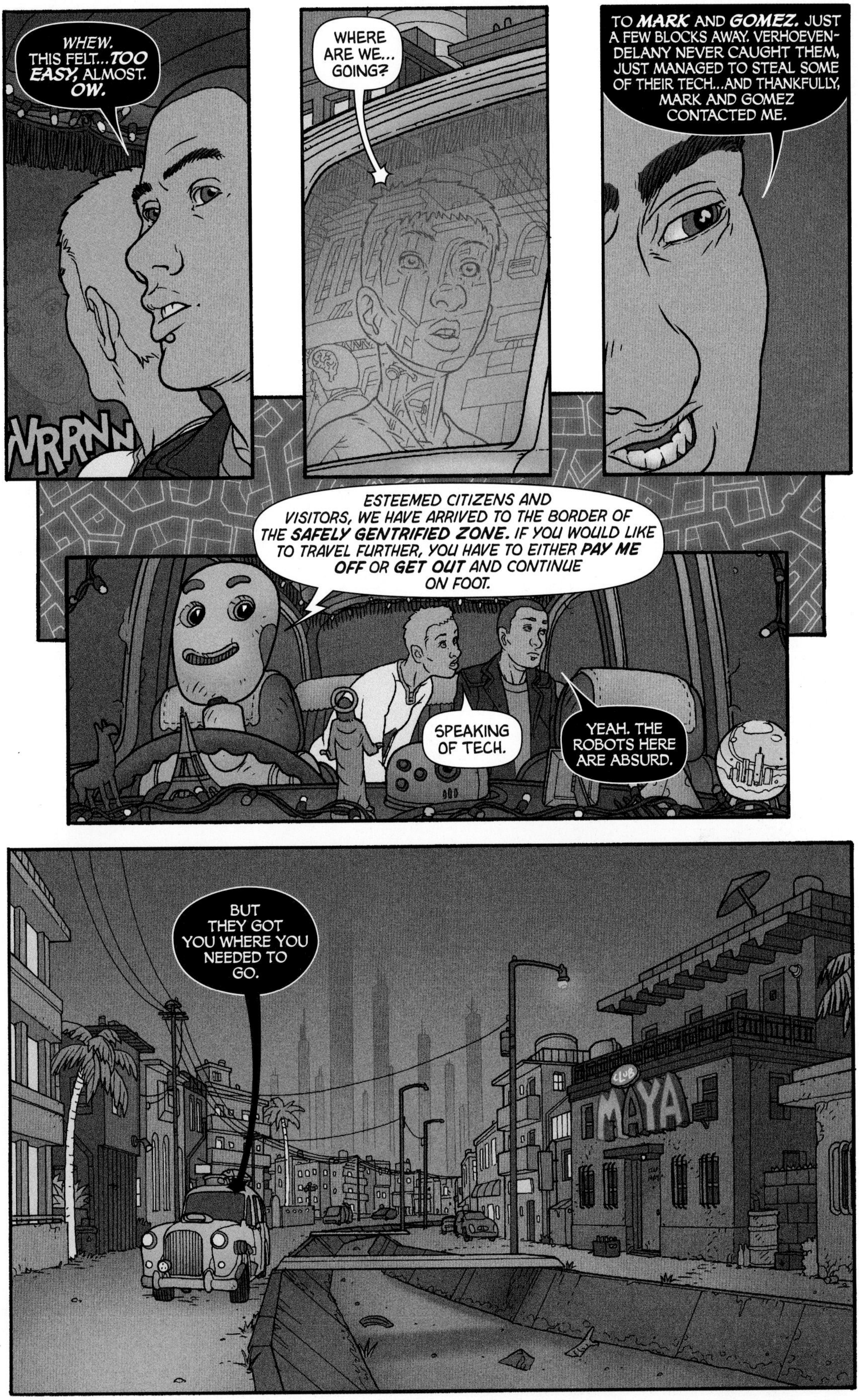
WHEW. THIS FELT...TOO EASY, ALMOST. OW.
VRRNN
WHERE ARE WE... GOING?
TO MARK AND GOMEZ. JUST A FEW BLOCKS AWAY. VERHOEVEN-DELANY NEVER CAUGHT THEM, JUST MANAGED TO STEAL SOME OF THEIR TECH...AND THANKFULLY, MARK AND GOMEZ CONTACTED ME.
ESTEEMED CITIZENS AND VISITORS, WE HAVE ARRIVED TO THE BORDER OF THE SAFELY GENTRIFIED ZONE. IF YOU WOULD LIKE TO TRAVEL FURTHER, YOU HAVE TO EITHER PAY ME OFF OR GET OUT AND CONTINUE ON FOOT.
SPEAKING OF TECH.
YEAH. THE ROBOTS HERE ARE ABSURD.
BUT THEY GOT YOU WHERE YOU NEEDED TO GO.
CLUB
MAYA

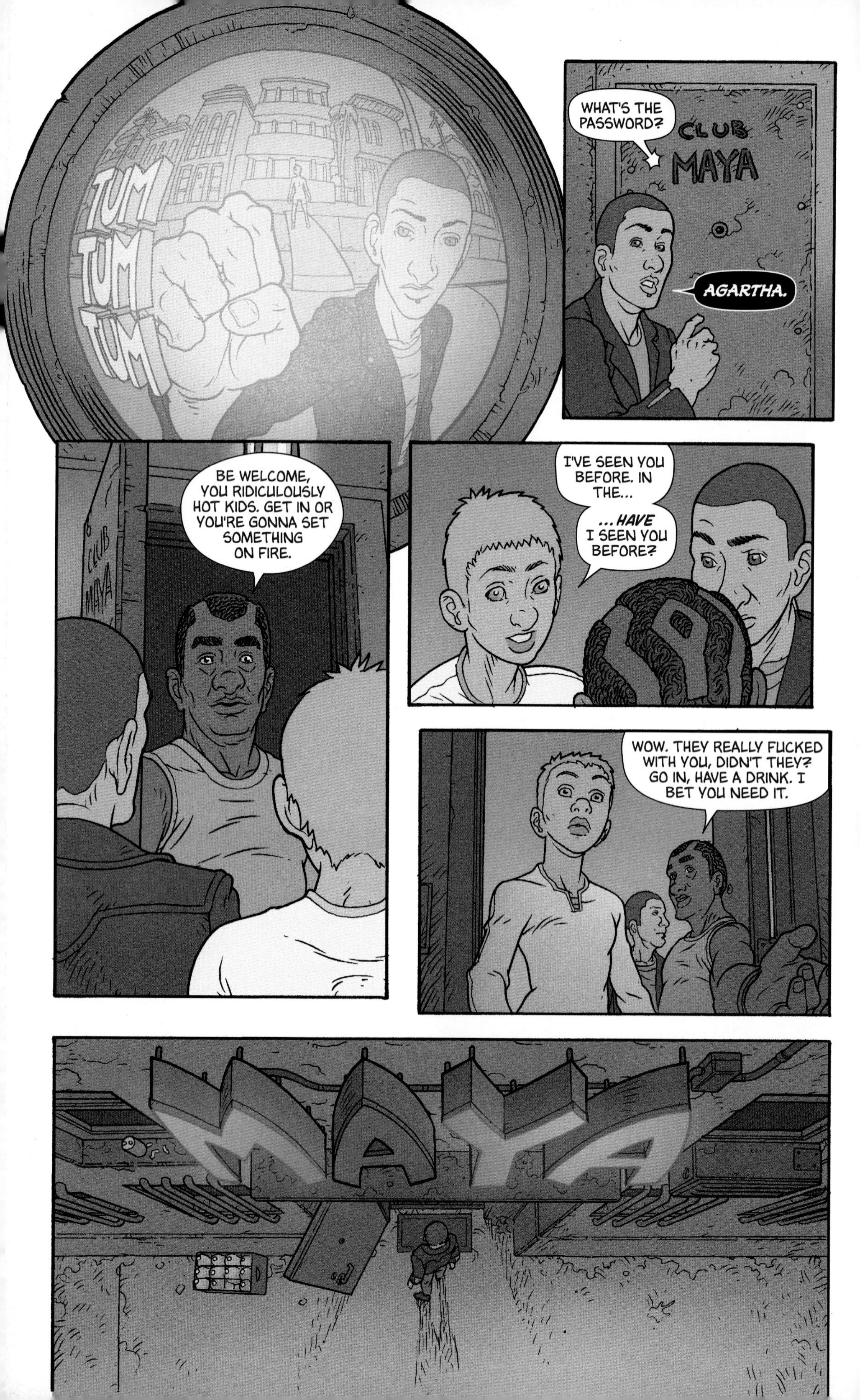
TUM TUM TUM TUM
WHAT'S THE PASSWORD?
CLUB MAYA
AGARTHA.
BE WELCOME, YOU RIDICULOUSLY HOT KIDS. GET IN OR YOU'RE GONNA SET SOMETHING ON FIRE.
CLUB MAYA
I'VE SEEN YOU BEFORE. IN THE...
...HAVE I SEEN YOU BEFORE?
WOW. THEY REALLY FUCKED WITH YOU, DIDN'T THEY? GO IN, HAVE A DRINK. I BET YOU NEED IT.
MAYA

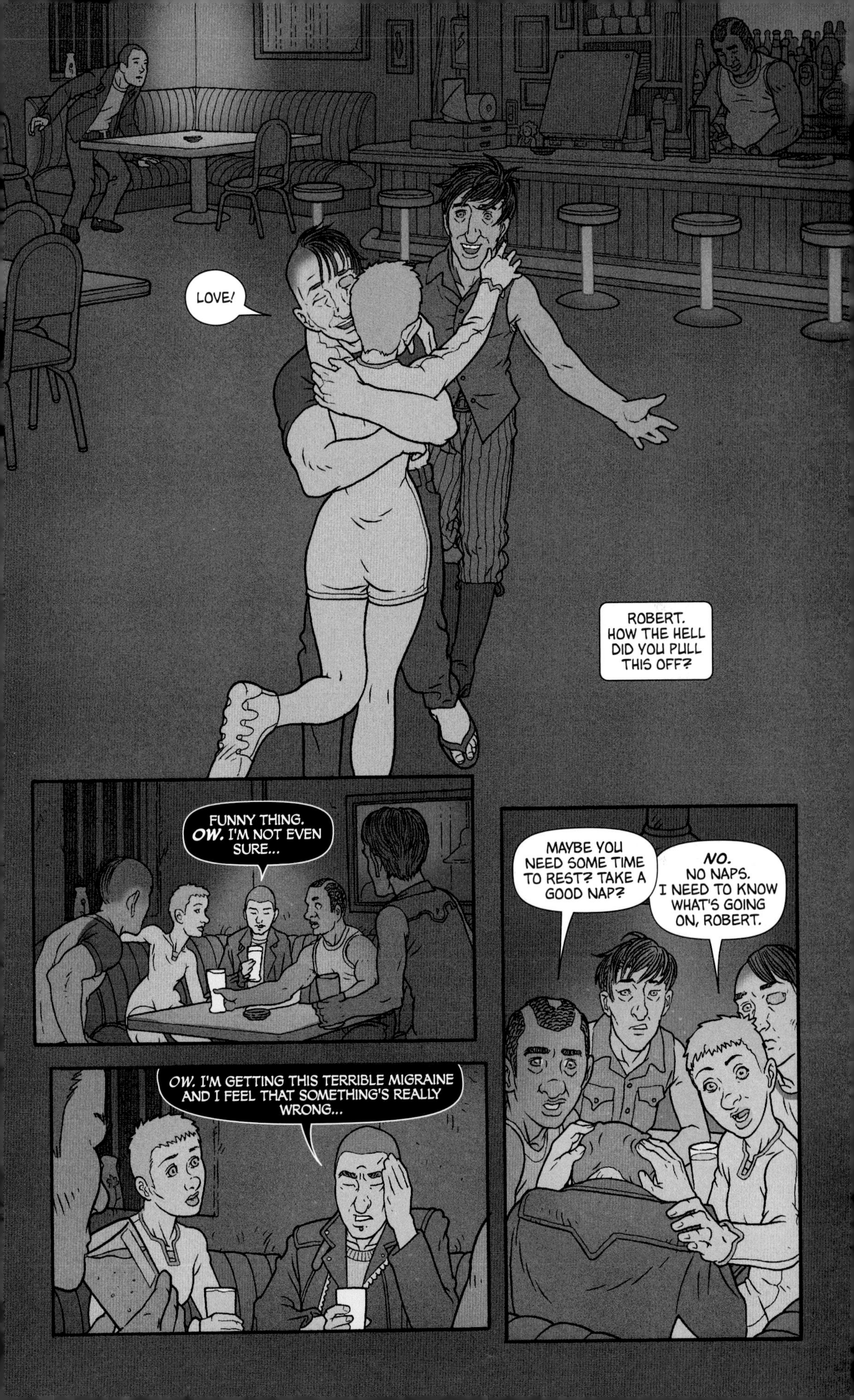
LOVE!
ROBERT. HOW THE HELL DID YOU PULL THIS OFF?
FUNNY THING. OW. I'M NOT EVEN SURE...
OW. I'M GETTING THIS TERRIBLE MIGRAINE AND I FEEL THAT SOMETHING'S REALLY WRONG...
MAYBE YOU NEED SOME TIME TO REST? TAKE A GOOD NAP?
NO. NO NAPS. I NEED TO KNOW WHAT'S GOING ON, ROBERT.

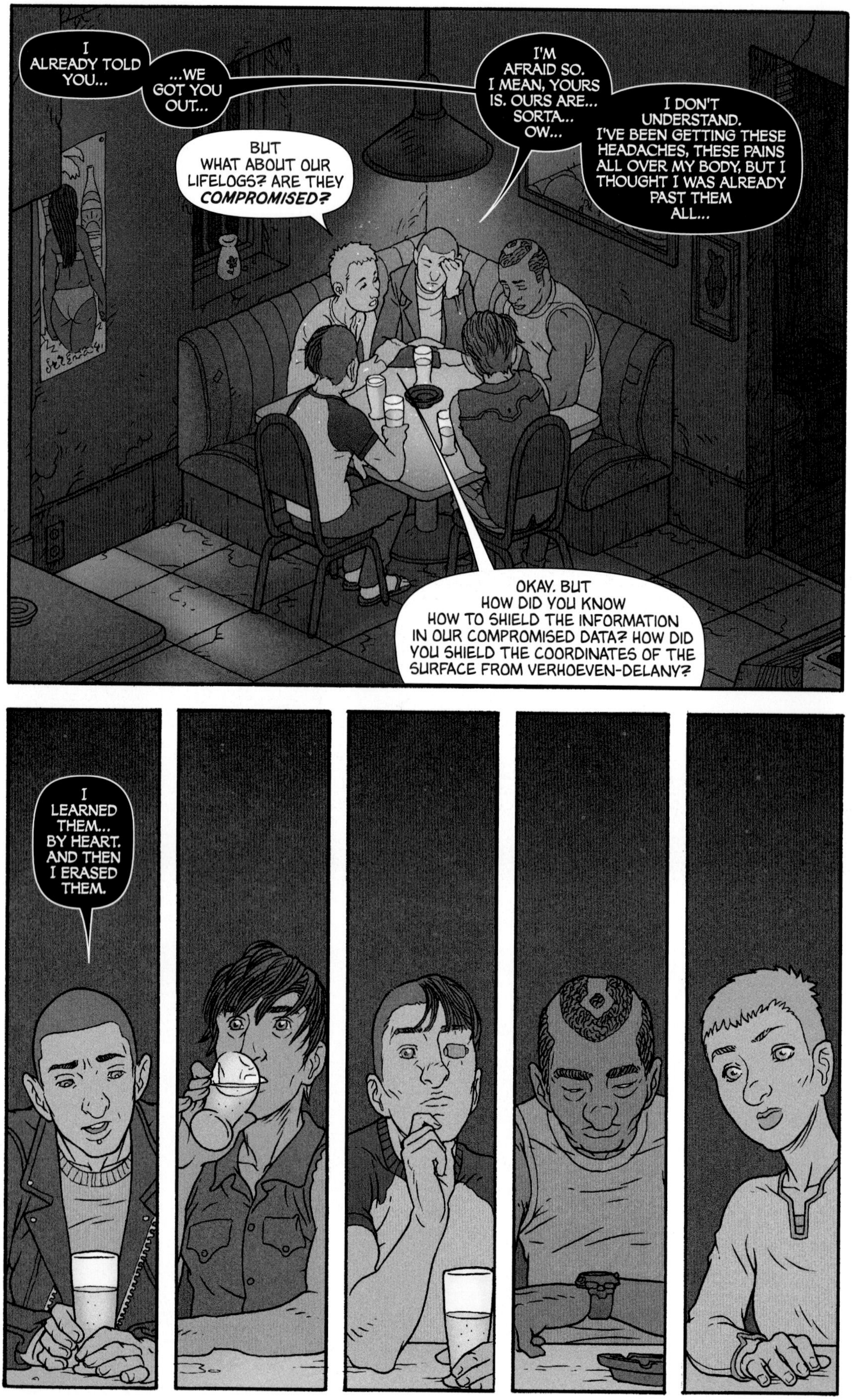
I ALREADY TOLD YOU...
...WE GOT YOU OUT...
I'M AFRAID SO. I MEAN, YOURS IS. OURS ARE... SORTA... OW...
I DON'T UNDERSTAND. I'VE BEEN GETTING THESE HEADACHES, THESE PAINS ALL OVER MY BODY, BUT I THOUGHT I WAS ALREADY PAST THEM ALL...
BUT WHAT ABOUT OUR LIFELOGS? ARE THEY COMPROMISED?
OKAY. BUT HOW DID YOU KNOW HOW TO SHIELD THE INFORMATION IN OUR COMPROMISED DATA? HOW DID YOU SHIELD THE COORDINATES OF THE SURFACE FROM VERHOEVEN-DELANY?
I LEARNED THEM... BY HEART. AND THEN I ERASED THEM.

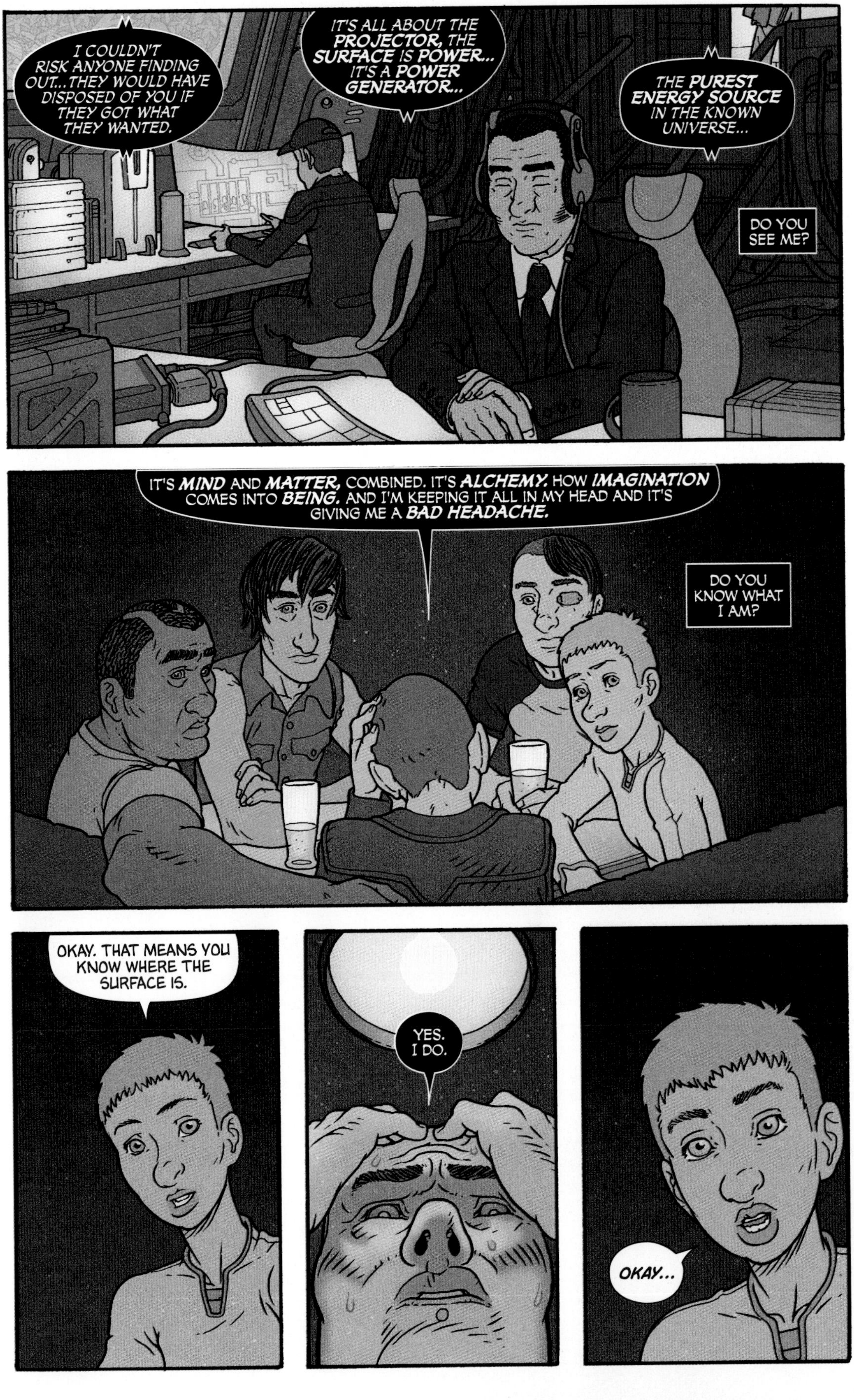
I COULDN'T RISK ANYONE FINDING OUT...THEY WOULD HAVE DISPOSED OF YOU IF THEY GOT WHAT THEY WANTED.
IT'S ALL ABOUT THE PROJECTOR, THE SURFACE IS POWER... IT'S A POWER GENERATOR...
THE PUREST ENERGY SOURCE IN THE KNOWN UNIVERSE...
DO YOU SEE ME?
IT'S MIND AND MATTER, COMBINED. IT'S ALCHEMY. HOW IMAGINATION COMES INTO BEING. AND I'M KEEPING IT ALL IN MY HEAD AND IT'S GIVING ME A BAD HEADACHE.
DO YOU KNOW WHAT I AM?
OKAY. THAT MEANS YOU KNOW WHERE THE SURFACE IS.
YES. I DO.
OKAY...

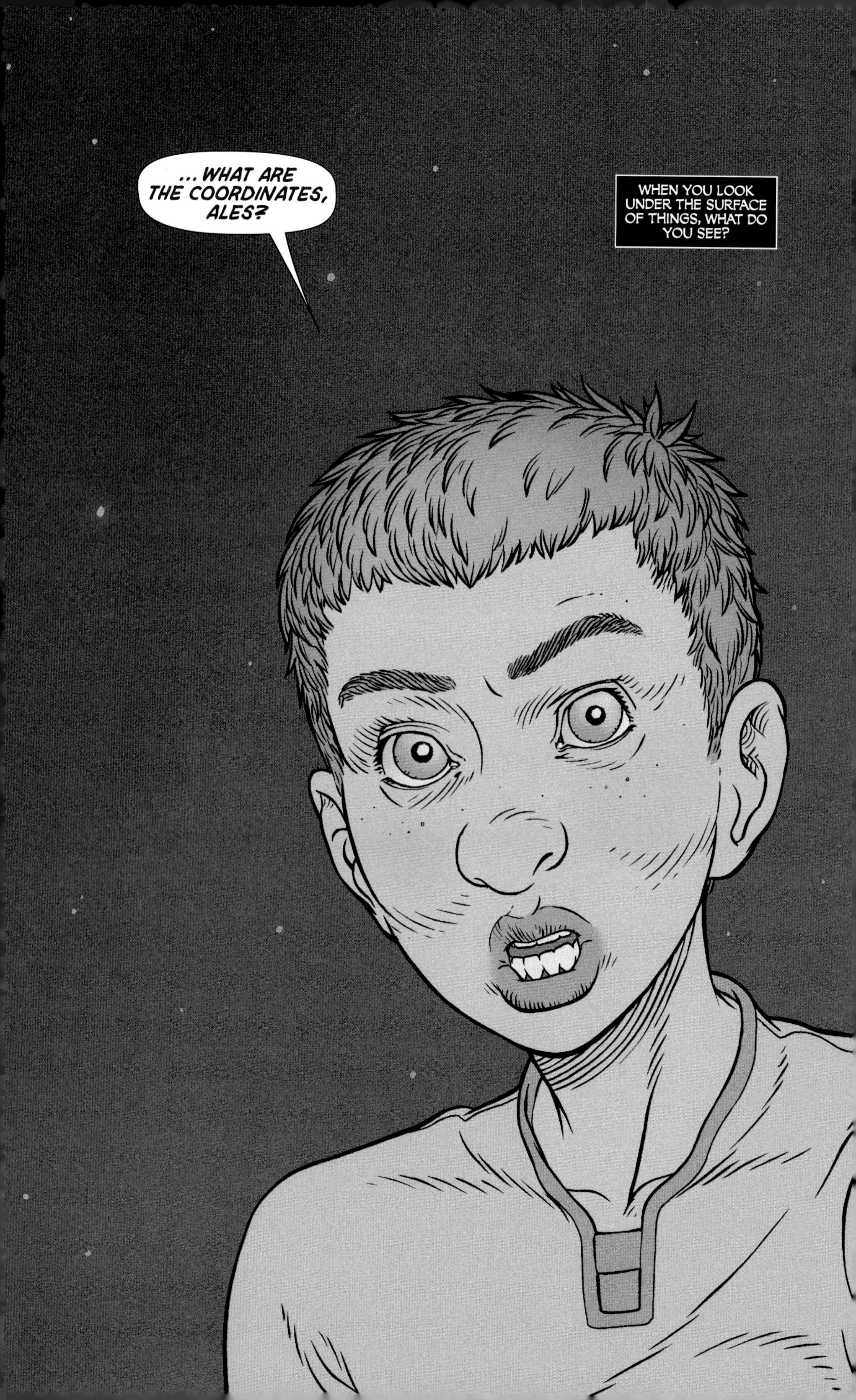
...WHAT ARE THE COORDINATES, ALES?
WHEN YOU LOOK UNDER THE SURFACE OF THINGS, WHAT DO YOU SEE?

THE LIFELOG PAGES

Model A.37-B Assembled in China
FCC 45B-AC731-G CE 89W-8-YD
LIFE LOG
VERSION 16.2.25 (19C1B9)
ACCESS

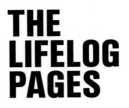

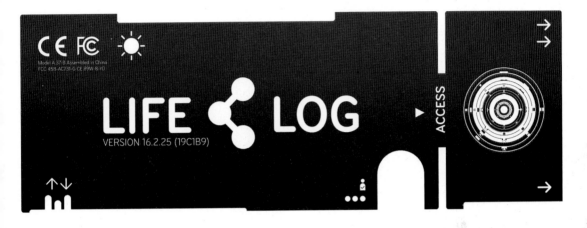

WHO WATCHES WITH YOU?

blinkfeed

WE HAVE NOTHING MORE TO SELL YOU

THE CLICKBAIT YEARS ARE OVER

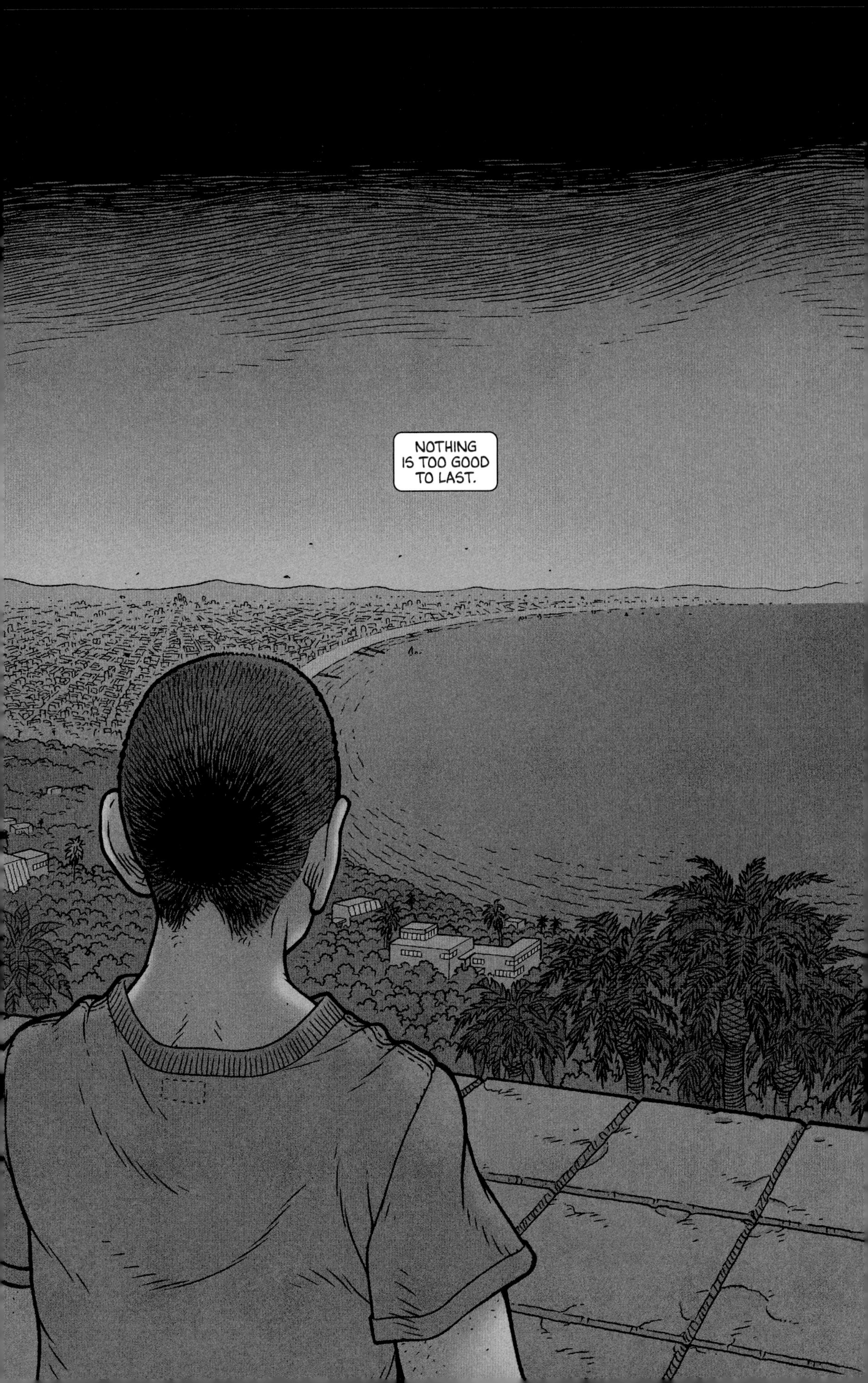
NOTHING IS TOO GOOD TO LAST.

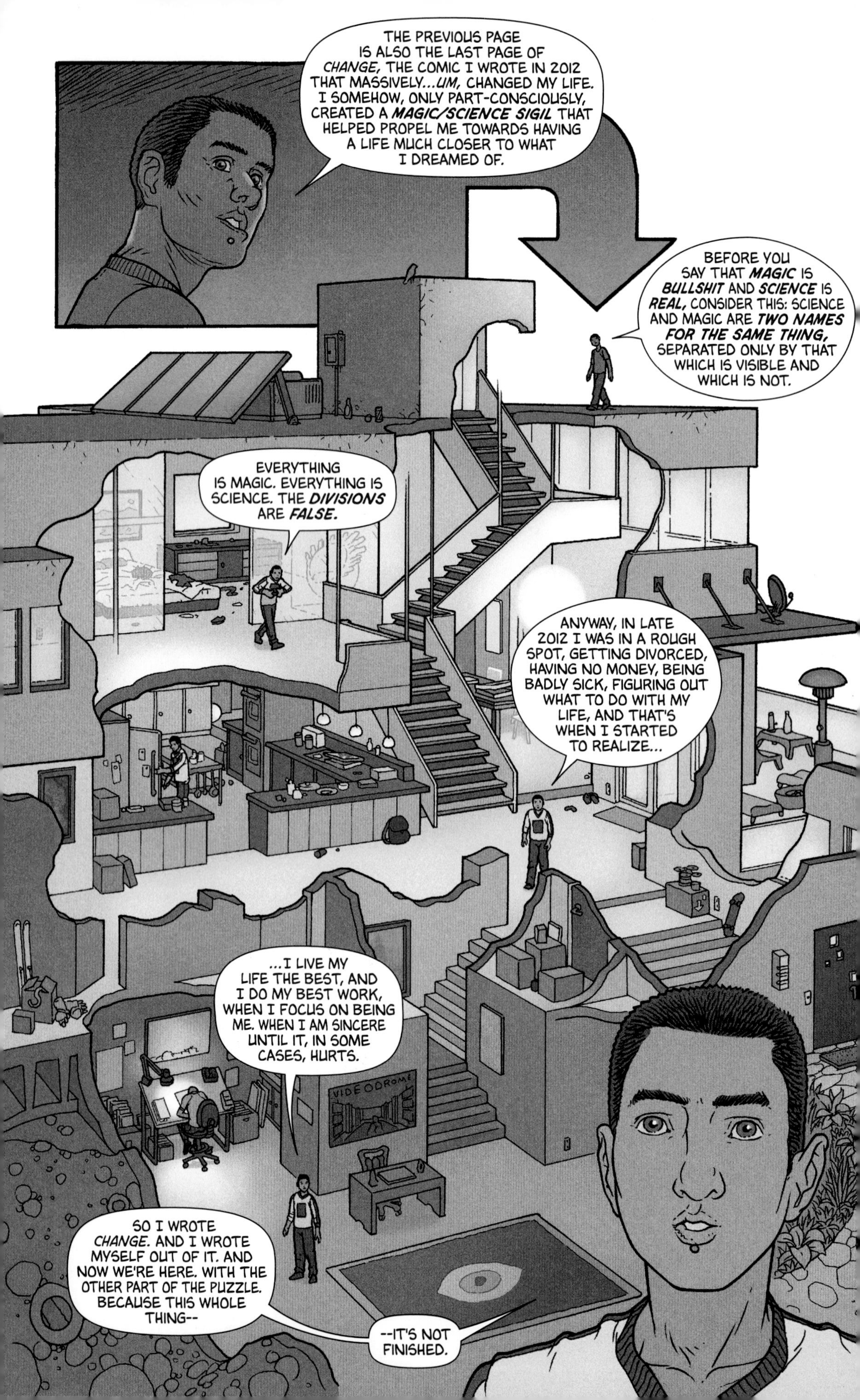
THE PREVIOUS PAGE IS ALSO THE LAST PAGE OF *CHANGE*, THE COMIC I WROTE IN 2012 THAT MASSIVELY...*UM*, CHANGED MY LIFE. I SOMEHOW, ONLY PART-CONSCIOUSLY, CREATED A ***MAGIC/SCIENCE SIGIL*** THAT HELPED PROPEL ME TOWARDS HAVING A LIFE MUCH CLOSER TO WHAT I DREAMED OF.
BEFORE YOU SAY THAT ***MAGIC*** IS ***BULLSHIT*** AND ***SCIENCE*** IS ***REAL,*** CONSIDER THIS: SCIENCE AND MAGIC ARE ***TWO NAMES FOR THE SAME THING,*** SEPARATED ONLY BY THAT WHICH IS VISIBLE AND WHICH IS NOT.
EVERYTHING IS MAGIC. EVERYTHING IS SCIENCE. THE ***DIVISIONS*** ARE ***FALSE.***
ANYWAY, IN LATE 2012 I WAS IN A ROUGH SPOT, GETTING DIVORCED, HAVING NO MONEY, BEING BADLY SICK, FIGURING OUT WHAT TO DO WITH MY LIFE, AND THAT'S WHEN I STARTED TO REALIZE...
...I LIVE MY LIFE THE BEST, AND I DO MY BEST WORK, WHEN I FOCUS ON BEING ME. WHEN I AM SINCERE UNTIL IT, IN SOME CASES, HURTS.
VIDEODROME
SO I WROTE *CHANGE*. AND I WROTE MYSELF OUT OF IT. AND NOW WE'RE HERE. WITH THE OTHER PART OF THE PUZZLE. BECAUSE THIS WHOLE THING--
--IT'S NOT FINISHED.

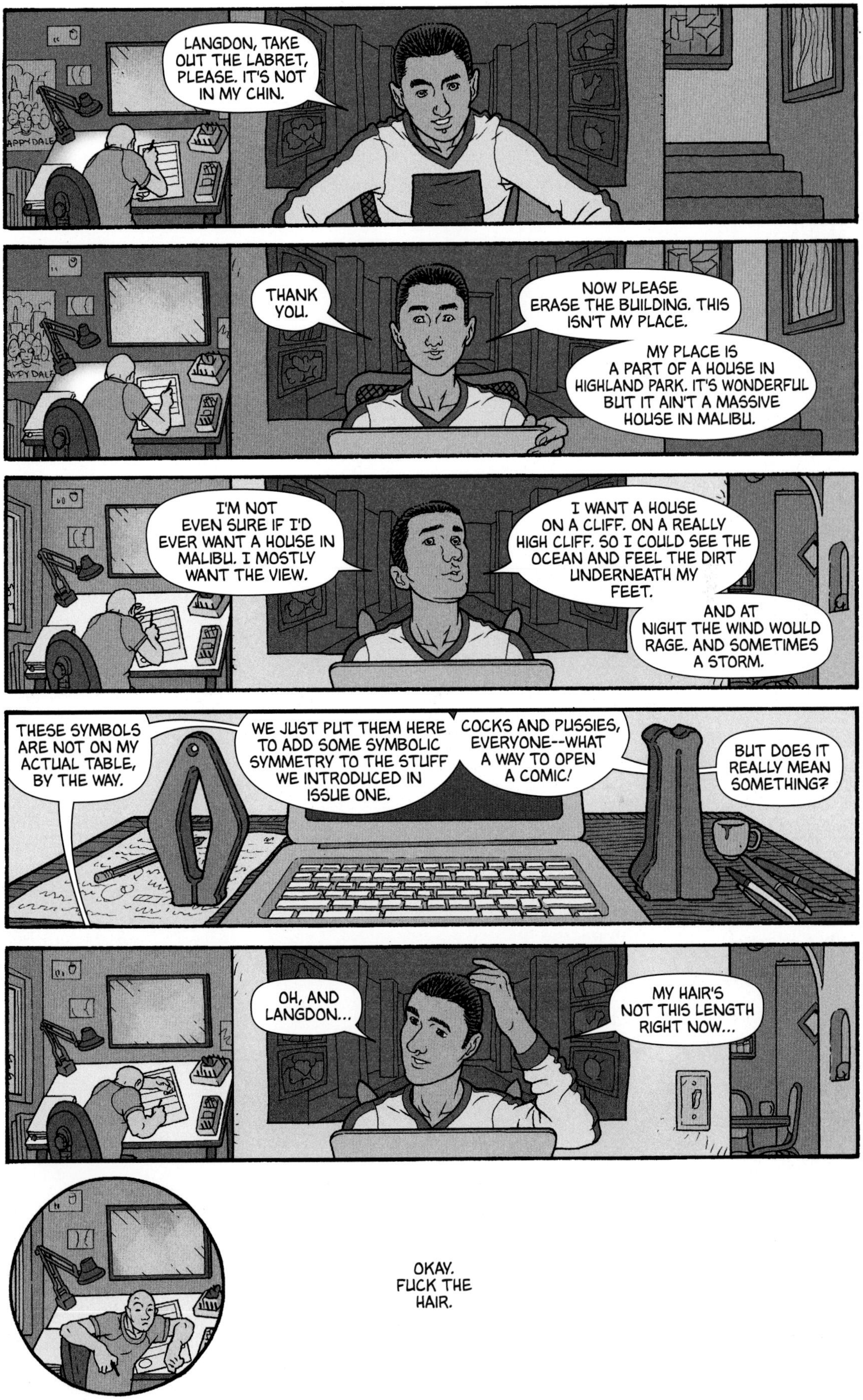
LANGDON, TAKE OUT THE LABRET, PLEASE. IT'S NOT IN MY CHIN.
THANK YOU.
NOW PLEASE ERASE THE BUILDING. THIS ISN'T MY PLACE.
MY PLACE IS A PART OF A HOUSE IN HIGHLAND PARK. IT'S WONDERFUL BUT IT AIN'T A MASSIVE HOUSE IN MALIBU.
I'M NOT EVEN SURE IF I'D EVER WANT A HOUSE IN MALIBU. I MOSTLY WANT THE VIEW.
I WANT A HOUSE ON A CLIFF. ON A REALLY HIGH CLIFF. SO I COULD SEE THE OCEAN AND FEEL THE DIRT UNDERNEATH MY FEET.
AND AT NIGHT THE WIND WOULD RAGE. AND SOMETIMES A STORM.
THESE SYMBOLS ARE NOT ON MY ACTUAL TABLE, BY THE WAY.
WE JUST PUT THEM HERE TO ADD SOME SYMBOLIC SYMMETRY TO THE STUFF WE INTRODUCED IN ISSUE ONE.
COCKS AND PUSSIES, EVERYONE--WHAT A WAY TO OPEN A COMIC!
BUT DOES IT REALLY MEAN SOMETHING?
OH, AND LANGDON...
MY HAIR'S NOT THIS LENGTH RIGHT NOW...
OKAY. FUCK THE HAIR.

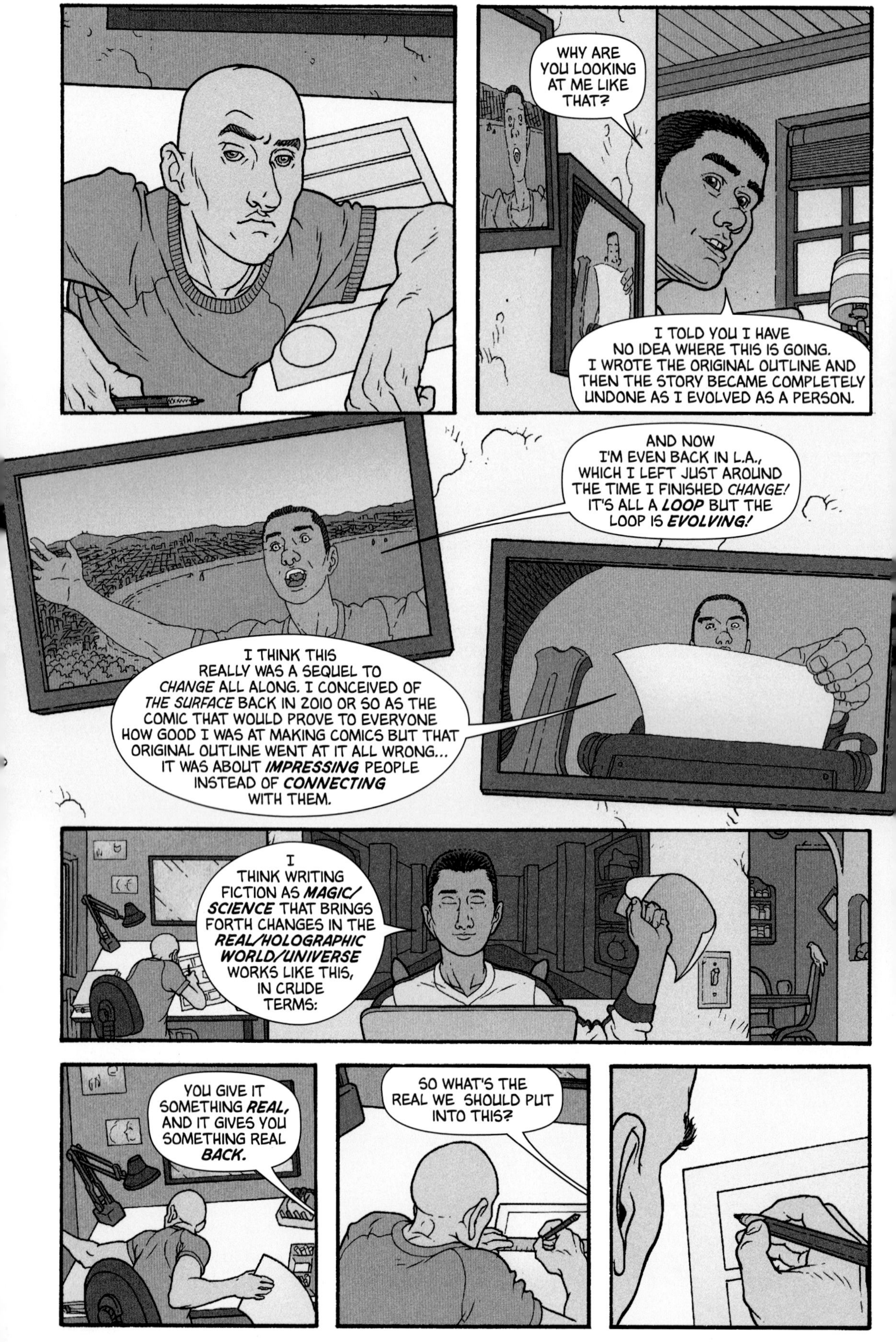
WHY ARE YOU LOOKING AT ME LIKE THAT?
I TOLD YOU I HAVE NO IDEA WHERE THIS IS GOING. I WROTE THE ORIGINAL OUTLINE AND THEN THE STORY BECAME COMPLETELY UNDONE AS I EVOLVED AS A PERSON.
AND NOW I'M EVEN BACK IN L.A., WHICH I LEFT JUST AROUND THE TIME I FINISHED *CHANGE!* IT'S ALL A **LOOP** BUT THE LOOP IS **EVOLVING!**
I THINK THIS REALLY WAS A SEQUEL TO *CHANGE* ALL ALONG. I CONCEIVED OF *THE SURFACE* BACK IN 2010 OR SO AS THE COMIC THAT WOULD PROVE TO EVERYONE HOW GOOD I WAS AT MAKING COMICS BUT THAT ORIGINAL OUTLINE WENT AT IT ALL WRONG... IT WAS ABOUT **IMPRESSING** PEOPLE INSTEAD OF **CONNECTING** WITH THEM.
I THINK WRITING FICTION AS **MAGIC/SCIENCE** THAT BRINGS FORTH CHANGES IN THE **REAL/HOLOGRAPHIC WORLD/UNIVERSE** WORKS LIKE THIS, IN CRUDE TERMS:
YOU GIVE IT SOMETHING **REAL,** AND IT GIVES YOU SOMETHING REAL **BACK.**
SO WHAT'S THE REAL WE SHOULD PUT INTO THIS?

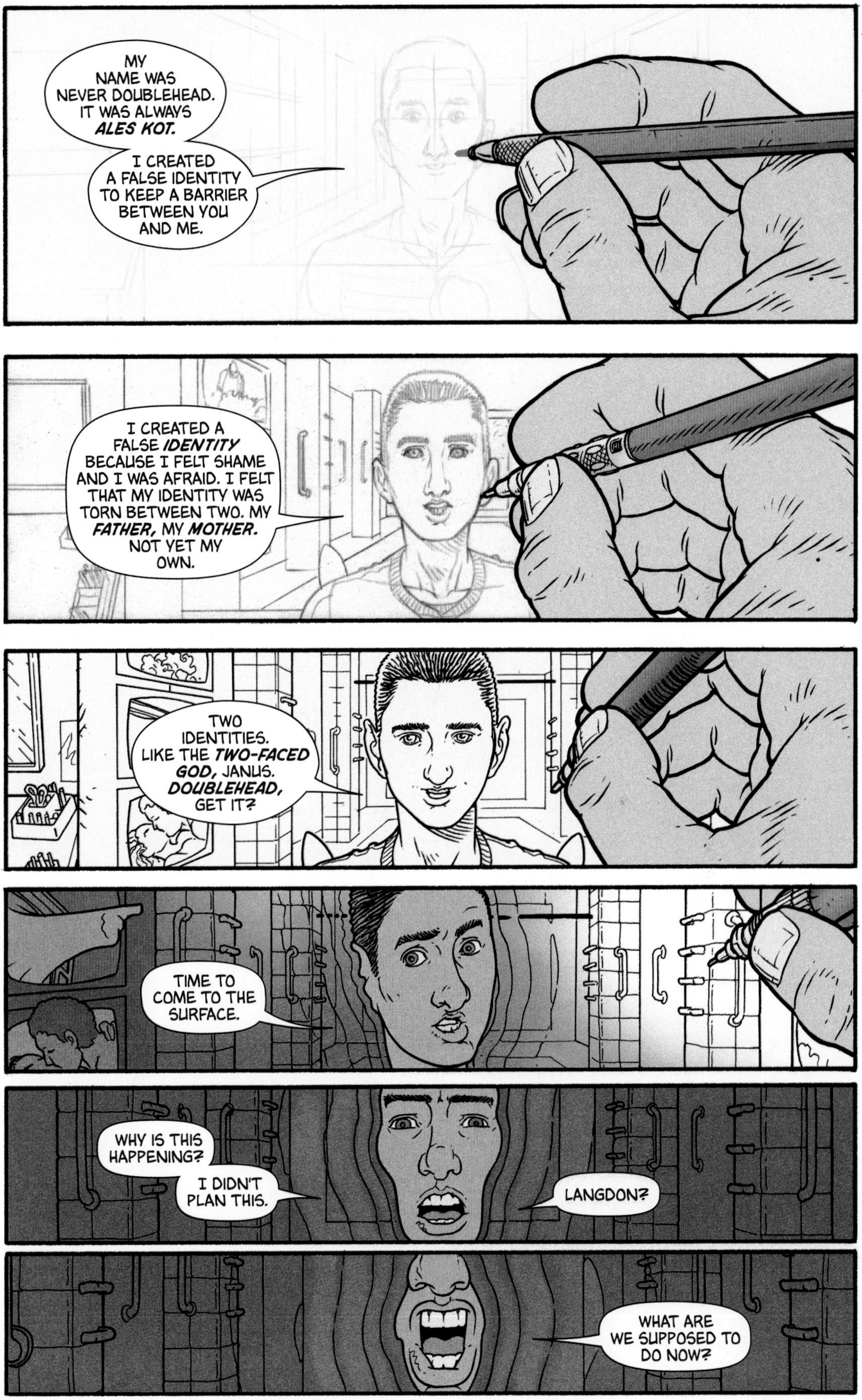
MY NAME WAS NEVER DOUBLEHEAD. IT WAS ALWAYS ALES KOT.
I CREATED A FALSE IDENTITY TO KEEP A BARRIER BETWEEN YOU AND ME.
I CREATED A FALSE IDENTITY BECAUSE I FELT SHAME AND I WAS AFRAID. I FELT THAT MY IDENTITY WAS TORN BETWEEN TWO. MY FATHER, MY MOTHER. NOT YET MY OWN.
TWO IDENTITIES. LIKE THE TWO-FACED GOD, JANUS. DOUBLEHEAD, GET IT?
TIME TO COME TO THE SURFACE.
WHY IS THIS HAPPENING?
I DIDN'T PLAN THIS.
LANGDON?
WHAT ARE WE SUPPOSED TO DO NOW?

oh,
to awake
from,
dreaming

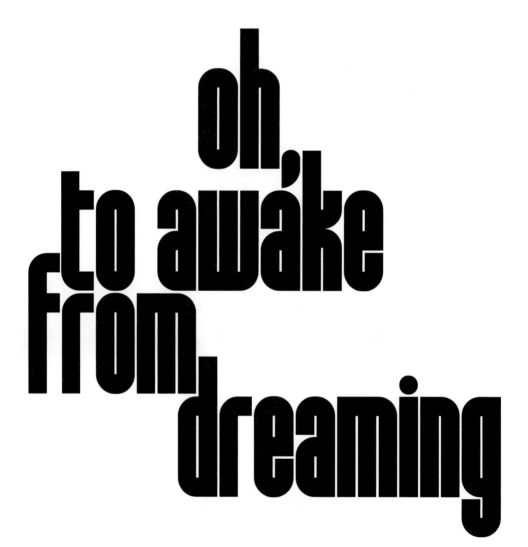

THERE WAS A MAN WHO USED TO BE LIKE ME BUT NOW HE'S GOING AWAY.

08.18.2015

"you are a puma" the woman in the dream says - is that -------?
there is a youthful energy to her. compatible energy. write down the
dream. in bed with her, whoever she was. research what puma means
as a spirit animal, what puma wisdom means.

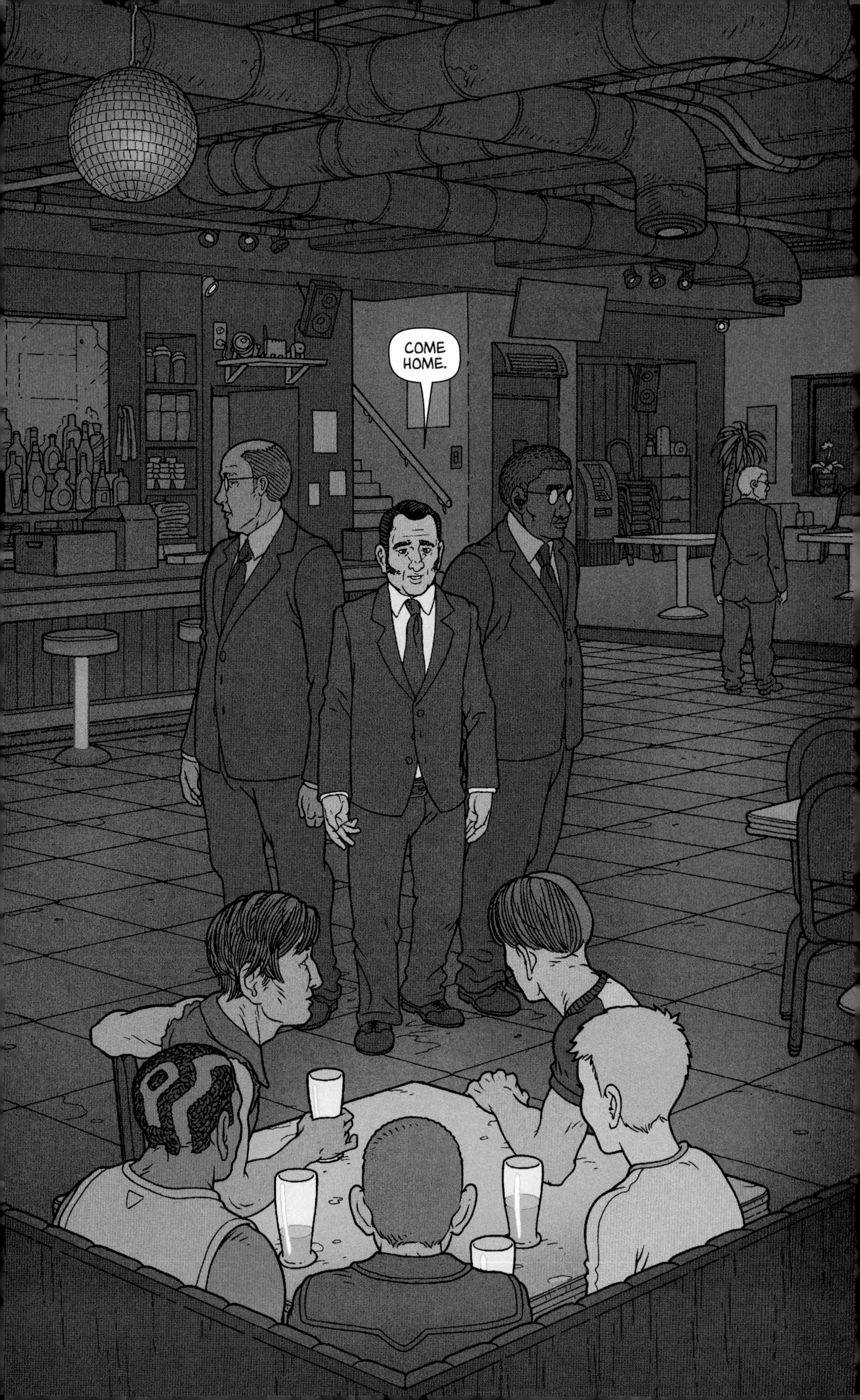
COME HOME.

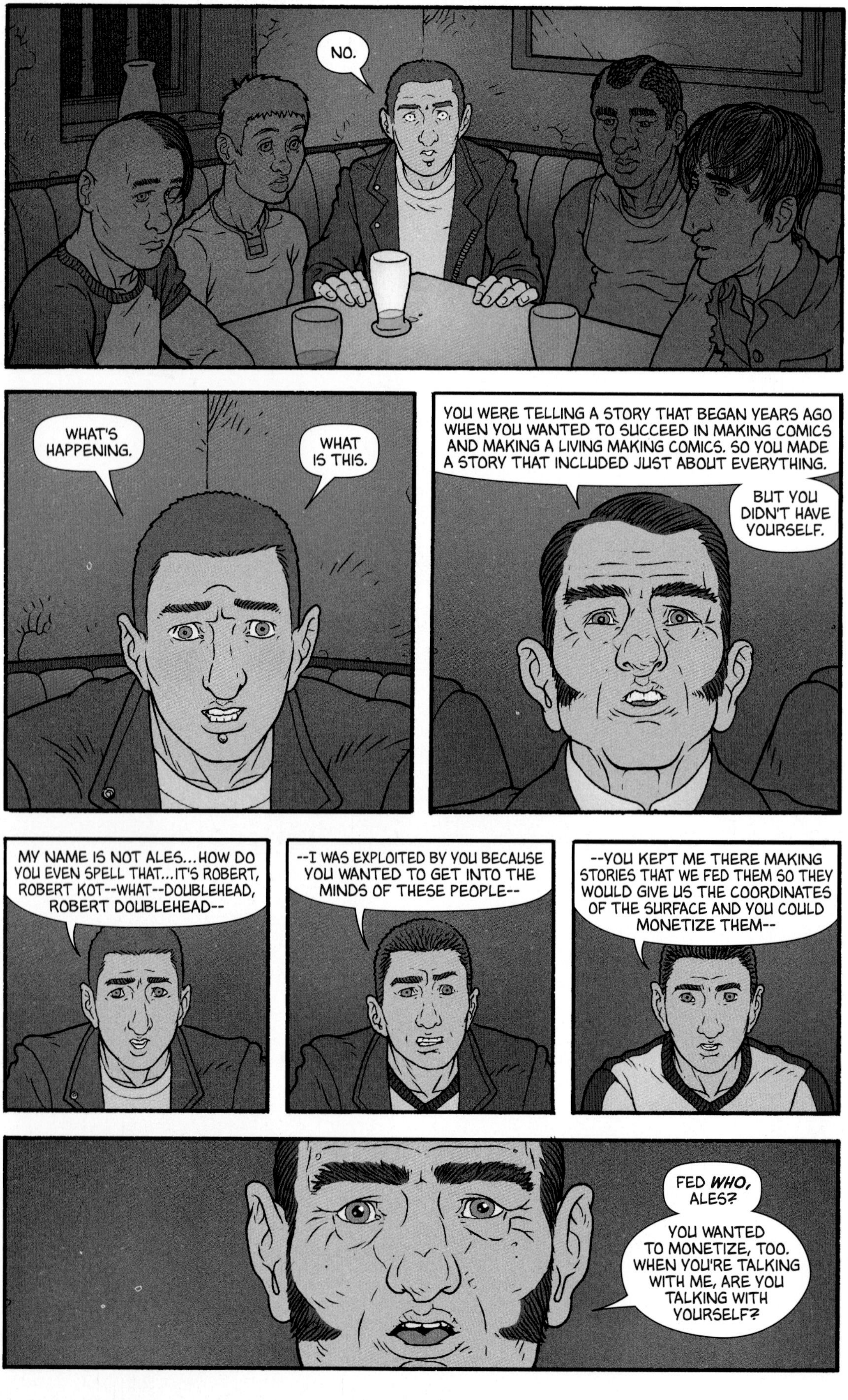
NO.
WHAT'S HAPPENING.
WHAT IS THIS.
YOU WERE TELLING A STORY THAT BEGAN YEARS AGO WHEN YOU WANTED TO SUCCEED IN MAKING COMICS AND MAKING A LIVING MAKING COMICS. SO YOU MADE A STORY THAT INCLUDED JUST ABOUT EVERYTHING.
BUT YOU DIDN'T HAVE YOURSELF.
MY NAME IS NOT ALES...HOW DO YOU EVEN SPELL THAT...IT'S ROBERT, ROBERT KOT--WHAT--DOUBLEHEAD, ROBERT DOUBLEHEAD--
--I WAS EXPLOITED BY YOU BECAUSE YOU WANTED TO GET INTO THE MINDS OF THESE PEOPLE--
--YOU KEPT ME THERE MAKING STORIES THAT WE FED THEM SO THEY WOULD GIVE US THE COORDINATES OF THE SURFACE AND YOU COULD MONETIZE THEM--
FED *WHO,* ALES?
YOU WANTED TO MONETIZE, TOO. WHEN YOU'RE TALKING WITH ME, ARE YOU TALKING WITH YOURSELF?

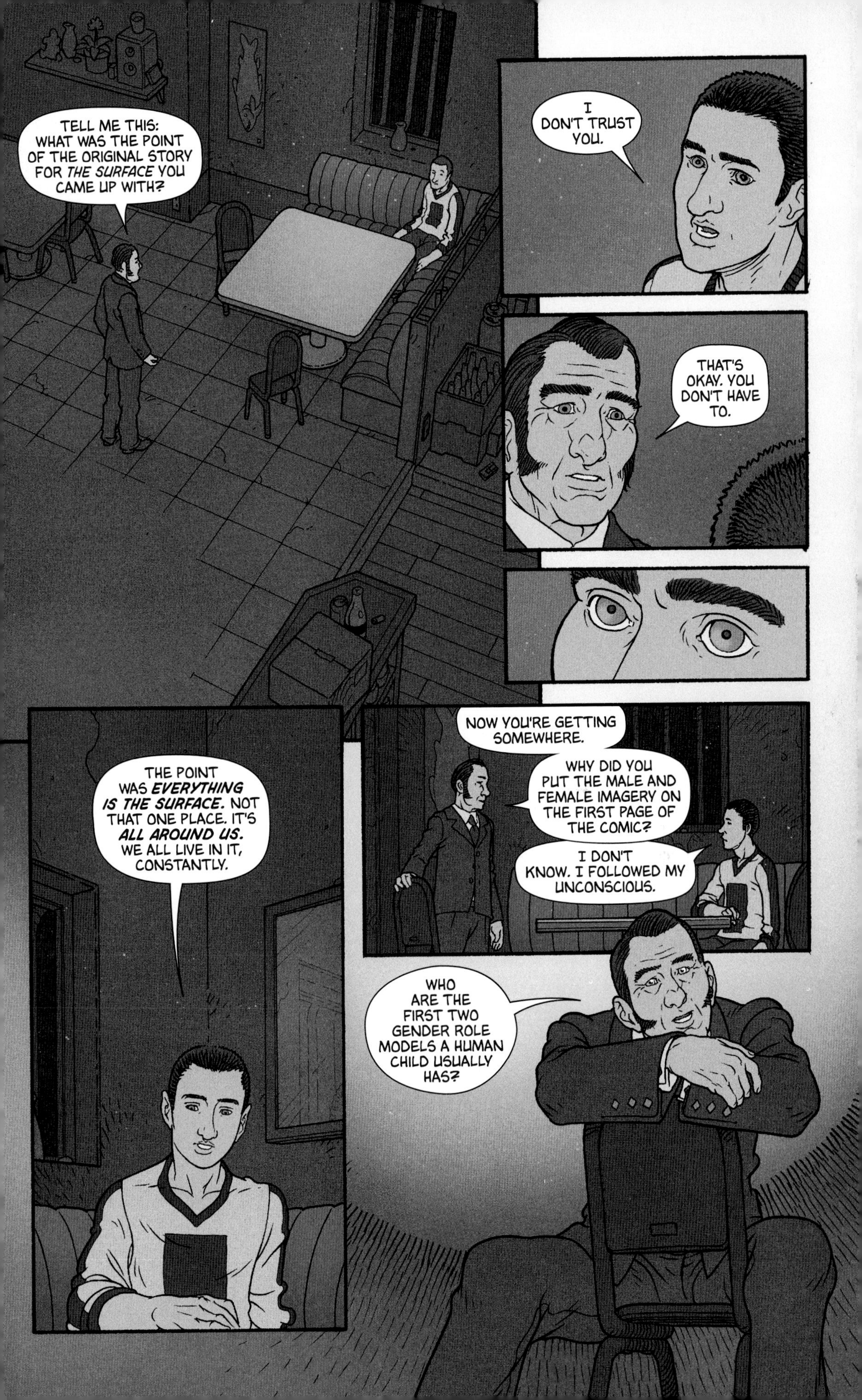
TELL ME THIS: WHAT WAS THE POINT OF THE ORIGINAL STORY FOR *THE SURFACE* YOU CAME UP WITH?
I DON'T TRUST YOU.
THAT'S OKAY. YOU DON'T HAVE TO.
THE POINT WAS ***EVERYTHING IS THE SURFACE.*** NOT THAT ONE PLACE. IT'S ***ALL AROUND US.*** WE ALL LIVE IN IT, CONSTANTLY.
NOW YOU'RE GETTING SOMEWHERE.
WHY DID YOU PUT THE MALE AND FEMALE IMAGERY ON THE FIRST PAGE OF THE COMIC?
I DON'T KNOW. I FOLLOWED MY UNCONSCIOUS.
WHO ARE THE FIRST TWO GENDER ROLE MODELS A HUMAN CHILD USUALLY HAS?

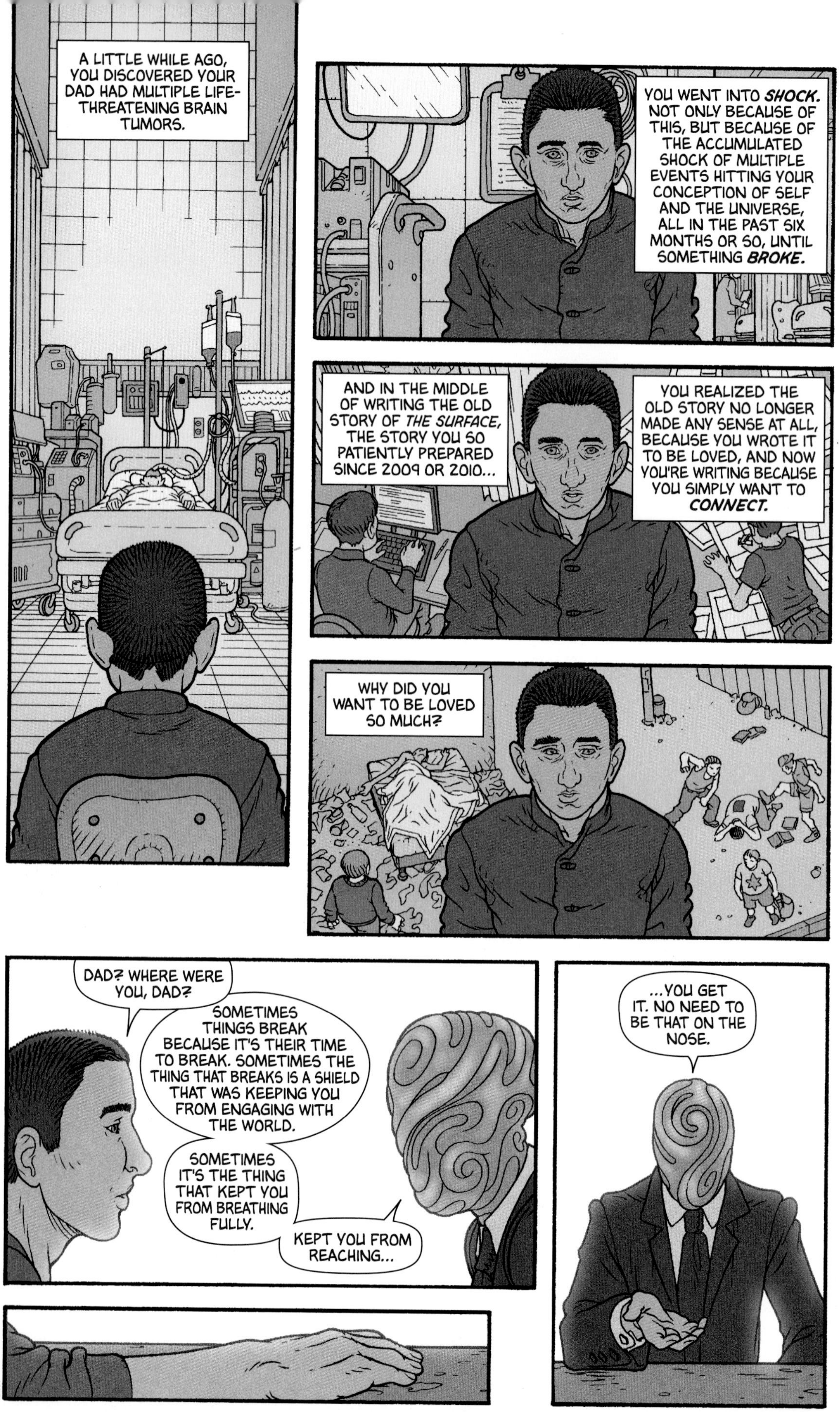

A LITTLE WHILE AGO, YOU DISCOVERED YOUR DAD HAD MULTIPLE LIFE-THREATENING BRAIN TUMORS.
YOU WENT INTO SHOCK. NOT ONLY BECAUSE OF THIS, BUT BECAUSE OF THE ACCUMULATED SHOCK OF MULTIPLE EVENTS HITTING YOUR CONCEPTION OF SELF AND THE UNIVERSE, ALL IN THE PAST SIX MONTHS OR SO, UNTIL SOMETHING BROKE.
AND IN THE MIDDLE OF WRITING THE OLD STORY OF THE SURFACE, THE STORY YOU SO PATIENTLY PREPARED SINCE 2009 OR 2010...
YOU REALIZED THE OLD STORY NO LONGER MADE ANY SENSE AT ALL, BECAUSE YOU WROTE IT TO BE LOVED, AND NOW YOU'RE WRITING BECAUSE YOU SIMPLY WANT TO CONNECT.
WHY DID YOU WANT TO BE LOVED SO MUCH?
DAD? WHERE WERE YOU, DAD?
SOMETIMES THINGS BREAK BECAUSE IT'S THEIR TIME TO BREAK. SOMETIMES THE THING THAT BREAKS IS A SHIELD THAT WAS KEEPING YOU FROM ENGAGING WITH THE WORLD.
SOMETIMES IT'S THE THING THAT KEPT YOU FROM BREATHING FULLY.
KEPT YOU FROM REACHING...
...YOU GET IT. NO NEED TO BE THAT ON THE NOSE.

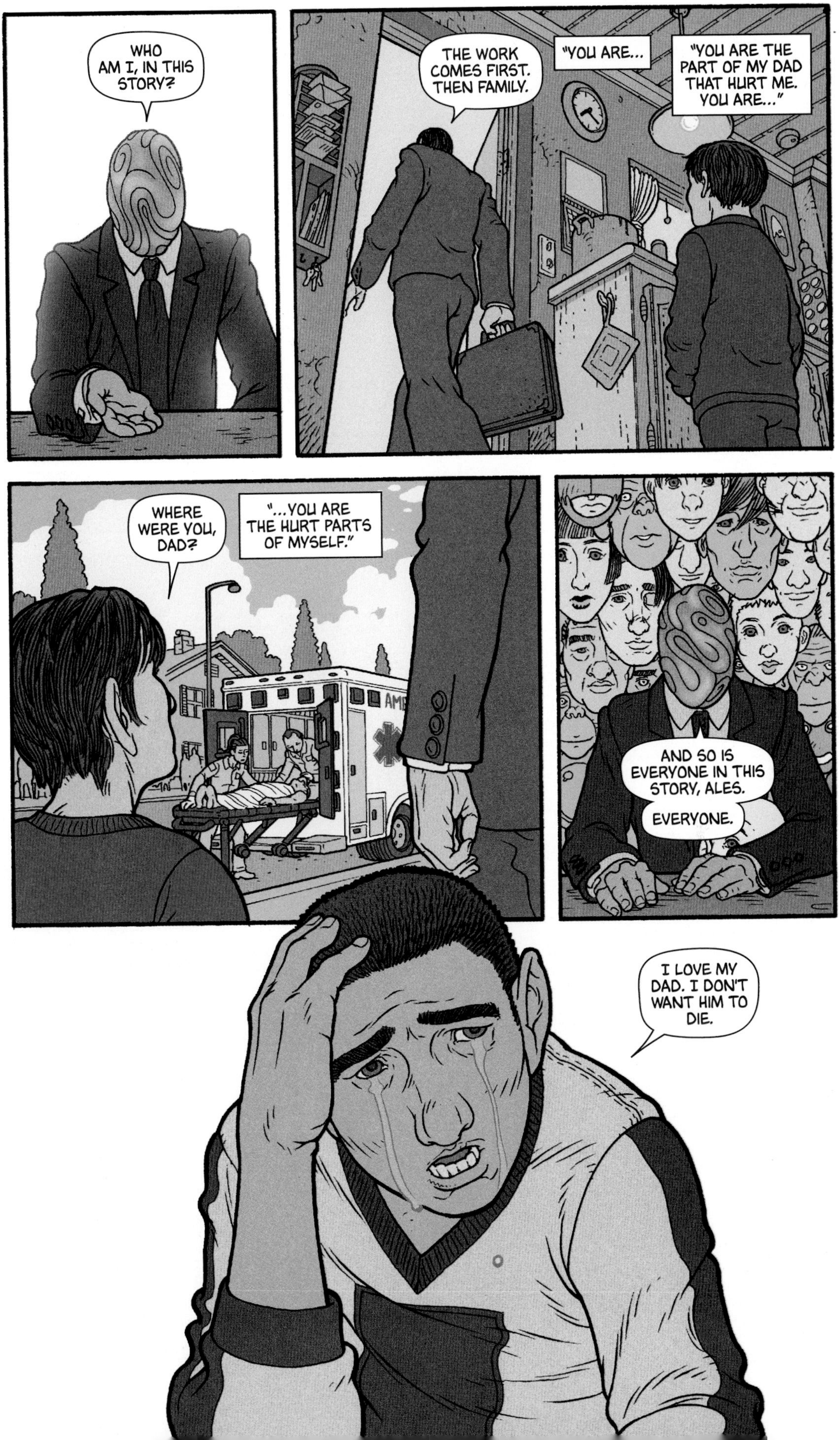
WHO AM I, IN THIS STORY?
THE WORK COMES FIRST. THEN FAMILY.
"YOU ARE...
"YOU ARE THE PART OF MY DAD THAT HURT ME. YOU ARE..."
WHERE WERE YOU, DAD?
"...YOU ARE THE HURT PARTS OF MYSELF."
AND SO IS EVERYONE IN THIS STORY, ALES.
EVERYONE.
I LOVE MY DAD. I DON'T WANT HIM TO DIE.

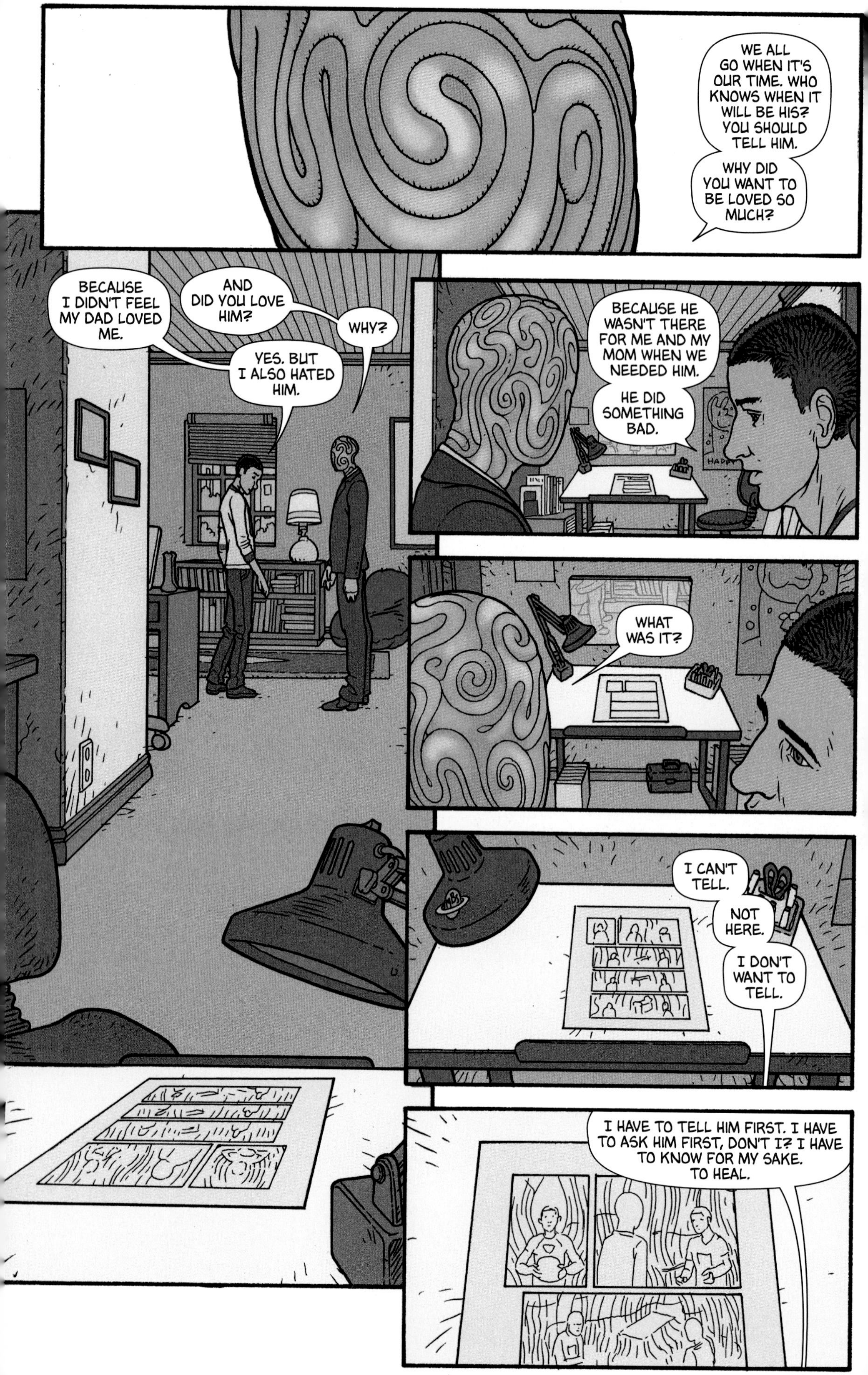
WE ALL GO WHEN IT'S OUR TIME. WHO KNOWS WHEN IT WILL BE HIS? YOU SHOULD TELL HIM.
WHY DID YOU WANT TO BE LOVED SO MUCH?
BECAUSE I DIDN'T FEEL MY DAD LOVED ME.
AND DID YOU LOVE HIM?
YES. BUT I ALSO HATED HIM.
WHY?
BECAUSE HE WASN'T THERE FOR ME AND MY MOM WHEN WE NEEDED HIM.
HE DID SOMETHING BAD.
WHAT WAS IT?
I CAN'T TELL.
NOT HERE.
I DON'T WANT TO TELL.
I HAVE TO TELL HIM FIRST. I HAVE TO ASK HIM FIRST, DON'T I? I HAVE TO KNOW FOR MY SAKE. TO HEAL.

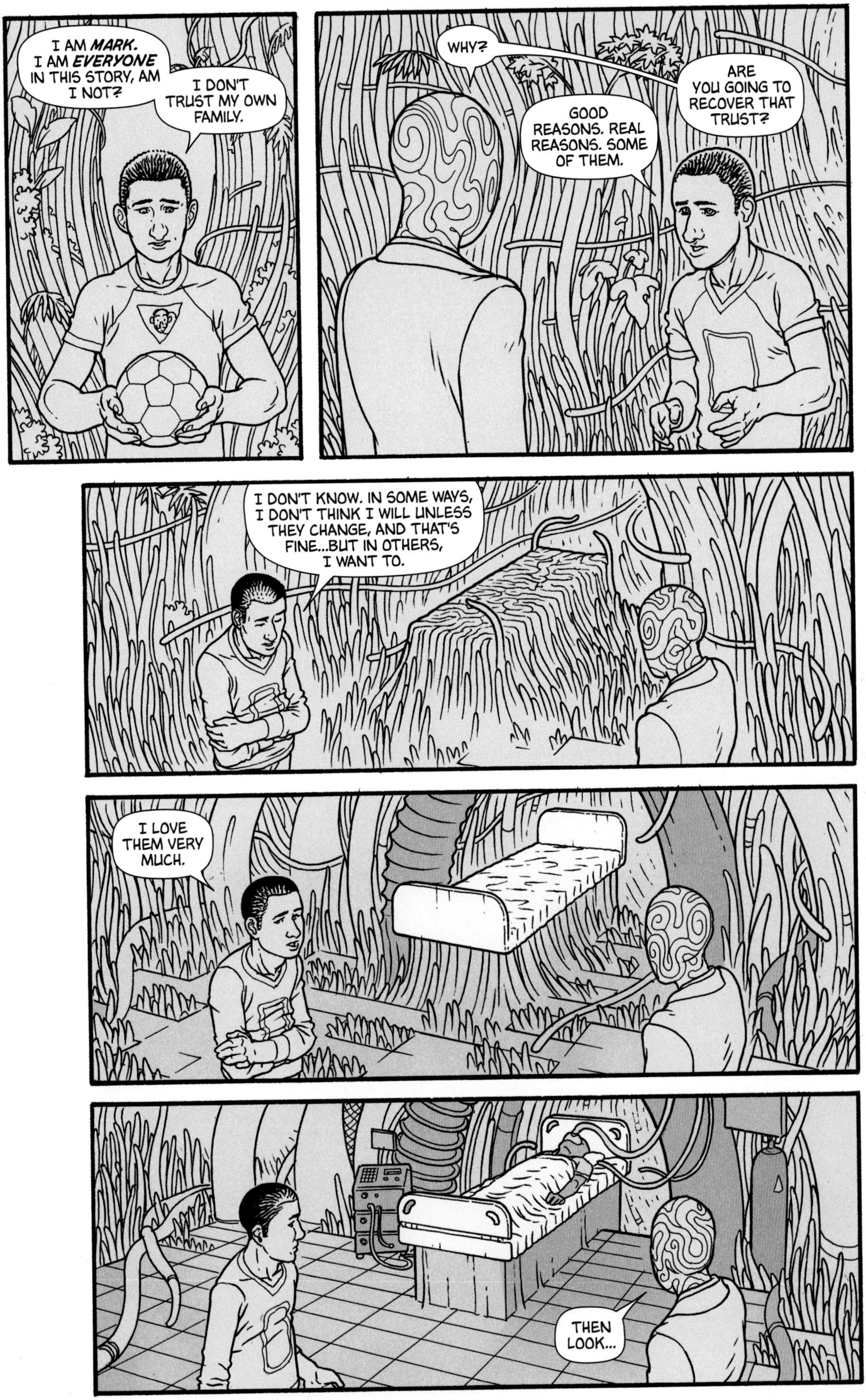
I AM *MARK.* I AM *EVERYONE* IN THIS STORY, AM I NOT?
I DON'T TRUST MY OWN FAMILY.
WHY?
GOOD REASONS. REAL REASONS. SOME OF THEM.
ARE YOU GOING TO RECOVER THAT TRUST?
I DON'T KNOW. IN SOME WAYS, I DON'T THINK I WILL UNLESS THEY CHANGE, AND THAT'S FINE...BUT IN OTHERS, I WANT TO.
I LOVE THEM VERY MUCH.
THEN LOOK...

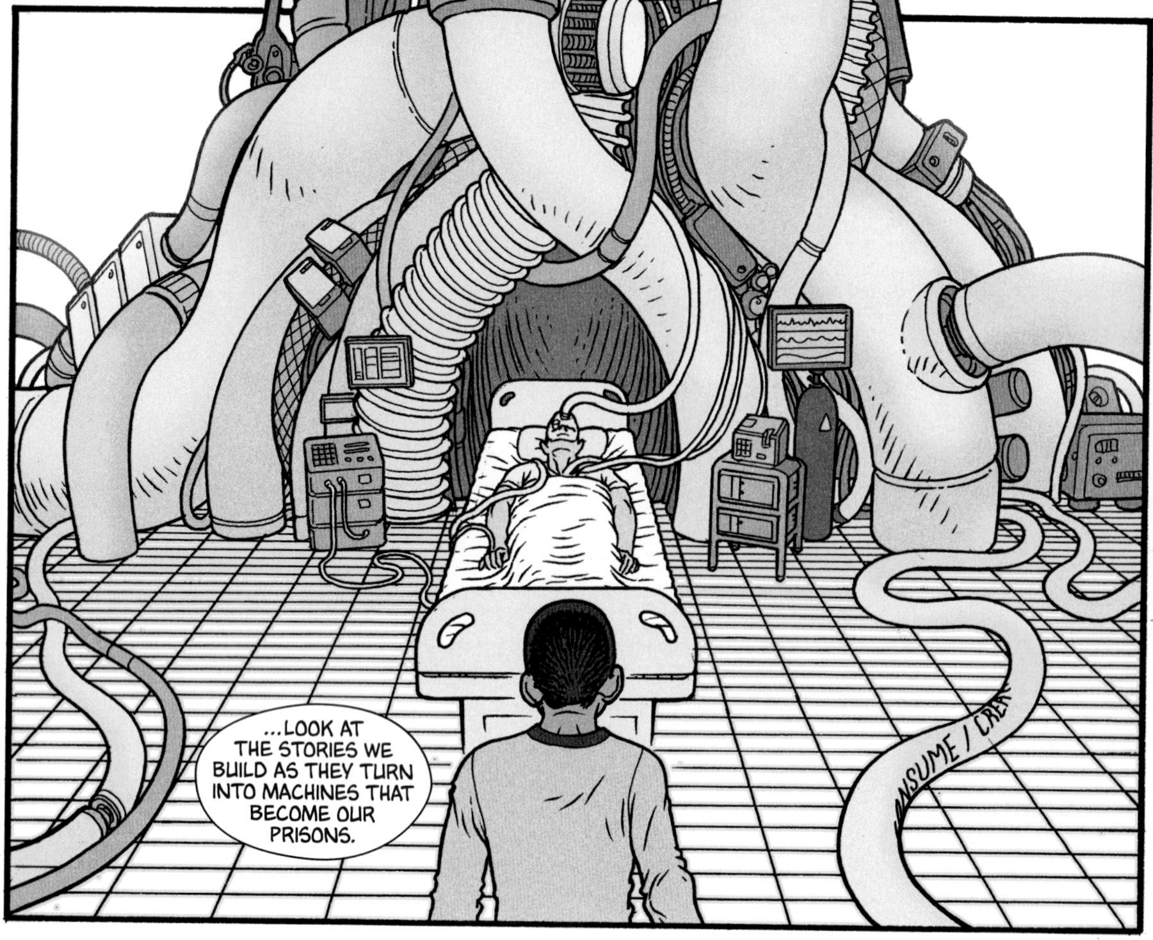
...LOOK AT THE STORIES WE BUILD AS THEY TURN INTO MACHINES THAT BECOME OUR PRISONS.

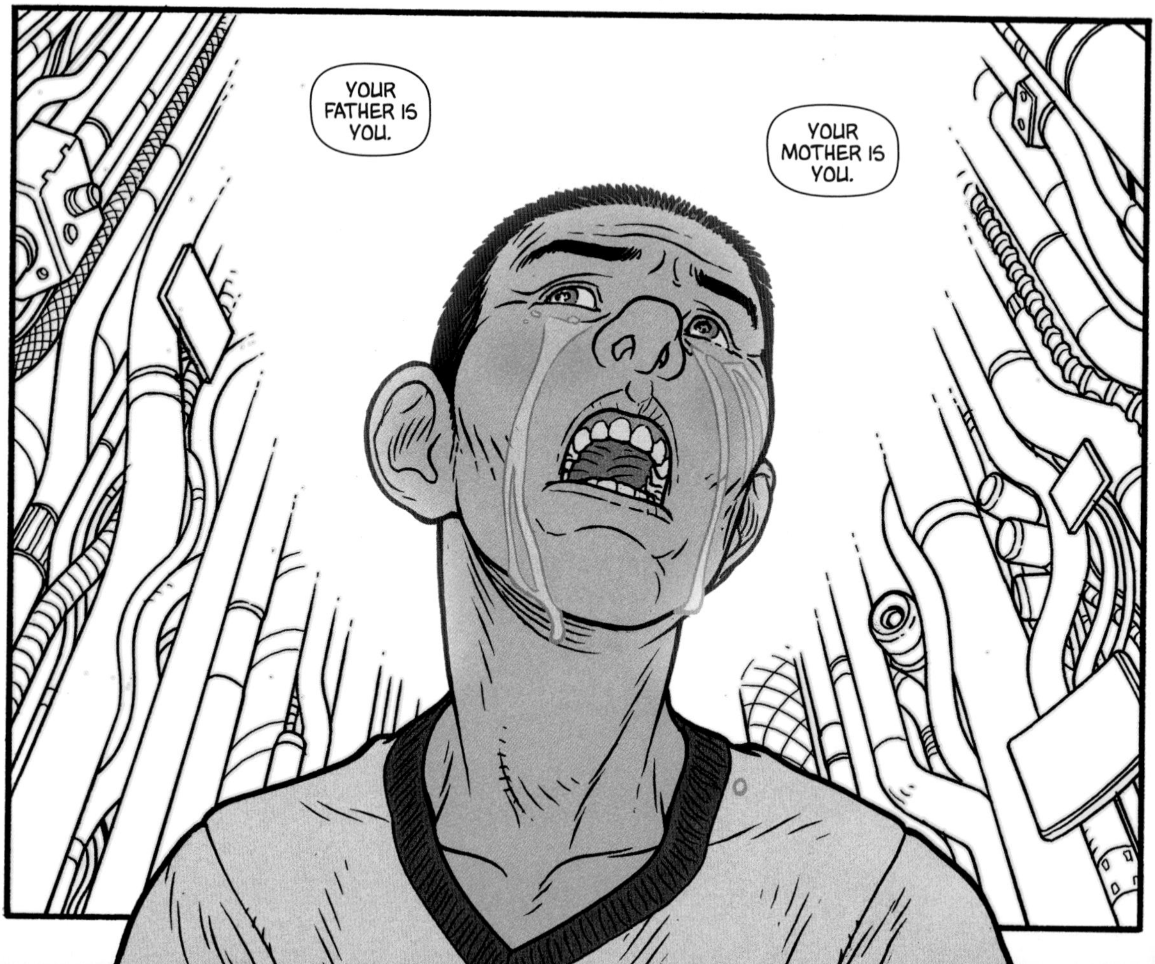
YOUR FATHER IS YOU.
YOUR MOTHER IS YOU.

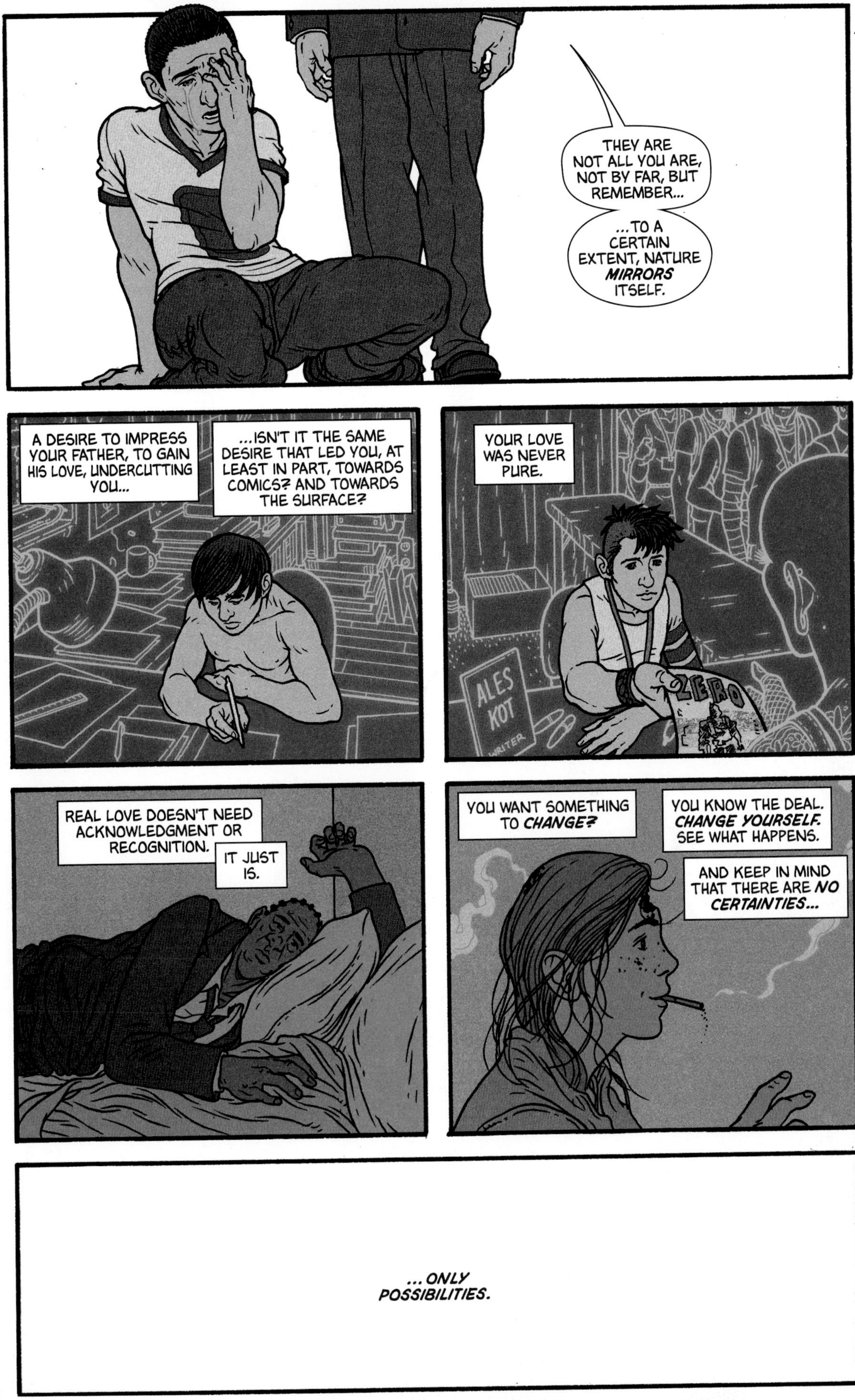
THEY ARE NOT ALL YOU ARE, NOT BY FAR, BUT REMEMBER...
...TO A CERTAIN EXTENT, NATURE *MIRRORS* ITSELF.
A DESIRE TO IMPRESS YOUR FATHER, TO GAIN HIS LOVE, UNDERCUTTING YOU...
...ISN'T IT THE SAME DESIRE THAT LED YOU, AT LEAST IN PART, TOWARDS COMICS? AND TOWARDS THE SURFACE?
YOUR LOVE WAS NEVER PURE.
ALES KOT
WRITER
ZERO
REAL LOVE DOESN'T NEED ACKNOWLEDGMENT OR RECOGNITION.
IT JUST IS.
YOU WANT SOMETHING TO *CHANGE?*
YOU KNOW THE DEAL. *CHANGE YOURSELF.* SEE WHAT HAPPENS.
AND KEEP IN MIND THAT THERE ARE *NO CERTAINTIES...*
...ONLY POSSIBILITIES.

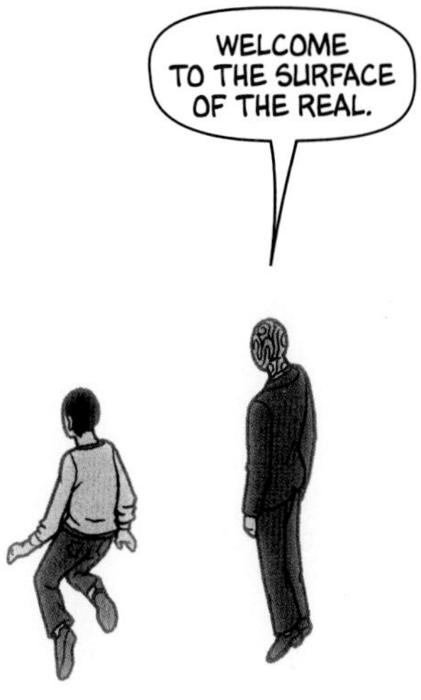
WELCOME TO THE SURFACE OF THE REAL.

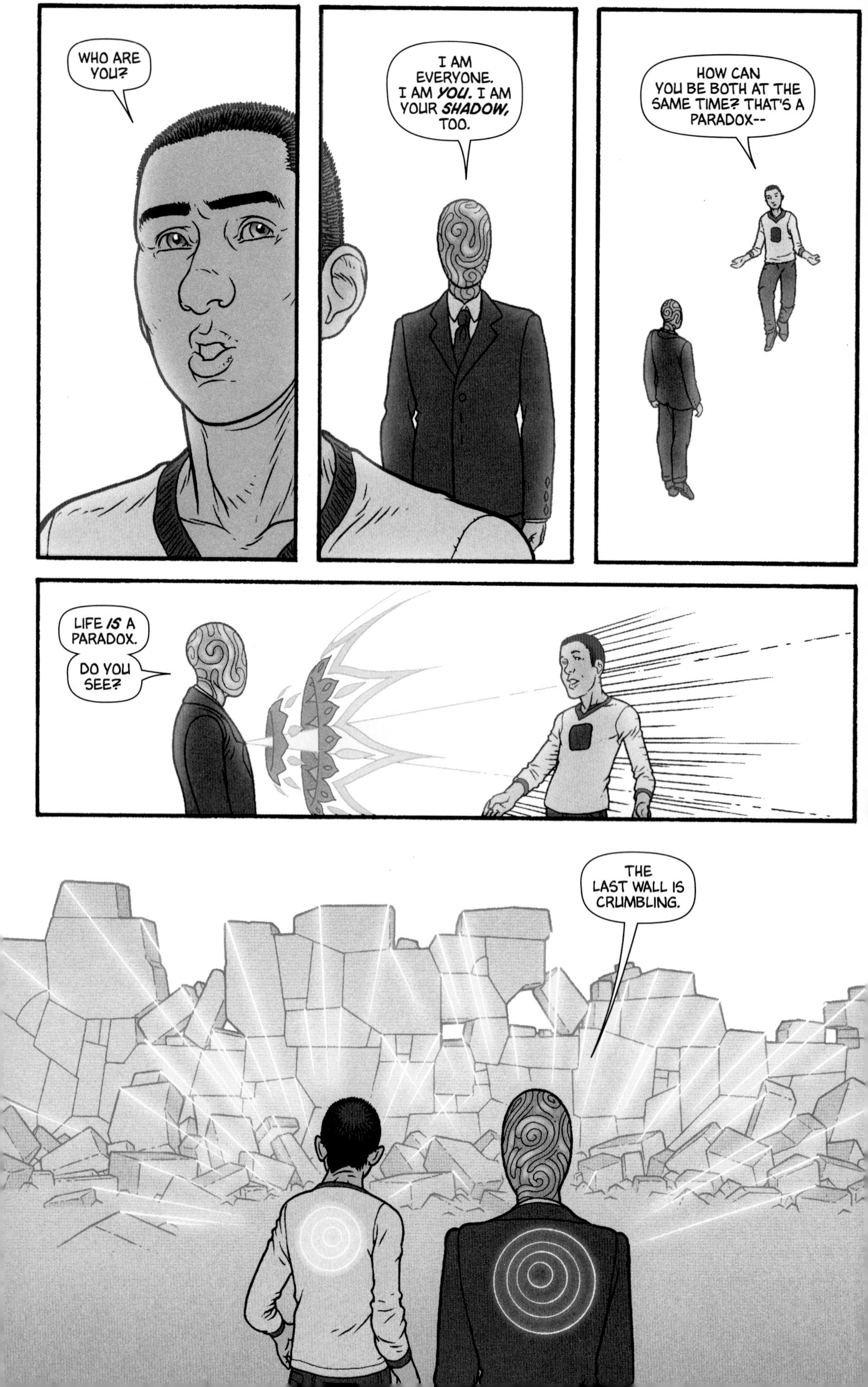
WHO ARE YOU?
I AM EVERYONE. I AM *YOU.* I AM YOUR *SHADOW,* TOO.
HOW CAN YOU BE BOTH AT THE SAME TIME? THAT'S A PARADOX--
LIFE *IS* A PARADOX.
DO YOU SEE?
THE LAST WALL IS CRUMBLING.

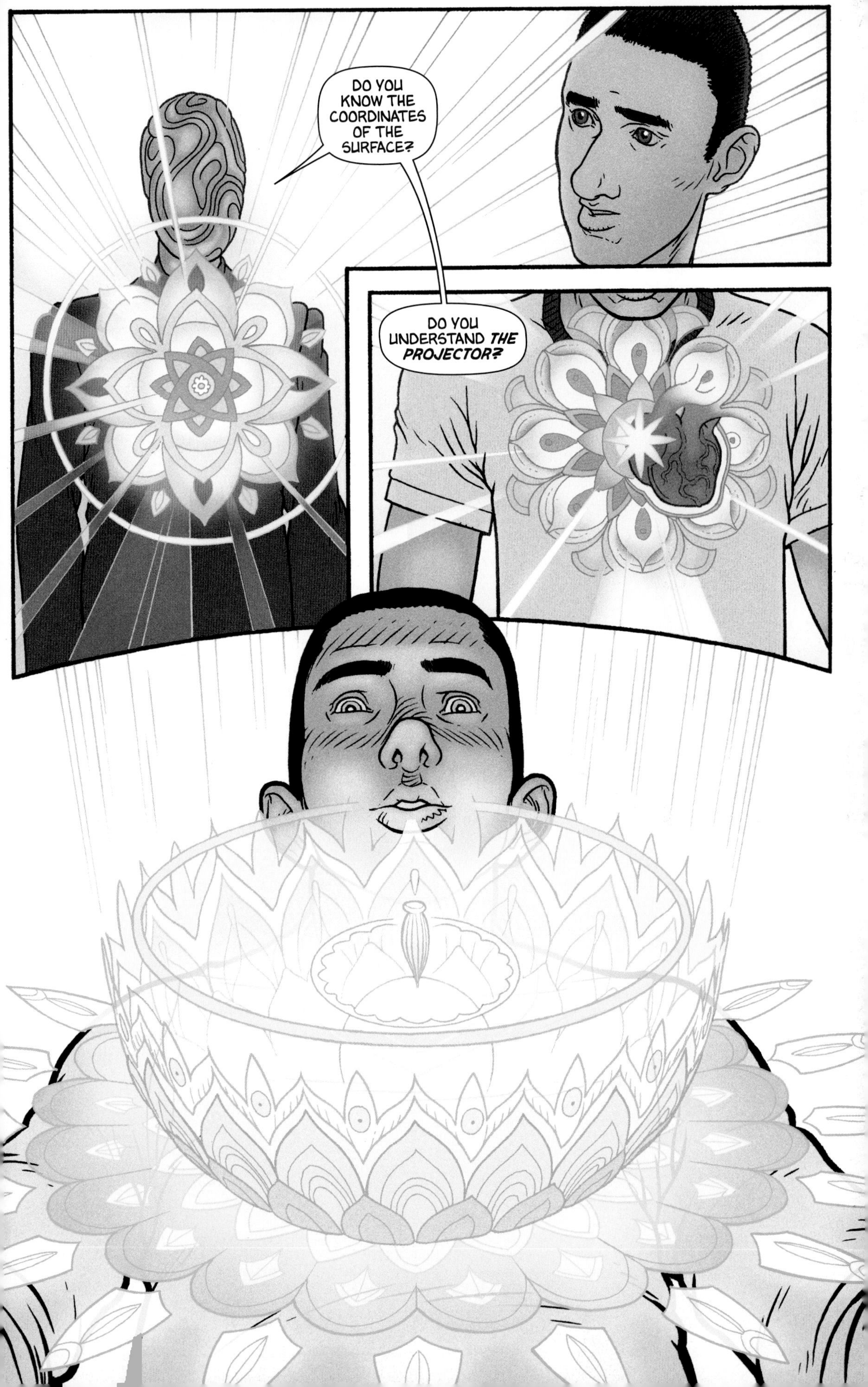
DO YOU KNOW THE COORDINATES OF THE SURFACE?
DO YOU UNDERSTAND *THE PROJECTOR?*

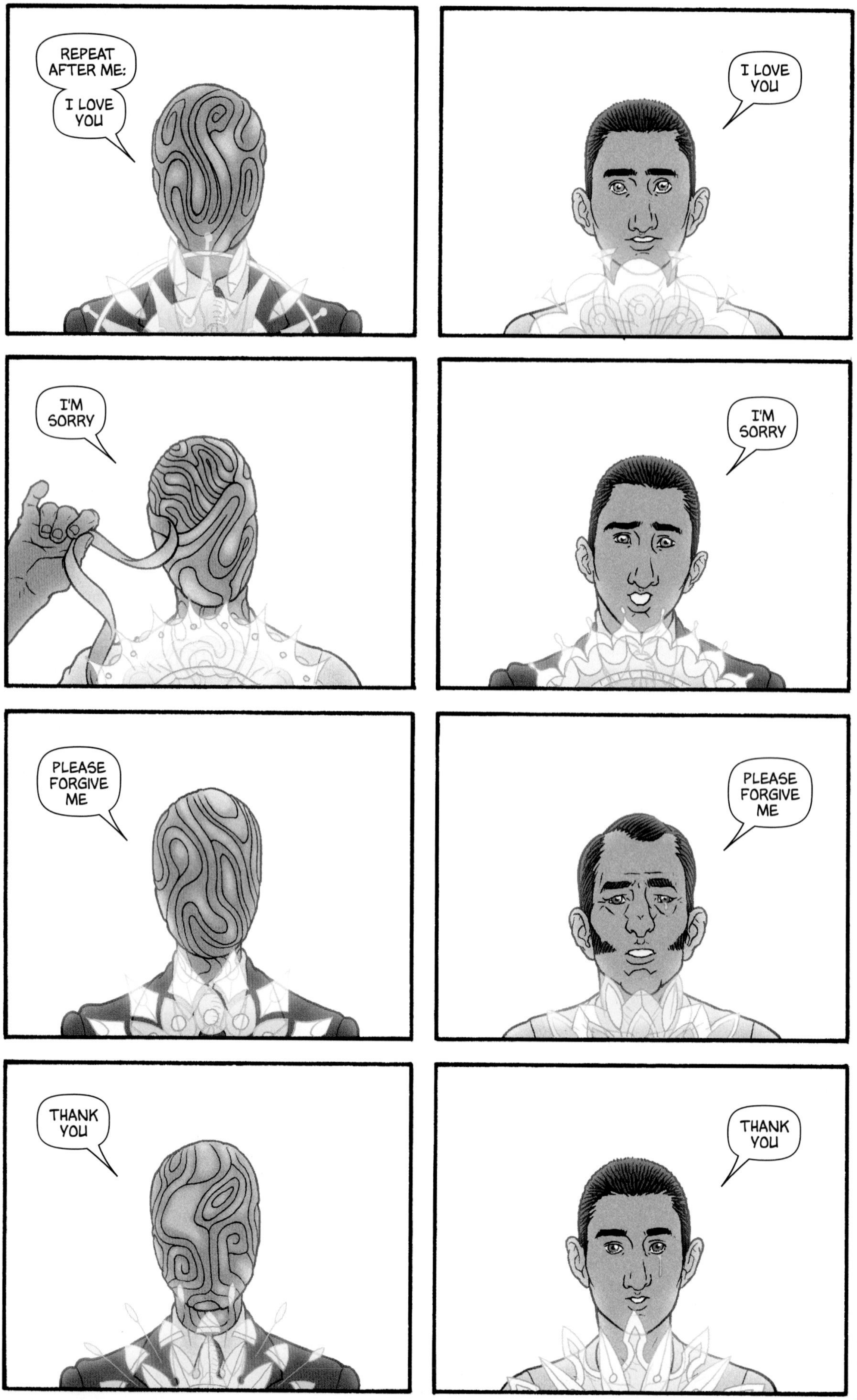
REPEAT AFTER ME:
I LOVE YOU
I LOVE YOU
I'M SORRY
I'M SORRY
PLEASE FORGIVE ME
PLEASE FORGIVE ME
THANK YOU
THANK YOU

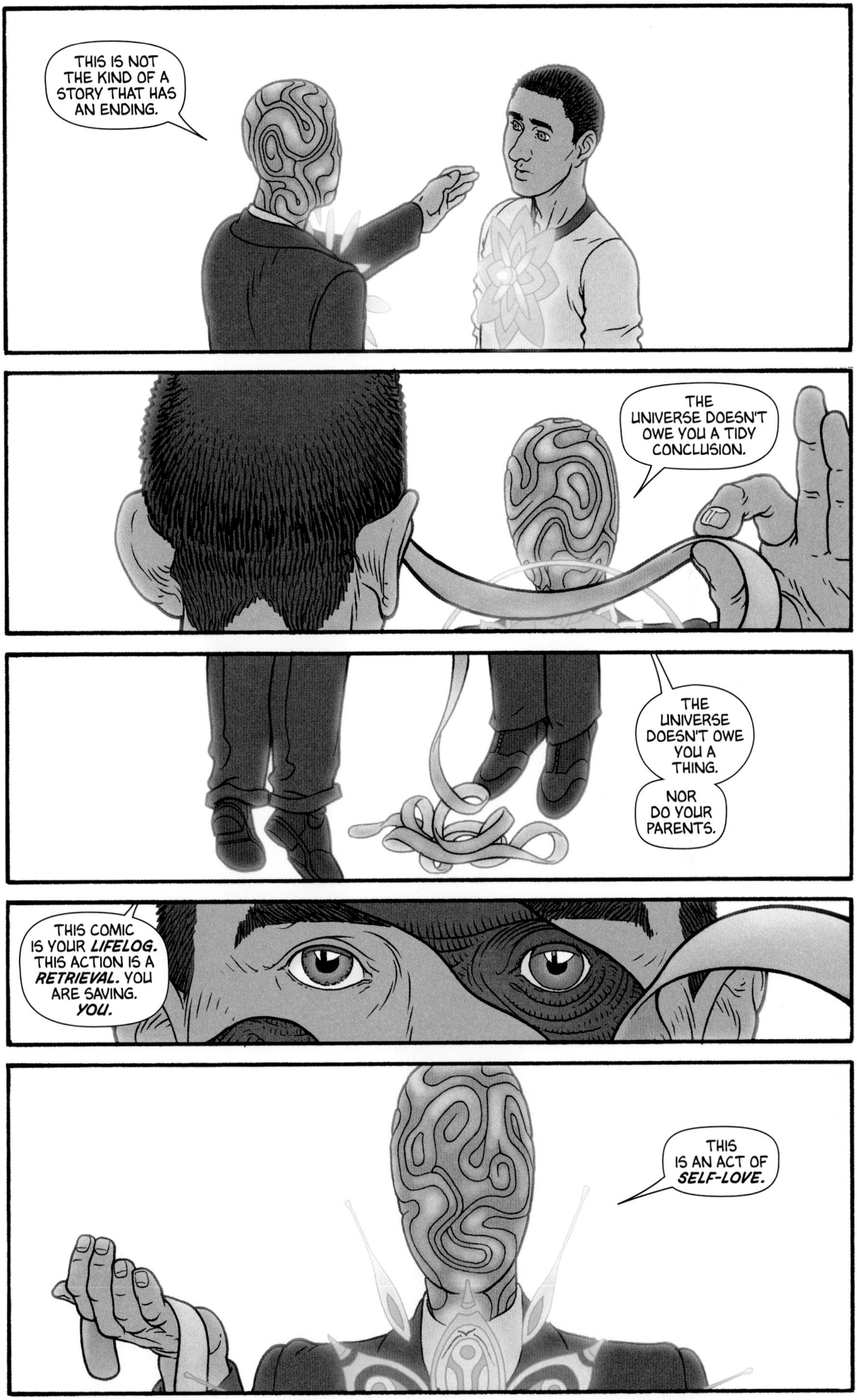
THIS IS NOT THE KIND OF A STORY THAT HAS AN ENDING.
THE UNIVERSE DOESN'T OWE YOU A TIDY CONCLUSION.
THE UNIVERSE DOESN'T OWE YOU A THING.
NOR DO YOUR PARENTS.
THIS COMIC IS YOUR *LIFELOG.* THIS ACTION IS A *RETRIEVAL.* YOU ARE SAVING. ***YOU.***
THIS IS AN ACT OF ***SELF-LOVE.***

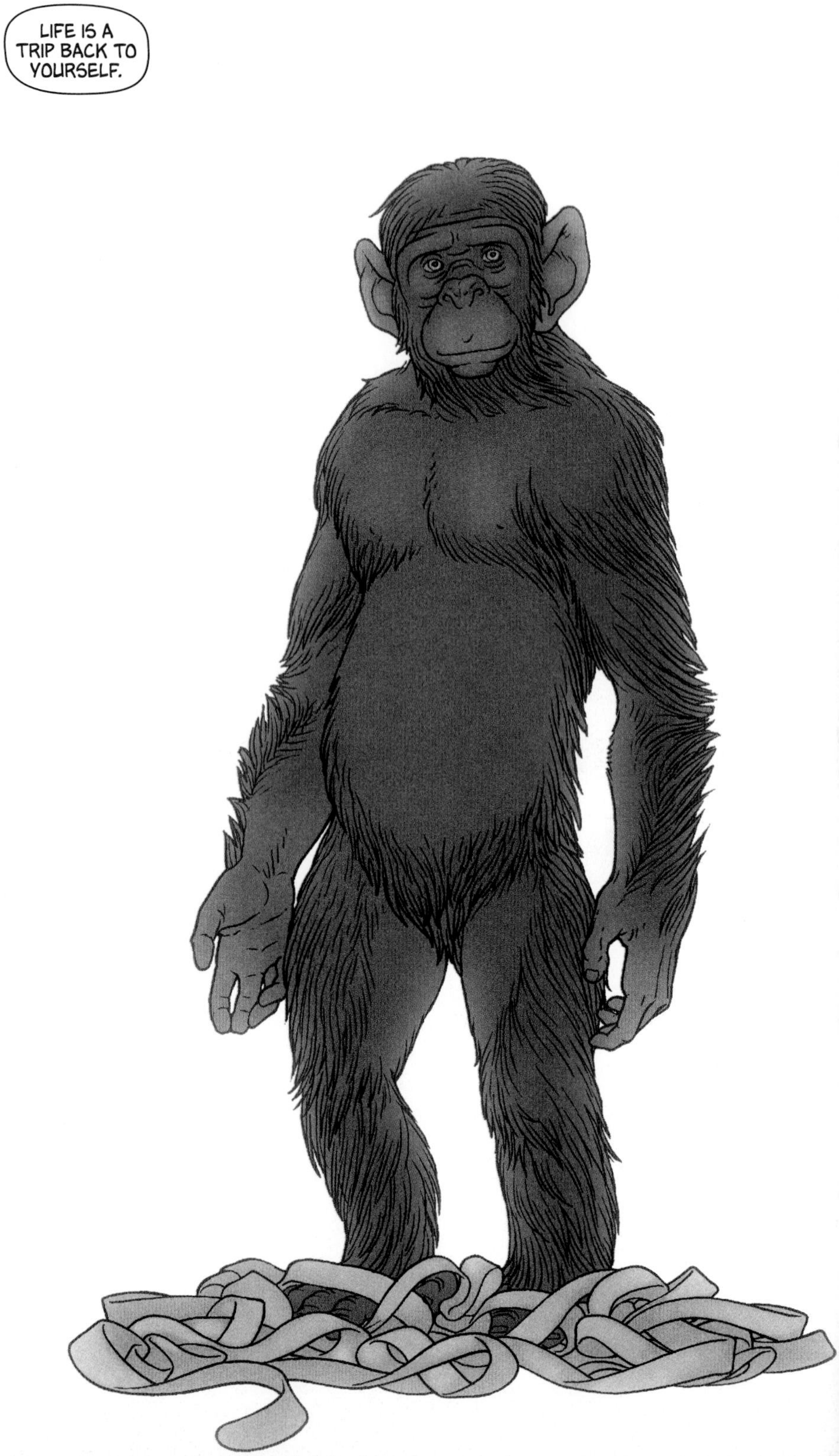
LIFE IS A TRIP BACK TO YOURSELF.

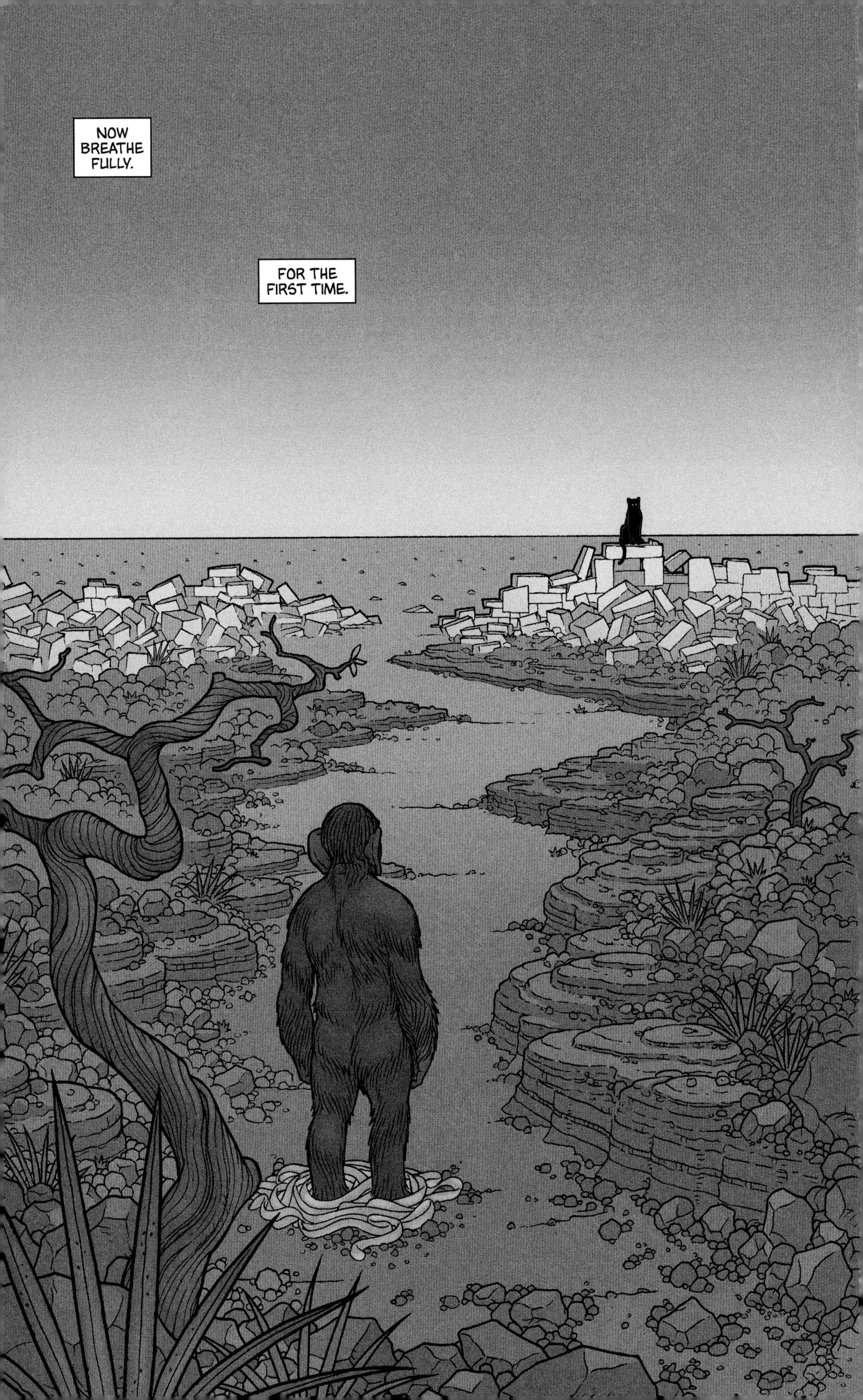
NOW BREATHE FULLY.
FOR THE FIRST TIME.

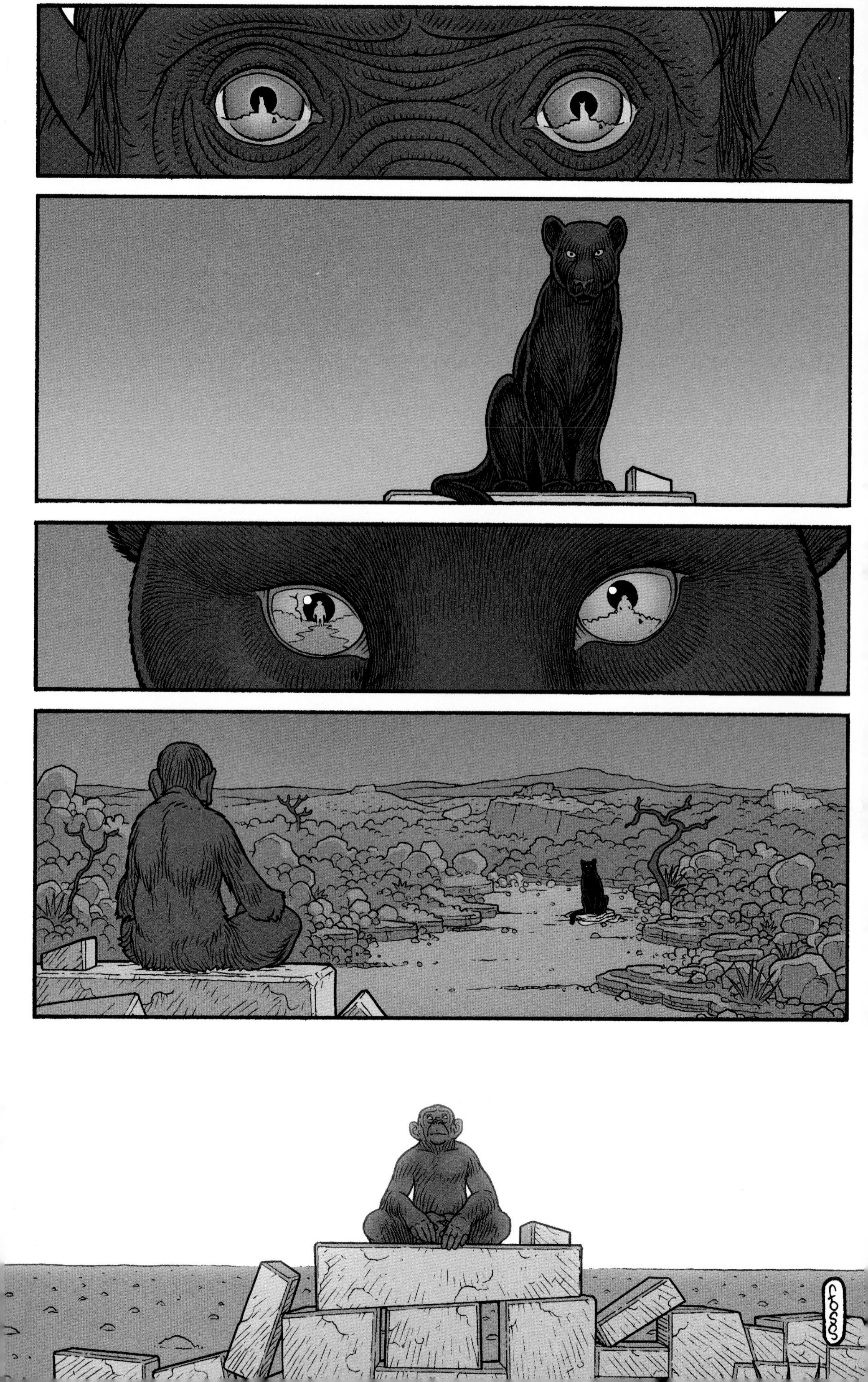

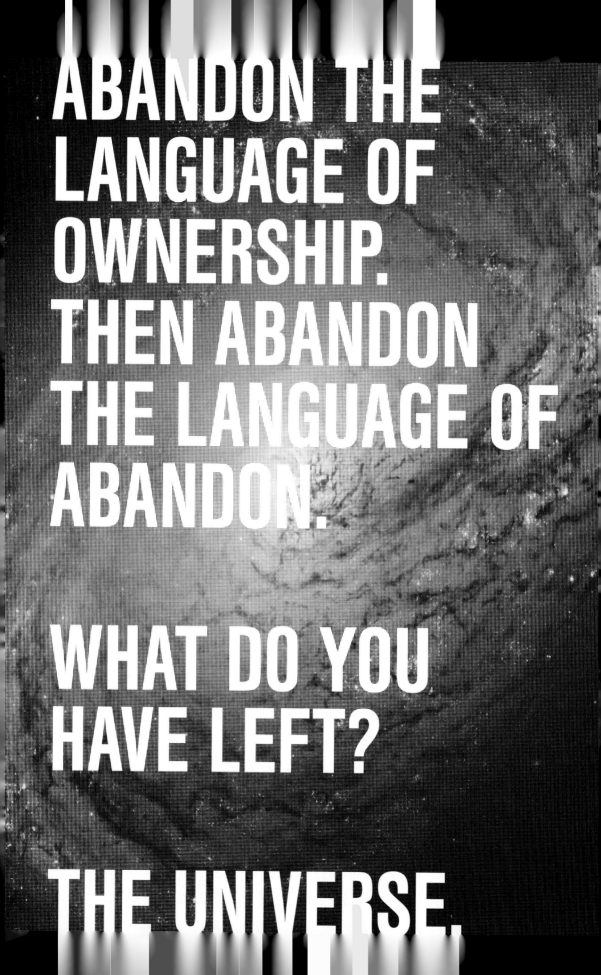

ABANDON THE LANGUAGE OF OWNERSHIP. THEN ABANDON THE LANGUAGE OF ABANDON.

WHAT DO YOU HAVE LEFT?

THE UNIVERSE.

ORIGINAL #1-4 COVERS BY LANGDON FOSS, JORDIE BELLAIRE AND TOM MULLER — #1 VARIANT COVER ART BY MARCO RUDY AND MICHAEL WALSH.

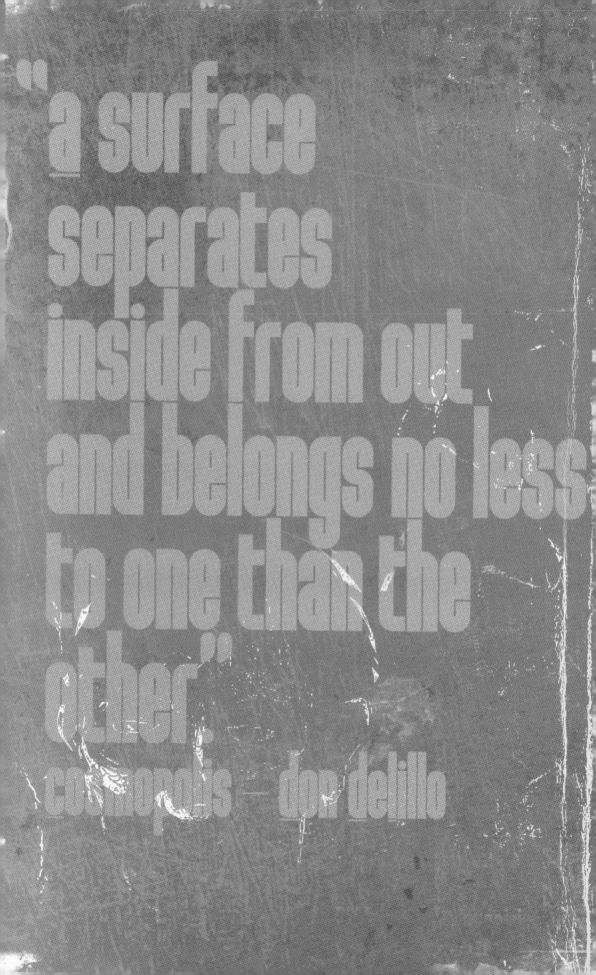

"a surface
separates
inside from out
and belongs no less
to one than the
other"

cosmopolis — don delillo

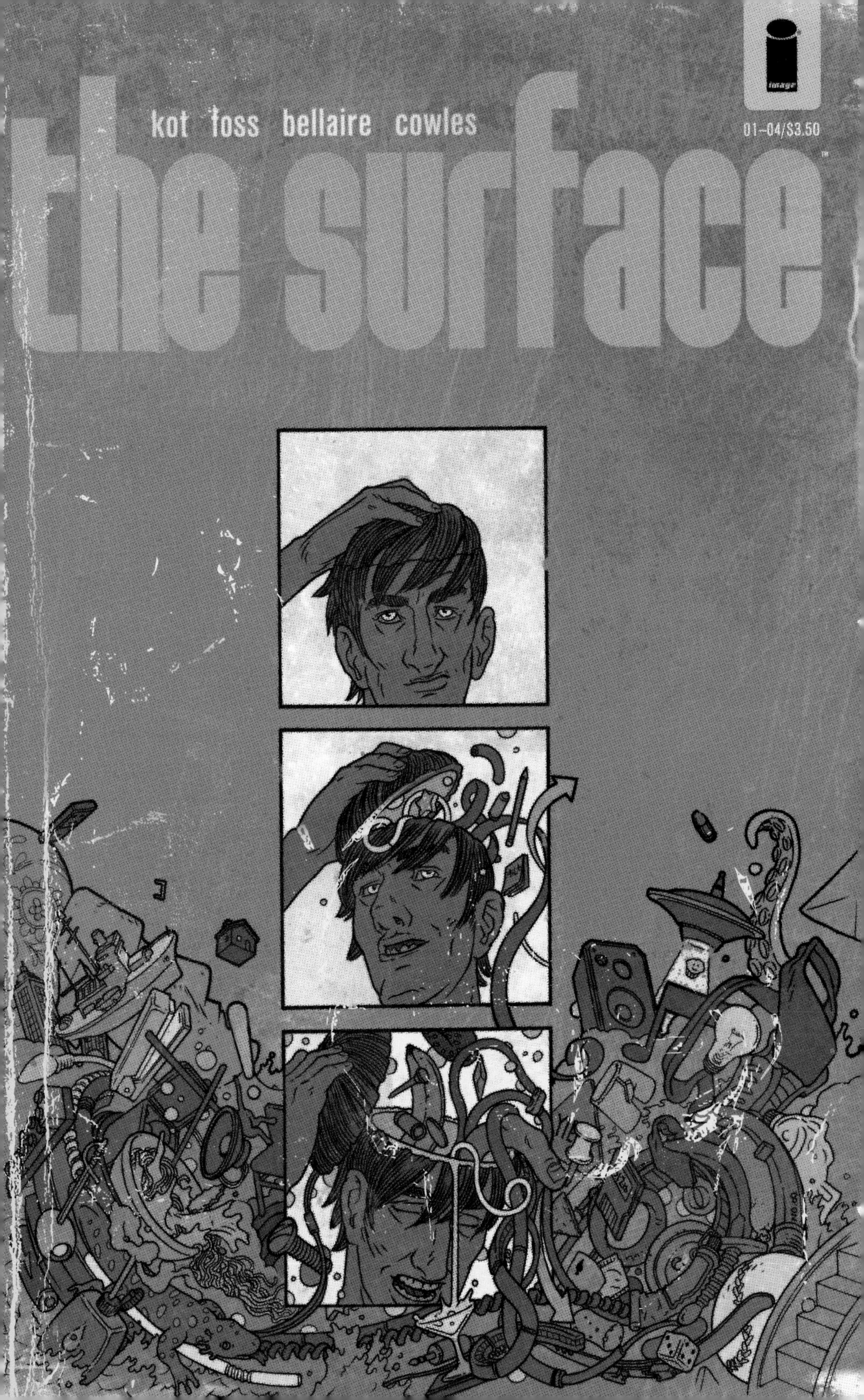
kot foss bellaire cowles
the surface™
01–04/$3.50
image

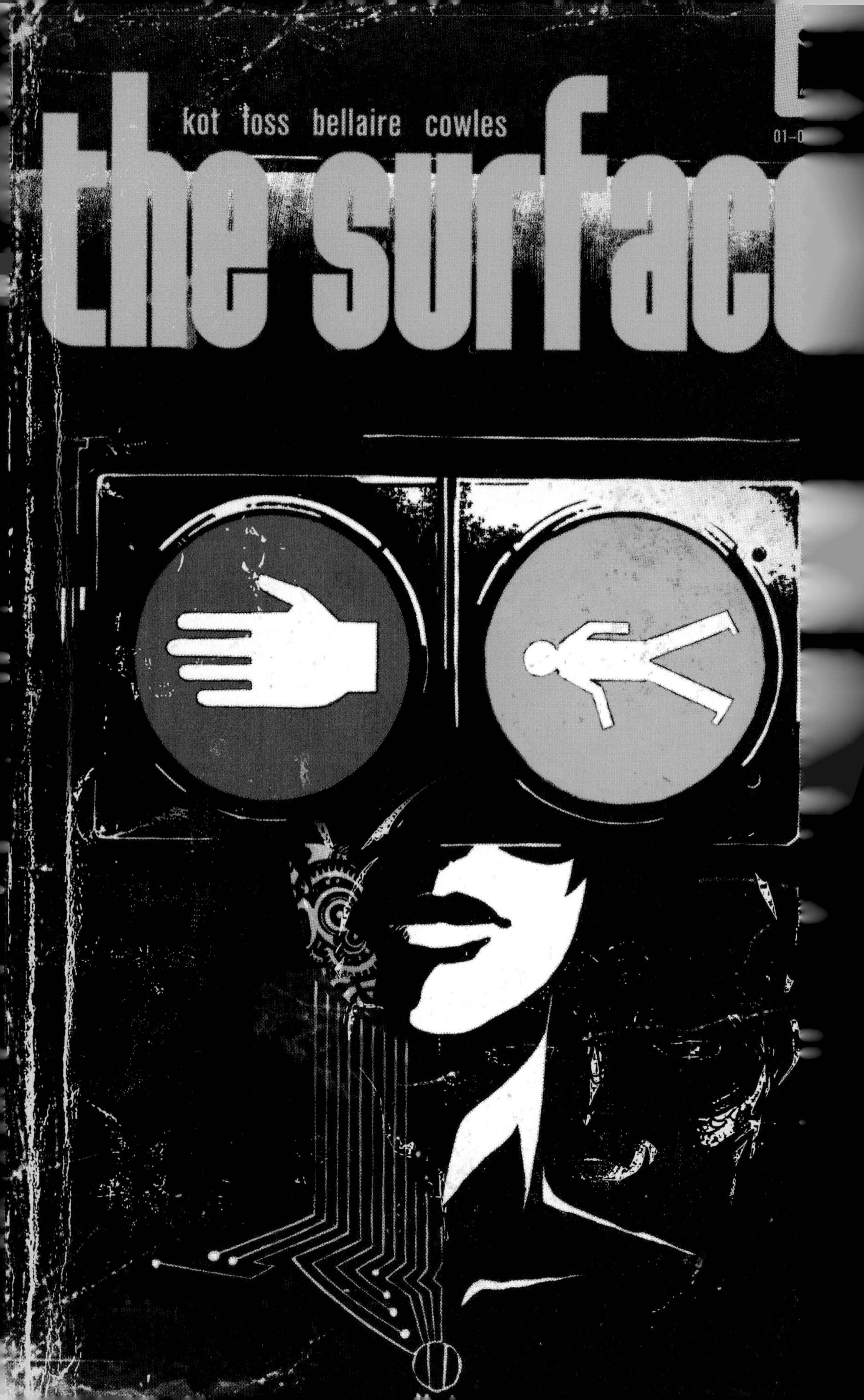
kot foss bellaire cowles
the surfac

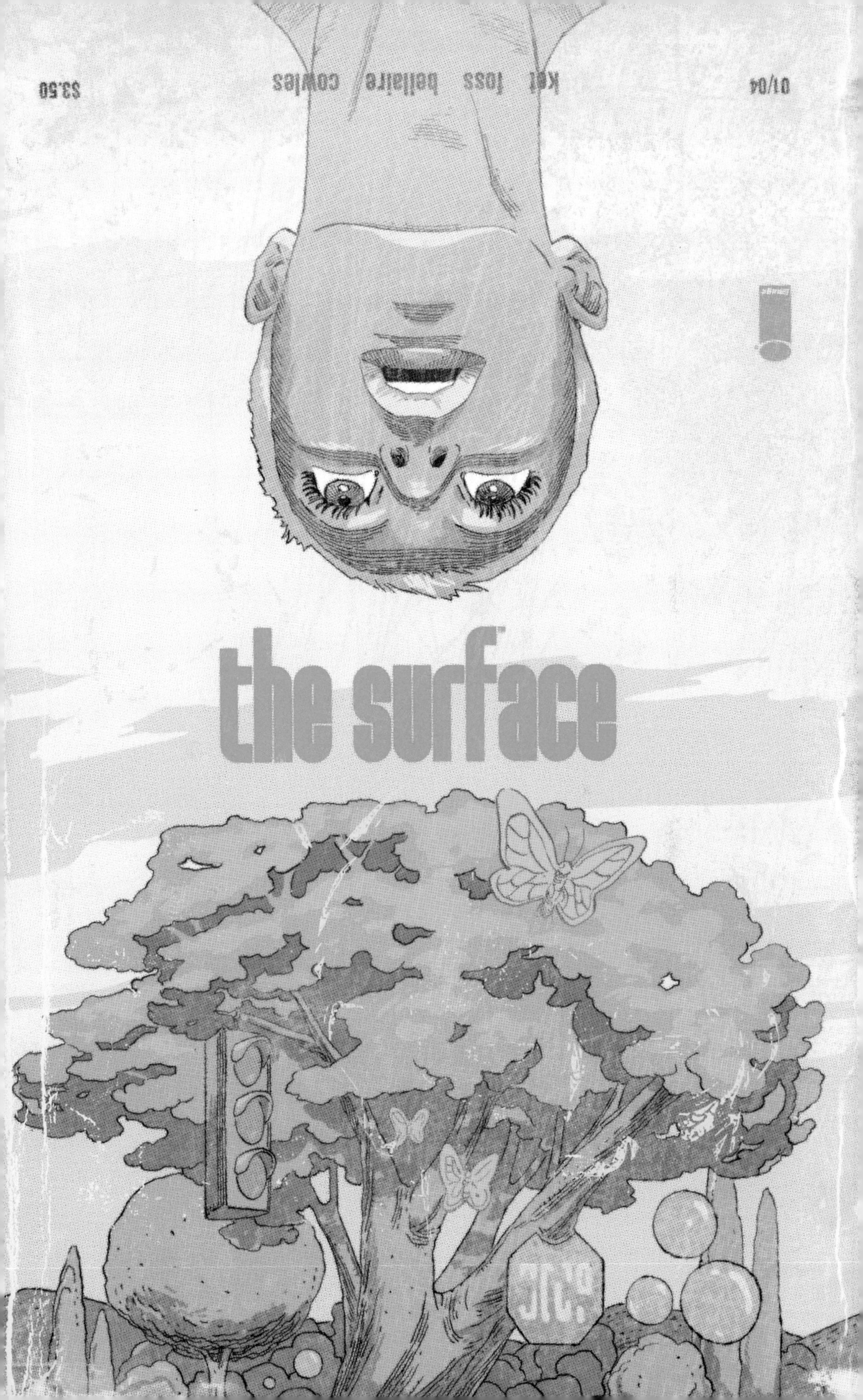
01/04
kat foss bellaire cowles
$3.50
the surface

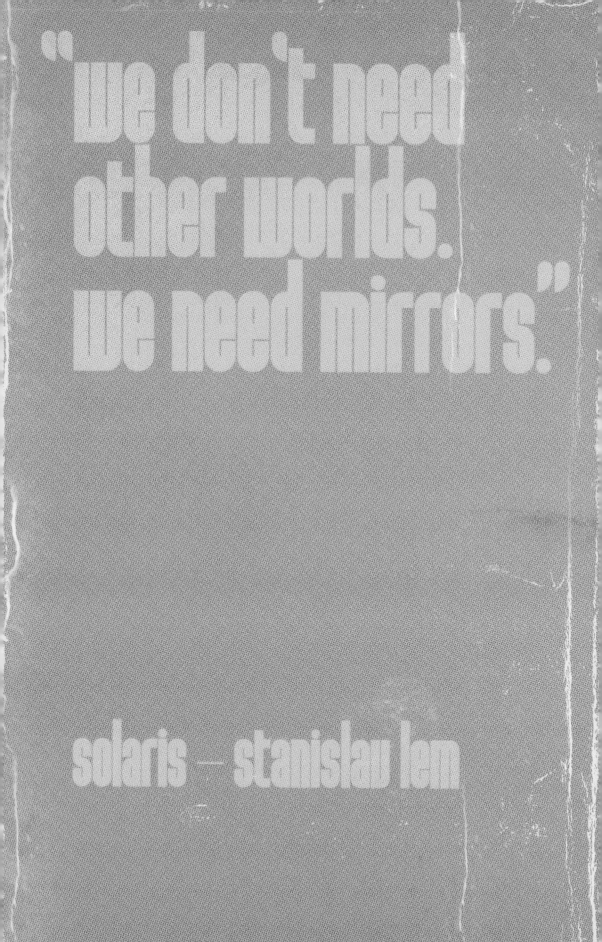

"we don't need other worlds. we need mirrors."

solaris — stanislau lem

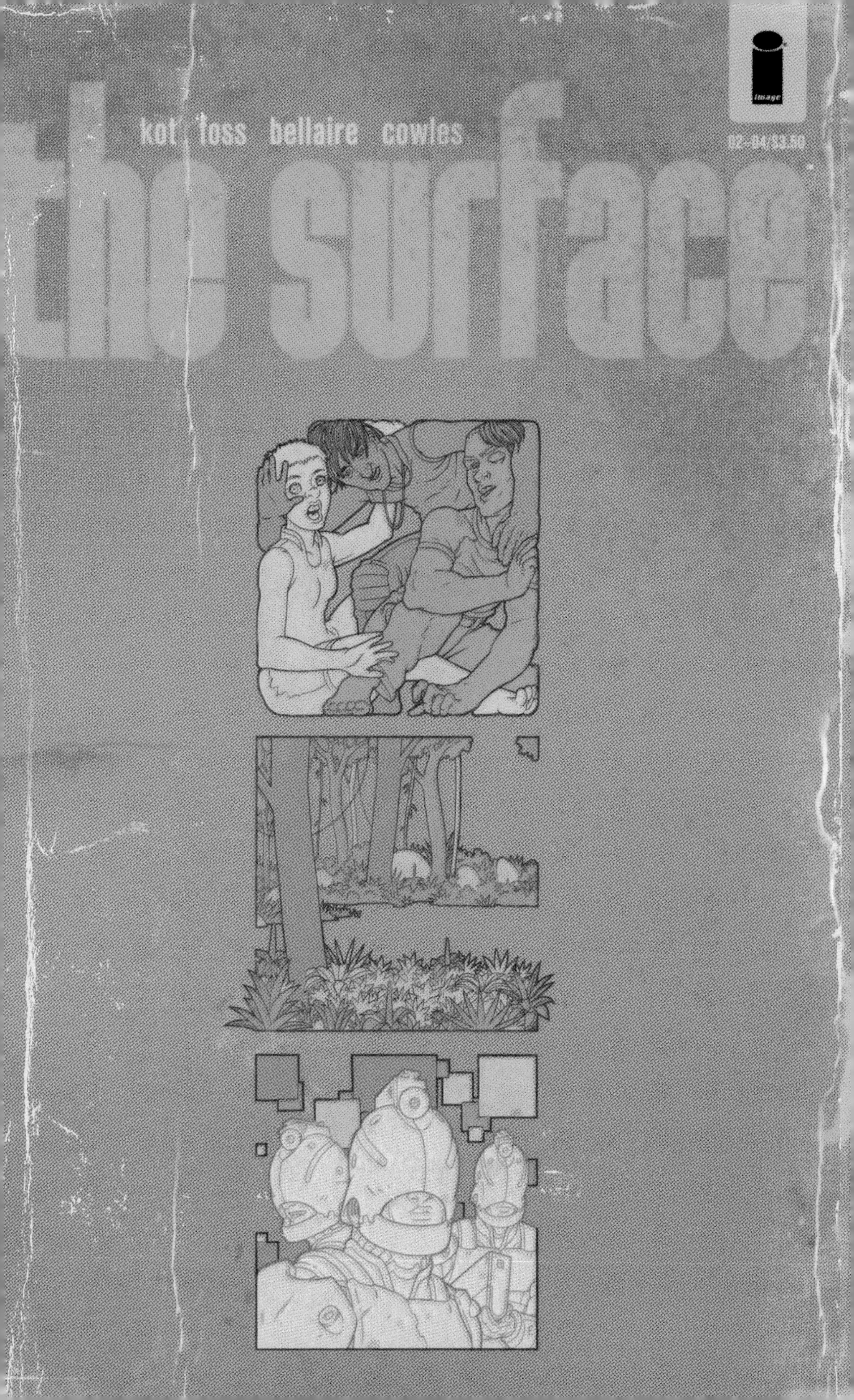

kot foss bellaire cowles
the surface
02-04/$3.50

"do i become my father during my sleep?"

philip k. dick — valis

kot foss bellaire cowles

03–04/$3.50

the surface

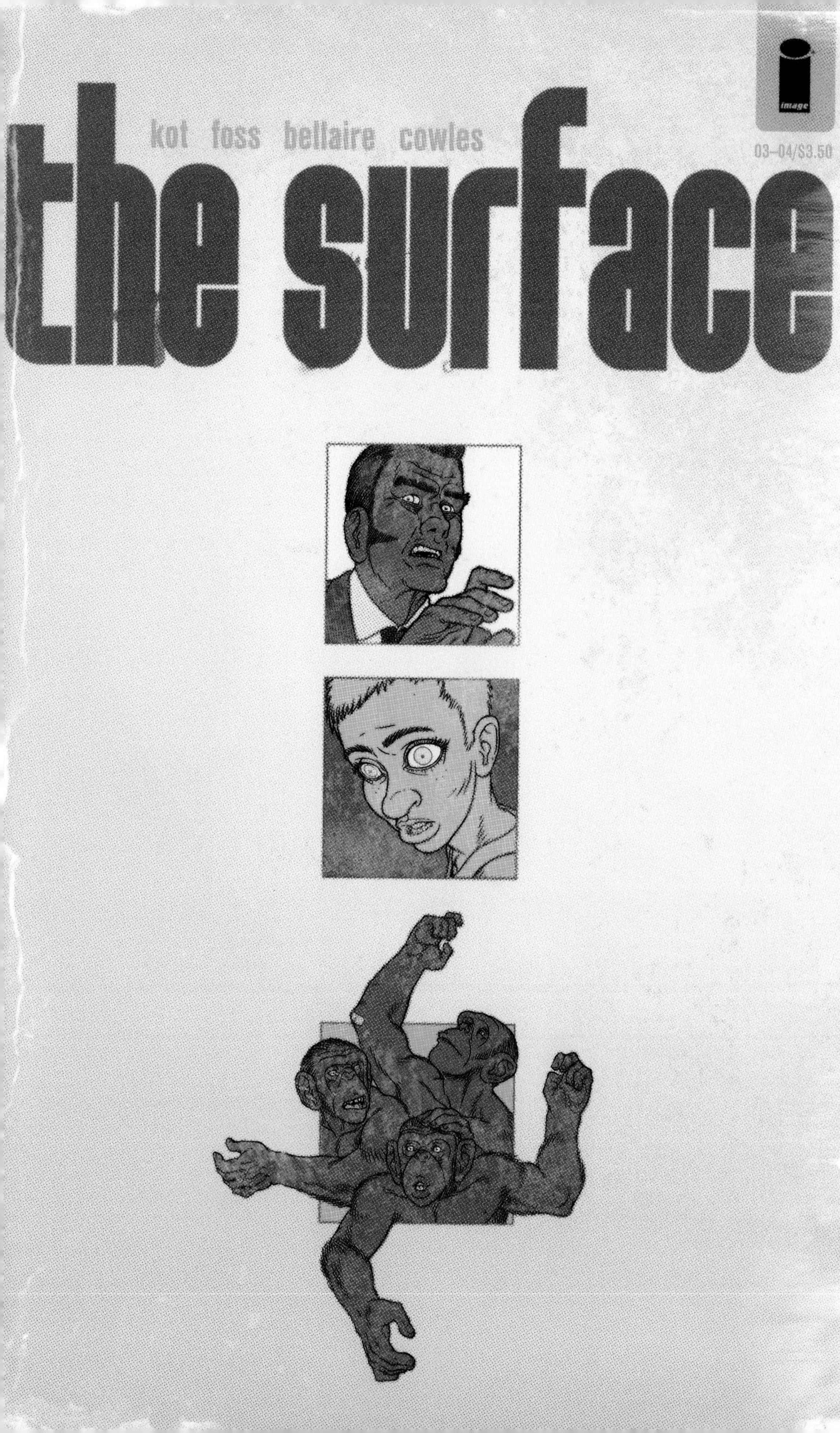

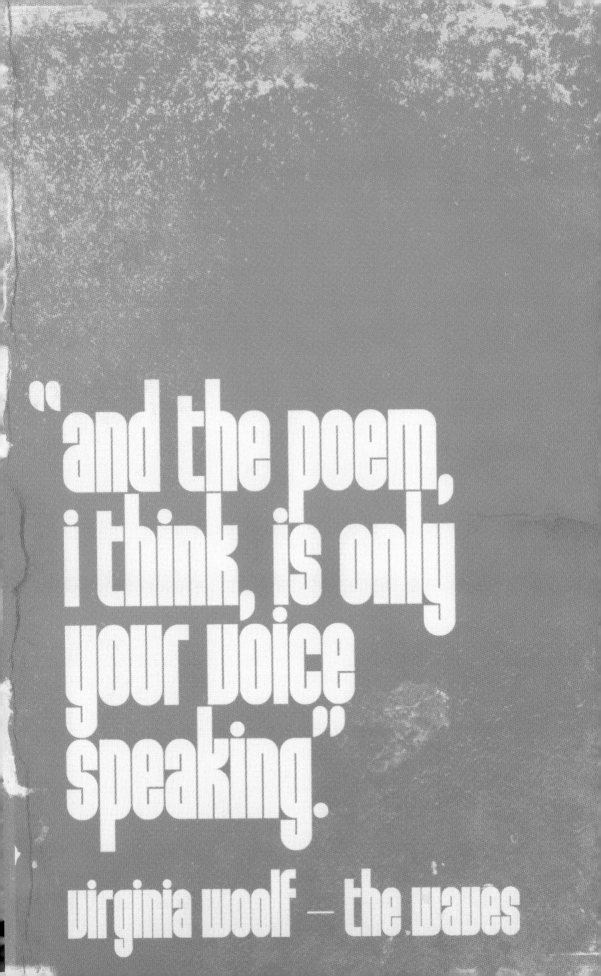

"and the poem,
i think, is only
your voice
speaking."

virginia woolf – the waves

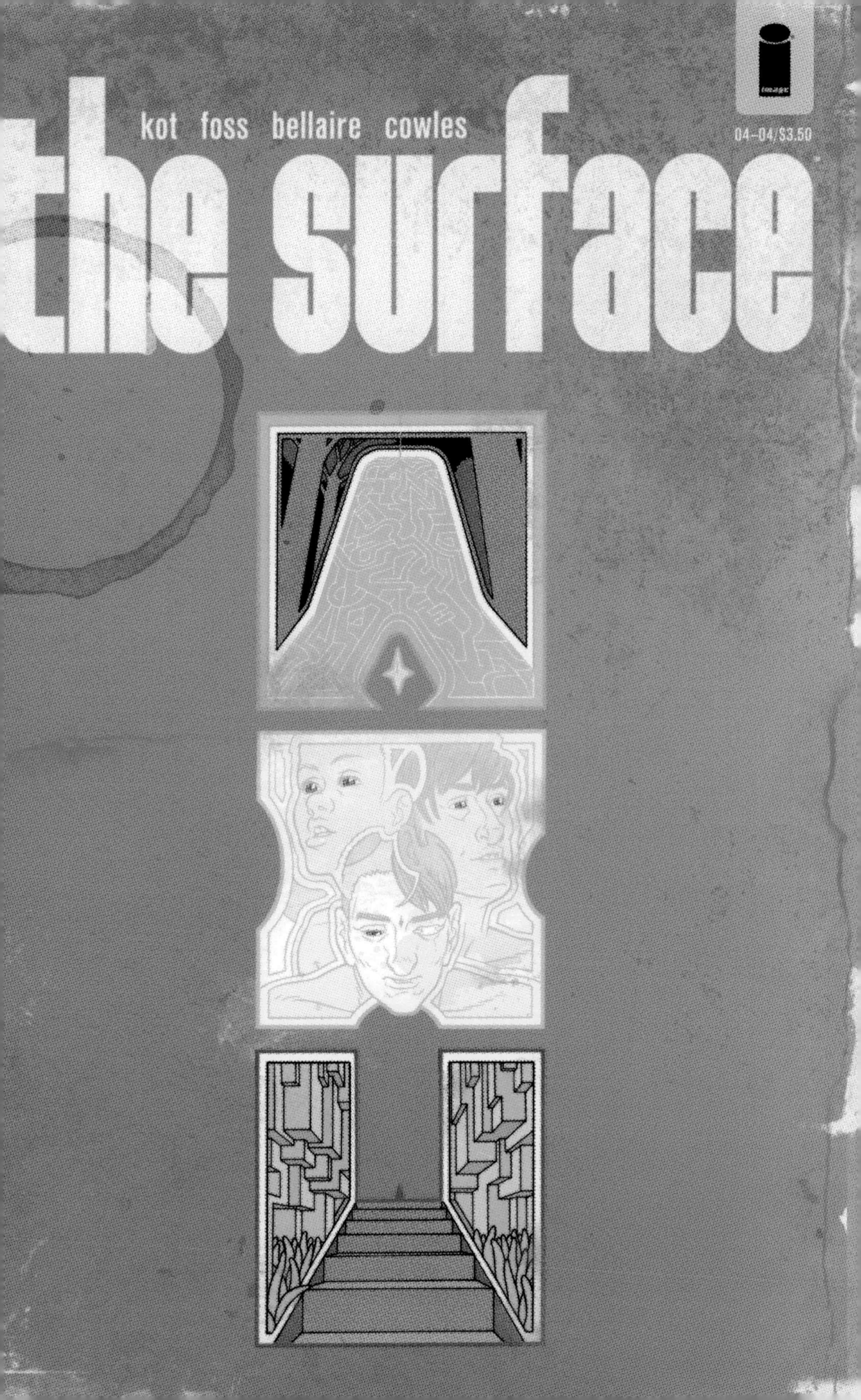
kot foss bellaire cowles
the surface
04-04/$3.50
image

made by:

ales kot

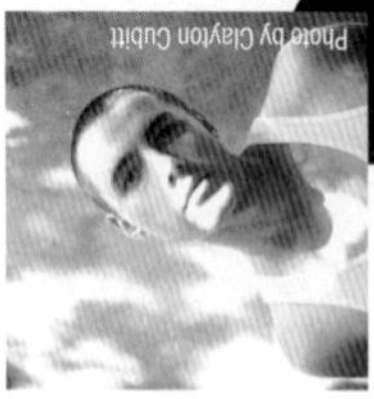
Photo by Clayton Cubitt

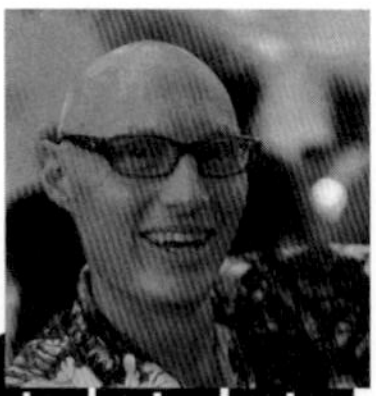

langdon foss

jordie bellaire

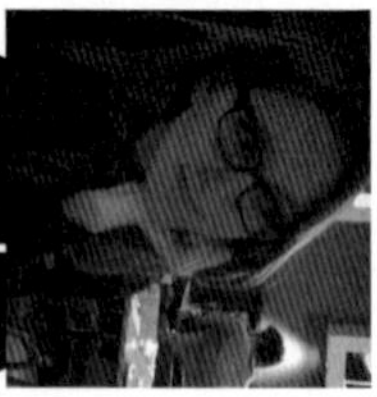

clayton cowles

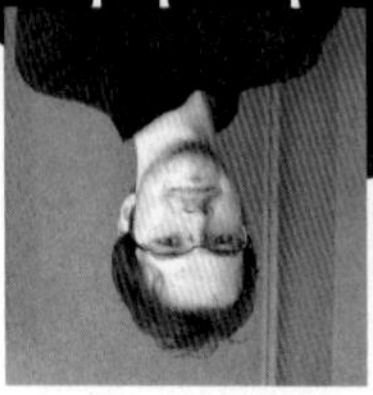

tom muller

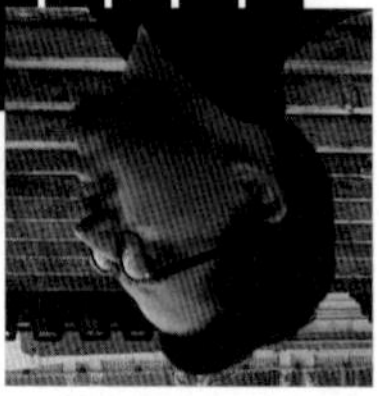

Clayton Cowles graduated from the Joe Kubert School of Cartoon and Graphic Art in 2009, and has been lettering for Image and Marvel Comics ever since. For Image, his credits include *Bitch Planet*, *Pretty Deadly*, *The Wicked + The Divine*, and less than ten others. His Marvel credits include *Fantastic Four*, *Young Avengers*, *Secret Avengers*, *Bucky Barnes: Winter Soldier* and way more than ten others. He spends his real life in upstate New York with his cat.

@claytoncowles

Tom Muller is an Eisner Award nominated Belgian graphic designer who works with technology startups, movie studios, publishers, media producers, ad agencies, and filmmakers. His recent comics design credits include Darren Aronofky's *NOAH*, *Zero*, *Material*, and *Drifter* for Image Comics; *Constantine*, *Survivors' Club*, *Unfollow*, and *Slash & Burn* for DC/Vertigo Comics; *Divinity* and *Book of Death* for Valiant Entertainment. He lives in London with his wife, and two cats.

@helloMuller

Jordie Bellaire is an Eisner Award winning colorist best known for her work on *Injection*, *Manhattan Projects*, *Pretty Deadly*, *Nowhere Men*, *Autumnlands: Tooth & Claw*, *Howtoons*, and *Three*. She lives in Ireland with her calico, Buffy.

@whoajordie

Ales Kot invents, writes & runs projects & stories for film, comics, television & more.
He also wrote/still writes: *Change*, *Zero*, *Wolf*, *The Surface*, *Wild Children*.
Current body born September 27, 1986 in Opava, Czech Republic. Resides in Los Angeles. Believes in poetry.

@ales_kot

Langdon Foss entered the comics scene with 2012's *Get Jiro*, and has since enjoyed working with DC, Image, Marvel, IDW, and others.
He's doing his best to balance comics, art, acting, family, friends, and his quest to find a formula for a correct and effective life.

He thinks he's close, the poor fool.

@LangdonFoss

Media inquiries should be directed to Roger Green &
Phil D'Amecourt at WME Entertainment and Ari Lubet at 3 Arts Entertainment.

ISBN: 978-1-63215-322-7

Published by
Image Comics, Inc.

IMAGE COMICS, INC —Robert Kirkman: Chief Operating Officer, Erik Larsen: Chief Financial Officer, Todd McFarlane: President,
Marc Silvestri: Chief Executive Officer, Jim Valentino: Vice-President, Eric Stephenson: Publisher, Corey Murphy: Director of Sales,
Jeff Boison: Director of Publishing Planning & Trade Book Sales, Jeremy Sullivan: Director of Digital Sales,
Kat Salazar: Director of PR & Marketing, Emily Miller: Director of Operations, Branwyn Bigglestone: Senior Accounts Manager,
Sarah Mello: Accounts Manager, Drew Gill: Art Director, Jonathan Chan: Production Manager, Meredith Wallace: Print Manager,
Briah Skelly: Publicity Assistant, Randy Okamura: Marketing Production Designer, David Brothers: Branding Manager,
Ally Power: Content Manager, Addison Duke: Production Artist, Vincent Kukua: Production Artist, Sasha Head: Production Artist,
Tricia Ramos: Production Artist, Jeff Stang: Direct Market Sales Representative, Emilio Bautista: Digital Sales Associate,
Chloe Ramos-Peterson: Administrative Assistant.

imagecomics.com